About the Authors

USA Today bestselling author **Jules Bennett** has penned more than fifty novels during her short career. She's married to her high school sweetheart, has two active girls, and is a former salon owner. Jules can be found on Twitter, Facebook (Fan Page), and her website julesbennett.com. She holds contests via these three outlets with each release and loves to hear from readers!

Besides writing, **Ann Major** enjoys her husband, kids, grandchildren, cats, hobbies, and travels. A Texan, Ann holds a B.A. from UT, and an M.A. from Texas A & M. A former teacher on both the secondary and college levels, Ann is an experienced speaker. She's written over sixty books for Mills & Boon and frequently makes bestseller lists.

Charlene Sands is a *USA Today* bestselling author of thirty-five contemporary and historical romances. She's been honoured with The National Readers' Choice Award, Booksellers Best Award and Cataromance Reviewer's Choice Award. She loves babies, chocolate and thrilling love stories. Take a peek at her bold, sexy heroes and real good men! www.charlenesands.com and Facebook

Scandalous Secrets

Scandalous Secrets:
His Hidden Heir

JULES BENNETT

ANN MAJOR

CHARLENE SANDS

MILLS & BOON

First Published in Great Britain 2020
By Mills & Boon, an imprint of HarperCollins*Publishers*
1 London Bridge Street, London, SE1 9GF

SCANDALOUS SECRETS: HIS HIDDEN HEIR
© 2020 Harlequin Books S.A.

The Heir's Unexpected Baby © 2017 Jules Bennett
His for the Taking © 2013 Ann Major
The Secret Heir of Sunset Ranch © 2013 Charlene Swink

ISBN: 978-0-263-28189-7

MIX
Paper from
responsible sources
FSC™ C007454

This book is produced from independently certified FSC™ paper to ensure responsible forest management.

For more information visit: www.harpercollins.co.uk/green

Printed and bound in Spain
by CPI, Barcelona

THE HEIR'S
UNEXPECTED BABY

JULES BENNETT

To everyone who has opened their homes and hearts to foster children...you are truly a blessing.

One

"What are you doing here so early?"

Jack Carson brushed past Vivianna Smith and stepped into her apartment, trying like hell not to touch her. Or breathe in that familiar jasmine scent. Or think of how sexy she looked in that pale pink suit.

Masochist. That's all he could chalk this up to. But he had a mission, damn it, and he needed his assistant's help to pull it off.

Wouldn't life be so much easier if Viv were only his assistant? He'd avoided the unwanted attraction for four years, yet the longer she worked for him, the more difficult that was proving to be. And lately, he'd been having dreams. Okay, fine. Fantasies. And she starred in every single one of them.

How the hell could he even have these thoughts about her? It was flat-out wrong, not to mention unprofessional.

"I need you to use that charm of yours and get more information." He turned to face her as she closed the door to her apartment. "You're going to have to dig deeper into the Parkers' lives."

Clint and Lily Parker were a young couple who had been killed two months ago in a robbery gone wrong. The perpetrators set the Parkers' house on fire. The only survivor was a sweet infant named Katie...a baby Viv now fostered.

The burn in his chest was still crippling. Jack wasn't going down the baby path, not even in his mind. He admired Viv for reaching out and helping a child, as she had so many times over the years. But babies weren't for him. They never could be if he wanted to keep his heart intact.

"You're positive the O'Sheas had something to do with that crime?" Vivianna asked, moving around him to head down the hall.

With no option but to follow her swaying hips, he fell in right behind her. He was human, and a guy. Where else could he look but those hips? She always had on those damn body-hugging skirts...he believed she referred to them as pencil skirts. Those curves would be the death of him.

"I know they did," he confirmed.

The infamous O'Shea family of Boston was always slipping around the law, ignoring the basic rules of human decency. Jack's main focus in life was bringing cocky bastards like that down. Every time he went against those believing they were above the law, he saw the person who had killed his wife and unborn child... and still ran free.

The O'Sheas might run a polished high-society auction house known around the globe, but he knew they were no better than common criminals. And Jack was about to prove to this arrogant family who was in charge. He would bring them down in a spectacular show of justice. And his ticket was the woman who fueled his every fantasy.

A year ago, Jack had set up the perfect bogus background for Viv. She was working only part-time for the notorious family, but that's all he needed for her to gain intel.

The FBI had sought him out, needing someone with his experience and resources to infiltrate the O'Sheas. Since Jack was the best in the business of investigating, of course they needed him. That wasn't vanity, either, just a fact. Jack could get things done when others couldn't.

The millions he'd made hadn't rolled in by him sitting back and delegating responsibilities. He'd worked his ass off, throwing himself into his work and opening Carson Enterprises when he got home from Afghanistan ten years ago.

He'd returned to find that he'd lost his entire family while he'd been overseas. What else had there been to live for other than seeking justice anywhere he could?

Since he'd already made a fortune, he often turned down jobs when they didn't appeal to him. But the O'Sheas were right in his wheelhouse. They had been in talks with the Parker couple about acquiring some of their antiques when the robbery happened. There wasn't a doubt in Jack's mind that this tight-lipped family knew what really went down that tragic night.

Viv went into the nursery. Heart clenching, Jack opted to wait in the hall—demons and all that.

He commended Viv for her love of children, the way she fostered with open arms. Over the time he'd known her, he'd seen her with various children, but never an infant. He couldn't get involved in any of that. The wounds he'd lived with for so long had never healed… probably never would.

Viv stepped back into the hall, Katie's head resting against her shoulder. "I need to drop her off at the sitter next door and get to work."

Viv was lucky that her next-door neighbor was a retired teacher and widow. She loved kids and took care of Viv's foster kids when she was working.

"I'm doing what I can, Jack." Her eyes held his and he hated how tired she looked. Beautiful, sexy as hell, but still tired. "They're already suspicious because of the missing data. If I press too hard, they'll know I'm not who I say I am."

Jack hadn't wanted to put her in this position. But he couldn't back down when he had a job to do. And that job wasn't staring at the V in her suit jacket as baby Katie tugged at the opening.

A flash of a white lacy bra taunted him, making him want to undo those few buttons to see if the lace…

Damn it. Get a grip.

She stepped forward, and Jack had to force himself to focus on her face. Which wasn't a hardship. Viv was part Native American. Her grandmother had been in the Sioux tribe, so Viv had inherited high cheekbones, long, dark hair and deep brown eyes. He'd seen more than one man do a double take her way…and each time, Jack had wanted to throat punch the stranger.

Guilt banded around his chest like a vise. He shouldn't be lusting after another woman. He'd had the love of his life; she was gone. Gone because he hadn't been there to protect her or their baby.

Getting drawn to Viv was just a by-product of working together for so long. She was the only woman he associated with, other than his housekeeper-slash-chef, Tilly. He admired Viv because she was strong, with an undertone of vulnerability. Add in her striking looks and perfectly shaped curves and it was only natural he be attracted to her. But he had to keep his emotions beneath the surface where he could control them.

"I'm on your side here," she told him with a soft smile, pulling him back to the moment. "Why don't you come over this evening and we can talk more."

"I have a conference call this evening with some clients in the UK."

Viv gave a slight nod. "Oh, okay. Then tomorrow? I'll make dinner and we can figure out our next step."

Dinner? With her and the baby? That all sounded so…domestic. He prided himself on keeping work in the office or in neutral territory. But he'd come here this morning to check on her…and he couldn't blame it all on work.

Damn it. The longer this case went on, the more protective he became—the more possessive.

"You can come to my place and I'll have my chef prepare something."

There. If Tilly was on hand, then maybe it wouldn't seem so family-like. Viv often fostered kids who had no place else to go. He had no idea why she'd never settled down and started a family of her own, when it was so obvious she loved caring for children. But that was none of his business. Just because they were associates didn't mean he had a right to pry into her life. Clearly, she didn't want to discuss such things or she would've brought them up.

"I can do tomorrow," she told him, her smile widening. "Katie and I would love to get out of the house.

I get off work around four, so I'll pick her up and be right over."

Jack hadn't had her over with a child before. On the rare occasions he and Viv got together outside the office, it was usually just the two of them. In the past couple years, ever since he started really noticing Vivianna as more than his assistant, he'd tried to keep their social interactions to a minimum.

"Any requests?" he asked.

Did her gaze just dart to his lips? She couldn't look at him with those dark eyes as if she wanted...

No. It didn't matter what she wanted, or what he wanted for that matter. Their relationship was business only. Period.

"Um...no requests." She shook her head, offered a smile. "Whatever you have will be fine."

Jack rubbed his damp palms against his jeans. He needed to get out of here. Between that telling look she'd thrown him, the precious baby still sleeping in her little pink onesie and his lack of sleep from working, his mind was throwing all sorts of impossible scenarios at him.

Jack crossed to the door and gripped the doorknob. He glanced over his shoulder as Viv closed in behind him. "Be careful, Viv. I don't want you to take unnecessary risks."

She shifted the sleeping baby and tipped her head. "You've taught me how to look out for myself. I promise I'll be fine. See you tomorrow."

Jack paused, soaking in the sight of her in that prim little suit, holding the baby. Definitely time to go before he forgot she actually worked for him and took what he'd wanted for months. He didn't need any more heartache or distractions in his life.

* * *

It was finally four o'clock and Viv couldn't wait to get out of her office at O'Shea's and go see Jack. Ridiculous, this infatuation she had with her boss. Clichés were definitely not her thing, yet she'd be diving headfirst into his sheets if he gave her the green light.

Sad. She was a sad woman hoping her boss would notice her. Like she had time for a torrid, steamy affair. She was caring for a child, an infant. There was nothing sexy about the haggard, overworked-mom look. But Viv would never give up fostering. She could still be a mother, yet not get too emotionally attached.

The heartache of knowing she'd never have her own children was somewhat pacified, yet the underlying hurt was never too far below the surface. But work kept her busy and her attentions focused elsewhere. It wasn't as if she didn't have a full load at the moment.

Viv started at O'Shea's part-time, which was perfect for her fostering schedule, not to mention that she still worked for Jack, as well. Being single, she had only a handful of people she could count on. Her parents were no longer around and she was an only child. She'd learned some time ago how to be independent, but even so, she needed some help when caring for a child and working outside the home.

Her quirky neighbor, Martha, was an adorable elderly lady who watched Katie most of the time, but when Viv was in a bind, she'd simply take Katie into the office. Well, her office with Jack.

Oh, she "worked" at O'Shea's, but that was only a cover created by Jack to get her on the inside, up close and personal. Her real employer was one sexy, rich investigator who couldn't move beyond his heartache to see there was still life out there.

If it wasn't work, he wasn't interested…which was the only reason he'd shown up so early at her house yesterday morning. The man had been through so much pain in his life, it was no wonder he was married to his job. He'd lost his mother when he'd been around nineteen, then he'd seen battle in war. His wife had been killed and he'd never known who his father was… Viv knew just enough details for her heart to break for him, but she wished he would try living again. She'd love to be the one to show him that not everything was harsh and cold…if he would only let her in.

Viv headed toward the back office of O'Shea's. Laney, the youngest O'Shea and the only female sibling, was out front dealing with a potential client. Since they had discovered some information had been leaked to the Feds, at least one member of the infamous family was here at all times…which made Viv's snooping a tad more difficult, considering she was here only about twenty hours per week.

Circling the antique desk that had been assigned to her in the office, she opened the top left drawer to find a pen. She wanted to jot down some items she needed to pick up from the store or she'd forget.

Katie was teething and the nights were getting longer and longer. Poor baby. She'd lost her parents and now she wasn't sleeping. Viv wanted to comfort the sweet girl while she was in her care.

All kids that came into Viv's home were precious, and they were all hard to say goodbye to. But Viv stayed strong for them. With this being her first baby, she worried how much more difficult it would be, both emotionally and logistically. She already had a demanding schedule, but she couldn't turn away this poor orphan who'd just lost both parents.

At the moment, Katie needed more pain reliever for her swollen gums, and Viv was out of nearly everything. Grocery shopping wasn't high on the priority list right now. Saving kids, helping Jack, trying to get Jack to notice her as more than a friend…would he ever? Her to-do list seemed to grow by the day.

Vivianna reached inside her desk for a pen and a slip of paper. She'd used this particular desk since coming here a year ago. During that time she'd earned the trust of the O'Sheas, and occasionally felt guilty about her act, but she wasn't naive. She'd heard the rumors around Boston. Anyone who delved into the art or auction world knew who the O'Sheas were. The terms *mafia* and *mob* seemed to follow them wherever they went.

Something brushed the top of her hand. Viv jerked back, bent down, but didn't see anything inside the drawer. If there was a spider in there tickling her skin there wouldn't be enough antibacterial gel to kill those horrendous germs.

She quickly reached back in for her pen and paper. And once again something brushed the back of her hand.

Viv reached for her cell phone and shone the light inside the drawer, fully expecting to see a family of hairy tarantulas.

When she bent down, she saw a sliver of paper sticking out…from the top of the drawer? Since Viv had used this desk for so long, she had no idea what that could be.

She listened. Laney and the client were still talking. Viv's desk sat in the corner, away from them, so the coast was clear. Pulling her chair over, she took a seat and bent to examine the underside of the desk. How had she not noticed anything before?

Gripping the paper between her thumb and index

finger, she tugged slightly. When it eased out further, she noticed some cursive writing she couldn't identify. Pulling a bit more, she felt something give. Putting her phone inside the drawer to shine upward, she reached with both hands. The board was loose.

Viv pulled slightly, careful to not make too much noise, but Laney and the client were now laughing. Perfect.

The board was a bit of a struggle, but it came loose. And a small book fell into the drawer.

Viv stared, curious about where it had come from and who'd hidden it in the desk. She quickly grabbed her purse from the bottom drawer and slid the book inside. She'd have to look at it later.

Grocery list forgotten—she could worry about that later—Viv grabbed her things. She belted her wrap coat and quickly hoisted her purse up onto her shoulder as she headed out the back door. The bitter wind cut right through her, but she was anxious to get to her car.

Once she settled into her older model car, Viv turned on her heated seat, locked the doors and pulled the small leather-bound book from her purse.

It didn't take her long to realize she'd struck gold. The author of this journal was none other than the late Patrick O'Shea. The patriarch of the Boston family Jack was hell-bent on bringing down. The family she'd been infiltrating for a year.

As she skimmed the pages, she knew when she got to Jack's house he'd devour this thing. She couldn't wait to get this to him, to show him she was valuable and actually had something concrete they might be able to use.

She flipped another page, then froze as she read the entry. Her blood chilled as each word sank in. There was no skimming this one. In fact, she read it twice to make sure she wasn't seeing things.

Heart in her throat, she knew there was no way Jack could ever see this journal. Everything he'd wanted to bring down the family was here…including the fact that Jack was Patrick's illegitimate son.

Two

Heels clicked on the hardwood, the echo growing louder as Viv approached. Jack came to his feet and turned toward the entryway of the patio room. He'd had his chef set up dinner out here so they could close all the French doors and have some privacy.

Jack sucked in a breath the second she came into view. The punch of lust to the gut was nothing new, though. More and more, when he saw her, she never failed to have a dramatic impact…an issue he'd have to deal with on his own.

Her pink suit jacket cut in at her narrow waist, the matching skirt fell just above her knee and her black heeled boots showcased just how long those legs truly were.

He'd traveled the world, both in the military and for pleasure, and had seen stunning women all over the globe. But Viv, who managed to embody innocence, class and a touch of sultriness, was one woman he couldn't get out of his mind.

Jack knew Viv would be gorgeous in anything she wore. That Native American heritage of hers set her apart from nearly every woman he knew. And the fact that she stood out in his mind only added to his guilt. He had to get a grip or he'd mess up their working relationship, and he refused to find another assistant. Viv was invaluable and they worked smoothly as a team.

And she was the only one he trusted to get inside the O'Sheas' inner sanctum and bring back information.

"Sorry I'm late." She blew out a breath, hugged little Katie closer to her chest. "She's been a little fussy and I'm pretty sure her teeth are bothering her."

Jack shoved his hands in his pockets. He had no experience with teething babies...not that he wouldn't have welcomed it once. But that chance was stolen from him the night his pregnant wife had been in the wrong place at the wrong time.

Working with Viv seriously hit his emotions from every single angle. Self-control was key to him not losing his ever-loving mind. And if he focused on the task at hand, at bringing down the O'Sheas, then nothing else mattered.

"I hope I didn't hold you up." Viv glanced at the table, her eyes wide. "Wow. You really went all out."

The yeast rolls, the turkey roulade with plum sauce, the roasted potatoes and veggies, wine...even pats of butter in the shape of doves. Tilly, his chef, housekeeper and wanna-be matchmaker, had gone a bit overboard. And Jack knew for a fact there was a homemade red velvet cheesecake waiting for them in the kitchen.

He gave a mental shrug. Tilly's attempts were all in

vain. Regardless of the fact that Jack had told her this dinner was strictly business, she clearly had ignored him and done her own thing…as usual.

Tilly had been his chef for nearly a decade and never missed a chance to set him up with a woman. Jack had turned down numerous blind dates she'd foisted on him. When he was ready, he could find his own damn date. Considering he was married to Carson Enterprises and dedicated to working for justice, he didn't have time to worry about dating or keeping a woman happy.

Jack glanced at the overly romantic table, then back to Viv. "I told Tilly this was a business dinner, but she's hell-bent on marrying me off."

Viv quirked a dark brow. "Well, this is already better than nearly every date I've been on. I'm still recovering from the last one."

Before Jack could ask what she meant, not that it was his business, Katie let out a cry. Viv patted her back and rocked back and forth, whispering comforting words in an attempt to calm the baby. Nothing seemed to be working, but he wasn't exactly an expert…nor would he ever be.

"I left the diaper bag up front where Tilly hung our coats. Could you grab it for me?"

Diaper bag. Sure. Maybe this meeting would have been better suited to a phone call. Viv had her hands full, technically working two jobs and caring for an eleven-month-old baby.

Jack refused to feel guilty as he headed to retrieve the diaper bag. Viv had been with him long enough and she was a strong woman. He wasn't worried she couldn't pull this off. He was *counting* on her to pull this off.

And that irritated him on a certain level. He hated relying on someone else to get the job done. He was a hands-on guy, so waiting for her to feed him information was not his idea of a dream job. But the FBI was counting on him to uncover something that would tie the O'Sheas to the crimes against the Parkers. Then they would have the open door to search the rest of their dealings.

The gray-and-white-patterned bag sat next to the accent table by the front door. Jack grabbed the strap and jerked the heavy bag up onto his shoulder. What the hell was in this thing? How could someone so small need so much stuff?

He started back down the hallway, but stopped short when Tilly stepped through the wide arched opening leading into the kitchen.

"Everything all right, Mr. Carson?"

Mr. Carson. She'd worked for him for nearly ten years and he'd given up trying to get her to call him by his first name. Tilly epitomized respect. Ironic, considering she didn't mind nosing right on into his love life…or lack thereof.

"Fine, Tilly. Thank you. Viv just needed her diaper bag."

Tilly smiled, the corners of her eyes creasing. "That little girl is lucky to have Ms. Smith in her life."

Jack nodded. "You're off duty from playing cupid tonight." And every other night.

A smile spread across her face, deepening the fan of wrinkles around her eyes. "I don't know what you're talking about," she claimed as she turned back to the kitchen. She stopped, threw a glance over her shoulder and added, "Just let me know when to serve the cheese-cake for two."

"I'll serve it," he told her with a laugh. How could he not admire her determination, even if it was wasted? "Why don't you go on home?"

Her eyes all but sparkled. "Want to be alone? I get it. Consider me gone."

He wasn't going to correct her. Yes, he wanted to be alone with Viv, but not for the reasons Tilly assumed. She'd draw her own conclusions no matter what Jack said, so he wasn't wasting his breath. Besides, he never let Tilly in on his cases. Keeping his work to himself was the only way he managed to crack cases and find justice for the people he helped. The money was just a bonus.

Tilly argued that he was too busy traveling for work and making money to find a woman. She often hinted that all that money was a waste if he had nobody to spend it on.

As much as the thought of another woman in his life terrified him, Jack couldn't fault Tilly for her efforts. The woman's heart was in the right place—he just wished she'd give up. He'd had the love of his life once. That kind of love didn't happen twice.

As far as dating, well, he didn't want to worry about that, either. He was perfectly content with the way things were. Worrying about himself was enough.

But part of him, okay a huge part, worried about Viv when she was with the O'Sheas. He'd be a fool not to worry. So much for not getting personally involved.

Katie's cry pulled him away from his thoughts as he headed back onto the patio. Viv sat in one of the cushioned chairs at the table. She was muttering nurturing words and holding Katie in a cradle position.

Jack froze when he spotted the pale pink lace peeking from beneath Viv's suit jacket. *Mercy, not again.* Katie had a white-knuckled grip on the V and was pulling the material apart.

The lace was quite the contrast against Viv's dark

skin…skin he shouldn't be looking at and lace his fingers shouldn't be itching to trace.

Pull it together.

He adjusted the diaper bag on his shoulder and attempted to ignore the fact this woman loved lace lingerie.

"What do you need out of here?" he asked, unzipping the bag.

She lifted her head and every time those dark eyes clashed with his, he struggled to look away. She had a power she wasn't even aware of and he'd do good to remind himself she was off-limits.

"Just set it down. I can get it."

Setting the bag at her feet, he stepped back and took a seat across from her. Unfortunately, when she bent down to dig inside the bag, Katie's grip tightened and that V only widened. A little pink bow was nestled in the middle of her breasts.

Damn it all. How the hell could he conduct a "business" meeting like this?

"Just tell me what you're looking for."

He got to his feet and picked the bag up, forcing himself not to look her way. *Focus on the bag.* That was the only way they were going to get anywhere this evening.

"Oh, the pain reliever." Viv shifted Katie on her lap, then adjusted her controversial jacket. "It's a small pink-and-white bottle with a dropper lid."

What the hell was a dropper lid? He shuffled through diapers, wipes, jars of baby food, lotion, a stuffed doll…

"Sorry. The outside pouch. I put it in there so it would be easily accessible."

Of course she had.

Jack finally pulled out the right thing and handed it

to her. With his hands on his hips, he stood back and watched as Katie settled back against Viv's arm.

"It's okay, sweetheart." Viv put the medicine in her mouth, then seemed to be rubbing it on Katie's gums. "You'll feel better in just a minute."

Viv had brought Katie into his office a couple times when her neighbor wasn't available to babysit. During those occasions, Jack found a reason to step out for the day. Being near this combination of beautiful woman and enchanting baby was like getting smacked in the face with all he'd lost...his family being the sole reason he was determined to bring down those who kept skirting the law.

As Jack watched Viv console a fussy Katie, he couldn't help but wonder what his life would've been like had his wife lived. He tried not to go there in his mind, but sometimes that just wasn't possible.

"Sorry." Viv looked up at him with a soft smile. "Why don't you go ahead and eat. I'd hate to hold you up any longer."

Thankful for the chance to focus on something else, Jack started filling both of their plates. "How was today? Did you work with Laney?"

Laney O'Shea, the baby of the clan, was now engaged to Ryker Barrett, right-hand man and family enforcer. The two were expecting their first child in the summer and Jack hated the jealousy that rolled through him. People like that shouldn't get to experience the happiness that had been robbed from him.

"What?" she looked up at him, then back to the baby. "Oh, yeah. Laney was there all day."

"Any interesting clients?" he asked. "Did Ryker or her brothers stop in?"

Viv eased the baby up onto her shoulder, patting her

back in an attempt to calm her. "Ryker dropped by and brought Laney lunch. He's been pretty territorial and protective of her since she got pregnant."

Gritting his teeth, Jack set her full plate in front of her. "Did he do anything else? Use the computers, make a call?"

"No. He was actually in and out in about ten minutes." Viv looked down to her plate. "There's no way I'll eat all of this."

"Eat what you want. Tilly takes any leftovers to the homeless shelter by her house. She actually always makes extra and takes it there anyway."

Viv stilled, her hand resting on Katie's back. "That's so sweet."

Jack shrugged. "She's got a big heart and she doesn't mind using my money to help others."

Katie's cries had calmed. Either the meds had kicked in or the poor thing was exhausted from crying.

Viv picked up her fork and stabbed one roasted potato. "And what about you? I'd say your heart is big or you wouldn't let her use your money for such things."

"I have no problem helping anyone when I see the need." He stared across the table, realizing she hadn't looked at him since mentioning work and was now trying to steer the conversation into another territory. "I grew up with a single mother who worked hard to make sure we never wanted for anything. I figure she struggled raising me alone. I would often hear her crying at night when she thought I was asleep."

Jack stopped, not wanting to dig too far into his suppressed memories. The past could easily cripple him, pull him down. The only thing he could use his past for was to propel him forward, to always remember where he came from. And he'd never forget the mother who sacrificed so much.

He pulled in a breath, determined to get back on track. "What happened today at the office?"

Her fork clattered to the plate, but she quickly picked it back up and shrugged. "Nothing. Just the same daily routine."

Again, the lack of eye contact. He'd known Viv long enough, hell, he'd been a soldier and investigator long enough, to know when someone was lying. What was going on?

Slowly, without taking his eyes off her, he leaned forward in his seat. "What happened today?" he repeated, slower this time until she finally looked directly at him.

"Jack, I'm telling you what happened." Now she held his eyes. Katie had fallen asleep and lay across Viv's arm, curled into Viv's body. "We were busy this morning with a new client and Laney handled that. I stayed in the back and logged inventory for the spring auction."

He listened, easing back in his cushioned seat. Why was he doubting her? He'd never second-guessed her before and she was his most trusted ally in this quest. He wouldn't have put her in this position if he didn't trust her completely.

"And then Ryker came with lunch," she went on. Her eyes darted down to the sleeping baby. "After that it was slow for about an hour and Laney and I ended up in the office talking baby things. She knows I foster and she had some questions."

"Like what?" He literally wanted every detail of what went on in that office. The key to his case was in there and he was not going to rest until every possible avenue was explored.

Viv shrugged. "She was asking about different milestones at different ages. But I've never had an infant until now. My foster children have always been older. The youngest I'd had was three."

Jack knew why Viv's taking Katie in deviated from her normal pattern of only fostering older children. One, she'd worked with the Parkers when they'd come into O'Shea's so she had a mild connection. According to Viv, she'd even played with little Katie during one of their visits.

Two, she knew the system was overloaded. Because she was certified to take in children, and since she was more than aware of the tragic situation, she'd actually asked to foster Katie.

"About an hour before we closed, an elderly lady came in and wanted to discuss some pieces she wanted to sell. She claimed they were from her honeymoon in Rome and thought they were valuable art."

Intrigued, Jack tipped his head. "What were they?"

Viv picked up her fork and took a bite of her potato. "I'm not sure. She had some pictures, but didn't want to bring the actual pieces without talking to Laney first."

That all sounded like a typical, boring day. A day that didn't help him one bit. But something was off. Viv had literally frozen when he'd first mentioned her workday at O'Shea's, then she wouldn't look at him.

"You're sure that's all?" he asked.

She shifted Katie to the other arm, which only aided in pulling her jacket open a bit more when Katie's hand got caught in the V. Viv did readjust the gap, but not before he was awarded another view of the swell of her breast.

"I'm just stressed," she assured him with a smile. "Katie is teething and the auction is going to be here before we know it. Working at O'Shea's isn't just me snooping and eavesdropping. They expect me to actually do a job, so it's tiresome at times."

Not to mention all the work she was doing for him. She was technically a single mother working two part-time jobs. But that part-time added up and when he was constantly meeting her outside of business hours, that didn't help. Damn it, he was ready to wrap this case up and let the justice system take care of this mob family. But he had to be patient. It was a trait he hated, yet it was necessary in his line of work.

With Katie resting peacefully, Viv continued to eat. Jack didn't press the topic again. He didn't know if he was just reading too much into her actions or if she was truly just stressed, but he wasn't about to add more to her plate.

"They don't suspect you, right?"

Viv took a sip of her wine. "They suspect everyone who's been in and out of that office. But, not me specifically. I'm careful, Jack."

Why was his name on her lips like a tight ball of lust hitting his gut? He couldn't afford the distraction—especially when it came to his damn assistant.

When this case was over, he'd head to his villa in Italy. He could relax, find a woman to spend a meaningless night with. He clearly was not thinking straight and he blamed everything on being overworked and sexually frustrated.

"There is a new shipment of paintings coming in on Monday," Viv went on, oblivious to the turn in his thoughts. "I'm supposed to be off, but I thought I'd see if I could come in and just tell them I'd like some extra hours."

Jack curled his fingers around the tumbler of bourbon and considered her idea. "I wouldn't. They already know someone is leaking information. If you ask for extra time, that could be a red flag. I need you to do everything as you always had before."

Viv nodded. "I guess that makes sense. I just wish there was more I could do."

Taking a hearty, warm gulp of his favorite twenty-year bourbon, Jack wished there was more to be done. But he wasn't inside, and using Viv as his eyes and ears was the only thing he could do at this point.

"I'd rather you explore the Parkers' angle," he told her, easing back in his seat and glancing at the sleeping baby. "You have the perfect lead-in, especially when you're with Laney. Continue to talk about Katie, discuss how she's adjusting, throw in the loss of her parents and you've opened up the floor."

Viv pushed her plate back, wrapped both arms around the baby and pursed her lips. "That could work. Laney and I tend to always discuss the baby when we're not talking about the auction."

"Now's the time. That's the angle we need to work. If we can find out more about the night they were killed, I know it will circle us right back to the O'Sheas."

Jack didn't care what the initial charges were. This corrupt family had plenty of crimes they could be pinned with. But first he needed concrete evidence that proved the O'Sheas weren't so squeaky clean.

No matter who was in charge now that Patriarch Patrick O'Shea had passed, this family was into illegals so deep, there was no way they could've gotten out in such a short time.

"I'll be there from eight to noon tomorrow," she reminded him, as if he didn't have her schedule memorized down to the very last second. "I need to take

Katie to the doctor for a checkup, so I'll text you when I leave work."

When Katie started to stir, Viv came to her feet. Rocking gently back and forth, Viv patted the baby's back in an attempt to calm her once again. Jack watched as she instantly went into mother mode. Viv was the most giving person he'd ever known. A born nurturer. He'd checked her background thoroughly before hiring her, so he knew she'd never married or had kids. He'd seen quite a bit of hospitalizations when she'd been young, but she'd never mentioned an illness, so he never asked. He could've easily found out, but he'd snooped enough and didn't want to betray her trust at this point. Honesty was of the utmost importance to him and he expected it to be a two-way street.

"I should get her home," Viv stated. "She needs to rest and I need to get my own downtime or I'll be of no use to anyone."

Viv wasn't a superhero, though she was a working foster mother juggling two jobs and carrying a colossal lie on her shoulders, so that was pretty much the same thing. Jack set his napkin on the table and rose to stand in front of her.

"Why don't you see if your neighbor can watch Katie for a few hours extra each day so you can relax?" he suggested. "I'll pay for it if that's an issue."

Viv's brows shot up. "I don't care about the money, Jack. The reason I became a foster mother was to care for children who don't have anyone. Pawning Katie off on my neighbor just so I can nap will never be an option."

"That's not what I meant," he retorted, though she'd made him look uncaring, which was not the case. He cared…too much. "If you don't look out for yourself, how do you expect to do everything else?"

Her lids lowered, her breath came out on a deep sigh. She shook her head before meeting his gaze. "Everything I do is for those I care about. This child, you. I have no family, Jack, so I work to fill a void. When I stop working, when I stop caring for those around me, I start to think. I don't want the down time. I can't mentally afford it. Do you get what I'm saying?"

Jack swallowed the lump in his throat. How could she put his thoughts, his emotions, into such perfect terms? It was like they lived a parallel life, and he desperately wanted to know what made her this way. Why did she use work as her coping mechanism?

He'd already known she had no family. He of all people understood the need to connect with something in life and he clung to work...apparently so did she. He'd never heard her so passionate about it before, but he understood the ache, the emptiness that needed to be filled.

"You're talking to the workaholic," he told her, trying to lighten the intensity of the mood. "I just wanted to make sure you were taken care of, as well."

Shoulders squared, she tipped her head. "I assure you, I'm fine. But I do need to get home and I promise I'll text you tomorrow. We'll get this," she assured him. "We've come this far, we'll make it the rest of the way."

Jack helped her with the diaper bag, then assisted her with her coat and Katie's coat—which was no easy feat, considering she was still asleep.

Once Viv was gone, Jack leaned against the front door and stared into the empty two-story foyer. Yeah, he understood perfectly about not having anyone. He'd bought this massive home in Beacon Hill after his wife died. He couldn't stay in the small cottage he'd bought for her, the place where they'd planned to start their family. While he'd wanted to burn the cottage to the ground, he ended up selling it to a young newlywed couple who had the same dreams he'd once had.

He'd moved on, made more money than he knew what to do with and when he started looking for a permanent residence, he knew he wanted something large…something he'd never be able to fill with a family. He wanted the space so it didn't feel like the walls were closing in on him.

Some might say he was flashing, living in a huge house all by himself, but he didn't care. His cars, his vacation home in the mountains, the two homes overseas, they were all material things he'd give up in a second to have someone in his life.

No. Not someone. His wife.

Yet lately, when he would think of someone to share his wealth with, Viv kept popping up. He wanted to scrub that image from his mind because thinking of another woman was surely a betrayal to Carly…right?

As he headed down the hall and passed the kitchen, he instantly remembered the cheesecake. If Tilly came back in the morning and saw that none of it had been eaten, she'd be disappointed.

Easy fix. He'd be gone before she came in and he'd take it to the office with him.

Or he could take it somewhere else.

Viv claimed she didn't need anyone to look after her, but that was a lie. And Jack would take on the role in the name of business…because that's all he had time for in his life.

Whatever notions he had in his head about Viv, he had to remember she was his assistant. She could never be anything else.

Three

With Katie turning one next week, Viv had decided that the baby's shots were going to have to happen on her half day at O'Shea's.

Now that the doctor's visit was—mercifully—over, Viv was convinced the shots had hurt her more than they'd hurt Katie. Viv had just walked into her apartment, dumped the diaper bag next to the sofa and put Katie in her Pack 'n Play when someone knocked on her door.

She couldn't suppress the groan that escaped her. She was soaked to the bone from the chilly rain. All she wanted to do was strip off her wet suit and get into her cozy pajamas. Viv had been able to shield Katie from the elements by wrapping her inside her coat and holding Katie's favorite blanket over the tot's head. Now Viv needed to get that blanket into the dryer or there would be hell to pay come bedtime.

The pounding on the door persisted. What were the

odds she could ignore her unwanted guest? If she lived in a house, maybe, but in an apartment building she couldn't have her neighbors put out.

"Vivianna?" Jack's voice boomed and Viv realized her wish to pretend no one was out there had just vanished.

She crossed the floor, her shoes squishing. She wasn't even going to glance at her reflection in the mirror next to the door. The drowned-rat look wasn't becoming on anyone.

Flicking the lock, Viv opened the door. Of course Jack didn't have one drop of rain on him. The large black umbrella he held at his side was dripping.

"You're…"

"Soaked," she finished. "I know. Come on in."

She stood back so he didn't have to brush against her as he stepped inside. Katie made noises and clapped when she spotted Jack. Inwardly, Viv tended to have that same reaction, but she wasn't too keen on the fact that he was seeing her look so haggard and frumpy.

She'd really been confident this morning when she'd left for work in her gray pencil skirt and fitted, pale yellow sweater. She'd even taken extra time with her hair, since Katie had slept in. Now Viv must look like all she'd done this morning was shower…with her clothes on.

She was so over this winter weather. One day it snowed, the next it rained. Spring couldn't come soon enough. But it was only February, meaning Valentine's Day was fast approaching. A holiday she could totally live without.

"I brought this for you."

Katie eyed the dish in his hand. She'd been too preoccupied with her looks to realize he held food.

Glorious food. She didn't even care if that domed plate held a bologna sandwich, her stomach growled at the sight. She'd skipped lunch because she'd left work late and had barely made it to Katie's appointment.

"Whatever it is, thank you," she said, taking the covered plate. She headed toward the kitchen, cringing as her shoes made the most unpleasant noises.

Of all the times Jack could see her, of all the times he *had* seen her, this was not her best moment. She set the dish on the counter and pulled the lid off. A laugh escaped her.

"Cheesecake?" she asked, turning to glance over her shoulder.

Jacked shrugged out of his suit jacket and hung it on the hook by the door…as if he'd done so a thousand times. Seeing a man's jacket hanging next to hers did funny things to her belly. Her eyes locked on the two pieces beside each other, and she didn't want to dwell on it too long, but couldn't get over the fact that this simple gesture seemed so intimate.

But he wasn't staying, he was visiting, for pity's sake. For a second, though, she wanted to pretend. He looked good in his all-black suit, with that rich, dark hair. He'd brought her cheesecake when she looked like a mess, and he didn't seem appalled by her appearance. If he wasn't the world's most perfect man, then one didn't exist.

Would he ever see her as more than an ally? As more than his assistant?

She hadn't missed the way he'd sneaked a peek at her cleavage last night. He was a guy; they all did it. But when she'd caught his gaze on her, everything inside her had warmed, tingled. Because he hadn't just looked and glanced away. No, there had been a hunger in his eyes she hadn't seen before.

"What are you doing here so early in the day?" she asked, turning to lean back against the counter. "Not that four o'clock is early, but you tend to work much later than this."

"I had a meeting today not far from here, so I thought I'd come by to see what happened at O'Shea's today."

Katie clanged her blocks together and squealed as she flung them out of her Pack 'n Play. Viv ignored them. This toss and fetch was an endless game and one she wasn't going to get sucked into.

"I need to get out of these wet clothes," she stated. "Can we talk after?"

His eyes raked over her wet body. Jack never needed words to get his point across. This powerful man had such a hold on her emotions, and he had no idea.

All this was her problem, she knew, but did he ever think of her outside of work? Not that she'd ever know. Jack's personal life was never on the table for discussion. She knew of Tilly, his right-hand woman, but that was all. Anyone else in Jack's life was there only because of work. To Viv's knowledge, he didn't even date…or if he did, he was extremely discreet.

"I'll wait in here," he finally told her.

Viv tiptoed through her kitchen and out into the hallway toward her bedroom. Once inside, she shut the door, thankful for the few moments to herself. She hadn't expected him to just show up, with carbs and calories no less, so she was even more taken aback than usual.

Before the O'Shea case, Jack had never showed up at her apartment. He'd texted and called after hours, but all pertaining to work. Granted, his recent home visits also centered around work, but he'd seriously stepped up his game in an attempt to bring the notorious family down.

Viv closed her eyes and pulled in a shaky breath. The fact that Patrick O'Shea's journal was hidden in her closet weighed heavily on her mind. Guilt, anxiety, fear…they all consumed her, making her question her next move.

She hadn't been lying when she said she had no one in her life. Keeping a relationship with Jack, no matter how platonic, was imperative.

She needed to tell him what she'd learned, but how did she do that without hurting him? The FBI trusted Jack, was counting on him, and he was counting on her. He sought justice like he needed it to live, so telling him about her discovery would cloud his judgment…and hurt him in a way that would alter their relationship.

She didn't want to hurt him, and finding out Patrick O'Shea was his father would most certainly destroy Jack. Still, he deserved to know. The question was, when should she tell him?

Viv made quick work of ridding herself of her wet clothes and shoes. She wasn't telling him today. She couldn't. There would be a right time, just…not now. Hopefully, a break in the case would come soon. Then she could give the journal to him and let him decide what to do with the information.

She didn't bother drying her hair, just twisted it up into a messy bun. After throwing on a pair of yoga pants and an off-the-shoulder sweatshirt, she headed back out into the living room.

Jack still remained closer to the kitchen than the living room. His gaze was directed across the open space at Katie, who was oblivious as she chewed on the fingers of her plush doll.

"Let's cut into that cheesecake and talk," Viv suggested. She needed something to occupy her hands, her mind, other than the journal in the other room and the unnerving effect Jack's presence had on her. "How did your meeting go?"

He didn't answer her. He never even looked her way.

"Do you think she knows the significant people in her life are gone?" he murmured, almost as if his thoughts had traveled out into the open without his knowledge. "I mean, she seems happy with you, but is she aware of the void?"

Viv thought of that often since Katie had come to live with her. The older kids she had fostered obviously knew all too well the reality of why they were in foster care. But sweet little Katie would have no idea why her world was suddenly so different.

"She says 'Mama' over and over, but I'm not sure if she's just babbling or actually asking for her. But I'm certain she notices the absence." Viv crossed her arms, stood beside Jack and watched his face. "Are you okay?"

He blinked as if waking from a trance. "It's been a long couple months. That's all."

When he turned to her, Viv stepped back. That intense gaze landed directly on hers and she had no idea what to do with the emotions stirring within her, from the guilt and anxiety over when and how to tell him about the journal, to the tension and chemistry that couldn't be ignored. It seemed unlikely she was the only one who felt the air crackling between them, yet Jack was in total control and never let on that he thought of her in any other way than simply his assistant.

But he'd shown up on her doorstep with red velvet cheesecake his chef had made.

"Tell me about your meeting."

He shook his head. "Later. I want to know what happened with you today."

"Not much," she admitted, then held up a hand to stop him when he opened his mouth. "But I overheard Laney and Braden talking. They said the FBI hadn't contacted them in a few days, but they were keeping their guard up. Braden told Laney not to erase any records and that he had nothing to hide in regards to the Parkers."

Jack's eyes held hers, but he said nothing. She wasn't delivering case-breaking news, but she had to tell him everything she'd heard, learned...except for the the piece of evidence that was burning a hole in her conscience.

"Something else happen?" he asked.

Viv pulled herself from her thoughts. Those midnight eyes still penetrated her, as if he were trying to read her thoughts...as if he *could* read her thoughts.

"Not today, but Braden said Mac was flying in on Monday and he'd be in the office all next week."

"Why?"

Viv shrugged. "They didn't say, but I'm working three full days next week and I'll find out then."

Jack raked a hand down his face and blew out a breath. "This is so damn frustrating. For years they flaunted their lifestyle in the face of law enforcement. Luckily, I work for myself and I don't have to stick so close to the rules."

Viv didn't want to see him struggle, didn't like that she'd found so little for him to go on. "I tried to engage Laney in conversation about the babies, but a client called and she was pulled away. Then I had to leave for Katie's doctor's appointment."

Jack shoved his hands in his pockets and glanced

at the ceiling. Watching him battle with this frustration was more difficult than Viv had thought it would be. But she had to keep the journal to herself for now. Everything—absolutely everything, from his life to this case—would change in the matter of seconds as soon as he learned about it.

"You're in my office tomorrow." He regrouped and focused his attention back on her. "I want both of us to go over every bit of intel we have on this family. Maybe there's some tiny nugget of information we're missing. Something that can put us on the right track. I want you ready for next week, when everyone is here."

He was getting desperate, yet she understood his need to protect his reputation as being the best. Unfortunately, the journal she'd discovered wasn't the master key to solving this equation, and she had nothing else.

"Tell the Feds that all the players will be available next week," she went on, hoping to give him something useful, to buy them a bit more time. "With everyone at the office, something must be going on, or else they're worried about this investigation."

Jack leaned a shoulder against the wall and pinned her with his stare. "Maybe they have an idea who's been leaking the information."

The thought sent a shiver up her spine. Taking this job had been risky, but she'd agreed to let Jack create a solid cover for her. She'd put her life in his hands... literally, if all those rumors surrounding the O'Sheas were true. But Viv hadn't been afraid. Jack wouldn't let anything happen to her.

"I'm not getting that vibe," she replied as she moved into the kitchen. "Do you want a piece of this cheesecake or not, because if I eat the entire thing, I won't fit into my pencil skirts."

His eyes traveled the length of her body. How in the world did that man evoke more emotions and glorious sensations with one look than some men did with foreplay? Seriously. How did Jack make her want him so much, so deeply, when he wasn't even trying?

"Your figure is just fine, with or without the cheesecake."

Viv turned away, because that sultry tone of his sent a combination of shivers and thrills darting through her. Add in the way he'd assessed her body—such as it was, clad in yoga pants and a sweatshirt—and she wondered if maybe she'd pegged him wrong for not showing any interest and keeping his emotions all closed off.

Katie let out a squeal, breaking the tension. She seemed quite content to sit and play with her toys for a bit. Thankfully, her pain reliever had kicked in fast after the shots.

Once Viv had generous pieces of the decadent dessert on a couple saucers, she crossed to her two-seater table in the breakfast nook. Well, technically it was her breakfast nook, dining room and home office, depending on the time of day. Her apartment wasn't big, but it suited her needs. She rarely had guests unless it was foster children, so she didn't require a grand table. Besides, the place was close to Jack's office and the rent was perfect.

Though right now she did feel a little inadequate, remembering how amazing Jack's patio had been. He most likely had an exquisite dining room and an eat-in kitchen, yet he'd still set up dinner on his screened-in sunroom. Just the little bit she'd seen of his house had left her in awe. The rich wood, the clean lines of the furniture, that grand entryway with a masculine yet impressive chandelier suspended from the second floor were worthy of a magazine. Her entire apartment could fit into that foyer alone.

Jack either had a perfect eye for detail and decor or he'd hired someone to tastefully, expensively decorate his mansion. He took a seat across from her, but her round table proved to be smaller than she'd thought when his knees bumped hers. Why did his every single action get her body all tingly and jittery? This was Jack. Her boss. Her very sexy, very single, very mysterious boss. Other than the fact that he was a widower, never dated and had served in the military, she didn't know much else about his personal life...but oh, how she wanted to.

He scooped up a bite. "Tilly will be thrilled we're getting to this."

"Trust me, I'm more thrilled." Viv wasn't going to even think about calories right now. Turning down red velvet cheesecake would be a sin. "She's going to be happier to know you came to my apartment."

His eyes caught hers. "For business."

Right. Business. What else would he want from her?

"Still, she seems ready to make sure you have a woman in your life."

When he remained silent, Viv kept going. She would crack his shell at some point. Over the past couple years she'd worked for him, he'd not volunteered any information unless it pertained to a case. And the only reason Viv knew about his mother was that he always referred to her in the past tense. His father was never mentioned.

And Viv would've assumed Jack was a regular single guy had Tilly not slipped and said something about his "late wife." That had been at the office. One sharp look from Jack and the woman's lips were still sealed to this day.

"I don't know how your dating life has been—"

"Nonexistent."

Viv swallowed. She'd assumed as much...but why? He was, well, hot. He had money, not that a bank account made a man, but it wasn't like he couldn't get a woman. Maybe he just didn't want to. Maybe he had some other reason for being married to his work and ignoring the world around him.

"I really should consider going that route, because I've had some doozies."

Doozies? Way to sound classy, Viv.

Jack took another bite, obviously not feeling so chatty about his own personal life. Whatever. She was chatty enough for both of them, especially when she was a bit nervous. And between the attraction and the journal only a couple rooms away, she had plenty of unease spiraling through her.

"One time, I had a guy who offered me dinner and a movie."

"Predictable," Jack muttered.

"I can handle predictable," she added with a laugh. "It was the expectations he had for the evening. Cooking me a frozen pizza and binge-watching old movies wasn't my idea of a night out. He was shocked when I made an excuse to leave. He seriously thought..."

Jack laid his fork down and narrowed his eyes. "You're kidding? Tell me you didn't."

Viv tipped her head. "I do have standards, Jack. It takes more than a frozen pizza to get me into bed."

Those bright eyes held hers, then dipped to her mouth before traveling back up. "What does it take?"

Four

Where the hell had that question come from?

This was why Jack had always refused to get personally involved with anyone. Yet here he was, asking his *assistant* what it took to get her into bed.

Clearly the case, and working so closely with this breathtaking woman, was making him delirious.

"Well—"

"No." Jack held up his hand. "Don't answer that."

Viv quirked a brow, taunting him with a teasing smile. "You're sure?"

There could be no flirting, no unwanted attraction. Too much was at stake—the case, his sanity.

When he remained silent, she laughed. "We'll just say that it takes more than a lame dinner and a black-and-white movie."

Jack laughed with her. He couldn't help himself. "Any man who doesn't pull out all the stops for you is an idiot."

She tipped her head again, pursing her lips. "You never do that."

Easing back in his seat, Jack met Viv's eyes across the small table. "Laugh? No, I don't."

She crossed her arms and rested her elbows on the table. "Why not? What do you do for fun?"

"Stakeouts."

She rolled her eyes just as Katie let out a cry. "I'm serious," she stated as she rose to her feet.

Jack watched as she maneuvered through the living room to Katie. The little girl instantly extended her arms to reach for Viv. Jack turned away. All this... familial life was digging into that past wound, threatening to tear it wide open.

Some might say he was hard, uncaring, detached. Whatever it took to stay sane, to stay on top of his game, to help bring criminals down—to find justice... Jack didn't care what label he was given.

He concentrated on taking the empty plates to the kitchen and placing them in the sink. Resting his hands on the edge of the counter, he pulled in a breath. He shouldn't have come by. Venturing into Viv's world, into her damn apartment, was not smart.

In his defense, he'd been close and she hadn't texted, and he wanted to bring the dessert, so he'd broken his own rule of not getting into someone else's personal space. Time to head back home, where he could hide in his office, drink his bourbon and contemplate his next move. He was done waiting around for the O'Sheas to slip up.

When he turned, he found Viv standing close to him...too close. So near he could see the dark flecks in her eyes.

"Something wrong?" she asked, her brows drawn in.

Katie pulled on Viv's still-damp hair. All that gorgeous, silky, midnight-black hair. He'd be lying to himself if he pretended he hadn't envisioned that mass spread out over his navy sheets. When had this woman gone from assistant to starring in his fantasies? Lately, the line between professional and personal was becoming more and more blurry.

Even from the start, when he'd interviewed her, he hadn't denied her beauty. But after a few years of working together closely, and especially this past year, the dreams were becoming more frequent. Forget the fact that he vowed never to open himself up again; he was a professional having extremely unprofessional thoughts.

"I'll let you get on with your evening," he told her, ignoring the worried look on her face. She need not be concerned about him. His emotions had been murdered along with his wife, years ago. "I'll be sure to tell Tilly you enjoyed her dessert."

Viv seemed as if she wanted to say something else, but finally nodded and stepped aside to let him through. "If she wants to bake anything else and send it my way, she's more than welcome. I have a sweet tooth."

"I'm aware." Jack nodded toward the bowl of chocolate candy on the counter. "Your desk at work has a matching bowl."

Viv shrugged as Katie continued to pull on her hair. "I won't apologize for my snacks."

If those snacks were what kept that body all curvy and mesmerizing in skirts, then he'd buy her a full year's supply.

No, damn it, he wouldn't. Admiring her body wasn't his job as her boss. He had to get the hell out of here before he made an absolute fool of himself. Sitting at her little table, watching her with Katie…it was all too much. She smelled too damn good and had that rumpled, sexy look down pat. The rain she'd been caught in hadn't done a thing to diminish her beauty.

If circumstances were different—if he wasn't a jaded widower, her boss and her protector on this job—then maybe he'd seduce her. Maybe then he'd exorcise her right out of his system.

"Why are you looking at me like that?" she asked.

He still hadn't moved, even though she'd made an opening for him to pass. Jack stepped forward, his eyes on hers.

"I've never seen you out of your professional element. I just…"

"What?"

Hell, he didn't know. Wanted to touch her? Kiss her? To know if either of those would compare to his detailed thoughts of having her in his bed?

Viv shifted Katie in her arms, reached out and placed her hand on his shoulder. Jack stilled. Such a simple touch shouldn't evoke instant bedroom fantasies.

"Everything will work out with this case," she assured him. "We're getting closer. I just know it."

Yes. Let her think his moment of becoming a mute, staring fool had to do with stress from the case. The last thing he needed was for her to believe he was attracted to her. Hell, if she thought that, who knew what would happen?

Wait. He knew exactly what would happen…which was why he had to get out of here before he turned his thoughts into actions.

"I'll see you in the morning."

With that, he got the hell out. Maybe the chilly rain would cool him off and draw his thoughts back to the job—and not his assistant splayed across his bed.

* * *

The rain had stopped, but had quickly turned to snow. As if in tune with the crappy, depressing weather, Viv's morning had gone downhill fast.

First her blow-dryer had gone kaput after about one minute of drying her hair. Then Katie had a blowout in her diaper, so that called for a change of every single item of clothing, from her onesie to her shoes. How did babies have that much in them that they could ruin an entire outfit?

To top everything off, Martha was sick and unable to babysit. Lovely. But nothing Viv couldn't manage.

She had thrown her wet hair in a side braid and changed Katie into something fresh. Unfortunately, there was no backup sitter. So here she was, wrestling the diaper bag, a sack of toys and Katie into the office. At least she was with Jack today and not at O'Shea's.

After Jack left her apartment last night, she couldn't help but reflect on their conversation…or the way he'd looked at her. The dynamics had silently shifted between them. She wasn't sure what had changed, what he'd been thinking or why he'd been staring at her like he wanted…well, her.

The shiver racing through her body had nothing to do with the February arctic breeze and everything to do with the possibilities swirling through her mind.

Maybe it was the fact that Valentine's Day was next week. Perhaps all the hearts and cupids in the storefronts were messing with her mind. When was the last time she'd actually had a valentine?

If Jack was having thoughts of her, would he ever act on them? Would he make a move, or was he that removed from the emotional world that he'd keep everything professional between them?

What if she weren't his assistant? Would that change the game?

So many questions. Thankfully, Viv had Katie to think about, and her first birthday was next week, which could cancel out any Valentine's Day celebration. Not that Viv had dates lined up, but now she had an excuse to ignore the day not created for single women.

Warmth enveloped her as she stepped inside the office. The inviting brownstone had once been Jack's apartment, before he turned it into a permanent office. The place was cozy, yet professional, with neutral colors and leather sofas. It felt more like a home than a workplace. Viv didn't mind bringing Katie here because she could easily section her off from the front area, where clients might be.

Once the door closed behind them, she breathed a sigh of relief and dropped her bags to the floor. If nothing else, by the end of her time with Katie, Viv would have toned arms.

She didn't want to think about giving Katie up to her adoptive family. Letting go of any child was always a bittersweet moment, but Katie was special.

Viv had never met the parents of any of her other foster kids. But she'd met with the Parkers on more than one occasion. She and Katie shared a unique bond Viv couldn't deny, but she would have to continue to guard her heart or she'd be crushed in the end. Not being able to have children of her own was a bitter pill to swallow, so getting too attached to Katie would only cause her more heartache.

Jack came out of his office and glanced at the mess at Viv's feet. "What's wrong?"

Holding a bundled-up Katie, Viv merely shrugged. "It's been a crazy morning of trying to get ready and learning Martha wasn't able to watch Katie. That snow is coming down pretty fast and I have no sitter."

He wasted no time in crossing to her and bending to retrieve her bags. "You could've taken the day off."

"There's too much work to do," Viv stated, as she wrestled the hat and coat off Katie.

Gripping her bags, Jack headed toward the back, where her office was located. "We could've phoned or emailed," he called over his shoulder. "I'm not that much of a slave driver that I expect you to take her out in this mess."

This wasn't the first time she'd had to bring Katie, so Viv had invested in a small play yard for her office. This way the door could stay closed, and there was an entertaining area for Katie to explore while Viv worked. The brownstone had two spacious bedrooms that Jack had converted into offices. He also happened to keep a sofa in his office that converted to a bed…which she knew he often used instead of going home.

Viv sat Katie in the designated kid area in the corner and turned to take off her own coat. Jack had set the bags on the long accent table against the back wall and was closing the distance between them.

Why did her boss have to smell so good? And why did she have to be tortured by it?

"I expect you to tell me when you need a break."

Viv untied her wrap coat and draped it across the back of her desk chair. Smoothing her silk blouse down over her pencil skirt, she attempted to calm her nerves. She'd lain awake most of the night worried about that journal.

Correction. She'd read the journal the first half of the night, then had stared into the darkness the other half, terrified of Jack's reaction once he discovered the truth.

From the veiled hints penned in Patrick O'Shea's neat hand, Jack was indeed the patriarch's son. Jack's mother had wanted to keep their affair a secret. Though, according to the timeline, Patrick and Jack's mother had been an item shortly after Patrick lost his wife.

Most likely the man had turned to her only for comfort. But according to the journal, he'd been torn up over not having his son in his life. The reasons seemed valid enough. Jack's mother didn't want her child to be exposed to the O'Shea lifestyle, and she worried what would happen if Jack were given the infamous last name. The affair wasn't created out of love, but from Patrick's tone, Viv could tell he cared for her.

Regardless of Patrick's past feelings or intentions, Jack wouldn't care. He'd be furious learning who his family was. All this time he'd thought he had nobody, but the family he was hell-bent on bringing down shared the same blood.

Every time he mentioned his mother, Catherine Carson, his tone held pure affection and adoration. Jack was a loyal man, which was why the pain he'd endured too often had hardened him. He was protecting himself.

"Sit down."

Viv jerked back. "Excuse me?"

Jack reached around her, turning her chair until it bumped the backs of her knees. When he curled his hands around her shoulders, she stilled. Oh, those hands were powerful as they pushed her into the seat. His eyes never left hers as he loomed over her.

"If you exhaust yourself to the point you can't work, you're no good to me."

Viv shivered, from her damp hair, from his stare... from his low tone that resembled anger, though there was concern in those eyes staring back at her.

"I'm off tomorrow," she reminded him. "I can rest up then. But if I needed a day off, I would've told you."

His gaze flickered to Katie, then back. This wasn't the first time she'd noticed how uncomfortable he seemed around the little girl.

"Does this bother you? Her being here?"

Jack shook his head. "Of course not. I'm just not experienced with babies, that's all."

She knew he had no kids of his own, and he was an only child, so it made sense that he was nervous. But there was almost a level of sadness there—an emotion she recognized all too well.

"What's got you so nervous?" she asked.

Jack eased to his full height, crossed his arms over his chest and stared down at her. The intimidating stance might work on some, but Viv saw right through him. She wasn't a stranger to defense mechanisms herself.

"I need to answer a couple of emails, then we can start working," he stated, obviously changing the subject.

Viv slowly came to her feet, not at all surprised when he didn't back up. "I never took you for someone who runs away from confrontation."

Jack's eyes swept over her, then up again to meet her gaze. "I never run from anything."

"No?" she retorted. "You're married to your job, you don't date and the sight of a child has you twitching. I'd say you're running from several things."

Viv ignored his sneer. Sometimes people just needed to be called out on things. Perhaps not her boss, but she couldn't stand her curiosity anymore. She'd worked for him so long, yet he never, ever opened up. How did anyone live so closed off for that long? It was like he bounced between the office and his mansion. What did he do at home in that empty, sprawling house?

He traveled for work, always alone, but that was all the man did. Living a robotic life with very little meaningful interaction sounded so hollow, so depressing.

"Not everyone is so open with their personal lives, Viv."

Why did her name sound so sexy coming through those kissable lips?

"When was the last time *you* dated?" he added, quirking a dark brow as if he'd bested her.

"The day before Katie came to live with me." There. That should wipe that smirk off his face. "And you?"

The muscles in his jaw ticked. "Instead of digging into my personal life, why don't we dig in to work?"

Viv shrugged. "Fine with me. I need to get Katie settled and give her a snack. Go send your emails."

When she turned to ease her chair back, Jack's hand curled around her arm. Viv glanced from his strong fingers over her silk blouse up to his eyes.

"You may want to rethink giving me commands." That low, throaty tone washed over her, the warmth from his touch piercing right through to her heart. "And always remember who's in charge."

Oh, he could be "in charge" of her any time he wanted. But now would be a good time to keep her mouth shut. Apparently she'd hit her mark. If the hunger in his eyes was any indication, Jack wasn't thinking of her as just his assistant anymore.

Good. It was time he was as uncomfortable as she was, because she'd been keeping her sexual frustrations in check for too long.

He released her, but didn't step back. "Be ready in twenty minutes."

Viv nodded, letting him think he could throw his weight around. Fine. Whatever. This was his office, he was her boss, but they both knew she'd knocked him off his game earlier.

Jack took a step back and shoved his hands into his pockets. "Call the deli on the corner and have lunch delivered at noon. I want—"

"A Reuben with half the corned beef, no pickle on the side, no chips and a piece of carrot cake."

When he raised his brows and smiled, Viv added, "This isn't our first lunch stuck in the office."

Katie started screaming, "Up, up, up."

Viv laughed. "Sorry. Her new word apparently is *up*."

Brushing past Jack, Viv approached the Pack 'n Play. Those sweet little arms stretched toward her. Katie clearly needed the comfort that only human contact could provide. Viv understood that yearning.

After settling Katie onto her hip, Viv turned back to Jack, who remained exactly where she'd left him. "I'll be ready in a few minutes. She just needs some love right now."

The muscle in his jaw ticked again. "Does she do that often? Want you to hold her?"

Katie rested her head on Viv's shoulder. Viv knew of nothing sweeter than to be a comfort for a grieving child. Even if there was no possible way Katie understood the grief, she understood the void.

"She seems to be clingier than when she first came." Viv wrapped her arms around the little girl, holding her firmly against her chest. "It's almost like she realizes now that certain people aren't coming back into her life."

Viv was extremely careful never to say *mommy* or *daddy*. She didn't want to trigger any painful emotions in Katie. But at the same time, Viv hated acting as if the Parkers had never been part of the child's life. Hopefully, the family that adopted Katie would tell her about the amazing parents she'd had.

Jack eased around the desk, but didn't get too close to her as he kept his eyes on Katie. "I will bring them down," he vowed. "It won't bring her parents back, but there will be justice."

The conviction in his voice, the anger flaring in his eyes, brought on a fresh wave of guilt. How could she help him bring down his own family? Would he want to bring them down if he knew the truth?

Pulling herself together, Viv crossed the office to the table. As would anyone experienced with children, she used a one-hand grab to find snacks in the diaper bag.

"Just give me a few minutes," she told him. "Then I'll be ready."

She continued to shuffle items until Jack left the room. Once he was gone, Viv closed her eyes, resting her forehead against Katie's. Because at the root of all this chaos, the lies, the unknowns…the fear, there was an innocent child who deserved to be Viv's top priority. Every action, every decision right now revolved around Katie and her welfare. The journal, the secret—none of that mattered in the grand scheme of things. Viv would put Katie ahead of her own needs, her own wishes and even what was morally right, if need be.

Even if it cost everything with Jack once he realized she'd lied and withheld the ultimate secret.

Five

Jack eased back in the leather club chair opposite Viv's desk as she reached for yet more pieces of candy from her little glass dish. He wondered if she even realized she was doing so. She scrolled through the items on her computer screen with one hand, and used the other for snacking.

He could watch her eat candy all day. His body tightened as her tongue darted out to catch a stray piece of chocolate on her bottom lip. Why was he so turned on by such a simple movement? He knew why—because it was Viv.

"The notes I have copies of are all clean," she stated softly. Katie finally had fallen asleep in her Pack 'n Play after lunch, so they had to talk quietly. "There's no red flags on shipments, nothing that looks suspicious in the days leading up to the Parkers' deaths. On the evening of the robbery, Ryker and Laney were out to dinner with Braden and Zara. Mac and Jenna were in Florida at the Miami location. They haven't deviated from their stories even once."

Jack eased forward, resting his elbows on his knees and raking his hands through his hair. "I'm going to call a meeting with Braden."

Viv jerked around in her seat. "What?"

He saw no other way. Jack had already put the pressure on Ryker, the family henchman. If that didn't work to Jack's satisfaction, he'd go straight to the top, and that meant the oldest of the O'Sheas.

"You can't do that," she went on. "They'll know who you are if you go to them."

"It's a chance I'm willing to take."

Viv leaned her forearms on her desk as her worried gaze held his. "You were at Braden's house with me for the Christmas party. Then you surprised them just a couple months ago with a visit. You think he won't start putting all this together?"

The Christmas party. As if Jack could forget. Viv had worn some emerald-green dress that hugged every damn curve she owned, and that memory had haunted his dreams, sleeping and awake, ever since. He'd been her faux date so he could get inside and eavesdrop. Not that he thought some epic family secrets would be revealed, but he wasn't letting the opportunity pass him by…and he sure as hell wasn't letting another man take his place.

Jealousy was an unwelcome bastard.

"That was months ago," he told her. "Besides, I had a full beard then and my hair was longer. And when I approached them after, I didn't look like the same man. They have no clue. They know now I'm onto them, but they don't realize I was the guy at the party with you."

He often changed his appearance, even in minor

ways, because the average person didn't look beneath the surface. With all the people milling about, Jack was confident nobody would remember him from the Christmas party...not when he'd been overshadowed by Vivianna's beauty. He'd also been sure to make himself scarce the times she'd chatted with the key players. This had certainly not been his first time sneaking around and altering his identity.

"And what are you going to say?" she demanded in a harsh whisper. "You can't very well ask him to spill all his illegal doings."

Jack wondered if she had any idea that her eyes widened when she grew angry, that one of her brows arched higher than the other.

"I've done this a long time," he assured her. "Trust me."

Viv closed her eyes, reaching up to rub her forehead. Glancing at his watch, he was surprised to see that they'd been at this for quite a while. Katie had been asleep for over an hour, and judging by the dark circles under her eyes, Jack guessed it had been a while since Viv had actually had a restful night's sleep herself.

"Go in my office and lie down."

Viv lifted her head, smoothing her hair behind her ear. Her braid had started unraveling, giving her that sexy, tousled look. As if she needed to look sexier.

"You're exhausted and she's asleep. I promise I'll come get you when she wakes."

Because he'd have no clue what to do with a baby, and attempting to learn now would not be wise for the sake of his sanity.

Viv shook her head. "I'm fine."

Not surprising that she refused, but he wasn't about to let her win this fight...or any other, for that matter.

"Thirty minutes," he stated. "The couch is more than comfortable."

"You're speaking from experience?" She tipped her head to the side, knowing very well he slept in his office on occasion.

"I'm not asking, Viv. I'm telling you."

She rubbed her temples, as she'd done several times in the past twenty minutes, and Jack wondered if her head ached from her hair being pulled back or because she'd been staring at her computer screen.

Pulling her braid over her shoulder, she reached up and jerked the rubber band out. After threading her fingers through the strands to loosen them, she gave her head a shake. There was no way he could take his eyes off her now. The simple move was just as sultry and seductive as a striptease. All that long, rich hair spilling down her back, the groan that slipped through her lips had his own body stirring. Again.

"Viv."

Damn, that had come out like a growl.

Her eyes snapped to his. They'd worked countless hours in her office, but this was the first time he'd locked the main door so they wouldn't be interrupted. This was also the first time they'd closed her office door, but that was for Katie's sake. Still, being so confined with Vivianna, knowing the crackling sexual tension wasn't going anywhere, Jack was having a difficult time focusing.

He rubbed his index finger against his thumb, practically feeling all that hair wrapped around his hand as he tugged on it…from behind.

Raking a hand down his face, Jack finally came to his feet. "Actually, head on home. We're not getting anywhere, and I'm going to call Braden anyway and arrange a meeting."

Viv continued to look up at him. All that hair spread around her, those midnight eyes wide... His body stirred again.

"Why are you angry?"

More like sexually frustrated.

Jack shoved his hands in his pockets. "I'm not angry with you. There's so much at stake here and I refuse to let those bastards get the best of me."

Katie made a whimpering sound and Jack realized he hadn't even tried to keep his voice down. Viv's gaze darted in the baby's direction, then back to Jack.

"They won't," she told him. "But don't be so hell-bent on destruction that you don't find the truth."

"What the hell does that mean?" he demanded in a harsh whisper.

Viv circled her desk to stand before him. "I'm just as eager to learn what happened to the Parkers as you are, but what if the O'Sheas truly had nothing to do with their murders?"

This was the first Jack had heard her even mention any doubts. Where were they coming from?

Viv smoothed her hair behind her shoulders. "Listen, I know you and the Feds want to nail the O'Sheas. I understand. I just really don't know that they had anything to do with that night."

Jack gritted his teeth. "If you're getting soft because you're working there—"

"I'm not getting soft." As if to prove her point, she tipped her chin and narrowed her eyes. "If anything, I'm getting to know them a bit better, and I can honestly say I just don't see it."

Jack couldn't believe this. He threw his hands in the

air. "Most criminals don't go around with a sign announcing their offenses. Of course they're going to be friendly toward you so you're not apprehensive. And why the sudden change of heart? You never questioned my suspicions before."

She said nothing, just kept staring at him as if she wasn't sure how to respond...or as if she knew something he didn't. His radar wasn't often off the mark. Why would Viv come to the defense of such seasoned criminals?

"Did one of them threaten you?" he murmured, taking a step closer to her.

"What? No, of course not."

She gripped his elbow and squeezed. A simple gesture any friend would use when trying to get his attention. Still, the touch from Viv was anything but friendly...at least in his own mind.

"Listen, I'm just saying they definitely had their share of, shall we say, questionable transactions in the past." Viv offered him a sweet smile. "But with Braden in charge now, I know they are trying to keep things on the up and up."

Viv clearly wanted to see the best in this family. Perhaps it was because Laney was pregnant and Viv felt protective—one woman to another. Jack wasn't quite sure, but he'd done this work long enough that he refused to be sidetracked by the family's sudden need to walk on the right side of the law.

He reached for Viv's hand on his arm. Sliding it between his, he held her still, ignoring the way her eyes widened in surprise.

"I need you, Viv." In ways he couldn't even let himself believe. "You're my eyes and ears on the inside.

You can't get caught up in this family when we're on the brink of shutting them down."

When she trembled, Jack gripped her hand tighter. She closed her eyes and pulled in a breath. Black lashes fanned out against her tanned skin. What was she so worried about?

"Is it because Laney is expecting?" he asked. "Is that what has you upset?"

Viv shook her head, lifting her lids to meet his eyes. "No. Well, that does bother me, but I just worry not everything is as it seems."

"Is there something you need to tell me?"

Katie belted out a cry, which had Viv jerking her hand away and heading toward the baby. And just like that the moment was gone. What was Viv hiding? He turned and saw that she had entered her comfort zone as she wrapped her arms around Katie and swayed back and forth.

Viv's hair lay in waves down her back, shifting as she moved. She seemed to be humming in an attempt to sooth Katie's cries. Jack watched, wondering again why Viv had never pursued a family of her own. Maybe it was time he dug a little deeper into his assistant's personal life. After all, she was so determined to dive into his.

Days off were absolutely glorious. To have a day off from both jobs was even more splendid. Viv actually welcomed lounging in her pj's and getting caught up on housework. She'd gladly take wielding a toilet wand over volleying back and forth between a rumored mob family and the sexy boss she was hiding the truth from.

Katie crawled behind her as they headed down the

hallway. With the baby still in her footed pajamas, her knees would occasionally slip on the hardwood, but she'd push herself right back up and continue on.

Viv didn't want to think about how she'd bounce back once this case wrapped up. Eventually Jack would learn the truth, in turn he'd hate her and at best she'd be fired. The fact she'd kept something so personal, so life altering from Jack would tear him apart. Plus, on top of the inevitable, the O'Sheas would likely learn she'd been spying. And Katie would find her forever home.

Viv pushed the negative thoughts away before they could consume her.

"Up, up, up."

Glancing over her shoulder, Viv laughed at Katie, who now sat at the end of the hall outside her bedroom. With her arms extended, she wiggled her little fingers back and forth and continued to demand, "Up."

Just as she started back down the hall to get Katie, Viv's cell chimed from the kitchen. She quickly scooped Katie up and played airplane as she ran the short distance to the galley-style kitchen. Braden's number lit up, instantly giving Viv's heart a few extra beats.

The new family patriarch for the O'Sheas had never been anything but kind to her, but she still worried at the random call. It wasn't typical of him to contact her when she was off, and with everything going on, she certainly didn't want to draw attention to herself.

Katie pulled on Viv's loose ponytail as she swiped her finger across the screen. "Hello?"

"Vivianna. I need you to come in to the office early on Tuesday."

That stern voice boomed through the line, reminding her of her father. Len Smith never let his children get out of line, except when Viv had wanted to leave home and live in a big city. But that was not a subject she wanted to think about right now.

"Of course," she replied, tipping her head when Katie reached for the cell. "Is one hour early enough?"

"That will be fine. The FBI needs to question all employees again." Braden blew out a sigh, as if echoing her own feelings. Fear also crawled up her spine, causing shivers. "It's a nuisance, but necessary to get them to back off. I apologize for putting you out. You've been an exemplary employee."

Well, either he didn't suspect her of anything or he was a really great actor trying to trap her.

"It's no bother at all," she replied. Katie lunged for the phone once more and Viv eased her back down to the floor. "I don't mind answering more questions."

Katie grabbed hold of Viv's plaid pajama bottoms and started her chant once again. "Up, up, up."

Braden laughed. "Sounds like you're busy, so I won't keep you."

The O'Sheas might be ruthless and known for their less-than-legal business dealings, but nobody could ever say they weren't a loving family. Family meant everything to them. And with Braden's wife and sister expecting babies, he apparently was in tune with little ones.

"I'll be there at eight on Tuesday," she told him, smiling down at Katie, who continued to tug, her tiny chin now quivering. "See you then."

She'd kept her voice steady, she hoped, while talking to him, but a new worry crept in. What if the FBI had found something? The Feds knew she was a plant; Jack was very thorough with keeping his contacts informed. Still, if they were questioning the whole office, maybe they were about to crack this case.

And then what? What would Jack do? The journal

was completely personal, so there was no need for the Feds to know about it at all. But she was the only living person who knew the truth. It was her moral duty to tell him, whether the case was blown open or not.

Katie started fussing, rubbing her eyes and biting down hard on her gums. Viv set the phone back on the counter and reached for her. It was getting later in the day, but Katie had been up nearly all night with teething pain. Viv would give anything if those teeth would just pop through and let Katie have some rest. Poor thing was turning one in a week and Viv wanted to plan a fun celebration, even if it was just the two of them.

"It's all right, sweetheart." Viv ran her hand up and down Katie's back as she headed toward the nursery. "Let's rock a bit and see if we can get you to rest."

Three hours, no sleep and an empty bottle of pain reliever later, Viv needed reinforcements. The bottle of medicine had only one dose left when she'd pulled it from the cabinet, but thankfully, she kept a spare in the diaper bag.

With Katie on her hip, Viv frantically searched her apartment. Where on earth could it be? She always kept it right by the front door so this didn't happen.

Katie's screams were getting worse and Viv's frustration level was soaring. How could she be so irresponsible and misplace the bag with the backup medicine in it? She'd put her spare bottle in the bag when she took Katie to the office yesterday and…

Oh, no. Viv's heart sank. The diaper bag was at the office. She'd completely forgotten it in her haste to get out of the confined space with Jack.

She could throw on clothes and run to the drugstore two blocks away, but she truly hated to take Katie out in this weather. She glanced at the clock hanging above her bookshelf and noted that it was much later than she'd thought. She really had only one option if there was any hope of sleep tonight.

Six

Jack felt like a complete fool. His instincts had gotten him through combat; he'd managed to make enough business deals in the past decade to make him a millionaire; he spoke Italian and Portuguese and owned homes in both countries. Yet as he stood outside Viv's apartment door with diaper bag in hand, along with a sack of extra items from the store, he cursed under his breath.

He should've just brought the bag Viv had requested and not gone the extra mile. The last thing he needed was her reading too much into his actions. He was having a hard enough time justifying them to himself. He'd come damn close to kissing her in her office yesterday so he needed to calm down and reassess exactly what he needed to focus on…and it wasn't his assistant.

A middle-aged woman walked by and stopped at the next door. She threw him a soft smile, causing her eyes to wrinkle in the corners.

"You're here for Vivianna?" she asked.

Jack nodded. "You must be Martha."

He'd never met the babysitter before, but he knew she lived just on the other side of Viv. Jack shifted the diaper and drugstore bags into one hand and stepped forward to take Martha's bag of groceries.

"Let me," he offered, not letting her argue. "I'll carry them inside."

"But you have your own load."

Jack flashed her a smile. "Then you better unlock your door so I can go in and set yours down. My mother raised a gentleman."

She fished out her key and threw a glance over her shoulder as she turned the knob. "I like you. Are you here to take Viv out? That girl never gets out except to work."

Jack secured the large brown grocery bag against his chest as he followed Martha into her apartment, which was the same layout as Viv's. Martha decorated quite a bit differently, though. There wasn't a shelf or stationary surface that didn't have a knickknack on it. The porcelain cats, ducks, random shot glasses from around the world…there was just so much to take in at once. How the hell did anyone watch a child here? Breakables were everywhere.

"I'm returning the diaper bag she left at work," Jack finally replied, once he got past the chaos of the place.

Martha motioned for him to set the bag on the dining table. "That's a shame. I was hoping some fine-looking young man was going to take her out on the town. I'd gladly watch Katie, if that were the case."

The naughty twinkle in the woman's eye had him inching toward the door. The last thing he needed was a meddling neighbor trying to play Cupid. He was getting along just fine on his own.

Who said money didn't buy happiness? He was happy, damn it.

When this was all over, he decided, he wouldn't vacation at his villa in Italy. He was buying a whole new house for a getaway. He'd always loved the beauty of Amsterdam. Maybe he'd go there and look into real estate.

"I'll let her know you're available." Jack started through the open door, but the woman wasn't done with him yet.

"The weather is getting bad out there." She wiggled her brows. "If you need to stay for a bit, just have Viv run Katie over."

Was this lady for real? Jack merely smiled with a nod and got the hell out. That was the babysitter? Jack needed to have a talk with Viv about this. Not that he had any say over whom she preferred to have babysit, and Katie sure as hell wasn't his kid, but Martha seemed a bit too eager to get a man alone with Viv.

How many other men had she tried to set Viv up with?

The thought irritated Jack as he pounded on her door. He had no right to be jealous, but damn it, he couldn't help where his thoughts instantly went. The idea of some faceless bastard—

The door jerked open. It took Jack a moment to fully assess everything before him. Viv's hair was half up, half down…and not in a stylish way. More like Katie had yanked on it in a fit kind of way.

Gone was her typical pencil skirt and silk blouse. She'd donned plaid pants—were those flannel?—and a long-sleeved T-shirt that was a bit damp in the chest region. And she wasn't wearing a bra. Maybe having Katie stay next door with the crazy neighbor was the safest option, after all.

"Thank God you're here." Viv blew out an exhausted breath. "She's been screaming for the past fifteen minutes. Sorry to bother you, but I figured you'd still be at the office this late."

The screamer in question turned from Viv's shoulder to look straight at Jack. Her little eyes were red and puffy, and drool covered her chin. Her blond curls were in disarray. The two females before him looked as if they'd been through a battle.

Jack stepped in and immediately put the diaper bag on the table just inside the door. Without asking, because he recalled from the last time, he reached into the front pocket and pulled out the pain reliever.

Katie let out a cry, and Viv grabbed the bottle from his hand. "I can't thank you enough. I really didn't want to get her out in this weather, and I can't believe I left the bag at the office. What kind of foster parent am I?"

She struggled with the lid and holding a fussy baby. Jack eased the medicine from her hands and twisted it open. "You're the best foster parent."

Tears welled in Viv's eyes. "She's been miserable and I couldn't do anything to help."

He understood that helpless feeling all too well.

As Viv administered the medicine, Jack shrugged out of his coat and hung it over the back of one of two kitchenette chairs. Then he returned to the accent table and started pulling things from the drugstore sack.

"What are you doing?" Viv asked.

Feeling like a fool at the moment.

"I didn't want you to run out of pain reliever tonight, so I brought a few backups."

He stacked the various boxes on the table, because he didn't know which brand was the best and had bought two boxes of each.

"A few?" she asked with a slight laugh. "That will last me forever. Maybe you should be a foster parent. Clearly, you plan ahead better than I do."

She had no clue that associating the word *parent* with him was literally like a knife to his chest. She didn't know, because he'd never told her.

When Viv swiped at her damp eyes, Jack nearly reached for her. And what good would come from that? What did he intend to do once he touched her? Console her? Tell her everything would be all right? He sucked at consoling, to be honest. He wanted to, damn it. She made him want to try. He hated that she obviously felt inadequate and second-guessed herself.

Katie whimpered a bit more and Viv patted her back, bouncing softly in an attempt to calm her. "I'm sorry you had to stop here on your way home," Viv told him, then blew a stray strand of hair from her eyes. "I'm even sorrier I'm a complete wreck."

"You're not a wreck. You look like a woman who's putting the needs of a child first." Which made her even sexier. "Never apologize for caring."

Viv kissed Katie on the forehead and smoothed back her unruly curls. "I just hate to see her in pain. Teething is no joke. We were up most of last night, then she was fine this morning and I managed to get my cleaning done."

He might not be able to do much, but Jack knew of one thing that would hopefully put a smile on her face. He reached for the last item in the bag.

Viv gasped as he held up her favorite candy. "I think I love you."

Jack froze. Viv's eyes widened. "I mean, thank you," she quickly added. "You don't know how low my stash was running, and these are the name brand. I always buy the generic."

Yeah, he'd seen the empty bags in her office, which was just one of the reasons he wanted her to have the real thing.

Jack tore the package open and crossed toward her kitchen. He dumped the candy into her glass bowl and tossed the empty sack.

"I met your neighbor," he commented, leaning back against the counter. "Does she always try to set you up with a booty call?"

Viv's eyes widened. Her hand, which she had been rubbing up and down Katie's spine, stilled. "Excuse me?"

Shrugging, Jack went on. "She was all too eager for me to let you know she'd watch Katie if I wanted to take you out, or if we wanted to stay in, since the roads are getting bad."

Viv closed her eyes and wrinkled her nose. "Please tell me she didn't really say that."

Jack bit the inside of his cheek to suppress his grin. "Do you think I would make that up?"

When she finally opened her eyes, she looked everywhere but directly at him. Vivianna was sexy as hell and adorable all at the same time…and that invisible string pulling him toward her kept getting shorter and shorter. There wasn't a damn thing he could do to stop it. He hadn't felt the stirrings of desire for another woman in years.

"She's tried to set me up on dates so many times, but this is a first."

Viv shifted Katie in her arms. Apparently, the medicine had started kicking in, because the infant had one fist in her mouth and was playfully tugging Viv's fallen hair with her free hand.

"In her defense, she was married to her high school

sweetheart for forty years. He passed from a heart attack a couple of years ago." Viv moved into the living area and started to put Katie in her Pack 'n Play. Having other ideas, Katie merely clung to her. "She's always looking for someone for me because she thinks I'm unhappy alone."

Jack navigated around the half wall separating the kitchen from the family room. "And are you unhappy alone?"

Finally, those dark eyes met his. "I'm not alone. I have Katie."

He came to a stop within a foot of her. "And when she's gone? Will you still be happy?"

Viv tipped her chin. "I'm always sad to see my foster kids leave. Saying goodbye to Katie will be harder to deal with because I'm so close to the story. But if you're asking if I need a man in my life to make me happy, the answer is no."

"What does make you happy?"

Why was he asking? Jack wondered. He should get his coat on and get the hell out. The roads weren't getting any better and…what other reasoning did he need? He was getting too cozy with his assistant.

"Right now?" She raised her brows and smiled. "A shower. If you'd watch Katie for me for just five minutes, I will put in all the extra hours you want and you won't even have to pay me."

Watch Katie? Jack would rather hand over his no-limit credit card and send Viv on a trip to Rodeo Drive. Not because he didn't like children. Quite the opposite. But there was that fear that had been ingrained in him a decade ago. He'd been so hyped up on the idea of becoming a father, and then when that dream vanished, he'd forced himself to shut down that side of his mind.

"It's okay." Viv shook her head with a wave of her hand when he remained silent. "I just appreciate you bringing the bag and all the backups, especially the candy. Having her medicine is clearly more important than my hygiene at the moment."

He was such a jerk. Here he was worried about his fears, when Viv was constantly putting everyone's needs ahead of her own. From being an incredible foster mother to Katie, to working at—no, excelling at—two jobs because of him, the woman was a marvel. And all she wanted was a damn shower.

"Go shower. I'll watch her."

Viv's eyes widened in surprise, mimicking his own feelings. The offer was out of his mouth before he could talk himself out of it, but he wasn't sorry. The second her shock wore off, her entire face softened and her smile warmed something deep within him... something he'd thought he buried with his wife and unborn child.

He thought Viv might argue or tell him not to worry about it, but she quickly handed Katie over and muttered a thank-you as she dashed down the hallway.

Gripping the child beneath her arms, Jack looked into her baby blue eyes. The irony that she'd lost her parents and he'd lost his own child was not wasted on him. But it wasn't like he was going to be in Katie's life permanently. Still, holding her didn't make him miserable. In some strange way he couldn't explain, having her in his arms was rather therapeutic.

Katie smiled as drool ran down her chin and dripped onto his hand. Even that didn't turn him off. When he tucked her against his side, he felt a bit awkward. But the way she kept her eyes on him, as if she fully trusted him, had his heart stirring.

He hoped like hell Viv stuck to that five-minute plan because he wasn't sure how much longer his emotions or his sanity could hold out against the power of this innocent infant.

Viv felt human again. She'd managed a quick shower, hair washing included, and she'd brushed her teeth. She'd been mortified that Jack had to see her so...so blah. There had been no way around it, though. She'd needed the bag and she'd known he would be at the office.

The fact that he'd brought her the name-brand candy had her wondering if he was reaching out to her on a personal level. Obviously, but why?

Viv wasn't going to dig too deep into this, because even if Jack was trying to become personal, she was harboring a colossal secret. Pulling in a deep breath as she tugged her tank top over her head, Viv realized this case might never be solved. Would she have to hide the truth from Jack forever? But he deserved to know, even though it might ruin his quest for justice...and her chance at a deeper connection with him.

Worry coiled low in her belly. She didn't like secrets and she'd never been a liar before.

Well, until she became a spy for Jack and started working for the O'Sheas. Her moral compass had never been so screwed up in her life.

As she came down the hall, she wondered how long she should give herself before she told him. Each day that passed only added more layers to her guilt. But before she could give herself a time line, the sight in the living room stopped her every thought.

Jack was the sexiest man she'd ever met and reduced her insides to mush every time he entered the room.

But seeing him cuddling a sleeping baby might just be the ovary buster.

Nestled in the crook of his arm, Katie seemed perfectly content to catch some much-needed rest against Jack's broad chest. And Viv was a tad jealous.

"I'm sorry," she whispered as she crossed the room. "I tried to hurry."

Jack's eyes met hers, then traveled down her body. Every part of her tingled just as if he'd touched her. Perhaps she should've put on more than a pair of sleep shorts and a tank, but she'd been in a rush and grabbed the first thing she came across.

"She was out almost as soon as you walked away," he stated, glancing back down at Katie. "Now what do I do with her?"

Inching closer, Viv brushed against his arm as she stood on her tiptoes to look down on Katie. Such a precious little girl, one who trusted so easily. Viv didn't want Jack to leave just yet, but she wasn't sure if he wanted to continue to hold the sleeping baby.

"Are you hungry?" Viv asked, looking back up at him. "I could make dinner for us. But if you want to get home, I totally understand. Nothing I make would compare to Tilly's cooking."

A smile flirted around the corners of his mouth. "I can stay. She isn't cooking tonight. I actually threatened to give her the week off, because she's about as subtle as your neighbor and wanted you to come back for dinner…and breakfast."

Viv couldn't help the images of all the possibilities surrounding that scenario that popped into her head. But she'd never spend the night in Jack's bed—especially after she revealed the truth.

"Then maybe Martha and Tilly shouldn't meet," she

stated as she moved around him. "Would you mind holding the baby for a bit longer while I get dinner ready?"

Jack's lips thinned as he stared at Katie. "Not one bit."

There was a sadness to his tone, one Viv wanted to explore but had no right to. She had bigger problems… like cooking a dinner that a millionaire would find appealing. She had a feeling microwave mac 'n cheese wouldn't make the greatest impression.

Viv tried to block out the image of Jack holding a baby in her living room while she made dinner. There was so much wrapped in this moment—fear, hope, nervousness, sexual tension. All she could do now was concentrate on cooking. Later, she'd sort out her emotions—and decide when to come clean to Jack about his birth father.

Seven

Jack held Katie while Viv ate her simple meal of hamburger, baked potato and salad. She had protested, but Jack had insisted, gentleman that he was. Or maybe he'd just taken pity on her after witnessing her tears and frustration earlier. She was so grateful he was here—not that she should get used to having him around.

Once she was done, Viv crossed to the living room, where Jack sat on her hand-me-down sofa. He looked so out of place with that designer suit, groomed hair and a baby sleeping across his chest. Still, he looked perfectly at home, too. How cruel of her heart to cling to such a ridiculous fantasy.

Viv eased the still-sleeping baby from his arms so he could get up and go eat.

"I never dreamed she'd sleep this long," Viv muttered. "I'm just going to lay her down in her room. I'll be right back."

Viv had gotten his plate ready and poured him a glass

of iced tea, which was all she had unless he wanted whole milk or water. Definitely nothing like the dinner he'd served her at his house. But she wasn't ashamed of how she lived. She wasn't a billionaire, but she rocked the thousandaire title pretty well.

As long as she had enough funds to keep fostering and caring for children who had nobody else, she didn't care how padded her bank account was. A trip to Tahiti would be nice, but was definitely not a necessity.

Viv took her time laying Katie down in the white crib she'd found in a secondhand shop and repainted. The yellow bedding was cheery, yet calm, quite the opposite of Viv's nerves.

The stress of the secret was weighing on her. The fear of the unknown, the future, scared her more than anything. But she had to remain quiet for now…all the more motivation to help Jack clear up this case sooner rather than later.

Darkness had long since settled in, causing the tiny night-light to kick on in Katie's room. Viv gave the baby one last glance before pulling in a deep breath and tiptoeing away. After being up all night and agitated all afternoon, Katie would sleep until morning, she hoped.

Viv backed out of the room, pulling the door closed. Jack's strong hands gripped her arms just as she was about to turn.

"Sorry." His whispered word by the side of her cheek sent shivers through her. His firm touch on her bare arms nearly had her leaning back against his chest. "I didn't want you to trip over me."

Viv turned, but Jack didn't take a step back. So close. He was so close, yet with just the soft glow from the kitchen light and the small lamp in the living room, she could barely make out his expression.

"I need to get going," he told her. "I just wanted to thank you for dinner. Tilly is the only one who cooks for me, so this was a nice change."

Viv refused to believe a man who'd traveled the globe, both for business and pleasure, was impressed by a meal she'd thrown together.

"Actually, before you go, could we just talk?"

She didn't want him to leave.

Jack tipped his head. "I don't think that's a good idea."

Viv stepped away from the door so she didn't wake Katie. "Why isn't it a good idea?"

He moved in front of her, raking a hand over his hair, ruffling it, reminding her of the unkempt way he'd worn it when they'd first met. The man could seriously shave his head or grow his hair long and still have just as much sex appeal.

His eyes narrowed. "Exploring this tension between us isn't a good idea."

Wait…what? He thought she was about to bring up the chemistry between them?

First of all, she wasn't that brave. Second, he clearly thought of her in that way or it wouldn't be an issue. Part of her wanted to jump up and down, but the realistic side remembered the damning journal in her bedroom.

She'd just wanted him to stay so she'd have some company. Okay, that was a lie. She wanted him here so they could talk about something that maybe wasn't only work. Perhaps if he would just slide into personal territory even once, maybe he'd see she was more than an assistant. She was a woman with a desire for her boss.

"I was—"

"I don't like tension in my work space," Jack continued. His broad shoulders blocked the light from the living area.

"And you think there's a problem between us?"

Why did she suddenly sound husky, like some seductress? She certainly wasn't trying to seduce him. Not that it would be a hardship.

"I think you drive me out of my mind." Jack took a half step closer, towering over her and doing nothing to slow her rapid heartbeat. "I blame myself for my thoughts, but I blame you for making me want things I have no business wanting."

Viv's breath caught in her throat. He'd never made such bold statements before. She'd caught him looking, but he'd never, ever been this audacious. She'd be lying if she denied the sudden thrill of knowing he couldn't ignore his feelings. All this time she'd thought he was made of stone. Clearly, this man was all flesh and blood. And sending her smoldering looks from mere inches away.

"I'm not trying to do anything to you," she murmured. "I'm attracted to you, but I know you're my boss and that's a line we can't cross, even if you were interested in me that way."

Jack muttered a curse, took a step forward and had her pinned between his hard chest and the wall. He propped one hand next to her head as he leaned in.

"*If* I was interested?" he repeated with a laugh of disbelief. "Do I look like a man who isn't interested, Viv?"

She bit the inside of her cheek. Treading this unfamiliar territory was not how she thought the evening would go down. She needed to tell him about the journal… That would squelch any interest he had. But now wasn't the time.

Jack placed his other hand on the opposite side of her head. He didn't touch her, but there was barely enough air moving between them in that miniscule gap.

"Just one taste," he whispered. "You should stop me now."

He didn't give her an option to answer before his mouth covered hers…not that she would've protested. She'd waited too long for this moment and she was going to savor each and every touch.

But the kiss remained his only touch. He didn't rush, didn't force. He didn't need to. The slow, sensual way his mouth moved over hers instantly had her wanting more.

He lifted his head slightly, just enough to change the angle before capturing her lips beneath his again. Viv couldn't hold back. She didn't have the willpower Jack apparently possessed.

She lifted her hands to his shoulders as he nipped at her lips. When he shifted slightly, bringing their bodies flush against each other, Viv let out a groan. If he'd offered to take her to her room right now, she wouldn't have objected.

Jack left her mouth to trail kisses along her jawline. Before she could stop herself, his name escaped her lips in a whispered plea.

He stilled beneath her touch and slowly lifted his head. When their eyes connected, there was enough of a glow for her to see he was done. His pained expression was back, the torment he inflicted on himself so evident from his thinned lips and the creases between his brows.

"Jack," she muttered once again. "You don't have to stop."

His hands fell to his sides as he took a step back. A chill enveloped her and she knew that self-erected wall was back in place.

"I need to go."

She didn't get a word in before he turned on his heel. In moments, the front door opened and closed, leaving her feeling even worse than before the kiss.

Viv slid down the wall, pulled her knees to her chest and dropped her head. Why did he have to kiss her? If she'd known he was going to have instant regrets, she would've preferred he leave her alone. Now all she could feel were his lips. He'd touched her nowhere else, but her entire body still hummed.

And from his reaction, she knew he would never touch her again.

Tears burned in her eyes. She'd practically inhaled her boss, then begged him not to stop. How the hell would she ever show her face at work tomorrow?

"If you have nothing to hide, then meeting me won't be a problem."

Jack's gloved hand gripped his steering wheel. Frustration rolled through him from all angles, especially concerning that kiss he'd experienced an hour ago. He could still taste her.

But now his anger shifted from himself to Ryker Barrett. This was one tough guy to crack, but Jack was tougher. He wasn't intimidated by the mob family's thug.

"Meeting you would be a waste of my time," Ryker replied.

"On the contrary," Jack countered. "You can't dodge the fact you all are the key suspects in the Parkers' murders."

"Nothing to dodge. Do you honestly believe we'd steal the items we wanted to auction? Pretty hard to pull that off, even for us."

Jack hated this man. Hated the way he blew off the

fact the Feds were swarming all around the O'Sheas. Either they were that arrogant or they truly had nothing to hide. Jack refused to believe this family had turned so lily-white after Patrick's passing.

The patriarch was notorious for getting deals done, no matter the cost. He'd been careful, had the right people in his back pocket and had never even gotten so much as a parking ticket.

And Jack would be the one to bring them all down.

"Come by the coffee shop next to my office tomorrow at eight," Ryker finally grunted.

Jack hung up and tossed the phone onto the leather passenger seat. Snow continued to fall and here he sat outside Viv's apartment. He'd battled whether to go back in and apologize, then he'd opted to call Ryker and set up a meeting instead. He wasn't worried about meeting with him, especially in a public place. The O'Sheas—and their henchman—were playing it smart now, anyway. They knew they were being watched and didn't want to bring more attention to themselves.

Jack would start with Ryker, then move to Braden, Mac, anyone who would talk and give Jack the lead he needed to crack this damn case.

It was getting late and he still had a call to make with one of his clients in the UK, to go over some security detail he was sending a team to cover. A simple job that would pay an easy seven figures. It was the one aspect of his life where he could maintain control and keep his sanity intact.

Because kissing the hell out of Viv had cost him everything.

He never showed weakness, never let his guard down, but he had done both with her. He'd gotten too damn cozy holding Katie while waiting on Viv to cook dinner. This wasn't some suburban family setting, yet it had sure felt that way to him.

Beyond the whole domestic feel of the evening, Viv had come out from her shower smelling like lilacs and innocence. They were both damn lucky all he did was kiss her. He'd at least held on to that last thread of control by not putting his hands all over her…but damn, how he'd wanted to.

She was his assistant. The only woman, other than Tilly, he'd let into his life on any level since his wife had passed.

Jack knew his wife would've wanted him to move on. That wasn't the issue. The issue was the pain he'd gone through when he'd lost her. Every single damn day since her murder, he'd had to live with the fact that he hadn't been there to protect her. Did he want to open himself up to even the slightest risk of that happening again?

No. He had business dealings all over the world, clients who demanded his full attention. There was no woman who would understand, not even Viv. Besides, he was a much different man than he'd been a decade ago. Life had blindsided him and left him to pick up each shattered piece. He hadn't even had the energy to put all the shards back together. Instead he'd opted for a fresh start, completely revamping his future goals.

Never once had seducing his assistant been on his list.

Jack put his SUV in gear and pulled from the curb. He had to put some distance between him and Viv. Had to get his head on straight so he could come out on top during tomorrow's meeting. And he had to forget the way Viv had kissed him back with total abandon and want. Because he knew if he went back up to her apartment to apologize now, they'd end up taking a step he wasn't sure he'd ever be ready for.

Eight

She hadn't had a good glass of wine in so long, but Viv was rewarding herself tonight. Katie had fallen asleep without incident. Martha said there had been no issues during the day, and Katie had two teeth popping through. Viv nearly wept with relief at the sight of those little white points.

She'd gone into O'Shea's earlier in the day. Even though it was Saturday, they were getting ready for the spring auction and there was a constant stream of data to be inputted.

Viv had left the office early and done some birthday shopping for Katie. She was turning only one and would never remember this time in her life, but Viv wanted to make the day special. She'd never had a foster child at birthday time before and she may have gone a bit overboard. Her credit card had definitely taken a hit, but she didn't care.

Once Katie had gone down, Viv had relaxed with a

bubble bath. The lavender lotion she'd applied afterward had instantly calmed the rest of her nerves.

She hadn't heard from Jack since he'd kissed her and bolted out the door. His silence spoke volumes, though. For a man who checked in with her almost hourly, he'd gone off the grid, most likely to analyze his actions. Knowing Jack, he was going to come back with some quick, stern apology and expect to move on like nothing had happened. He would shut down once again if she didn't do something to make him realize that the kiss had not been a mistake.

If it had been, she wouldn't still be tingling and reliving every glorious detail.

Viv settled back against her pile of pillows, propped her feet on her bed and reached for the book on her nightstand. Armed with a glass of wine and a good novel, she didn't care what went on for the next hour or so. She was taking this time for herself.

With the snow blowing around outside, being cozy in her apartment was the perfect setting for getting lost in a good book. Unfortunately, she'd started this one so long ago she'd have to start over to refresh her memory.

Viv had just opened the hardback when she heard a thump. She glanced to the video monitor screen on her nightstand. Katie hadn't moved one inch since being laid down. Viv strained to hear another sound, figuring it must be one of her neighbors.

Just as she dismissed the noise, she heard it again. Sounded like someone was at her front door. Viv quickly set her glass and book on the nightstand, grabbed her phone and the monitor and tiptoed across the hall to Katie's bedroom. If someone was trying to get in, she wanted to be in the same room as the baby.

Her building had security, but nothing like the fingerprint scanner at Jack's office and his home. Her heart beat too fast as possible scenarios flooded her mind. Was someone trying to get in? Was this related to the case she was working on from both sides?

It was too late for visitors and the only people who ever dropped by her place were Jack and Martha. Viv didn't figure either of them would be attempting to get in to her apartment.

Viv heard a creak, very faint. She couldn't just open the door and look, because if someone was there, they could hurt her and take Katie. Right now, Viv needed to stay with the baby.

She dialed Jack and willed him to answer and not still be sulking about their intense kiss.

He answered on the second ring. "Viv."

"I think someone is in my apartment," she whispered. She kept her eyes glued to the crack beneath the bedroom door, praying she wouldn't see a shadow.

"Don't move," he said, his tone suddenly alert. "I'll be there in five minutes."

In other words, a lifetime.

"Don't hang up," he told her. "Keep this line open while I drive so I know you're okay."

Beneath the bold, firm command, Viv caught an underlying sense of fear.

"Don't be reckless," she whispered. "The roads are—"

"Damn the roads," he growled. "Talk to me. Where are you and Katie in the apartment?"

"I came into her room."

She heard another faint thump and squeezed her eyes shut. She'd never been one to rely on someone else to get her out of a jam, but this was different. Fear gripped her as she stood by the crib, clutching the phone and watching the door. She'd at least turned the simple lock when she'd come in.

"Viv."

"I'm here."

"Don't talk anymore," he ordered. "I'm almost at your street."

Still minutes from getting in to her apartment. But just knowing he was close, knowing he was on the other end of the line, was a comfort.

Thankfully, Katie slept on, unaware of any turmoil.

Viv hadn't heard anything in the past couple minutes, but she wasn't ready to step out of the room and leave Katie yet.

"I just parked and I'm heading inside."

He already knew the building code and the code to her apartment. Viv waited, hearing random clicks and footsteps through her cell phone.

He was in her building and she was going to be just fine. But was someone out there waiting for him?

"Be careful," she whispered.

Then she heard a few beeps seconds before her apartment door opened.

"The door was closed and I don't see anyone in here."

The heavy weight lifted from her shoulders as she tucked the monitor under her arm and quietly stepped from Katie's bedroom. Jack stood at the end of the hall, filling the opening with his broad shoulders. She'd never seen a more beautiful sight in all her life.

And it struck her that her first instinct had been to call him and not 911. Jack was the only protection, only security she wanted.

With the monitor and phone clutched to her chest, she moved on into her bedroom and dumped them on the bed. The wine and the book remained on the table where she'd left them what seemed like hours ago.

Wrapping her arms around her waist, she tipped her head down and drew in a shaky breath. Strong hands gripped her shoulders and Jack pulled her against his firm chest.

"You're fine now."

She nodded, afraid to speak. His heartbeat at her back was nearly as frantic as her own.

"Sorry I bothered you so late," she muttered.

"I would've been pissed had you not."

She turned, not caring how utterly unprofessional this entire scenario was, and wrapped her arms around his neck.

"Give me just a minute," she murmured against his chest. "I just…need to get my heart rate back under control."

When his arms circled her, tugging her tighter against him, Viv melted right into his embrace. The woodsy cologne he always used filled her senses. The warmth from his touch had her nerves settling. Just knowing she'd called and he'd beat feet to get here had her heart swelling.

"Thank you." Viv eased back to look up into his eyes. "I probably should've called 911, but I thought of you and then I heard another noise. I just dialed your number without thinking and didn't know who else to—"

Jack placed a finger over her lips. "I'm always your first call. Always."

Viv nodded, never taking her eyes off his. She noticed then that she wasn't the one trembling now. Every part of him, from his hand touching her face to his body pressed against hers, had a slight tremor.

Curling her fingers around his wrist, Viv pulled his hand away. "Are you all right?"

"Of course I am."

The words came out on a huff, as if she were asking an absurd question. But worry was etched all over his face. The drawn brows, the thin lips. Jack had been just as scared, maybe more, than she had been.

"You're shaking."

"Adrenaline." He kept her close, his gaze on her face. "It's not often I get a phone call after midnight unless it's business, and even then I'm expecting it."

She noticed then that this was quite possibly the first time she'd ever seen him sporting something other than an Italian-cut suit. He wore jeans and a long-sleeved black T-shirt. He hadn't even bothered with a coat.

And she was even more aware of how little she wore, considering she'd gotten ready for bed. Suddenly her silk tap shorts and matching pink tank seemed like nothing. The thin material was barely a barrier between them.

Viv took a step back, hating how her body cooled instantly once away from his touch. "Um…sorry you came for nothing. I think I'll be fine now."

Jack's eyes raked over her. "I'm not leaving."

Heart in her throat, Viv crossed her arms over her chest—the only defense she had, given the nearly sheer material and no bra. "It's fine, Jack. I'm sure it was a neighbor and my mind just played tricks on me. I'm sorry I dragged you out in this weather."

"Never apologize and never call me second when you need someone." He took a step forward, closing the gap between them. "I'm staying on the couch tonight."

"But—"

"I'm not asking your permission." He glanced around

her bedroom, his eyes landing on the nightstand with her wine and book. "Pretend I'm not here."

Viv snorted. As if that were even a possibility.

Once again, he was visually sampling her—and he wasn't hiding the fact. Having Jack on her couch all night would ensure one thing…there was no way in hell she'd get one wink of sleep.

Nine

Jack was used to sleeping in random places. The military had instilled that ability in him from the get-go. Then, when he'd started doing surveillance, he spent many nights holed up in his car or a van with video equipment. While he might have eight bedrooms, in his home here and villas in two other countries, he wasn't pampered and didn't need the finest accommodations. He was comfortable anywhere.

Or so he thought.

Viv's sofa smelled like flowers, like her. And he could possibly get beyond that, but every time he tried to close his eyes, images of her in that damn silky pajama number flooded his mind.

Hell, he didn't even need to close his eyes to see that glorious view.

And how much of a jerk was he, sitting here fantasizing about her, when she'd been scared out of her mind earlier. When she'd called him, Jack hadn't even thought. There hadn't been time. The fear in her tone, the way she whispered that she needed him, had absolutely gutted him…and thrown him back ten years.

Letting anyone else get hurt, or worse, on his watch again was not an option. Especially someone he cared about. And he did care about Viv—more than he would ever admit.

Jack dropped his head back against the cushion and stared into the darkness. Viv was only a few walls away, still wearing that outfit that dreams were made of. How much willpower did a man have?

Part of him wanted to ignore the fact that she was his assistant, and to go take what they both wanted. The boss part of him knew there would be no turning back—and the boundaries he'd so carefully constructed would be permanently blurred.

Did he really want to risk that for one night?

Before Jack could think too much, he came to his feet. Hell, yes, he wanted to risk it. If anything, he'd learned to take what he wanted out of life…and he wanted Vivianna Smith.

She'd stared at the same page, the same paragraph, for the past fifteen minutes. She'd downed her wine immediately, because she'd needed something to calm her nerves…nerves that had nothing to do with the scare she'd had earlier and everything to do with the man keeping guard in her living room.

That whole protective nature of his was such a turn-on, as if she needed more reasons to want him. So far the only flaw she'd discovered was his inability to let anyone behind the wall he'd erected around himself.

But after the way he'd kissed her, the way he'd looked at her and proved to be a white knight, Viv wasn't letting her desire go. She had to know if there was more passion in him where that came from.

Her mind made up, she set the book on the nightstand next to her empty glass. Just as she rose to her feet, there was a creak outside her bedroom. A second later, the door eased open.

Viv stood next to her bed, eyes locked on Jack filling her doorway. The small accent lamp on her nightstand was the only thing illuminating the space. Jack raked his gaze over her as he'd done earlier…as if he couldn't get enough. She was counting on just that.

"What took you so long?" she asked. "I was coming to you."

He stayed in the doorway, but Viv wasn't deterred. She knew he'd come this far and wasn't about to leave. She remained by the bed, because there was no way she was going to cross that space now. The next move was his.

"This is it," he murmured, stepping over the threshold. "Tonight has nothing to do with tomorrow."

If that's what he chose to believe, whatever. She knew better, but she wasn't about to argue, not when she was so turned on she was about ready to pounce on him.

"What changed your mind?"

He stalked closer, until they were toe to toe and she had to tilt her head to look into his eyes. "Does it matter?"

In the grand scheme of things maybe, but right this second? No.

Anticipation had her stomach quivering. Now that he was in her bedroom, Viv really wished he'd do something rather than stand so close with no contact. Throw her down on the bed, for starters.

Jack's fingertips traveled up her bare arms, across her collarbone, before slowly sliding the straps of her tank out of the way.

"Do you always wear sexy silk things to bed?" His eyes remained on the task of undressing her as he spoke.

"Yes."

He eased the thin material down until the tank pooled around her waist. Instinctively, her body arched, reacting to the cooler air and the anticipation of his touch. He was slowly killing her.

"If you don't move faster, I'm going to take over."

Jack's eyes darted to hers. "I've waited for this. I'm going to take in every single second."

He'd waited? For how long?

Before she could analyze his statement too much, Jack hooked his thumbs in the bunched material around her waist and slid everything lower. When he crouched down, she lifted one foot, then the other, until she was completely bared to him.

If any other man was at her feet, Viv would think him submissive, but she knew better with Jack. He was in control at all times.

Jack curled his fingers around her ankles, then pushed his way up her body, over her hips to the dip in her waist, until he was on his feet again. Viv let out a moan when he finally palmed her breasts.

"You're so responsive."

Now wouldn't be the time to tell him she'd never been this responsive to another man. She'd never ached for a man like this before. Viv wanted to see him, too, all of him. She reached for the hem of his shirt and jerked it up. Jack released her long enough to whip the garment over his head and toss it aside. Keeping his eyes locked on hers, he quickly rid himself of his jeans and boxer briefs, until he stood before her in all his glorious masculinity.

"I'm not—"

Her thoughts were lost as he snaked his arms around her waist and pulled her against his body. His mouth crashed down onto hers as if every shred of his control had snapped.

The backs of her knees hit the edge of her bed. Jack followed her down, never breaking away from her. The weight of his body pressing her into the duvet was a welcome sensation. She'd dreamed of this moment, never thinking he'd be in her bed. In her imagination they'd always been in one of the rooms of his grand home.

Jack pulled his lips from hers as he looked down into her eyes. He rested his elbows on either side of her head, smoothing her hair away from her face.

"Be sure."

Viv bent her knees, sliding her ankles around his waist and locking them behind his back. When he closed his eyes and pulled in a deep breath, she stilled. Realization hit her.

"You don't have protection, do you?" she asked.

He shook his head. "I clearly didn't plan this when I left."

"I don't keep anything here."

The corners of his mouth tipped up. "On one hand that makes me happy. On the other hand, I'm dying."

Viv wasn't the most sexually active woman and pregnancy wasn't an option with her history. But now was definitely not the time to start verbally going through her medical chart.

"I'm clean," she told him. "And you don't have to worry about pregnancy."

His eyes turned darker as he lowered his lids once again. Before she could question him, he slid his mouth across hers and murmured, "I'm clean, too."

Viv tightened her grip around his waist, urging him to take what they both were so desperate for.

The second he joined their bodies, he locked his eyes on hers. This was what she'd been waiting for. This man, this moment.

Viv arched into him, her fingers gripping his shoulders as he set the pace. Jack captured her mouth, nipping at her lips over and over as his hips met hers. He reached down, curling his hand around the back of her knee and lifting just enough for her to feel even more sensations rushing through her.

Viv tore her mouth from his the second her body started to climb. She squeezed her eyes shut, not wanting him to see just how affected she was by the intensity of their passion.

Jack's lips on the side of her neck, drifting down to her sensitive breast, was all she needed to peak. Her body clenched around him as she cried out. He jerked against her, his own body stilling as he followed her into oblivion.

Moments later, Viv continued to tremble. Jack kissed her once more, then rested his forehead against hers. His heart beat harshly against her chest and she wanted desperately to know what he was thinking. Then again, the silence of the moment was perfect. She could relish the fact that she'd made love with the one man she'd wanted for years. He'd come to her because he'd been unable to fight the attraction any longer.

Could he just walk away after this? Could he be satisfied with just one night and then go on as if this didn't alter their lives?

Viv turned her head aside as guilt and fear trickled through the euphoric state she'd been floating in.

The journal was behind her closet door. The key to Jack's past was only feet away. She'd been looking for the right time to talk to him, but this certainly wasn't it.

"You were right earlier," he murmured against the side of her neck. He rolled slightly so his weight wasn't directly on her, but he kept an arm around her waist. "I was scared when you called. It's not an emotion I connect with or have often."

Viv jerked her thoughts from the journal and shifted to face him.

"My wife died when I was overseas, and I wasn't there to protect her." He held Viv's gaze as his thumb stroked her abdomen. "She was in the wrong place at the wrong time. I know I may not have been with her even if I had been stateside, but knowing I was so far…"

Viv slid her palm over his stubbled cheek. "You don't have to explain why you were afraid. I know your wife died while you were overseas. I didn't know specifics, though. You aren't to blame. You have come to grips with that, right?"

Jack eased away and rose to his feet, instantly leaving her chilled. When he started gathering his clothes, Viv knew he was holding true to his word. What just happened was all he would give. There would be no opening up and sharing past stories now.

And how could she expect him to reveal a part of himself, when she held such a damning secret?

"I'll be on the sofa."

His parting words left her cold. She wished he would have just gone home, because what had taken place in her bed hadn't drawn them closer together at all. If anything, she felt more distanced than ever.

Ten

Jack glared across the coffee shop, willing Ryker Barrett to step through the etched glass doors. After last night, Jack wasn't in a great mood, which was perfect for a meeting with the man who knew all the O'Sheas' secrets.

Sipping his black coffee, Jack tried to ignore the ache in his chest. Last night had been everything he'd wanted, everything he hadn't known he'd been missing. But there was no way anything could ever come from hooking up with Viv. She was all about taking care of children, and he refused to allow himself the luxury of even entertaining the idea of a family life.

He'd had sex. He certainly wasn't looking for holy matrimony. Once was enough. The risk of going through such heartache again wasn't something he was on board with. Besides, no permanent relationship could come from an affair with his assistant, even if he were looking for something long term.

Which was why he'd found himself hightailing it from her apartment before she and Katie woke. He'd gone back to his Beacon Hill home to change, dodged all questions from Tilly and had made it out to Bean House, hopefully in time to catch Ryker.

Jack had done enough surveillance to know the man frequented this coffee shop next to the O'Shea offices. He wasn't surprised that Ryker had picked this neutral territory for their meeting.

Jack waited nearly twenty minutes before he spotted the man in the dark leather jacket, with coal-black hair and a menacing look in his eyes. Ryker Barrett was exactly what he portrayed: mysterious and standoffish, and exuding a go-to-hell attitude.

Well, too bad. Jack was eager to get this little pow-wow started.

After Ryker placed his order, Jack stepped to the end of the counter and met the man's gaze, relieved not to see recognition there.

"Get your coffee and meet me over in the corner."

He didn't wait for Ryker to answer. Even though Jack had been at the O'Sheas' Christmas party, he hadn't spoken to Ryker that night, so it was unlikely the family's right-hand man would link him to Viv.

Just as Jack took a seat, Ryker came to stand on the other side of the table. Coffee cup in hand, he glared down at him.

"You can sit or stand, but you may not want everyone to hear our conversation." Jack wasn't in the mood for games.

Ryker sipped his coffee, then slid the wooden chair out and casually dropped into it. He glanced around the café as if he didn't have a care in the world. Arrogant jerk. Jack wanted to reach across the table and punch the smug look off his face.

"I've already told you everything, which is more than you deserve." Ryker flung an arm across the chair beside him and set his cup on the table. "You have two minutes."

Jack knew if he wanted to get to the bottom of this case once and for all, he'd have to take a different approach. "I'm willing to work with you to find out who committed the crime against the Parkers," he said grudgingly.

There was a ring of truth to the saying about keeping your enemies closer, even if Jack hated every second of it.

"And why would I want to work with you?" Ryker countered.

Jack shrugged, leaning forward on his elbows. "Because you want to clear the O'Shea name and I want to find out who made an orphan out of an innocent child."

Even though Jack had a gut feeling he was looking at the main suspect. But if he could work closely with Ryker, and Viv kept digging at the office, there was no way they could miss the truth.

"You've been hell-bent on pinning this on us," Ryker stated. "Why the change now?"

"I'm determined to get to the truth. You can either work with me or get out of my way."

Ryker's dark eyes narrowed. "Threatening me isn't your smartest move."

Jack couldn't help but smile. "That wasn't a threat. That was a promise."

Determined to keep the upper hand, Jack pushed himself to his feet. "Talk it over with your friends and let me know."

Gripping his to-go paper cup, Jack headed out the café door and into the brisk February air. There wasn't a doubt in his mind he'd be contacted by Ryker or another member of the O'Shea clan in short order. If they were truly going legit in the legal sense—and Jack wasn't so sure about that—then they'd want to work to clear their name and get the Feds off their backs.

Jack sipped his hot coffee as he made his way to his SUV. He'd head into the office, because he wasn't in the mood to go home and face Tilly. After he'd spent the night at Viv's apartment, there was no way Tilly wouldn't know something was up. She'd caught him sneaking in this morning and he'd dodged her questions, but he couldn't forever.

First, he had to come to grips with what had happened last night before he could even attempt to make excuses to his nosy, yet loving, chef and maid.

Logically, he knew he shouldn't have slept with Viv, but there was no way he could've avoided her forever. The more he worked with her, the more he wanted her. The physical aspect he could deal with, and thoroughly enjoy. It was everything else that came after the sex that had him questioning what the hell he was doing.

Like why he was still thinking of her. Thinking of the way her hair had spilled around him, the way she'd looked at him with hope, as if their one night could lead to something more.

Jack climbed in behind the wheel of his SUV and brought the engine to life. He'd been up front with Viv, telling her that he was unable to give more, and she'd agreed. But her face as he'd dressed and left the room said differently.

They both needed time apart. Unfortunately, that

wasn't possible, since they were working so closely together. Jack had to keep the upper hand on his emotions or he'd find himself falling deeper for Viv. And that was a heartache he couldn't afford to revisit.

He'd avoided her for two days.

Viv sat behind her antique mahogany desk and willed her door to open. She'd come in and gone straight to her own office like she did every morning she was scheduled to work with Jack. But this morning was unlike any other. This was her first day back to work after sleeping with her boss.

The phrase sounded so clichéd and tacky, but there was no sugarcoating the truth. He'd left her bed before she'd fully recovered, and spent the night on the sofa, then slipped out before she was up for the day. Clearly, he meant what he'd said about one night being all he could give.

Viv would be lying if she didn't admit she'd hoped he'd change his mind. Did he feel anything at all toward her? Was a one-night stand all he wanted? The man was so closed off, she honestly had no clue.

In his defense, he hadn't lied to her.

Viv dropped her face into her hands as guilt consumed her. Jack may have had sex with her and left, but at least he'd been totally up-front with her. As opposed to Viv, who was still hiding a secret that would completely change his life and everything he thought to be true.

The timing hadn't been right, then their attraction had snowballed and they'd slept together. Now here she sat, half in love with her boss and trying to help him bring down the family that was his by birthright.

From this point on, nothing would be easy. Not her feelings, not her actions…absolutely nothing.

Viv jumped when her cell rang. Glancing to the ID on the screen, she quickly slid her finger across to answer.

"Hello."

As if her heart wasn't already beating fast enough, now she waited to see what the social worker wanted. If it was time to say goodbye to Katie, then she'd have to let the precious baby go. But Viv wasn't ready.

"Vivianna, I hope this is a good time."

"Of course." It wasn't like she was actually working. "What can I do for you?"

"I'm calling with a question that I'd like you to take your time to consider."

Viv eased back in her leather chair and crossed her legs. "All right." Smoothing her pencil skirt down her thigh, she gripped her cell in anticipation.

"Before you took Katie in, you had expressed interest in full adoption. Is that still an avenue you'd like to explore, or are you content with fostering? I'd like to make it clear that Katie has no other family members."

Hope blossomed in Viv's chest. Being a parent had been a dream she never thought she'd reach. She'd put her forms in to adopt because she did want a family. She'd thought someday she'd be okay with erasing that distance between her and the foster children she helped, but honestly hadn't known if that day would ever come. Was Katie the one to be part of her family?

To know she could fully adopt a baby so sweet, so perfect… Viv was almost afraid to get too excited.

"Adopting is definitely an option," she replied, unable to hide her smile. "But I have questions and concerns."

"Of course. I'm happy to answer anything. Would you like to take some time to think, to fully process what this means? There are so many things to consider. Cost, time, paperwork. You're a fostering veteran, so you've already gone through a great deal of the process."

Viv came to her feet just as her office door opened. Of course Jack would decide to barge in now. She held up a finger and he nodded as he sauntered over and took a seat in the leather club chair across from her desk.

Viv turned her back to him and concentrated on the view out the window. Snow swirled around, piling on top of the three inches that had already been dumped on Saturday.

"I'm definitely interested in talking with you further," Viv stated, well aware that Jack was likely hanging on her every word. "Why don't I call you in a day or two? Maybe by then I'll have my questions all made out and we can go over everything at once."

"Perfect. And Vivianna, there's no pressure here. We can find a home for Katie. I just thought you would be the best candidate for her."

Viv blinked as tears burned her eyes. "Thank you. I'll be in touch."

She disconnected the call and held on to her phone as she crossed her arms. Adopting Katie would be a dream come true. The little girl she'd come to love and care for could possibly be hers forever. Her heart swelled nearly to bursting.

"Viv?"

Jack's voice pulled her from her daydream. Composing herself, she turned to face him, thankful the desk still sat between them as a barrier. She could handle only so much at once.

"Everything all right?" His eyes held hers and he frowned. "You're crying."

Viv swiped at the stray tear that had escaped. "Everything is fine. What did you need?"

"First I need to know why that call has you upset."

Viv leaned over her desk chair and placed her phone back on her calendar. "Nothing that has to do with work."

Slowly, he pushed himself to his feet, never taking his eyes off her. "Is this how things are going to be?"

"You mean a professional relationship?" she asked, crossing her arms. "Isn't that exactly what you decided on? I'm just following orders like a good assistant."

Jack rounded the desk, those green eyes never wavering from hers. He came to stand toe to toe with her, forcing her to tip her head back. Viv didn't step away, but nerves spiraled through her.

"Don't make things difficult," he growled. "When I see you upset, I have to know why."

"And you have no right to ask." Oh, how she wanted to share this news with him, but after he'd all but sprinted from her bed, she just couldn't expose herself to any more hurt and rejection. "My personal life has nothing to do with you. Now, I'll ask again. What did you barge in here for?"

The muscles in his jaw ticked. "I spoke with Ryker on Saturday. I offered to work with him in order to solve this case."

Now Viv did step back, mostly from shock. "What? What did he say?"

Shoving his hands in the pockets of his Italian suit, Jack shrugged. "We battled back and forth. I left before he could turn me down, but I'm sure he'll think about it. He'll discuss the offer with Braden and Mac, and with Mac coming into town, one of them will reach out to me."

"You think they'll agree to work with you?"

"I have no idea, but I'm not giving up and I had to find a new tack."

Viv closed her eyes. If he knew about the journal, perhaps he could approach them in a different way. Maybe they'd be more willing to speak if they knew Jack was family.

But first and foremost, Jack was an investigator and security specialist. He was still the enemy, according to the O'Sheas. So for now, the journal and the secrets would remain locked safely in her closet.

"I'm going in early tomorrow to talk to the Feds," Viv told him. "I know everyone will be at the office."

"There's nothing to be nervous about." Jack reached for her, then dropped his hand before he could make contact. "They haven't discovered anything to incriminate you."

Oh, but *she* had. Something much more life-altering than clues that might solve a mysterious case.

"I told you about the files I copied," she countered. "That was months ago and I haven't taken anything else, but the O'Sheas are convinced someone on the inside is betraying them."

"The Feds won't ask you anything that will be damning in front of Braden or Mac."

Jack did reach for her now. His hands curled around her shoulders and she couldn't help but stiffen at his touch.

"I don't want you worried. I'll take care of you."

Viv laughed. "Right. For the case, I know." She shrugged away from his touch. "I have work to do."

Jack fisted his hands at his sides. "And ignoring the other night is part of that?"

Oh, that was rich coming from him. "Says the man who couldn't get out of my bed and dressed fast enough."

Eleven

There was no way to avoid this conversation, but Jack just wished like hell he didn't have to see that hurt in her eyes. How was he protecting her when he was the one causing her pain and frustration? He should've kept his damn hands to himself. But the slippery slope he'd been clinging to for months had become too much.

"Don't do this."

"What?" she asked, tilting her chin in defiance. "Call you out on the truth?"

"Damn it, Viv." Jack raked his fingers through his hair. Propping his hands on his hips, he forced his eyes to stay on hers. "You're everything I used to want."

Great, now he'd exposed a portion of himself. Letting anyone see that side of his heart wasn't an option, but the words hovered in the air between them and he wished like hell he could snatch them back.

Viv's brows dipped as she frowned. "I don't even know what that means."

He'd come this far. Viv deserved the truth after the way he'd blurted out half of it.

"As you know, my wife died while I was overseas."

He hated thinking about that time in his life, let alone talking about it. Yet somehow he felt the need to open up to Viv about it for the second time.

Other than Tilly, Viv had been in his life the longest since his darkest hour. If anyone deserved to be let in, it was her. Besides, he prided himself on being truthful whenever possible.

Viv had always been an open book, never pushing for more in return. Her loyalty, her honesty and her commitment to stand by him even during his moody days were humbling…and that was the only reason he was opening up to her. It had nothing to do with the fact he'd felt a connection while he'd been in her bed. That connection couldn't go any deeper and she would understand why soon enough.

"My wife was shopping when a robber decided to randomly open fire. He turned the gun on himself before the cops arrived."

Jack swallowed, turning away when moisture gathered in Viv's expressive brown eyes.

"She was shopping for baby furniture," he whispered, when his own emotions threatened to take hold.

Viv's audible intake of breath pulled his focus back to her. "I wasn't there with her. I only had one month left in the service and I was getting out, because we were planning the family we always wanted."

"Jack."

Viv reached for him…and he let her. Perhaps he needed the contact, or maybe he was just a glutton for punishment, because he wanted more of her touch whether it was the right thing to do or not.

She took his hands, squeezing them in hers as she stared up at him. "I don't even know what to say."

Tears spilled down her cheeks. He'd never had someone shed a tear for him before, never let anyone get close enough to care.

"I know that pain," she whispered. "Losing what you want more than anything in this world."

He opened his mouth to question her, because there was definitely a story there, but she kept going as if she hadn't just alluded to a dark past of her own.

"But you're the strongest person I've ever known. Don't you want to move on and take back what was stolen from you?"

Jack gritted his teeth. "I want to bring down criminals who skirt the law and believe they're above reproach."

She let his hands drop as she reached up to frame his face. "And what about your personal life?"

When she stared at him in such a caring way, Jack realized that, their passionate night of sex aside, she got him. She understood him because she had her own demons.

"I opened myself up once, Viv." He gripped her wrists and eased them away from his face. "I won't make that mistake again. I've chosen to devote my life to seeking justice."

"Even at the cost of your own happiness?"

Jack let go and stepped back. "I have homes in three countries, so much work I'm turning clients away and I'm about to bring down the biggest Mafia family Boston has ever seen. How could I not be happy?"

The corners of Viv's mouth tipped in a sad smile. "The fact you equate happiness with material things tells me all I need to know."

She pulled her office chair out and took a seat. Jiggling the mouse on her computer, she brought her screen to life. "I have some emails to sort through. Go ahead and close the door on your way out."

Jack stared at the back of her head for a split second before he whirled her chair back around. Leaning down, he curled his fingers around the arms. Her eyes widened in shock as he jerked the chair even closer, so their faces were only a breath apart.

"I warned you once about dismissing me," he murmured against her mouth. "Just because I refuse to commit doesn't mean I don't still crave you."

He crushed his mouth to hers, damning himself for letting his emotions guide his actions. Reaching up to grip his hair, she didn't hesitate in opening for him.

Encircling Viv's waist with his hands, Jack hauled her up against him. Without breaking contact, he shifted until he was leaning against the edge of her desk and she stood between his legs.

One taste wouldn't be enough. He'd known that the moment he'd stepped into her bedroom. He was doomed to repeat the performance, and he didn't give a damn if they did it right here in her office.

A chime interrupted erotic thoughts of Viv spread out on her desk, begging. He wanted to ignore the cell in his pocket, but business always came first.

Viv tore her mouth from his, taking a step back and smoothing her skirt down. Shoving her hair behind her ears, she turned to face the window, as if she were ashamed.

He'd have to deal with that later. He'd wanted a kiss, and damn it, he wasn't going to deny himself anymore when she wanted it, too. Jack pulled the cell from his pocket and answered without looking at the screen.

"Jack Carson."

"Jack, Braden O'Shea. I hear you're looking to work together."

In an instant, Jack's back straightened. "Braden."

Viv jerked around, eyes wide. Jack had to ignore the swollen lips he'd just tasted. His body was still revved up from having her plastered against him. Her curves were something he couldn't deny himself…and that was going to have to be addressed sooner rather than later.

"I'll meet with you on my terms," Braden stated.

"Depends on the terms," Jack retorted. He wasn't about to hand over control so easily.

"You can come by our main office on Friday after we close. We're a bit busy this week."

Yeah, with the Feds breathing down your neck.

"Friday it is," Jack agreed. "See you then."

"One more thing."

Jack gripped the phone, pinning Viv with his gaze as he listened. "What's that?"

"If you try to play both sides, you'll regret it."

Jack laughed. "Threats don't work on me. You'd do best to remember that."

He disconnected the call, making sure Braden knew full well going into this little meeting who was in charge.

"He threatened you?" Viv whispered.

Jack slid the cell back into his pocket and waved a hand. "We came to an understanding."

Viv wrapped her arms around her abdomen. "If you get hurt…"

"I'm fine. This all will come to an end soon."

Pursing her lips, Viv glanced down at the floor. She was a confident woman, one of the qualities he found so damn sexy, but something was wrong.

"About earlier—"

She jerked her eyes back up to his. "Don't apologize."

"Fair enough, since I wasn't going to." He reached out, palming her face with his hand. He stroked her full bottom lip. "I want you in my bed. *My* bed. I won't make excuses or promises. You're what I crave and I intend to have you again."

She swiped the tip of her tongue across her lip, catching the pad of his thumb and sending another jolt of arousal through him.

"Maybe I want more than just to be the one to scratch your itch."

Jack laughed as he hauled her against his body once again. "Honey, you're not just scratching an itch. I've had that before."

"So what am I?" she pressed.

"You need a label? Can't this just be simple?"

Viv laughed in turn. "No, it can't."

Jack pulled in a deep breath, careful to choose his next words wisely. "I can't name this, Viv. What we have…I've never done this before. You're my assistant, my friend."

"Your lover."

He nodded. "That's what I'm offering, no more."

She cocked her head with a quirk of her brow. "Is everything a business deal with you?"

"There's no other way to live."

Viv stared back, silence heavy in the narrow gap between them. "There's every other way to live. Happiness, building on your dreams, raising a family."

And all that had been robbed from him, making him detach from ever wanting such luxuries again.

"Looks like I only scratched that itch, after all," she murmured. "I have goals I'm moving toward and I won't let anyone get in my way…no matter how much I may care for him."

Viv turned away and circled her desk as she headed out of her office. That jasmine scent clung all around him, mocking him with the promise of a woman he'd had, but never would again. And he had nobody to blame but himself.

Twelve

Viv sank into the desk chair in her office at O'Shea's. After an hour of answering questions from the Feds, with Braden, Mac, Ryker and Laney all present, her nerves were shot and she needed a moment to herself.

She was still reeling from the emotional roller coaster she was on with Jack. One minute he was telling her no, the next he was kissing her as if he needed her more than air. She wanted him, that was never in question. But she'd also come to realize she deserved more than an occasional romp whenever *he* wanted...which was exactly the tacky proposal he'd delivered.

Katie's adoption was another emotional standoff Viv found herself in. Her first instinct was to say absolutely yes, but that was the selfish side of her. She wanted to truly think about this from every angle. Viv had lain awake most of the night worrying if she could provide the best environment for Katie to grow up in.

She lived in an apartment, with no yard for a child to play. She was a single parent, and Katie deserved two.

But Katie was comfortable with her. They were already a team in the short time they'd been together. Letting Katie go to another family would be crushing, not just for Viv, but possibly for the baby, too. Even though she was just shy of a year old, Katie had already experienced enough trauma in her life. Stability was essential for children.

Approaching footsteps had Viv snapping out of her reverie. Braden.

"You have a second?"

As if she'd tell him no. Viv nodded and came to her feet.

"Sit down." He motioned with his hand as he crossed to the accent chair across from her desk. "I appreciate you coming in early and going over the Feds' questions with me. They have a tendency to be redundant, trying to get us to slip up."

"I have nothing to hide." Lie of the century. "So there's no slipping up."

He gave a clipped nod as he crossed his ankle over his knee. "Loyalty is of the utmost importance in our line of work. We appreciate you hanging in there through this past year. It's been a bit of a rocky road."

Viv offered a smile, despite her stomach clenching in knots. "I need the job and I value family. Working here is a perfect fit for my lifestyle."

Braden laced his fingers over his abdomen and held her in place with those intense green eyes of his. "How is the foster situation going with Katie?"

As tightly as her lies were woven, she always had to prepare a quick response in her head before she delivered it. One misplaced word or action could be detrimental to not only her, but Jack, as well. Despite whatever was going on with them personally, she would never jeopardize his work.

Viv let out a sigh. No way was she going to reveal the fact she might be adopting Katie, either.

"It's going really well. Katie has adjusted and I'm planning a little cake and a fun outing for her birthday next week. If the weather cooperates we'll go sledding."

"Bring her out to the estate. We have plenty of room and slopes."

Viv stilled, hoping her smile didn't falter. She'd been to Braden's home only once, for the Christmas party where Jack had insisted on being her date, albeit in disguise.

If she was invited to their house again, clearly they continued to trust her and didn't suspect a thing. Yet Viv couldn't help but wonder if any of them even knew that journal existed. Most likely not. She'd found it shoved in the secret compartment in the top of her desk...a desk they'd assigned her to.

Unless it had been a plant. Would she be pulled into some downward spiral by failing a test?

Paranoia was not her best quality, yet she couldn't help but look at this scenario from every possible angle. That's the only way she could be prepared for the fallout.

"I may take you up on that," she replied. "I know she's only turning one, but I want her first birthday to be special."

"She's lucky to have you." Braden eased forward in his seat, planting his elbows on his knees. "I'd like to ask you something."

Why did she have to be so on edge? He was just a

man. A powerful, mysterious man who might or might not be on his way to prison.

"What's that?"

"Would you consider coming on here full-time?"

Shocked, she shifted in her seat. Definitely not what she thought he was going to ask. Not that she had a clue as to what he'd been thinking, but never once did she consider they'd want her here more often.

"I know you have Katie to think about, as well, but we'd be more than happy to accommodate you if you need to bring her in every now and then." Braden's chiseled face broke out into a wide smile, softening his harsh features. "It's not like this place won't be filled with babies soon enough, anyway."

With his own wife and sister expecting, Braden was definitely immersed in the baby world. This was one area he was going to get a crash course in very shortly.

"How soon do you need my answer?" She'd have to discuss this with Jack, and see if it was even possible for Martha to watch Katie more often.

"Laney would like to start working from home more, so you'd be picking up a little of her work, plus Zara and I would be coming in to take up the slack, as well. If you could just let me know in the next few weeks."

Hopefully, in that time the case would be wrapped up and she wouldn't be here. Part of her couldn't help the guilt that settled heavily in her chest. Over the past year, she'd gotten to know the O'Sheas. No matter the rumors surrounding them, or how Jack felt about them, she truly believed they wanted to move forward and just focus on auctions and growing their family. They might obtain some of their items through less than legal ways, but they weren't hardened criminals. Or murderers.

Patrick O'Shea may have done things differently, but Viv would bet just about anything that Braden, Mac and Ryker had nothing to do with the Parkers' deaths. Still, there was no evidence either way.

"I'll think about it," she assured him. "Katie is my top priority right now, so I need to do what's best for her."

Braden came to his feet. "I wouldn't expect any less from you. I'll let you get back to work. We have the final inventory list coming in this morning. I believe there are seventy-two pieces for you to input."

Viv nodded with a smile. "I'll be looking for the email."

Once she was alone, she blew out a breath and rubbed her temples. If she were a drinking woman, she'd take a whole bottle of something strong right about now. But she was a simple girl, and a scented bubble bath and a good book would do the trick... Too bad she had no time for the mental breakdown she deserved.

And at the heart of everything going on was Jack. He'd gotten her into this impossible situation with the O'Sheas, he'd turned her emotional life inside out and he'd left her wanting more. She'd walk through fire for that frustrating man and he was willing to settle for a romp in the sack.

Some fantasies weren't meant to be fulfilled. She just wished she could get the image of him in her bed out of her mind. Each time she lay down, she felt him, ached for him. And she didn't know if she'd ever get over that need.

Tilly had the week off, but she'd come by and prepared food to keep him going and promised to leave him alone. She was either worried he'd starve or she was nosy...and he knew the answer.

She'd given him a wink and told him she'd made more cheesecake. Damn it, the woman knew his plans for the night and he hadn't even said a word. Which was why their relationship was utterly perfect.

Still, she could make all the cheesecakes she wanted, could throw him that knowing grin and think she knew what he was up to during his personal time, but she had no idea.

In all honesty, he couldn't grasp his own thoughts lately, not when it came to Viv and all the unwanted emotions she'd conjured up.

Tonight, though, he'd called her to his house because of business. No other reason. He wouldn't even let his mind go down the path toward anything personal. He'd offered her all he had to give; she'd turned him away. They wanted completely opposite things in life, which he'd known going in. But that didn't stop him from wanting her.

Jack downed the rest of his whiskey just as his doorbell rang. He slammed his tumbler onto his desk and headed down the curved staircase. The exterior lights shone on Viv, revealing her shape through the etched-glass door. There was no mistaking that luscious figure. His hands itched to touch her intimately. Hell, he'd been aching for her since he'd left her bed days ago.

As soon as he used his fingerprint on the security panel and opened the door, he knew the possibility of having her tonight wasn't on the table. Not that Katie on her hip was the issue, because she'd fall asleep eventually, but Viv's eyes narrowed on his a half second before she pushed her way into his foyer.

"Good evening to you, too," he muttered as he closed the door.

"You demand I come by after work and won't tell me why." She slid the hood off Katie's head and Jack reached over and eased the baby from Viv's arms. "So I rushed to pick her up and get here, thinking something was wrong, but as I'm driving in this hellacious weather, I realize nothing is wrong and you're just being you."

Jack unfastened Katie's coat as Viv jerked her own off and flung it over the banister. She took Katie back, then removed her coat and tossed it there, as well.

"So, now that we're here, what could you possibly want that you couldn't text or call about?"

Jack crossed his arms and didn't even try to hide the smile that spread across his face. Was now a bad time to tell her how damn hot she looked when she got worked up? Because this fire and passion shooting from her was seriously turning him on.

Damn it. He didn't need to be more turned on by her. He needed to cool it. She wanted things he'd given up on. And she deserved every bit of what she worked for. He just wished she'd give in to what they both wanted while she was on the path to her dreams.

"What's the smirk for?" she asked, her eyes narrowing even more.

"I've never seen you so…"

"What? Frazzled? Losing my sanity? Confused and terrified all at the same time?"

Jack closed the space between them, instantly regretting that he hadn't taken better care to protect her. She was fine physically, but he should've seen that this entire process would take its toll on her emotionally. Not to mention the fact that she was a single mother. She gave to everyone but herself, always and in all ways.

"Something happen?" he asked, searching her eyes for the hint of tears. If she shed any, he'd be a goner. He could handle anything but the vulnerability of a woman, especially this woman. The instant tears came onto the scene, he was ready to slay any proverbial dragons on her behalf, even if that meant himself. And he'd hurt her, he knew that, but he was trying like hell to never do it again.

"Just the Feds in today, questioning me again."

"I listened to the audio. You did amazing."

He'd been so damn proud of her for sounding so confident, giving the same answers she'd given time and time again. But with the Feds still working the case, things would look suspicious if Viv wasn't questioned just as much as the rest of the staff and family at O'Shea's. He and Viv had gone over her story and background so much before she'd ever started working for them, there was no way she would flub up. He'd made sure she was mentally armed before going into enemy territory to do his battle.

And that still pissed him off. He hated placing her inside, knowing she was getting tangled up in that corrupt family. The sooner he could bring them down, the better off they'd all be. At this point, he was itching for them to screw up and just get a parking ticket—anything to open up the field to investigate every aspect of their lives.

Katie struggled in Viv's arms and Viv eased her down onto the floor. Jack watched as the infant pulled herself up, holding on to Viv's legs. She gripped the hem of Viv's pencil skirt and started glancing around the unfamiliar territory.

Yeah, his house wasn't kid friendly.

"So what was so important?"

He focused back on the woman before him, the woman he shouldn't want, but did, almost as much as he wanted to solve this case.

"You're moving in here with me."

Thirteen

Viv laughed, sure she'd heard him wrong. "Nice try. What do you really want and where is our chaperone?"

Jack rested his hand on the newel post and leveled his stare at her. "Tilly is on vacation for the next several days and you are moving in. It's not up for debate."

Who the hell did he think he was?

"I don't know what plan you have in that overactive mind of yours, but I can't move in here." She pointed down to Katie, who had started crawling around the hardwood floor of the foyer. "We're a team."

"Move her in, too," Jack stated, as if things were that simple.

Viv shook her head and crossed her arms. "What has gotten into you? I turn down your oh-so-romantic proposal of sleeping with you at your beck and call, so now you're trying to overcompensate by having us live together?"

"Damn it, no." He blew out a breath and rubbed his

hand over the back of his neck. "I think you'd be safer here. If Braden were to piece things together or get a hint that we're working together... It's just too risky. You've already heard suspicious noises at your apartment. Next time I may be too late to help."

Viv nodded, fully in agreement about the safety issues. "I can work from home for you, so why jump to the conclusion that I'd be safer here?"

"First of all, the security in your building is ridiculous."

Viv rolled her eyes and crossed to the entryway to the formal living room. Katie was off exploring and Viv knew from experience that she needed to keep her eyes on the active child.

"You have to have a code to enter my building. I'm perfectly safe. I'm sure a neighbor was moving furniture or something and I just overreacted."

When Katie started crawling toward the stone fireplace, Viv intervened. The last thing she needed was the baby climbing up onto the hearth and falling. As if sensing the end to her fun, Katie turned and speed-crawled toward the low coffee table. Thankfully, there was just a variety of classic novels on display and nothing breakable.

When Viv turned toward the wide, arched doorway, Jack met her gaze. Leaning against the frame, he had his arms crossed and that look on his face that said he wasn't in the mood to argue. *Welcome to the club.* She wasn't too keen on having been summoned here to have this insane conversation.

"If there was nothing else, we'll head back home. I've never been a fan of driving in this crazy weather."

Didn't matter that she'd lived here for years, she still

didn't like navigating the narrow Boston streets when they were snow covered.

"We need to talk, so if you want to go home tonight, I can drive you, or I can take you home in the morning."

Viv glanced at Katie as she pulled herself up with the help of the coffee table. Maybe Viv could lower her blood pressure if she counted backward from one hundred. She doubted it, and she didn't have the time. Jack seemed to be under the impression that she would just do anything he commanded.

"You should know me well enough to understand I don't do demands." Viv circled the table and took a seat on the leather sofa. The thing looked like nobody had ever sat there, which was probably true, considering Jack wasn't the most social of butterflies. "I'm safe where I am, but I will agree to not go into your office until this is all over. That's the compromise."

Jack pushed off the door frame and stalked toward her, his eyes never wavering. When he stood only inches from her, Viv smiled.

"Intimidation may work on your adversaries, but I'm not afraid of you."

Turned on, reliving every moment of their night together in vivid detail, but not afraid.

"I won't let you get hurt. And if Braden figures all of this out…"

Jack's growl sent shivers through her. Knowing what she did about his past, about the crippling loss he'd suffered, was the only reason she wasn't grabbing Katie and leaving. He was scared…for her. How could she be angry about that?

Still, she wouldn't be bullied into staying here. For her own sanity, she couldn't. She was half in love with him, and being under the same roof, faux playing house, was not an option.

"I'm not going to get hurt," she informed him. "Actually, I was offered a full-time position at O'Shea's."

"When was this?"

"Today." Viv peered over her shoulder just in time to see Katie heading back to the fireplace. "Braden came in and talked to me after the Feds left."

Katie protested when Viv picked her up. Jack's house was definitely a bachelor pad. Yet another reason they wouldn't be staying here.

"And what did you tell him?"

Viv pulled off her bangle and handed it to Katie. Promptly, the gold bracelet went into the infant's mouth, but at least she wouldn't choke on it. Jewelry, the new teething ring for on-the-go mommies.

"I said I'd think about it and get back to him."

Exhaustion set in and Viv went back to the unused sofa and sank down. She slid her shoes off, not because she was staying, but because there was only so long she could be "on." She'd reached her limit for the day.

"I explained that I needed to think about what was best for Katie, but I knew I needed to talk to you, as well."

Jack came to sit next to her. Resting his elbows on his knees, he leaned forward and stared across the room. "I don't like this," he murmured.

Confused, Viv shifted in her seat, tucking Katie into the crook of her arm. "I thought you'd jump on board. Having me there every day would give us the leverage we need."

"I think they know something."

Viv shook her head. "I don't agree."

Jack's dark brows rose. "And why is that? Because you've become so chummy with them?"

The hurt in his tone made her feel guilty. She certainly had plenty to feel guilty about, but not because she'd gotten to know the notorious family on a personal level. She wanted justice for whoever killed Katie's parents, but didn't happen to think it was her fake employer.

"I don't want to argue with you."

Viv started to rise when Jack placed his hand on her knee.

"Stay."

The simple command had her stilling beneath his touch. Jack had a way of looking at her that made her want to obey his every word, and that irritated her. She couldn't let herself get swept into his world. He didn't want her there on a personal level and she had a damning secret that would blow everything out of the water.

Inevitably, the situation would come to a head, and she knew for a fact they'd both be hurt in the end. "I'll take the full-time position," she told him. "It's the smart move. I can work from home in the evenings for you, plus I'll be alone some if I'm a regular employee there. This will bring us closer to solving the case, I know it."

Jack blew out a sigh and shook his head. "I don't like it, Viv. If you find something incriminating, you can't take it. They may not suspect you yet, but this is a test. If anything at all happens, you'll be to blame."

Katie wiggled down once again, taking Viv's bangle with her. "I'm aware of that. I won't do anything to raise a red flag."

Viv knew where all the security cameras were, knew nearly all the passwords to various accounts and she'd be the contact people would speak to if she was the only one there.

The irony in all this? She'd been completely innocent in her actions when she'd stumbled upon Patrick's journal. When she actually tried to snoop, she'd discovered very little. She'd copied those files in the hopes something would be in them, but no such luck.

Which only went to confirm her own suspicions about the O'Sheas being exactly who they claimed to be.

"I want to know your every move, every contact, even what you eat for lunch."

Viv laughed. "Don't you think that's a bit much?"

He leveled his gaze at her. "Where your safety is concerned? It's not enough."

Shivers slid through her at his throaty tone. That whole dominating, protective trait was the sexiest part about him…and he had a whole lot of sexy going on. There was no way she could be this close, inhaling his masculine scent, and not recall exactly how he felt with his weight pressed against her. The way his hands had traveled over her body was a memory she'd carry forever. Even though he hadn't stayed in her bed, their intimacy was one of the best moments of her life.

She needed to leave. Unless they were strictly discussing business, she needed to keep her distance, because she only wanted him more, and she had no right to.

Every part of her wanted to tell him about that journal, but trumping her need to be truthful was the guilt she felt about being the one to hurt him. And knowing who his father was would destroy him. His passion for justice would come second to the cold, hard truth of his paternity.

Jack jumped up from the sofa and sprinted across the room. Viv came to her feet in time to see him grab Katie before she could climb onto the stone hearth.

Great. She'd been fantasizing about her boss and totally ignored Katie's safety. If that wasn't a sign she needed to get her priorities straight, she didn't know what was.

"Nice try, speedy." Jack scooped Katie up and did some mock airplane moves around the room. Frozen in place, Viv could only take in the sight. He would've been a great father. His protective side was obvious, but this playful side was something she hadn't seen. Jack would've put his family first, above all else. He might be a big shot in the industry and moving into global territory of security and investigating, but the smile on his face right now told her everything she needed to know.

The man wanted a family. He didn't want to be as closed off and hard as he came across. She'd witnessed his caring nature time and time again. And watching him right now had Viv's heart tumbling in her chest. Jack would be the perfect husband, father. He'd be the fiercest protector and greatest provider.

There was no denying the fact, now that she'd fallen face-first in love with Jack Carson. She'd tried to dodge her deeper emotions, hoping she was just physically infatuated. But no. She admired everything about him, and at this point, being with him would never be an option.

Tears pricked her eyes. Blinking them away didn't help as they slid down her cheeks. She swiped at the dampness with the back of her hand and pushed her hair behind her shoulders.

As Jack spun around, he zeroed in on her and stilled. Pulling Katie close to his chest, he strode over to Viv.

"She's fine," he assured her.

Viv nodded, emotions too thick in her throat to form words.

"What is it?" he pressed, patting Katie's back.

His large hand covered Katie's entire pink floral jumper. Such a strong man who'd had so much taken from him, and Viv was only adding to his heartache... only he had no idea.

Another round of tears hit and she didn't even try to hide them. She needed to tell him the truth. Viv loved him and he deserved to know. In the face of her feelings, this case was nothing.

Jack's free arm wrapped around her shoulders as he pulled her to his side. Viv instantly rested her head on his shoulder, even though she had no right to. Seeking comfort from the man she was lying to was hypocritical, at best.

"Jack, I—"

Katie reached out and fisted a handful of Viv's hair.

"No, no." Jack twisted his body, pulling Viv slightly to the side. "She's a grabber. Apparently, everything goes into her mouth."

Viv squeezed her eyes shut. The words weren't coming. She'd just fully confessed to herself that she loved him, and here she was, ready to tell him a secret that would destroy him. Why did life have to be so complicated?

"What were you saying?" he asked.

"I'm sorry," Viv sniffed in an attempt to compose herself. "I guess I'm just tired from work and trying to figure out what to do for Katie's party."

"I'll help plan the party. Tell me what to do."

Viv laughed, the room blurring before her from the moisture in her eyes. "You plan first-birthday parties often?"

Jack glanced down at her, his crooked smile melting her heart. "Never, but how hard can it be? She's one. She has no expectations yet."

"I know." Viv moved from his hold, because it was so easy to lean on him, to draw from his power and strength. "I just want her to have the best."

"She will. I'll make sure of it." Jack glanced at Katie, who was toying with the tiny button holding down the collar of his dress shirt. "Right, speedy? You'll have the biggest cake and a roomful of presents—"

"Let's not get carried away," Viv interrupted. "My apartment isn't that big."

She smoothed her silk blouse back in place and dabbed beneath her eyes, sure her mascara had run against her splotchy skin. If there was ever an Ugly Crier award, she'd win hands down.

Of course, if she weren't waging such an epic internal battle, then there wouldn't be an issue.

"Stay here tonight," Jack told her, looking back her way. "You're exhausted."

Viv shook her head. "I'm fine. Besides, there's only a few diapers left in my bag and Katie doesn't have the stuffed animal she hugs when she falls asleep."

The intensity of his gaze warmed her. The man inside who had loved and lost was still there. Would he ever make a full appearance? Would he ever let down that guard again and open himself up to a relationship?

She hurt for him. She hurt for the life he'd been through and the truth he'd yet to discover. She loved this man, wanted more than anything to be with him, but she couldn't form the words.

"Don't look at me like that, Viv."

"I see the truth," she whispered. "I know you want more and you just won't let yourself feel."

His jaw clenched. "I can't afford to feel. Not anymore."

"Then I'll be living in my own apartment and working from there." Viv reached for Katie, who protested and reached back for Jack. "We're going home, sweetie."

Turning from Jack and those mesmerizing eyes, Viv made her way to the foyer. He fell in step behind her, but she ignored him as she busied herself getting her and Katie's coats on.

"I want to know when you're home."

Viv picked Katie up, securing her on her hip. "You don't have that luxury, considering I'm only your assistant."

She circled around him and jerked the door open. "I'll see you in the office—actually, I won't, because I'll be working from home—"

Jack's hand flattened on the door, slamming it shut and closing out the cold air. She whirled around, but before she could say a word, he kissed her hard and fast before he released her.

"You're more than my assistant, so quit throwing that in my face," he commanded. "You will tell me when you reach home because I care. Damn it, Viv. I care too much and that's the problem."

When he said things like that he made it damn near impossible to stay angry.

Reaching behind her, she turned the knob. "It's only a problem for one of us."

Fourteen

Four days had passed without any real contact from Viv. Without hearing her laugh, her soft tone of voice. Without seeing those expressive eyes as she watched him when she thought he wasn't looking.

Four. Days.

Evidently, Viv was holding her ground and not having anything to do with him if it didn't involve work. She'd been only emailing or texting. He hadn't even heard her voice over the phone. Fine. He could handle this switch.

But he didn't like it. He hated every moment that had passed without her. Damn it, he missed her.

He'd noticed a void by the end of day one. A hole in his life that only Viv filled. When had she become so important, so permanent in his life, that he was miserable without her?

The office was boring as hell and it smelled...not like her jasmine scent. Her cheery yellow-and-white office mocked him every time he passed by. He finally closed the door on the second day.

But having her work from home was the smart move to make. Wasn't it? He wanted her safe, out of harm's way as much as was possible with this messed-up case.

Now, after four days of not seeing her face, Jack stood at her apartment door with an insane amount of shopping bags—he'd left the boxes in his car. Katie's birthday was today and Viv had texted him that she was doing a cake and maybe taking her sledding in the park. There was no way in hell Jack was going to ignore that invitation.

Because not only had he missed Viv, he'd missed Katie. He wasn't quite sure when he'd become attached to the innocent girl, but he couldn't wait to wish her a happy birthday.

As he gripped the bags, he wondered if he'd done too much. What was the protocol for buying presents when a child was in temporary housing after being orphaned? In Jack's opinion, there was no maximum amount...as he'd just proved with his no-limit credit card.

The neighbor's door opened and Jack groaned inwardly, pasting a smile on his face as he turned to see Martha poke her head out.

"Oh, nice to see you again," she said with a wide smile. Her eyes darted to the bags in his hands. "Are those for Katie? That is one spoiled little girl."

He wasn't about to mention the dollhouse or the motorized convertible toddler car he'd left in his SUV.

"You only turn one once, right?"

Viv's door opened, saving him from further conversation with the nosy babysitter.

"Jack. Come on in." Viv peeked out the door and

waved to Martha. "Thanks again for the stuffed elephant. She loves it. I'll bring you some cake in a bit."

Her neighbor winked. "Take your time."

Ushering Viv back in, Jack threw Martha a nod and followed her. Once they were inside, Viv closed the door with a giggle.

When she laughed her beauty was like nothing he'd ever seen. She was absolutely breathtaking. With her hair down around her shoulders, a simple cream sweater hugging her every curve, Viv was the quintessential girl next door, but she was as complex as any woman he'd ever known.

And he wanted her. The attempt to get her to move in with him was legit; he was worried about her safety. But he wanted her under his roof where he could keep his eyes—and his hands—on her.

Damn it. He shouldn't want this. Yet there was no way he could stop the ache, the need.

"I've never seen anyone scare you." She continued laughing. "Yet you're afraid of my elderly neighbor."

Jack didn't reply. There was no denying the truth. That woman terrified him.

He glanced around the open apartment. A bundle of pink balloons lay on the small dinette table, while white and pink streamers were twisted around every stationary object. Two cakes sat on the kitchen counter, a small one with a large purple *1* in the middle and a larger one that was pink with white-and-purple polka dots.

"You've been busy," he commented, setting the bags down.

Her eyes darted to the load he'd carried in. "I hope all of that is not for Katie."

"I actually have more in the car," he told her, feeling like a fool when her eyes widened. Perhaps he had gone too far, but whatever. He wasn't sorry and he still believed Katie deserved everything and more. "I had a problem choosing just one item."

"Jack." Viv closed her eyes and sighed before meeting his gaze again. "Go get the rest."

Stunned, Jack tilted his head, narrowing his eyes at her. "You're not angry?"

"Does it matter?" she laughed.

"Not really. Once I got to the store and the clerk started showing me all the new things that had arrived, I just kept adding to my pile. Honestly, if I'd had more room in my car, I would've bought more."

Viv's hand went to her forehead and she began rubbing her temples. "I don't know why I'm surprised, but…okay. Just go get the stuff and I'll get Katie into her birthday outfit."

Jack darted out the door and made quick trips, grateful not to get caught by Martha again. He was nearly out of breath by the time he'd carried everything into Viv's apartment. Obviously, he needed to up his workout routine. He'd been a little preoccupied lately to get in all the miles and lifting he was used to.

As he closed the door the final time, he realized his purchases had pretty much overtaken her apartment. Wrapped boxes in various colors, with thick bows, littered the living area; the bags he'd brought in first circled the dining table. Between all the variegated shades of pink, there was no denying this was a little girl's birthday party.

Katie came crawling out of the bedroom wearing a polka-dot top with some ruffles around the hem. She seemed to match the theme of the newly decorated apartment. He may have gone overboard monetarily, but Viv had seriously thought this out and wanted something special for the little girl.

Viv stood over Katie, reached down and took her hands. Suddenly, Katie was on her feet, wobbling toward Jack.

His heart swelled. How could he be so excited to see her learning to walk? He wasn't invested in her... was he?

No. Absolutely not. She wasn't staying with Viv. One day, probably soon, Katie would move on to the family that would give her a forever home.

Still, he couldn't help but smile. He wasn't completely detached from emotions.

"When did she start this?" he asked.

Before he realized his actions, Jack found himself squatting down and reaching for Katie. That wide, two-toothed smile tugged at strings he thought had been severed years ago. This sweet child didn't have a care in the world. How could he not smile back? How could he even think of anything going on in the outside world when she was teetering toward him, those bright blue eyes locked on his?

"She started a week or so ago, but she's getting stronger."

Viv let one of Katie's hands go and Jack took hold. Together they walked toward the dining area. The image of a family hit him hard and he attempted to tamp it down, but damn it, this was everything he'd wanted. A woman like Viv was exactly what he'd be looking for if he wanted a family. She was perfect in the way she cared for Katie, the way she was sexy and sweet, the way her cheeks flushed when he caught her looking at him. She'd called him first when she'd been scared, so she trusted him to protect her. At one time that's all it would've taken for him to get her and keep her in his bed, his life.

But that man was gone. His dreams had been murdered. There would never be a future with Viv. His sexy assistant would have to remain just that. And working with her day in and day out was wearing on him.

Somewhere along the way, though, his wants had changed, and they looked too much like everything Viv was offering.

Was it even possible to have that life he'd once wanted? After ten years of grieving, of burying himself in work and building his empire, could he actually put a personal life back in place?

Katie let out a squeal. "Up, up, up."

Jack didn't hesitate and didn't even question who Katie was requesting pick her up. He merely reached down and swung her into his arms. The weight of her little body, the slender arm that rested behind his neck... There was something so special, so perfect about her.

And maybe he could slowly ease back into the idea of having his own family one day. He knew his wife would've wanted him to move on.

"I've never done this before," Viv stated. "Should we just let her dive in to her cake first?"

Jack laughed. "I don't think there's a rule here."

Pulling out one of the chairs, he took a seat and situated Katie on his lap. "Bring her cake over and let's see what she does."

Viv's eyes widened. "She's going to get you filthy. Put her in her high chair."

Jack shrugged. "We'll be fine. I have other dress shirts."

He maneuvered his arms around Katie so he could fold up his sleeves while Viv went to get the cake. She placed one white candle in the top and set the confection in front of Katie.

"Hold her arms back while I light this."

Viv pulled out a lighter and lit the candle. With a smile, she pulled her cell from the pocket of her jeans and held it up. "Should we sing?" she asked.

"Sure."

Jack started "Happy Birthday" and didn't feel silly at all, sitting in a sea of pink. If anything, he felt...hopeful. Damn it. He deserved to have this. He *wanted* to have this.

While Viv sang and snapped pictures with her phone, Jack motioned for Katie to blow out the flame. Of course she had no clue what was going on. Jack met Viv's eyes, the smile on her face making something inside his heart clench. Before he could assess the emotion, she leaned toward the candle. Together, they blew it out.

Jack reached out and slid his finger along the icing. He showed the glob to Katie, then took one of her hands and guided it toward the cake.

And that was all he needed to do. She dived in to the white cake and colorful icing with both hands, bringing fistfuls of the clumpy mess to her mouth. She rubbed her hair, rubbed his pants, turned and smeared some across his lips.

Viv laughed, still snapping pictures.

Jack licked his lips. "This is really good. You made this?"

"I did. I'm not much of a baker, but I figured I could handle a simple cake recipe."

Viv set her phone down and went to get napkins— pink-and-white polka-dot ones, of course.

"About the other day—"

She shook her head, cutting him off. "I don't want to discuss it. Forget about it."

Surprised at her flippant response, Jack eased the cake closer to Katie before meeting Viv's intense stare. "Isn't that supposed to be my line? I wanted to forget everything, but I can't."

"For now, let's focus on Katie." She smiled, warming him in places he thought would always be cold, empty. "And discuss where you think I can possibly keep all the toys you bought."

He didn't want to discuss toys. He wanted to discuss how he'd ached for her since he'd last seen her. He wanted to discuss how he'd handled the situation poorly.

But mostly he wanted to discuss how they could erase this sexual tension between them, which was more prominent than ever. And he had a feeling there was only one way.

Fifteen

Jack discarded his dress shirt straight into the trash. It wasn't even worth having Tilly take it to the cleaners at this point. The icing appeared to be permanently embedded, which was just fine. He honestly didn't recall when he'd had a better time…at least not in the past ten years.

His dress pants weren't faring much better, but he couldn't exactly walk around in his black boxer briefs and light gray T-shirt. He'd scrubbed out as much of the pink icing as he could, but only managed to grind it in more. Tilly would scold him, but whatever. His tailor in Italy wouldn't mind making a new suit.

Viv had taken a sugar-loaded one-year-old back to the bath. Poor Katie could barely keep her eyes open, but her ringlets had been dripping icing and she needed a good scrubbing.

While he was alone, Jack attempted to tidy up, but he was wondering if he should just buy Viv a new condo. It would take days to get her tiny apartment looking like it once did. Granted, with all the purchases he'd made, the living area would look like the toy department at Saks as long as Katie lived here.

Unwelcome emotions suddenly clogged his throat. He'd gotten attached to the innocent child, when he'd told himself he wouldn't. But only a heartless person could look in that sweet baby's face and not feel a connection. She demanded affection and damn if he didn't want to give her everything. Toys were one thing, but he wanted her to have the perfect family. That would mean leaving…which would destroy Viv. Hell, he was beginning to think it might destroy him, too.

He'd give Viv the world and her every desire if he were in a better place. She deserved to have everything handed to her. More than anything, he wanted to be that man who could do that. But he couldn't risk the pain to his already battered heart.

Attempting to focus on things he could actually control, Jack took a trash bag and started gathering up the wrapping paper and empty boxes. Once that was done, he piled the toys on one side of the living room. When he turned back to the dining area and kitchen, he groaned inwardly. There was no way that was going to come clean without something akin to a pressure washer.

When Viv stepped into the living area, she glanced around and let out a laugh. "We survived."

Jack took in her disheveled hair, ends damp from the bath and a glob of icing dangling on one side. She'd stripped off her sweater and now wore a simple white tank that hugged her breasts and dipped in at her waist. As messy as her appearance was, Jack wanted his hands on her. Now that he knew the way her silken skin felt beneath his palms, his need for her was all-consuming.

But after this family moment they'd just shared, seducing her wouldn't be the wisest decision. Everything from this day was temporary: Katie, Viv, Jack, the party, the appearance of domestic bliss.

"Why don't you go shower and I'll figure something out in the kitchen."

Shaking her head, Viv crossed to the chaos on the table. "I'll clean this up. You didn't come over to get assaulted by a birthday cake. You can head home."

She threw him a glance over her shoulder. "Where's your shirt?"

"Trash."

Her eyes widened. "I can wash it for you. There's no need to just throw away a good shirt."

He shrugged. "I have more at home."

Viv rolled her eyes and focused on gathering everything inside the plastic tablecloth she'd laid out. "I'm not going to offer to wash your pants."

Jack couldn't hold back the smile. "If you want me to take them off, just ask."

Flirting was dangerous, but he could control himself. He'd help her clean up and then be on his way. It was getting late, but where else did he have to be? Nobody was at home, and for the first time in years, he didn't want to go back to that empty place where his own breathing echoed in the halls.

"Keep your pants on and help clean if you insist on staying," she said with a laugh. "Just grab a garbage bag and hold it open."

Jack pulled another bag from the roll beneath her sink and shook it out, holding it in front of her. When she turned with the bundled tablecloth and pieces of mashed cake, she tripped, sending the whole gooey mess onto his chest.

Her eyes immediately went to his. "I'm so sorry," she gasped.

Jack dropped the sack on the hardwood floor, scooped up a hefty amount of icing with his hand and flung it. The glob landed just at the scoop of her tank, disappearing into her cleavage.

Her eyes narrowed, but the glimmer of mischief there warned him this war had just begun. He quickly picked up the discarded bag and held it out as a shield, but not before she scooped up another chunk of hot-pink icing and smashed it into the side of his head.

As he reached down for more discarded cake, Viv ran toward the living area, her hands stretched out in front of her. "Okay. Truce."

The wide smile, the brightness in her eyes... Even smeared with cake—especially smeared with cake— she looked sexy as hell.

"I don't think so," he stated, stalking toward her. "You got me twice. I owe you one."

"Jack, it's in my shirt," she argued, taking another step back until she hit the side of the sofa. "We're even. I didn't intend the first attack—I tripped."

He jerked one hand out to grab her arm, pulling her against him, then smeared the icing over her chest with the other. Slowly, he stroked that exposed skin just above her tank, keeping his eyes locked on hers. Viv shuddered beneath his touch.

"You're not...playing fair," she murmured.

Jack snaked his arm around her waist. Trailing his fingers up to her mouth, he spread the last of the icing across her lips.

"I'm not playing at all, Viv."

Tipping his head down, Jack held her close as he slid the tip of his tongue over the icing just below her collarbone. Her breath hitched, so he did it again.

"Jack."

The way she whispered his name set off a fire inside him he didn't know existed. Gripping her hips, Jack aligned her body perfectly with his.

"You drive me crazy," he muttered against her lips. "I tried to ignore you, ignore this. Damn it, Viv, I want you."

Her fingers threaded through his hair, urging him closer, and it was all he could do to not rip her clothes off and take her to the floor.

"Then have me."

She covered his lips with hers, demanding he turn his words into actions. No problem. He slid his hand inside the back of her tank, palming her bare skin. Her body arched against his as she tore her mouth away and started licking the icing off his jawline, his neck. His body was strung so tight, but he didn't want just a quickie.

"I want more than just your bed tonight," he told her.

Viv lifted her head and smiled. "Then maybe we should start with a shower, where I can thoroughly clean you."

Every part of Jack's body tightened as he lifted her off her feet and headed toward the hallway. Viv wrapped her legs around his waist.

"Go to the bathroom in my bedroom," she whispered in his ear. "My shower is huge."

Anticipation gnawed at him as he turned the corner to her room. The second he set her on her feet, he grabbed the hem of her tank and yanked it over her head. Icing and cake crumbs covered her lacy white bra. Jack wasted no time in bending down to lick every last bit, until she gripped his shoulders and trembled beneath him.

Reaching behind her, he flicked the closure of her bra until it sprang free. She flung it aside.

Jack fisted his T-shirt and slid it over his head, sending it to the floor. Her eyes raked his chest before she reached for his pants. Jack glanced down, watching as she continued to undress him. Those delicate hands shook as she eased the zipper down.

He toed off his shoes and kicked away his pants.

"I want you in that shower now," he growled. "So if you don't want to go in with your pants on, I suggest you take them off."

Her eyes widened as she quickly went to work, and within seconds she was gloriously naked before him. Jack reached for her, seizing her by her waist. He backed her into the bathroom, keeping his eyes on hers.

"I've never had a food fight before," he told her. "I better be thorough with the cleanup."

Viv reached between them, covering him with a gentle stroke of her hand. "I like a man who's thorough."

Mercy, she was going to be the death of him. There was nothing sexier than a woman who took charge and knew what she wanted.

The corner shower had two glass walls and a rain head. Jack opened the door and reached in to turn the water on, testing the temperature before stepping in and pulling her with him. He positioned her directly beneath the spray, smoothing her hair away from her face.

Droplets dotted her skin. Jack's hands roamed up and down her sides, needing to feel every bit of her.

"Tell me what you want," she murmured.

He spun her around until her back hit the tiled wall. "Every inch of you."

Sliding his hand between her legs, he stroked her. Viv's head tipped back, her eyes lowered. Every time he touched her, she shook with need—a need he completely understood.

Her hips pumped against his hand and Jack couldn't take his eyes off her. There was nothing more erotic than a woman about to come undone at his touch...*this* woman. She was different than any other, an epiphany he'd come to so recently, he was still reeling from the shock to his system.

Viv panted as she turned her head to the side, squeezing her eyes shut. Water trickled over her flushed skin, catching on her lips a second before she slid her tongue out to wipe it away.

The moment her body tightened, Jack captured those lips. He hadn't been kidding when he'd said he wanted every single inch of her. He swallowed her groan as she gripped his biceps. Having her cling to him was everything right now.

When she finally stilled and pulled away, she blinked against the water and met his gaze. When she bit that swollen bottom lip, Jack removed his hand and reached up to frame her face.

"Whatever you're thinking, leave it." He kissed her fast, hard. "It's just us here. Nothing else matters."

Wasn't that what she'd been trying to get him to see? She'd been urging him to live again, to find happiness again. Part of him, a part he'd just revived, desperately wanted to risk his sanity for that happiness. He wanted to know what taking a chance on a relationship would do.

Tears filled her eyes. "I need to—"

He nipped at her lips. "I need *you*. Nothing else right now."

Her brows drew in as she studied him. Her hesitation had worry spearing deep inside him. "Are you having second thoughts?" he asked.

"No." She shook her head and reached up to grip his wrists. "No. I'm just…nothing. I want this, I want you. Are you sure? Because the way you left the other day…"

"Right now, right here, this is all that matters." He couldn't express his feelings, was still struggling to come to grips with them himself. "I need you, Viv."

Admitting that was a leap for him. He never needed anyone, ever. But Viv was his. She had been for a while and he was finally realizing just how much he ached for her…and not just physically.

Her arms circled his neck and her ankle locked behind his knee. "Then take me."

Jack lifted her against the wall, pinning her in place with his body. She wrapped her legs around his waist and began to rock her hips against his.

Staring at him from beneath thick, dark lashes dotted with water, she whispered, "Make me yours again."

How could he deny the lady?

Jack gripped her hips and joined their bodies. With no barrier between them, he stilled, taking just a second to bask in everything Vivianna. She was utterly perfect and she was completely his.

With an arch of her back and a moan, Viv urged him to move. She closed her eyes and bit down on her lip as he complied, but he was having no part of that. If she was going to be his, then she was going to damn well know it.

"Look at me," he commanded.

Her dark eyes locked on to his. Jack kept one hand firmly on her hip and gripped her jaw with the other before crushing his mouth onto hers. He craved more.

She was like a drug and he couldn't get enough. Would he ever?

Her knees dug into his waist as Viv pressed even closer. The warm spray beat all around them and Jack knew he'd never take another shower without imagining her thrusting her body against his with total abandon.

Viv's body quickened and she gripped his shoulders. He eased back, needing to see her come undone again.

She held his gaze as her body tightened around him, thrusting him into his own release. He didn't look away, couldn't if he wanted to. Viv's expressive eyes most likely mirrored his own. So many unspoken emotions...

Jack clenched his teeth, fighting the urge to say something. Any confessions stemming from feelings during sex were not smart. Later, when they were lying in bed, he'd say what he needed to, what she deserved to hear.

When her body went lax, Jack rested his forehead against hers as he came down from his own release.

"Jack—"

He kissed her. Whatever she was about to say would have to wait. Right now, he was reeling from the fact he was falling for a woman, the first in over a decade. And he had no idea how the hell that would fit into the life he'd created...a life he'd intended to live alone.

Sixteen

He'd wrapped her in a thick bath towel and carefully laid her in bed before climbing in beside her—as if this was part of their daily routine.

Viv blinked back the tears, thankful for the darkness. His feelings for her had changed. Somewhere along the way, he'd started falling for her. She'd seen it in his eyes, tasted it on his lips and felt it with every single touch.

There was so much he didn't know, so much he deserved to know. She had to stop being such a coward and just tell him, reveal the most damning secret. But the words wouldn't come. Viv lay in the crook of his arm, her hand resting directly over his heart. "I can't have children," she whispered into the darkness.

As if that was the only secret she'd been keeping from him. Nerves spiraled through her as the inevitable conversation hung in the air. But this was at least one truth she didn't mind sharing. The reality of never having her own children had caused an open wound so deep inside her, she hadn't revealed it to anyone. She wanted to with Jack. She wanted to share everything... but the lie that she'd held on to for weeks would likely be the hurdle they could never jump together.

"Have you tried?" he asked. He stroked her shoulder with his thumb, sending a shiver through her.

Viv pulled in a shaky breath. "I'm infertile. I was sick when I was younger. The choice was never mine."

He squeezed her tighter against his side, turning to kiss her forehead. "That's why you foster."

Wrapping her arm around his waist, Viv nodded. "I don't have to give up my yearning for children, and I can help many. Fostering is the best fit for me. I'm single, so it would be more difficult to raise a child on my own."

As she explained her reasoning, the heaviest weight she'd ever known crushed her chest.

"You're an amazing woman, Viv."

She didn't want his praise, and she sure as hell didn't deserve it.

"I'm actually thinking of adopting Katie. I was asked and I...I think I'm going to move ahead with the process."

The idea both thrilled and terrified her. She was so excited to be a mother, and sweet Katie was an angel. But could she do it on her own? At least with fostering she had gaps between children, could decide when she was ready to open her home again. She could keep her heart from getting involved—though with Katie she was already a goner. But adoption was permanent and Viv wanted to make sure Katie was getting the best life possible. Would one parent be enough?

Jack shifted to lie on his side, facing her. "I can't

think of anything better for you or her. She's lucky to have you."

"I want to give her everything," Viv confessed. "I just don't want to make a mistake."

Jack's soft laugh filled the room. "You wouldn't make a mistake. When you come into anyone's life, they're better for it. Katie… Me…"

Viv's heart clenched. "Jack—"

"I need to tell you that you mean more than—" He broke off with a muttered curse before continuing on. "Damn it, I want this, Viv. I want to see where this will go, how we can make this work. I can't promise anything. Hell, this is all still new to me, but I know when I'm not with you—"

"Stop."

She couldn't listen to his declaration. Once he knew everything, every last part that she had to share, then he could decide…and Viv knew in her gut that he wouldn't feel the same. Still, she had to tell him. This wasn't about the case anymore, this was about family. If they were going to have any chance at being a couple, a family with Katie, he needed the truth now.

In the glow from the baby monitor, she found it hard to look at him. But she couldn't wait another minute. The dynamics in their relationship had shifted immensely and as much as she wanted to wait for the right time, she knew in her heart such a moment didn't exist.

It was now or never.

"I—I've learned something about the case," she whispered, tears threatening to clog her throat.

Jack propped his head on his hand and stared down at her. "When? Today?"

"A few weeks ago." She closed her eyes. "I didn't know how to tell you."

"Weeks?" he repeated. "What don't you know how to tell me? Damn it, Viv, I need to know everything. Don't worry about how to break news to me."

Silence settled between them and already the wall separating them was being erected. She'd been building it brick by brick the second she'd opted to keep that journal hidden.

"How the hell could anything you discover be upsetting to me?" he went on. "What could you possibly have learned?"

Viv never wanted to be the one to destroy Jack. His need for justice overrode everything in his life. She knew he had to have all the facts. But even now, on the brink of blowing this case, she couldn't tell him.

She rolled over, flicked on the lamp and headed to her closet. Without a word, she reached up to the top shelf and pulled down the leather journal. She'd read it front to back, twice. She knew the secrets Patrick O'Shea had kept, knew more than just Jack being his son. She'd read about how his children wanted him to go in a more legal direction, but he'd been hanging on to contacts he couldn't cut ties with.

Turning back around, she met Jack's gaze. Those green eyes pierced her from across the room. He glanced at the book she held.

She'd never been more vulnerable in her entire life. Viv stood before Jack wearing absolutely nothing...except the truth clutched in her hands. Completely bared to him, Viv willed herself to push through this, to do the right thing.

With her arm extended, she walked to his side of the bed and handed it to him. Jack kept his eyes on her as he took the journal.

Finally, he shifted his focus to the leather-bound

book in his lap. He opened the cover, immediately seeing Patrick O'Shea's name.

Jack jerked his attention back to her. "You've had this for how long?"

Viv swallowed against the guilt, the remorse. There was no going back now. "Too long," she whispered.

Unable to look at his face, coward that she was, Viv grabbed her robe from atop the comforter and jerked it on before heading to the antique trunk at the end of her bed. She took a seat, facing away from Jack. Twisting her hands in her lap, she imagined each word he was reading. She knew where the bombshell was located within the pages; he had a few more to go.

Each time he turned another, Viv cringed.

Jack's audible gasp gutted her. Still, she couldn't face him.

"You read this."

His accusing tone was like a slap. "Yes."

"And you didn't think I deserved to know this bastard was my father?"

Viv came to her feet, tightened the belt on her robe and turned to face him. The pages lay open, Patrick's dark penmanship mocking her.

"Of course you needed to know," she said, knowing she had no right to feel wounded. "I wanted to tell you the second I found it. But I—"

"What?" he demanded as he jerked the sheet aside and came to his feet. He reached for his boxer briefs from the floor and tugged them on. "You got too close with the family and shifted your loyalties?"

Stunned he'd even think that, Viv shook her head. "No. Never. I never shifted my loyalties to them. I may believe in my heart they're innocent, but I am on your side, Jack."

His laugh mocked her. "Really? I'd hate to see if you were my enemy. How the hell do I even know this journal is real? It could've been a plant. Did you ever think of that?"

Viv nodded. "I've thought of this from every perspective. But I wasn't snooping when I found it. The one time I was actually just doing my job, I stumbled upon it."

In a rush, she explained how it was caught in her desk, but the way it was wedged in, she truly didn't believe it had been placed there to trick her.

"Conveniently, it was *your* desk," he replied in that dry, disbelieving tone. "So why now? You waited until we'd grown closer for what? Because you thought it would soften the blow somehow?"

"No," she whispered. "I just…I couldn't keep it from you any longer. I'm falling for you and—"

"Don't say it," he demanded. When he started gathering the rest of his clothes, Viv's heart sank. He wasn't even going to stick around to hear her defense…not that she hadn't seen this coming. "Don't even try to tell me that you love me, or any other feelings you're having. At this point, what you want, what you feel, is irrelevant."

He stepped into his pants, shrugged his T-shirt on, then grabbed the journal. "You know how much this case means to me. You're the only person I've confided every damn thing to. I've confessed my fears to you because I knew you understood from being on the inside."

The disappointment in his tone was worse than the rage. He'd trusted her. He'd placed her on this particular case because he knew she'd always been loyal and honest.

She'd failed him.

"I can't take back what I did," she explained, crossing her arms over her chest. "I was scared when I first found it, worried I was being set up to see what I'd do with it. But as I read on, I figured there was no way the O'Sheas knew you were their half sibling. Braden would've confronted you. So then I tried to find the right time to tell you."

"The second you found it was the time," Jack countered, narrowing his eyes at her. Only moments ago those eyes had held her in place with passion and signs of love. "But you clearly chose the team you're on. And it's not mine."

Katie's cry blared through the monitor. Viv jumped from the unexpected intrusion, then glanced at the screen. Katie turned, grabbed her favorite blanket and quieted down.

Jack sat on the edge of the bed to pull on his socks and shoes. "Everything you've learned, from the journal and otherwise, needs to stay with you until this case is wrapped up. Clearly, you'll need to stay at O'Shea's, because the Feds are counting on you, but I no longer need you to do work for me."

He didn't look at her as he delivered the toneless speech. Cutting her out of his life was that quick, that final. As much as she wished he'd listen to her reasoning, she knew Jack wasn't that man. He saw things as black-and-white, and his once-glossy perception of her had been tainted. Quite possibly, his need for justice had been tarnished, as well. How could he take down the only family he had left?

As much as it hurt to let him walk away angry, she truly had no choice. He needed to think, and she needed to let him go. She loved him, more than she thought possible. But for now, she'd keep things professional—and live with the gaping hole he'd left in her heart.

She hoped in time he'd come around, hoped he'd realize that she loved him and had done everything to protect him.

"Do you want me to stay on with the O'Sheas full-time?" she asked.

Jack's mocking laugh rang out as he rose to his feet. "I'll text you the name and phone number of the contact from the FBI. You can direct all of your questions to him from here on out. I'll have your things from your office sent over."

With the leather journal in hand, he headed toward the bedroom door. He stilled at the threshold and threw a heartbreaking look over his shoulder.

"This isn't how I planned the night to end." His eyes held her in place from across the room. "And to think I nearly let my guard down and told you how I truly felt."

By the time she processed exactly what that veiled statement meant, he was gone.

Viv clutched the V in her robe as she sank to her knees. Tears gathered and fell as she struggled with the reality that Jack had fallen for her. He didn't need to say those exact words; he'd shown her.

Swiping at her eyes, she glanced at the monitor. Sweet Katie slept peacefully now. Viv had done the right thing in finally telling him. It didn't matter what her heart wanted, all that mattered now was that child and giving her the best life.

But that didn't mean Viv would let go of what she'd found with Jack without a fight.

Sometimes seeking comfort is the only way to get through the mourning process. I had no idea a child would come from our intimacy. As much as I want to be part of his life, I respect Catherine Carson's wishes. I came into her life, offering nothing, so the least I can do is stand by her in a silent manner and support her from a distance.

It kills me. Goes against everything I stand for. I take what I want, what's mine. And this little boy with green eyes like my own is mine.

Sending checks isn't the same, but he will want for nothing.

Jack stared at the words, hating every single one of them. At this point he even questioned his loyalty to his own mother. She'd lied to him by remaining silent. She'd never once hinted that his father was the notorious Patrick O'Shea, but here it was, in plain sight.

Easing back in his leather office chair, Jack stared at the open pages, willing them to rewrite history. He didn't want to be the son of such a criminal. He'd done nothing these past ten years but take down jerks like him.

Yet here he sat, at a crossroads, and he had no idea how the hell to move forward. What direction did he take at this point? Did he confess to the Feds that he was too close to the case now? Did he go to Braden, Mac and Laney and tell them…

What? What would he say? "Congratulations, it's a boy"? Somehow that didn't sound right. There was no "right" way to go about this, yet Jack had to make a decision and he needed to make it fast.

He swiped a hand over his face, instantly smelling something floral. Jasmine. The shower he'd taken with Viv had left its mark on him. There was no escaping her.

The idea that she'd had this information for weeks tore him up. He'd lost sleep over the case, had gone to the enemy, had quizzed her over and over. Yet she had remained silent.

He'd slid right into her world, trying like hell to remain closed off, but where Viv was concerned, he hadn't had a choice. Everything about her drew him in, from the way she took in foster children to the way she called him out when he was being difficult.

She had curves that any man would beg to touch, and he'd done so much more. He literally craved her, ached for her. How did he just turn that off?

And sweet Katie had gotten into his heart, too. How could he ignore that emotion? An innocent baby had stolen his heart when he wasn't looking.

But Viv made him smile, made him want... Made him realize there was enough life left in him to do exactly what he'd intended, and that was to have a family of his own.

She'd helped him in a sense, but in the end, she'd destroyed him. If she cared for him the way she claimed, she would have come to him first.

Falling for Viv wasn't what hurt. Knowing she didn't trust him with the truth cut him so deeply, he didn't know if he'd ever recover from the wound.

But there was only one thing he could do at this point. The Feds didn't need to know about Jack's biological connection to the O'Sheas—at least Viv was right in that area. They only wanted Jack's help with proving or disproving the theory that the family had something to do with the Parkers' deaths.

Uncovering the truth about his past, his family, was more important to Jack than any damn case.

For once in his life, something was coming before work.

When he glanced at the antique clock on the corner of his desk, he realized time had literally slipped away from him. It was nearly six in the morning. He'd left

Viv's house so late, then come straight to his home office and bottle of twenty-year-old bourbon. He'd read Patrick's damn journal cover to cover, trying to make sense of it all.

Jack had no doubt this book was legit, and he highly doubted the rest of the O'Sheas—*his siblings*—knew anything about their father's deepest secrets.

Tapping the edge of his desk, he continued to glare at the black ink. He'd wait a bit longer before making the call. A call that could change his entire future.

Jack tipped back the rest of the bourbon in his tumbler. His thoughts drifted to Viv again, and he damned himself for ever letting her into his life.

He cursed himself further for still wanting the hell out of her.

But that was something he'd have to address later... after he met with his newfound brother.

Seventeen

Neutral ground was always his first choice, but for this little meeting, Jack had agreed to go to O'Shea's. Mac was still in town and Jack wanted to meet him and Braden together. He wanted to go through this story only one time, though he knew that wasn't likely.

Jack entered the offices an hour before they officially opened. He'd been up all night and called promptly at seven. Braden had agreed to the emergency meeting, though Jack could tell the tycoon wasn't too thrilled with the demand. Too damn bad. Jack's life had spiraled into a cursed mess in the past twelve hours and he was done getting smacked in the face by fate.

He figured the only way to get them all together was to tell them he had information about their father. Which was the truth.

Clad in a black dress shirt and black pants, Braden stepped out of the back. Jack couldn't stop the punch to the gut as he stared into the man's green eyes. The same shade he saw every morning in the mirror. How had he never noticed the resemblance?

Because there had been no reason to until now.

"This better be good, Carson." Braden motioned for him to follow. "Come on back. Mac is here and Laney will be along shortly."

And where Laney was, Ryker was. Arrogant prick.

Jack clutched the journal in his hand and headed toward the back. He expected to feel a little fear, if he were being honest with himself, but right now all he wanted to do was get this over with. The odds of losing control were in his favor; after all, this meeting was going to be four against one. But he'd gone against odds before. Jack never backed away from a challenge. Besides, he held the journal—of which he'd made copies—and he also had more ties with law enforcement than the O'Sheas could ever hope to have.

Jack stepped through the doorway to the back office and met Mac's angry stare. With a clipped nod in greeting, Jack surveyed the rest of the space. He hadn't been in this part of O'Shea's before. He knew from Viv's description that the mahogany desk in the corner was hers.

Bringing Viv into his thoughts right now would not help him get through this meeting. He needed to focus 100 percent on what was about to happen, because this journal didn't affect just his life—he was getting ready to drop a bomb directly onto the people he'd despised for so long.

Ruining them had to take a backseat to the truth. He wanted them to know exactly what he'd discovered.

And after reading Patrick's words, Jack had a gut feeling he might be trying to bring down the wrong individuals. His father—it still hurt to think of Patrick O'Shea in those terms—had been the one who'd needed to be brought to justice for his past crimes. Braden, Mac and Laney were all guilty by association, but they'd pleaded their innocence in this case all along. Ryker... well, he brooded and threatened, but he'd maintained his story, as well. Perhaps Viv had been right all along. Maybe this family was innocent and were only hypothetically guilty because of their notorious name.

"What couldn't wait?" Braden asked as he took a seat behind the oversize desk in the middle of the room. "It must be something big for you to agree to come here."

The journal felt heavy in his hand. "I've stumbled upon some information."

And he'd thought hard about how to admit where it came from. He might be feeling hurt and betrayed by Viv, but he wasn't about to out her in front of this family. Even he wasn't that big of a jerk.

"There's no easy way to do this," he admitted as he crossed into the room and laid the journal at Braden's fingertips. "This was your father's."

Mac, who'd been silently leaning against the desk, glanced down to the leather book. "How did you get this?" he asked, turning his focus back to Jack.

"That's not important. What's important is what is inside." Jack swallowed, but he kept his features taut. "Halfway in, you'll see a date flagged—June 30."

Braden blew out a sigh, as if he'd rather be anywhere else than talking with Jack barely after sunrise. Well, Jack would rather be anywhere else, as well, but there was no escaping the inevitable.

Keeping his eyes on Braden, Jack propped his hands on his hips and waited. Moments later, the man slid the open pages to his brother.

"Where the hell did you get this?" Braden demanded. "I suppose you believe you're the son?"

Jack nodded. "I know I am. Catherine Carson was my mother. Patrick refers to her often, and my mother never told me who my father was. I know we were taken care of, because when I turned eighteen, I received a lump sum of money. There's no way it came from my mother, who worked in a flower shop."

Mac held the journal in his hand and gestured with it. "So because you find this out of the blue, and the time line adds up, you just assume—"

Jack held out his palms. "I'm not assuming. I'm willing to get a DNA test."

Mac set the journal back on the desk and eyed his brother.

"Sorry I'm late." Laney swept in, Ryker right on her heels. She tugged her coat off as she glanced between Jack, Mac and Braden. "What did I miss?"

"Here." Braden held out the journal, open to the page that changed Jack's life.

Ryker took the book and read with Laney. Her gasp filled the room, but he just grunted out a laugh.

Ryker took Laney's coat and folded it over the back of a leather chair. "Where did you find this?" he asked.

"He won't say," Mac stated.

Jack wasn't about to let the power slip through his fingers. "Where I found it doesn't matter. Is that Patrick's writing?"

Laney nodded. "Yes. How do we know you're the son he's talking about?"

She eased down into the seat and leaned against her coat, her hand covering her swollen abdomen. "All this time Dad knew he had another child out there and didn't say a word," she murmured. "I bet that tore him up inside."

Jack gritted his teeth. He didn't care what it did to the old bastard. The man was a crooked liar. He'd done vile things to innocent people.

"Your eyes," Laney stated, looking back up at Jack.

He nodded. The eyes clearly told the truth. Everyone in this room, save for Ryker, had the same shade of green eyes.

"That doesn't mean a thing," Ryker snarled. "If you're trying to get money—"

Jack laughed. "Don't be absurd. I couldn't care less about your money. I'm here for the truth."

"You're here with a new approach to try to pin a crime on us we didn't commit," Braden stated.

Jack shrugged. "I could use this information to my favor if I wanted. But I'm starting to believe you."

All eyes turned to him. Yeah, the revelation was just as shocking to him as it was to them. He didn't want to admit he was wrong—who did? But he wasn't going to make excuses for his actions. He'd gone on his instincts and past scenarios, and believed he was working the right angle.

"This is all too coincidental." Mac rose to his full height, crossing his arms over his chest. "Suddenly our long-lost brother comes in and wants to help us save the day against the big, bad Feds."

Jack's cell vibrated in his pocket. Nothing was as important as this, so he ignored it. Again, he was putting his personal life ahead of work.

"I didn't say I believe you completely," he retorted. "I'm willing to work together, and if that clears your name, then so be it."

"What exactly do you want from this meeting?"

Braden asked, narrowing his eyes and leaning back in his chair. "You expect us to welcome you to family gatherings or reveal our deepest secrets?"

Jack glanced around the room. Ryker and Mac seemed to be angry, Braden still skeptical, while Laney looked at him as if she wanted to reach out and hug him, but was afraid. So many mixed emotions, so many lies swirling between them, and Jack was trying to set straight as many as he possibly could.

"I don't expect to be trusted, by any means," he stated, glancing back at Braden. "I wouldn't believe me if I were in your shoes. I wanted to present you with what I'd found. The journal is yours to keep. I made copies."

Braden closed the book and tapped his fingers on the leather cover. "I'd still be interested in knowing how this fell into your hands."

The same way everything else lately had fallen into his hands…by chance. Viv had entered his life when he hadn't been looking, just like the journal.

"I have a large reach," he replied. "Same as you. I doubt you give up your informants."

There was no way he'd ever give up Viv's name. No matter what happened between them on a personal level, Jack cared for her, and he'd never want to see her hurt. She'd come to work for him when she'd needed a job, and he'd thrown her into the lion's den. She'd never complained, but had stuck by his side and worked double duty.

And when she'd discovered a journal that uncovered a lie over three decades old, she'd panicked. Jack would be a jerk not to realize that she'd been scared, that she'd been trying to protect him while he finished this case. She knew the amount of time and mental effort he'd put into seeking justice.

And as furious and hurt as he was that she'd kept something so pivotal from him, he'd have to be blind not to see her reasoning.

"You don't have to give up your informant," Braden stated, shifting Jack's focus back to the present. "I know you and Viv have been working together. I've known for some time."

Keeping his cool, refusing to show any sign of affirmation, Jack merely asked, "And what makes you think this?"

Braden shrugged and came to his feet. "She's the likely candidate, but Laney didn't want to believe Viv would turn on us. She's the only reason we kept Viv here."

Jack flashed Laney a glance. The sadness in her eyes proved how much this family had come to care for Viv. Damn it, this was a debacle of epic proportions, because he, too, cared for her. Too much.

"Leave Viv out of this," Jack stated. There was no reason to try to hide the facts or treat them like fools. "She worked for me, but she's no longer in my employment."

"Relax," Mac interjected. "We also kept her here because we have nothing to hide. We know the Feds want to pin the Parkers' tragedy on us. If you want to stop snooping around and actually work together, maybe we can find the guilty parties and clear our name."

Jack tried to process everything happening. First and foremost, Viv's true identity had been discovered long ago and they'd still kept her on. They could've done anything to her, given the rumors surrounding the family. But now that Jack was getting a glimpse inside their lives, inside Patrick's journal, he was starting to see that maybe this family wasn't all death and destruction.

"So you're agreeing to work together?" he asked, taken aback.

"The truth goes both ways," Braden said. "We don't trust easily, but if you want to do this, then we're all-in."

Jack needed Viv, he realized. She had ties to this family that he didn't, and they obviously respected her.

Damn it, that wasn't the only reason he needed her. He missed her, and it had been only hours since he'd seen her, touched her.

But the O'Sheas wanted to work together to clear their name. Jack wanted justice for the Parkers...justice he'd never been able to deliver on behalf of his wife and unborn child.

His family.

And he might have another chance at a family yet. Viv had made a mistake, but she wasn't malicious.

"I'd say with our combined resources, we can solve this case together," Jack agreed. He had to focus on this moment, and deal with his personal life later.

"Get that DNA test," Braden demanded. "I see it, though. I know the truth just by looking at you. What my father wrote may be shocking, but it's the truth. Eyes aside, you've got the O'Shea attitude."

Jack didn't want to have the O'Shea name tacked on to his life. In his line of work, he couldn't afford it. But at the same time, he wanted a family of his own. Only time would tell if this group would be his or not. He wasn't quite ready to cozy up to the idea of holiday dinners or family portraits.

"I'll have it done, but the result stays inside this room." He glanced around at the people who were family by biology...nothing more. "I have a business, a reputation to protect."

Braden smirked. "Can't be associated with the no-torious family? I get it. No problem."

Mac glanced at his watch. "I need to pick Jenna up at the airport. She caught an early-morning flight."

Braden nodded. "Go ahead. We'll discuss a game plan and I'll fill you in later."

Once Mac stepped out, Jack and Braden sat down at the desk. He wanted to solve this damn case the FBI had entrusted him with. His priorities had shifted, but he was still keeping his guard up, as he suspected Braden was, too.

"I'm going to go out front and get the store ready to open," Laney stated. "I'll keep this door shut for pri-vacy."

Ryker pulled up a chair beside Braden, his dark eyes narrowing in on Jack. "You need to talk to Viv before we get started?"

Jack shook his head. "No. She has nothing to do with this anymore." But even as he said the words, he knew they weren't true.

"I don't know what's going on between the two of you, but—"

"No, you don't." Jack settled back in his chair as he cut off Braden's words. "Now, let's get to work."

Jack pushed Viv out of his mind so he could concen-trate on this all-important meeting.

Too bad he couldn't push her out of his heart.

Eighteen

Martha was all too eager to watch Katie for the evening, but Viv assured her she wouldn't be long. Valentine's Day sucked, and heading to Jack's house was just salt in the wound. But she had things that needed to be said. Once she got all this off her chest, maybe…

No. She wouldn't feel any better. She'd still feel empty inside, but she had to tell him how she felt and had to defend herself. Added to that, she needed to return all these presents.

She'd piled the ridiculous toys he'd bought into her car. Where on earth would she house a tiny sports car, anyway? Katie didn't need such extravagant gifts and Viv was doing her best to cut all ties with Jack. That was what he'd wanted, after all.

He'd made it perfectly clear that she was of no use to him any longer. But she knew he still cared for her. He wouldn't be so hurt if he didn't care. Plus, she'd seen the way he looked at her, felt how perfectly he'd touched her. They shared a bond whether he wanted it or not. Viv just wished that was enough to get them back where they needed to be. She'd give anything to be able to turn back the clock and hand him that journal the second she'd discovered it.

But she'd made the best decision at the time. At least she thought she had. Hindsight and all that.

Viv pulled in a breath as she tugged her coat tighter around her neck. The snow would not let up. This would be a great night for all those lovers to stay indoors.

She cursed Valentine's Day again as she rang the bell at Jack's Beacon Hill home.

In moments, the wide door swung open and Tilly greeted her with a smile. "Honey, come on in. It's freezing out there."

Viv stepped into the foyer, forcing herself not to look around the house for the man she'd dreamed about all night. She needed to drop the toys off and leave. That's all. Now that she was here in his domain, she couldn't talk to him. What would be the point? He was so furious with her. He hadn't spoken to her or reached out to her at all since he'd left her bed.

"I can't stay," Viv informed Tilly. She needed to get out of here. "I have some things in my car that belong to Jack."

Tilly's brows rose. "Oh, well. I'll go get him—"

"No!" Viv didn't mean to shout, but she didn't want to make this evening any more unbearable than necessary. "I mean, I can carry them in."

Tilly tipped her head to the side, reaching out to grab Viv's hands. Her warm touch threatened to break Viv. She was already so close to an emotional breakdown... she just didn't have time for one.

"I don't know what happened with you guys," Tilly

started. "But he's a grouchy bear. I can't get him to eat. He stays in his office and only asks me to bring him more bourbon. I've seen him like this just one other time."

When his wife died. The words hovered in the air as if she'd said them.

Viv swallowed the tears clogging her throat. "It's all my fault," she whispered.

"I'm sure it can be fixed." The elderly woman wrapped her arm around Viv and squeezed. "Go talk to him."

Viv shook her head. "He's angry, and rightfully so. I just think it's best if I drop off all these things and be on my way."

Tilly eased back and patted Viv's hands. "His wife was taken from him too soon. You're the first woman I've ever seen him interested in since that time. Are you sure you want to throw all of that away because you're afraid?"

Viv closed her eyes. Was she willing to risk more humiliation and rejection?

"He's upstairs in his study." Tilly took a step back and gestured toward the grand stairway. "I'll be finishing up in the kitchen before I go. You can bring the toys into the foyer and take off, or you can do what you know in your heart is the right thing. Either way, I'll be leaving shortly."

Tilly headed down the hall to the kitchen.

Viv's chest was heavy as she eyed the steps. She'd never been upstairs, but she wasn't going to let this moment pass her by. She'd say her piece, put the ball in his court, then be gone.

If he truly wanted to sever all ties, then at least she'd know she'd done her part.

Viv gripped the carved newel post and willed her legs to carry her up the steps. Nerves threatened to take over, to force her to turn back around and get out. But Jack was facing one of the most difficult situations of his life and he was justified in his feelings toward her. She couldn't apologize enough, but she wasn't going to miss the chance to say it one last time.

The wide hallway was dark, except for the dim light shining beneath one closed door. Viv pulled in a shaky breath and crossed the distance. She tapped lightly on the door with her knuckles.

"Go away, Tilly. I'm fine."

He didn't sound fine. He sounded...crushed.

Viv didn't knock again, but merely turned the knob and pushed the door open. He was already angry at her. Barging in on his personal space was nothing compared to what she'd done.

"Tilly, I..."

He glanced up from behind his desk, the words dying on his lips as he met her gaze across the room. Viv's heart beat heavily against her chest. She clutched the knob for support as she remained frozen in place.

"I came by to return the toys," she stated. "I, um, well, Tilly said you were up here and..."

The way he sat unmoving, without saying a word, had her nerves spiraling out of control. But she'd come this far and she was going to get this out.

"I know you hate me." She eased forward, one slow step at a time, across the expansive office. "You have every right and I don't blame you. But when I found that journal, I was stunned. My immediate thought was to get it straight to you, but then I realized what that truth would do to you. You think of nothing but justice. When

I learned about your wife and child, I understood how deep your need for justice went. You've been trying to bring the O'Sheas down for so long and I didn't want to be the one to crush you."

Motionless, Jack stared at her. The bottle of bourbon sat on the corner of his desk, and he clutched an empty tumbler in his hand. Was he drunk? Was he even listening?

"I kept it hidden, waiting for the right time, hoping the case would wrap up and I could present it to you. I wanted you to be able to separate work from this bombshell because I knew the case was so important."

She stopped at his desk. Tugging the tie on her coat a little tighter, she wished she had something else to do with her shaky hands. Those green eyes held her in place, pinning her with an unreadable expression.

"But then the timing didn't matter," she went on, biting her bottom lip to prevent the trembling. She attempted to tamp down the tears, but her eyes filled. "I started falling for you. The attraction I'd had for so long turned into something I didn't expect."

Jack came to his feet, setting his glass aside. "Viv—"

"No, let me get this out, then I'll go."

She didn't want him to kick her out, not until she explained herself and apologized the proper way.

"When my feelings got stronger, I cursed the day I found that journal. I didn't want to know that truth, didn't want to carry it around with me, to hold such a burden. I knew it would hurt you no matter when I told you. But I didn't want to be that person, Jack. I didn't want to be the one who had to drop this bomb into your life."

Viv swiped at the tear that slid down her cheek. "I'm sorry I lied. I'm sorry I kept something so vital from you. But at the time, I thought I was doing the right thing by saving you heartache."

Viv took a step back, blinking the moisture from her eyes. "I'm sorry," she whispered. "That's…that's all I wanted to say."

She spun on her heel, more than ready to get out of this room, this house. The ache of seeing him again spread through her and she had no idea how the hell she was going to recover, but she had no choice. She would get through this, in time…she hoped. A little girl was depending on her.

Firm hands gripped her, hauling her back against his chest. "Don't go."

Viv's heart slammed against her chest. "I can't stay, Jack. I've said all I need to say."

He spun her around to face him. The intensity of his gaze had never been so powerful, so raw.

"Well, I haven't said all I need to, and you're going to listen."

She nodded. He deserved to say whatever he wanted, and the hell he was about to throw at her was completely justified.

Jack stepped aside and pointed to the chaise in front of the wall of books. On any other day, she'd marvel at the entire wall of hardbacks, but since she would never be here again, she'd have to just commit the scene to memory.

"Sit down."

Viv shouldn't have been surprised at his aggressive tone, but, well…she was. Without a word, she crossed and took a seat, sliding her fingers along the velvety arm of the chair.

"I've thought about nothing else since I saw that journal," he began, pacing like a caged animal. "My father was a criminal, I've been working to destroy my half siblings, only to find they are legit, and the woman I trusted most lied to my face."

Viv glanced down to the ends of her coat ties. She toyed with a single dangling thread.

"No, you don't get to look away."

She glanced up to find him standing before her. Hands on his hips, he glared down at her.

"You came to me. Now you're going to listen."

She glanced at the bottle on his desk. "How much have you had to drink?" she asked.

Jack snorted. "Not enough to dull the pain, but I'm not drunk."

Viv bit her lips, nerves dancing in her belly, because she had no clue what he was about to tell her. And he was right. She'd come to him, so she would listen.

"Braden and I have come up with a plan and I've gone to the Feds with it. They don't need to know any more than the fact Braden and I are working together. They trust me and they know I'll find the people responsible for this crime."

Viv nodded, glad for that at least. Maybe if he and Braden did this together, Jack would slowly ease into the idea that the O'Sheas weren't monsters.

"That's great," she told him. "I'm happy for you."

He raked a hand over his face and stared up at the ceiling. Only the Tiffany lamp on his desk cast any light in the room. But she saw the pain in his eyes, sensed the frustration rolling off him. She'd hurt him, but he still cared. She felt it.

"I only want what's best for you," she went on. "I know it doesn't seem like that, but I do."

"That's the other thing that has haunted me." He spread his feet wide, crossed his arms and pinned her with that sultry gaze. "I've looked at this from every angle. Mine, yours. I want to push you out of my life for hurting me."

"I understand and I don't blame you." Guilt fueled another round of tears. "I'll just go."

She'd started to stand, when Jack's hands came down on her shoulders and forced her back down.

"You're staying right here." Viv didn't know what to say, especially when Jack squatted down in front of her. "I'm not done talking."

"I get that you're hurting, but we've said everything." She had to get out of here. "Let me unload my car and I'll be out of your life for good."

Jack dropped his head, blew out a breath before looking back up into her eyes. "I don't want you gone, Viv."

Hope slammed into her. "What?"

He reached up and gripped her hands. "I'm upset, yes, but I understand why you did what you did. Hell, I don't know that I'd have done things differently had I been in your position."

Viv blinked, sure she'd heard him wrong.

"When I was torn over what to do about approaching Braden and Mac, I caught a glimpse into what you must have gone through. And that was for people I didn't particularly care about. I know you care about me, so I can only guess how much that tore you up."

Viv pulled her hands from his and stood, causing him to rise, as well. "No. Don't forgive me, Jack. That's not why I'm here. I just—I wanted you to accept my apology. I know we can't go back to where we were. I don't deserve it."

She shoved her hands inside her coat pockets. "I need to get back home."

"Will you just stop?" he demanded, when she started to move past him.

Standing shoulder to shoulder with Jack, she froze, not glancing to her left, where he stood a breath away.

"Damn it, Viv. You love me. Why are you doing this? I'm trying to forgive you. I'm trying to tell you that I'm sorry, too, for thinking the worst. For not listening to your side from the beginning."

Air caught in her lungs as she turned fully toward him. "What?"

"You love me," he said softly, smiling this time. "I know you do or you wouldn't have been so upset about the journal."

She closed her eyes. "You're sorry," she whispered. "I hurt you and you're apologizing. You had every right to—"

He slammed his mouth down onto hers, gripping her wrists at her sides. Jack wasn't gentle, wasn't slow. He consumed her as if he were claiming her all over again. Jack nipped at her lips before easing back to look her in the eyes. "I may not like what you did," he murmured. "But I understand why you did it. And don't bother fighting me or telling me you don't love me, because that won't work at all with my plans."

"What are your plans? To kiss me like you love me, when you know exactly how I feel?"

He laughed, easing her arms behind her back to draw her arched body into his. "Oh, but Viv. I do love you. And that's why I was so hurt."

Viv's heart quickened as she stared up into his eyes. "You what?"

His mouth quirked. "I can admit when I was wrong and I can admit that I love you. I knew I was falling for you, but when I left your apartment, I realized it was love. Someone I didn't care about couldn't get close enough to make it hurt so bad."

Viv closed her eyes. "I never wanted to hurt you. I wanted the exact opposite."

"I know." He nipped at her lips again. "I know you didn't want to hurt me."

Jack pulled back, stared down at her, making her wonder what was going to happen next. Where they would go from here. *He loves me.* The words swirled in her head, her heart. She'd never expected him to return her feelings, never thought he'd forgive her, let alone love her.

"I'm waiting."

Viv narrowed her eyes. "For what?"

He leaned into her, causing her body to arch even further into his. He continued to hold her arms behind her back and Viv ached for his touch, sans clothes.

"For you to tell me you love me. I want the words."

Viv licked her lips, pleased when his eyes watched her mouth. "I love you, Jack. I'm sorry I hurt you. I'm sorry I ever made you doubt my loyalty. But I love you more than I've ever loved anyone in my life."

He started for her mouth again, but Viv turned her head. "Wait."

"What?"

She glanced back. "If you love me, why were you holed up here worrying Tilly to death?"

"I was in a pissy mood about how to approach you," he confessed. "I was coming to your place tomorrow, but I was working through my plan of action to get you back."

Viv raised her brows. "And what was the plan you'd concocted?"

Jack released her hands and immediately went for

the tie on her coat. After he peeled the garment off and sent it to the floor, he tugged at the closure on her jeans.

"My plan was to strip you naked, have my way with you and tie you to my bed until you believed me."

Arousal shot through her. "You can still do all those things, but I'm going to have to text Martha first and tell her I'll be a little later than I thought."

Jack gripped the V of her button-up shirt and jerked, sending buttons flying across the room. "I have a feeling she won't mind."

Viv tipped her head back as Jack feasted on her neck, then made his way down to her chest. She'd text Martha…in a bit.

Epilogue

One year later...

"Happy Birthday to you," the whole crew sang.

"Hard to believe she's two already," Jack stated, as Viv helped Katie blow out the two little purple candles on her three-tiered cake. Maybe he'd gone overboard when he ordered the cake, but he did tell Viv she could handle everything else.

"Time flies once you become a parent." Braden held his own baby, Michael, who was six months old now. "I can't believe all the things this little guy is doing on his own already. He's army crawling across the house. Zara went nuts and baby gates are everywhere."

"They're not everywhere," Zara chimed in, sliding a party hat over Braden's head.

"I don't want a hat," he grumbled. "It has a ballerina on it."

"It's not your party," Zara stated, as she patted the side of his face.

"Who wants cake?" Viv announced. "We have plenty and we'll all be eating it for the next week."

She sent Jack a look and a wink. He'd never thought he'd find love again, but everything was different with Viv. She was perfect for him and had come into his life at exactly the right time.

After he'd discovered he was actually an O'Shea, Jack and Braden had worked around the clock to clear their name. It ended up that some wannabe gang members had botched the robbery and tried to cover their tracks. Once Jack had gotten the proper intel, it took only one stakeout to bring down the criminals.

And after all this time, the O'Sheas were completely legit. Braden hadn't been lying; the family had cut ties with all illegal dealings. Their worldwide auction house was more lucrative than ever. It had taken some time, but Jack and his new siblings were all meshing perfectly together. Jack had wasted no time in marrying Viv and they'd adopted Katie together. They were in the process of adopting another child. He and Viv both wanted a large family and he was more than ready to fill up his large home. Tilly was overjoyed, of course.

As Viv passed out pieces of cake, Katie played with her own layer of purple icing and pink cake.

"More, Mommy." Katie held up her sippy cup with one hand and shoved icing in her mouth with the other.

"I'll get it," Jack said, taking the sticky cup. "You're a messy monster."

Katie smiled at him, her purple teeth flashing. "Wuv you, Daddy."

Those words never failed to make his heart clench. As a man who had thought he'd lost everything, he was beyond blessed with Katie, Viv and the O'Sheas. He literally had every single thing he'd ever wanted at his fingertips.

As he filled Katie's cup with juice, Mac let out a whistle. "While we're all here, I have an announcement."

Jenna stepped close to his side and smiled. Mac wrapped an arm around her, pulling her in tight.

"We're having a baby," he yelled.

Laney squealed, rushing for Jenna and enveloping her in a hug. Ryker stepped up and smacked Mac on the back with one hand, while he held his baby girl on his other arm.

All these kids... Jack smiled as he twisted the lid back on the cup. "Looks like there will be a whole new generation of O'Sheas," he proclaimed, crossing back to the dining area. "Just when I thought my house was big enough to host this family..."

"We're going to need a compound if we keep wanting to have family events," Zara said with a laugh. "I'm okay with that, since we plan on having more."

More O'Sheas. At one time that thought would've angered Jack, but now...well, he couldn't be happier.

He threw a glance at Viv, who mouthed, *"I love you."* He sent her a wink and knew he was the luckiest man alive...and that included being an O'Shea.

* * * * *

HIS FOR THE TAKING

ANN MAJOR

To Ted

One

The last thing John Coleman had planned to do when he woke up to the stench of petroleum and the roar of his oil rig was to go chasing after Maddie Gray.

Jamming the phone against his ear, Cole—as everybody from Yella, Texas, called him—leaned back in his leather office chair and rubbed his throbbing temple. "What do you mean Maddie's come back to Yella and she's nursin' Miss Jennie?"

Miss Jennie had been their beloved high school English teacher.

Cole knew his soft drawl sounded mild, even disinterested, as he spoke to Adam, his older half brother, yet Cole was anything but calm.

During his marriage to Lizzie, which had ended when she'd died almost a year ago, he'd dreaded the thought of his childhood sweetheart coming back to town. Because he'd feared how he might react. But he was a widower now, and he'd been thinking about Maddie of late, thinking he might just drive to Austin and look her up. So far he'd always managed to talk himself out of it.

What kind of sap carries on a secret teenage affair with the town's bad girl and then can't move on after she treats him like dirt?

Hell, six long years had come and gone. And still his mind burned with memories of Maddie's fine-boned face, her heart-shaped lips, her violet eyes and ebony hair, and ample breasts. Why couldn't he forget how radiant her face had been every time she'd lain beneath him? Because she'd been more than beautiful. She'd been smart and gifted, especially with contrary horses.

But she had bad genes. Maddie's mother had stolen husbands, fathers—indeed any man who would have her. And in the end, her own daughter had turned the tables on her by stealing her boyfriend and running off with him, leaving Cole behind.

"Miss Jennie fell over a garden hose and cracked her pelvic bone," Adam said, interrupting Cole's thoughts. "Maddie's here to take care of her until Miss Jennie's niece from up in Canada can get down here. Nobody in town can stop talking about Maddie. About how well educated and classy she is now. About how's she's got herself a college degree and all. Cole, she's so damn beautiful she takes your breath away."

"You've seen her?"

His half brother hadn't moved to Yella until after their dad's death, which had occurred shortly after Maddie had run off, so Adam hadn't known Maddie when she and Cole had been together.

"I dropped by first thing this mornin'! All the guys have been stopping by Miss Jennie's place to check on her, so I figured I'd better check on her myself."

"Right."

"Just to make sure she's gettin' proper care and all. Oh, is Maddie ever beautiful. All curves and creamy skin. She has the softest voice and the sweetest smile—one that lights everything up."

"Enough!" Cole growled.

The brothers' telephone call had centered on ranch business until this last bit of local gossip. When Cole was away from Yella, Adam usually ended their calls about the family business by filling him in on the latest scuttlebutt.

"Well, don't you be going back there just to see Maddie, you hear." It was strange how much more annoyed than usual Cole suddenly was with his older brother. "You're to steer clear of Maddie Gray. I don't care how polished she is now, she's no good. Never was. And never will be."

"Something's sure got you riled this morning." There was an edge in Adam's voice now, too.

"Pressure here on the rig. You know how I was telling you this damn drought has shale frac water in short supply? Well, I'm facing the possibility of having to drill a deepwater well. All the drillers are overbooked except for one bandit who says he'll put me first, but only if I make it worth his time by paying him triple. And now you're distracting me with idle gossip about a no-good woman like Maddie."

"She's the interim CEO of some nonprofit in Austin called My Sister's House. She's worrying herself to death over some fundraiser she's in charge of in a couple of weeks. Sounds like she's trying to do some good, at least, doesn't it?"

"Camouflage! It's an ancient trick."

"Well, I liked her. Oh, and she's got a little boy she left back in Austin at camp. He's six years old. Noah. Miss Jennie's got loads of pictures of him. He's cuter than a bug. Black hair... green eyes. He reminds me of someone." There was an odd note in his brother's voice. "All in all, Maddie didn't seem the least bit bad. She's nothin' like her mother."

The last thing Cole wanted to hear was praise for Maddie, or her son. Especially not from his half brother, who often resented him because of their father's mistakes, so he told Adam he was a fool to fall for anything Maddie Gray said and ended the call.

So, Maddie was back, dazzling the town, even his brother. And she had a kid. Who was the father? Vernon? The timing would be about right. Cole had always been careful to protect her, so he knew the boy wasn't his.

Cole pushed his mug of strong black coffee aside so roughly, the steaming liquid sloshed onto several important drilling leases. With thoughts of Maddie stirring his blood, he didn't need more caffeine.

Edgily he shoved the papers aside and stared out the window. He slid his jean-clad legs onto the top of his desk and stacked one scuffed, black, ostrich-skinned cowboy boot on top of the other. It was early yet, but already a brilliant sun blasted the desolate Texas landscape. Thanks to his air conditioner, the interior of his trailer was icy. That was the only thing he liked about living at the drill site for weeks on end while he worked a field. But even the chilled air couldn't keep out the hot memories of Maddie.

Too well he recalled the first time he'd actually spoken to Maddie, who'd been younger and poorer than him, and hadn't run in his social circle.

He'd driven home from the University of Texas on a Friday and had gone looking for his girlfriend, Lizzie Collier, over at her daddy's ranch. It had been spring and the pastures had been filled with bluebonnets.

When Cole had stepped inside the barn and hollered for Lizzie, one of the horses, Wild Thing, had gone off like dynamite, neighing and kicking his stall door. Cole thought Wild Thing was too dangerous to fool with but Lizzie had the softest heart in the world. When she'd found out Old Man Green was starving Wild Thing and beating him, she'd talked her dad into buying the horse. Her father had hired more than a dozen horse whisperers to save the animal, and when they'd failed, Lizzie's father had wanted to put him down. Lizzie wouldn't hear of it.

Cole hadn't thought too much about the ruckus the horse was making until he heard a crooning voice inside the stall. Thinking Lizzie might be trapped, Cole had rushed toward the stall door.

"Lizzie?"

"Shh!" chided a young, defiant voice from inside the stall.

Since Cole couldn't see too clearly in the shadows, he took the slim figure wearing jeans and a baseball cap turned backward for the young male groom who worked for Lizzie's dad.

Fixating on Cole, the gelding's ears swept so far back against his narrow gray skull they all but vanished. Then the big animal lowered his head as his pale forelock shot over terrible eyes that rolled backward. Half rearing, the animal charged, his hooves splintering a board.

"Get out of that stall, boy!" Cole commanded.

Wild Thing's eyes rolled crazily. Again the gelding reared to his full height and heaved himself with murderous intent against the stable door.

The boy jumped back and flattened against the wall. "Are you trying to kill me?" In the confusion the kid's baseball cap hit the sawdust, and a lustrous mane of black hair tumbled down the imp's shoulders. And across *breasts*.

"Maddie Gray?"

What male with an ounce of testosterone wouldn't have recognized her sinfully gorgeous, exotic features—Maddie's creamy pale skin, her voluptuous mouth, her violet-blue eyes? Hell, she looked exactly like her no-good mother, Jesse Ray Gray, the town's most notorious slut.

Cole's gaze seared her ample breasts, which heaved against

her faded blue cotton work shirt. She'd filled out since he'd seen her last. If her tight clothes were any clue, she'd probably be up to her mother's tricks—if she wasn't already.

"You're Maddie Gray," he repeated accusingly, disliking her more than a little because she stirred him.

"So what if I am?" Her beautiful mouth tightened rebelliously.

Wild Thing's eyes rolled, and he neighed shrilly.

"Please lower your voice and start backing away," she ordered.

At least she wasn't a total simpleton. She saw the folly of being penned in such a small enclosure with a monster like Wild Thing.

"I said back away!" she repeated. "Can't you see you're scaring him?"

She began to speak to the startled horse in a sweet, soothing murmur Cole would have envied if he wasn't so furious at her for her foolhardiness and willingness to blame him for her own stupidity.

"It's okay, big baby. Nobody's going to hurt you," she said huskily in a purr that would have oozed sex had she been talking to a man.

A gray ear perked up. Not that the large animal didn't keep his other ear flat and a suspicious eye on Cole.

"You've gotta go," the girl urged when Wild Thing danced impatiently.

"Not until you get out of that stall," Cole said.

"I will, you big idiot—just as soon as you shut up and leave." For the horse's sake, she kept her insult soft and sweet.

Cole's stubbornness made him stand his ground a few seconds longer, but her pleading eyes finally convinced him. After Cole left, it took another minute or two before the horse settled and the girl was able to slip out. Strangely, no sooner was she safely outside the stall than Cole's temper flared again. He knew he should forget about her recklessness and go to the Collier house and wait for Lizzie, but Maddie had his blood up. So when he heard her light, retreating footsteps as she lit out the back to avoid him, he rushed after her. When she caught sight of him, she let out a cry of alarm.

Grabbing her arms, he shoved her against a wall. "You have no right to be on this property! Or to be in that monster's stall!" Cole yelled. "You scared the hell out of me!"

When Wild Thing screamed and sent his hooves crashing against wood again, Maddie stilled.

"I was just doing my job, okay?"

"Your job?"

"I'll have you know Liam Rodgers hired me."

Liam, Lizzie's daddy's foreman, was no man's fool. "Why you? Why would he hire you, of all people, when he could hire the best?"

She frowned. "Maybe because I know what I'm doing. While you've been off at college driving your fancy cars and chasing girls, I've been mucking stalls to get free riding lessons. Maybe I've learned stuff. When he saw Wild Thing stand calmly and let me saddle him in the round pen, Liam about fainted. When I rode the horse just as easy as you please, Liam hired me."

"Well, you can't possibly know enough to work with that monster."

"I did what twelve men couldn't do!"

"You got lucky! Now you listen to me. A normal horse weighs half a ton and has a brain the size of a tomato. Such an animal is wired to defend himself against predators, which includes humans, even half-pint girls like you."

"I know all that!"

"That horse is a maniac. You shouldn't be anywhere near him—not in the round pen, not in his stall, not ever!"

Her chest swelled, and her eyes narrowed rebelliously.

Her dark look only fueled his fury. "Don't you get it? Next time he'll kill you!"

"Not if you stay out of this barn and let me do my job!"

"Right! So, it's my fault? I have half a mind to report this to Mr. Collier."

"No! If I don't save him, Mr. Collier will kill him."

"Good."

"No! Please… He's better. I know he's still easy to startle, but he'll get even better. It's just going to take time and patience. He's been through a lot."

"He's a killer."

"Not many living creatures get the easy, pampered start in life you've had. That's why you can't possibly understand what it's like for the rest of us!"

Her lovely voice had softened with desperation and love for Wild Thing but it didn't hold a trace of self-pity. When her impassioned eyes misted, he noticed they were as beautiful as sparkling amethysts.

"I know you don't care what I think, but Lizzie loves him. Spare him for her sake!"

The girl was passionate, compassionate…and despite her ragged jeans and faded shirt, gorgeous, as well.

Damn those eyes of hers. Again they reminded him of jewels, with lavender facets of light and dark that made his blood run hot and cold. Those damn eyes, coupled with having held her too close for too long in a shadowy barn that afforded him the privacy to follow through on his desire, had him hard as granite. Aware of her soft, slim body pressed tightly into his, he didn't even try to defend himself from the heat that her sexy curves generated.

It would be so easy to take her right here.

Her mouth was full and luscious and suddenly he wanted to kiss her, to dip his tongue inside and taste her. Would she open her mouth and let him?

The heat in her gaze was generated from *some* emotion. Maybe she felt what he did.

"What?" She had gone still. Her eyes never left his face. "Let me go!" Her voice was shallow.

"You don't want me to do that, and you know it." In the grip of a need too fierce to deny, his voice was raspy.

His gaze moved hungrily lower. She had soft, lush breasts. Hell, he wanted way more than a kiss, and he wanted it very badly. She was Jesse Ray's daughter, so she probably wanted it, too.

Feeling justified in testing a girl of such easy virtue, he gripped her shoulders and pulled her closer. Before she could react, he lowered his mouth to hers so he could take his first taste of her. His lips were hard and demanding because he expected easy compliance. And for an instant she responded just as favorably as he'd imagined, by gasping and sighing and clutching him closer. Her lips did part, and he felt her tongue, if only for an instant. Then almost immediately she stiffened. Recoiling, she balled her hands and began to pound at his chest, thrashing wildly.

When he didn't immediately let her go, her face flushed with anger. "You wouldn't treat Lizzie like this! You wouldn't try to take her in a barn like she was something cheap and easy without ever even having a single conversation with her!"

"Well, you're not Lizzie Collier, are you? You're Jesse Ray's girl."

"And that makes me too low to have feelings like you and your kind? Well, I do have feelings! And I'm not like my mother, you hear! So, go find your precious, saintly Lizzie Collier, and leave me in peace! She's your girlfriend. Not me! And I wouldn't ever want to be!"

But the last was a lie. The quick tears of shame and desolation in her lovely eyes and the thick pain in her ravaged tone told him so. She wanted him, but on equal terms. She didn't want to be someone cheap in his eyes. Her pride, as well as her longing for him, tugged at his heart and made him feel ashamed even as it made his desire for her increase a thousandfold.

He hadn't misread her. She had wanted him, badly. But Jesse Ray's daughter had as much self-respect as Lizzie Collier did any day.

For a long moment, she gazed at him as if pleading for something he was at a loss to give even as her look tore his heart. Then, with a desperate cry, she pushed free of him and ran out of the barn. As he watched her retreating across the pasture, he was stunned by her grace and vital beauty and by how much more he wanted her than he'd ever wanted Lizzie. He was baffled by how low and ashamed he felt by that fact. She was just Jesse Ray's girl. Why the hell should he feel such an overpowering need for her, such a need to apologize to her?

For weeks afterward, he'd tried to put the scent and softness and taste of the spirited and unsuitable girl out of his mind, but she'd been too lovely, too passionate, too brave, too forthright—too sexy. He'd dreamed of her, dreamed of making love to her.

He tried to forget her, but then his friends began to tell him stories about Maddie—marvelous stories he'd hungered to hear. How Maddie raced with the other kids, mostly the boys, in the pastures outside town. How she always won on the back of that prancing demon, Wild Thing. They said that she'd tamed him, that she was fearless, that she would ride bareback, that the pair could jump anything.

Why, one day after school when Cole's friend Lyle had been smoking in his vintage Mustang with the top down, she and Wild Thing jumped over him and the car.

"Crazy horse came so close to my head I dropped my cigarette in my crotch. Burned a hole in my best pair of jeans," Lyle had complained.

Such stories had impressed Lizzie, but they'd merely proved to Cole that Maddie was a headstrong fool—and brave, stubborn and determined. Even if the older generation in Yella wouldn't change their minds about her because of her mother, some of the kids began to think she wasn't as bad as they'd been taught. Maddie was smart in school, too, and Miss Jennie, whose approval was hard to win, thought she was as good as anybody.

For all that, Cole knew his mother would never approve of Maddie as his girlfriend. After his mother had married into the legendary Coleman family, she felt her children had a position to uphold. Still, despite his better judgment, his fascination with Maddie began to consume him. Thus, it hadn't been long before Cole started coming home from the university every weekend to seek her out.

He'd go to the barn and watch her train Lizzie's horses, especially Wild Thing. Maddie worked hard, giving more than she should to that monstrous beast, who now behaved like a docile pet to please her. Not that she said "I told you so" when Cole admitted he'd been wrong about her horse-training abilities. She simply basked in his praise, and he'd realized how much she enjoyed being admired rather than scorned. She was sweet when he apologized for kissing her, too.

Cole broke up with Lizzie and, with immense determination, began to court Maddie—but secretly.

He decided the gossips were wrong. Although she resembled her mother physically, she had a different character. Yes, mother and daughter shared the same jet-black hair, the same smooth, pale skin and the same lavender eyes that could turn blue when impassioned. Yes, their curvy bodies and sensual natures had been designed by God to drive men wild. But unlike her mother, Maddie was sweet and true.

Then she'd jilted Cole for Vernon Turner and left town,

proving his assessment wrong. She was just as feckless and promiscuous as her mother.

If she was trash, why couldn't he forget her? Why did he care if she was back in Yella?

She doesn't matter anymore. Hell, she never should have mattered.

So why did every nerve in his body feel taut? Why was his heart racing at the possibility of seeing her again?

Women like Maddie Gray, women who roared into a man's life and then left him like so much roadkill when they'd finished with him, were a dangerous breed. A smart man learned his lesson the first go-round and steered the hell clear of them.

So why was he standing up and slinging his jacket over his shoulders?

Cole had about a million things to take care of on the rig, like dealing with that crooked driller. He didn't have time for an unscheduled trip to Yella. Nevertheless, he scooped his cell phone and the keys to his Ford Raptor off his littered desk. Then he grabbed his sweat-stained beaver Stetson and rushed out of his trailer. Scanning the well site, which reeked of acrid fumes, he hollered for Juan.

After the air-conditioned trailer, the thick summer heat felt suffocating. Briefly he informed Juan that there was a problem at Coleman's Landing, his family's legendary ranch on the southern tip of the Texas Hill Country. Cole said he had to get down there fast, but that he'd be back soon. He told Juan to get the water well drilled and to damn the expense.

Then Cole was in his truck. Tires spinning, gravel and dust clouds flying, he set off for Yella.

After three miles of graded dirt road, his tires hit the main highway. He drove down that straight stretch of asphalt through parched, open country of scrub oak, mesquite and huisache like a madman, hating himself for being so all fired up to see her. She'd ruined his life…or at least several years of it, and she'd hurt sweet Lizzie, too.

Lizzie had loved him with every bone in her body, but because of Maddie haunting him, hard as he'd tried, he hadn't ever been able to love Lizzie as he should have. Or at least he'd never craved her, if that sort of cravin' counted for love—not the way he'd craved Maddie, with every fiber of his being.

Even Lizzie's dying words had been about Maddie, and he'd hated Maddie for distracting him at a time when he should have been concentrating solely on Lizzie.

But he had to see Maddie again. Hopefully all he needed was closure to get her out of his system. Something about the way she'd left him six years ago—without even so much as a goodbye—bothered him.

He had to know how she could have been so unfailingly thoughtful and kind during their long-ago summer romance, how she could have loved him so sweetly that final afternoon in August—and then run off with trash the likes of Vernon Turner that same night.

Who was she: The bad girl her own mother and the town claimed she was? Or the sweet, pure girl he'd fallen in love with?

He hoped to hell he wasn't fool enough to chase after a dream again.

Two

If Maddie felt nervous and out of sorts just being back in Yella, she felt even worse to be chasing Miss Jennie's dog onto Cole's wooded land. What if Adam was wrong? What if Cole came back to town before he was supposed to?

She dreaded seeing him more than anyone else in Yella, which was ridiculous. How could his rejection and contempt still hurt so much after six years, when she'd told herself repeatedly that the past—that who she used to be—no longer mattered?

Maddie hadn't been back to Yella since the night she'd run away because there were too many memories here, both good and bad. For years, she'd made the future her focus and only rarely looked back. Besides, coming here meant she'd had to leave Noah, who was enrolled in a summer day camp on Town Lake, with a dear friend. She missed him, but she wouldn't have people here judging him because of her—or noticing how much he resembled Cole and putting two and two together.

She'd only come back now because she owed Miss Jennie for everything good in her life.

Maddie wiped her damp brow with the back of her hand. Had Yella always been this suffocatingly hot in the summer? Of course it had. She just hadn't noticed when she'd been a skinny, fearless kid wearing a thin T-shirt and shorts, running wild in the woods.

Today, with the sun beating down out of a bright sky, the heat felt thick and ferocious, and it wasn't even noon yet. Strands of her long black hair had come loose from her ponytail and stuck to her cheeks and neck. Her T-shirt and cut-off jeans felt as if they were glued to her perspiring body.

Still, despite the oppressive heat and humidity and a faint sense of uneasiness, she loved the scents and sounds of the woods. The smell of grass and dust, the chorus of insects that hummed along with the birds, made her remember some of the brighter moments of her youth. Long ago she'd ridden in these woods. Here, on horseback, a slim, despised girl had acquired the magical power that riding a powerful horse could bring. Riding had taught her to be brave and strong.

Most of all she remembered riding here with Cole.

Don't think about him.

Better to fret about her company's fundraiser than Cole. Even though she dreaded the annual event and the stress of dealing with wealthy donors, especially the women who knew how to dress and where to shop and where to lunch, she preferred worrying about all of that to thinking about Cole.

He'd rejected her, had made her feel more unworthy than anybody else here ever had. Why couldn't she simply forget him? Even after Greg had come into her life last spring— solid, reliable Greg, who didn't know her secrets, who approved of her and wanted to marry her because of who and what she was now—she remained confused about her obsession with Cole, who'd never seen her as his equal.

He'd rejected her soundly—so why couldn't she let him go? Why was she so afraid of seeing him?

When she'd fled Yella six years ago, she'd been too traumatized to ever imagine coming back. In Austin, she'd tried to better herself, tried to live down the mother who hadn't wanted her, the sorry trailer in Yella where she'd been raised, the terrible night that had driven her away. Most of all, she'd fought hard to be a better mother to Noah than her mother had been to her.

Not that juggling single motherhood while working full-time and going to college had been easy. Especially not when the nagging fear that she really was what everybody here had believed—no good—had remained.

Then, five days ago, just when she'd been on the verge of setting a date for her wedding to the man who valued her, Miss Jennie had called from the hospital and said she'd fallen. Miss Jennie was the one person in Yella who'd always believed in Maddie, the one person who'd been there when Maddie had been terrified and desperate. So, when Miss Jennie had mentioned she'd just love it if Maddie could come for a few days because her niece, Sassy, lived in Canada and needed some time to wrap up her affairs before she could fly to Texas, Maddie had agreed to come.

Not that Miss Jennie's neighbors hadn't all offered to fill in, but Miss Jennie had made it clear that she would prefer spending a little time with Maddie...if only that were possible. "Time seems more precious as you get older," she'd said, her voice sounding frail.

Still, since Miss Jennie had helped her relocate and had lent Maddie money to go to college, there was no way she could say no, even if it meant facing Cole and the prejudiced town.

Up ahead Maddie heard the jingle of dog tags. Just as she was about to call him, Cinnamon barked exuberantly from the sun-dappled brush. Her heart sank as she realized that he'd set off for the swimming hole on the Guadalupe River where she and Cole used to secretly meet. Where they'd made love countless times. Of all the places she would have preferred to avoid, the icy green pool beneath tall cypress trees on *his* land topped her list.

For here she could be too easily reminded of Cole, of their brief affair. Back then she'd been young and in love and filled with anticipation for their every meeting. She'd been so sure that he'd loved her and would love her forever, and that his love, once known publicly, would change other people's opinions and she'd gain the respectability she'd craved. Even when he'd insisted on keeping their relationship a secret from everyone important to him, especially his mother, she'd believed in him.

It had taken a crisis of the worst magnitude to make her see him for what he really was—a typical boy in lust out for a few cheap thrills with the town's bad girl, a boy who'd never respected her and couldn't be counted on to save her. No, she'd had to save herself.

Maddie had had six years to deal with the trauma of the past. She was all grown up now. She knew that life wasn't a fairy tale, that she needed to get over the hurt that Cole and his mother had inflicted on her.

The last thing she wanted or needed now was to see him again and reopen all those old wounds. If she were lucky, Cole would keep to his oil fields while she was here with Miss Jennie.

Maybe then she would escape Yella unscathed.

Three

Two hours after he'd left the drill site, Cole pulled up to Miss Jennie's white house on the edge of town where her property backed up to a corner of his own estate. Miss Jennie's house, with its sagging wraparound porch, was a sorry sight in the middle of an overgrown, brown lawn. Not that Cole's mind was on the lousy condition of her house and yard as he slammed the door of his big, white truck and strode up her walk.

He was a little surprised when Miss Jennie's fool of a dog didn't race up to him, yapping. Whenever Cole rode on this part of his ranch he usually ran into the mongrel. On hot summer evenings Cinnamon loved nothing better than lying on a shady rock along the bank where the river was spring-fed and icy cold.

That particular swimming hole had often been Cole and Maddie's secret meeting place.

All he could think of was Maddie.

He knocked impatiently, but when the screen door finally

opened, it wasn't a reluctant Maddie prettily greeting him, but sharp-eyed Bessie Mueller from next door.

Cold air gushed out of the house around her as she set fists on her solid hips. Her wrinkled face was brown from working outdoors. She had a way of standing that made her look bolted to the earth.

"Your mother told everybody you weren't coming home till tomorrow, so, what has got you planting your dusty boots on Miss Jennie's doorstep today?"

It went without sayin' that everybody in Yella knew everybody else's business.

"Ranch affairs," he drawled, hating the way the lie made heat crawl up his neck. "Is Miss Jennie doing okay?"

"She's just fine, but she's restin' for a spell. She's had so much company this mornin'—all male. She's plumb tuckered out."

"And Maddie Gray?"

Bessie grinned slyly. "Oh, so, it's *her* you've come to see... like every other man in town?" The knowing glint in her black eyes irritated the hell out of him. "Well, she's out looking for Cinnamon, if you have to know. That's why I'm here. I told Maddie it wasn't no use chasin' that mongrel. When that fool dog isn't barking loud enough to wake the dead, he's after my poor chickens or diggin' up my pansies. He always comes back—when he takes a mind to."

Like all mammals, human or otherwise, living in Yella, Cinnamon had acquired a reputation.

Cole tipped his hat. "You tell Miss Jennie I'll be back a little later, then."

If Maddie was chasing Cinnamon, he knew where to find her.

When Cole tugged lightly on the reins, Raider snorted and jerked his head, stopping just short of the small creek that fed

the river where ancient trees grew in such dense profusion
they were almost impenetrable.

"The brush is too thick from here on," Cole said, "so this
is where I'll leave you."

On a hunch that Cinnamon would lure Maddie to the pool
by the dam, he'd saddled his large, spirited bay gelding and
set off.

Dismounting, Cole looped Raider's reins over a fallen log
near the rushing water and left the horse grazing in the shade.

Pushing back a tumble of wild grapevines that cascaded
from the highest branches of a live oak, Cole made a mental
note to get his foreman to send a hand out to clip the vines
before they smothered the tree. Then, as he stalked through
the high brown grasses toward the emerald pool, memories
of Maddie played in his mind.

He and Maddie had ridden these trails together. When
they'd dismounted they'd often played hide-and-seek. How
he'd loved catching her and pulling her slim body beneath
his. She would smile up at him, her flushed face thrilled and
trusting in the pink glow of a late-afternoon sun.

After she'd left, he'd posted signs that read No Trespassing and No Swimming.

At the sound of a dog barking, Cole's heart began to race.
When he recognized Maddie's low, velvety voice, he went
stone-still.

"We shouldn't be here. We're trespassing. But you don't
care."

Stealthily he inched forward until he caught glimpses of
dewy skin and ebony hair through the trees.

Sitting on the dam, dangling her long legs in the water, she
wore nothing but a blade of wet grass on her left nipple and a
pair of black thong panties. Her exotic face with those arched,
slanting brows was lovelier than ever. Not that his gaze re-

mained on her face. Her naked breasts and slender waist and her legs that went forever stole his breath.

He gulped in air while his heart thudded so violently he was sure she'd hear. He could turn and go, but why should he? He'd come here to find her, hadn't he?

Slowly she dipped a rag—no, it was her T-shirt—into the water and squeezed it so tightly that rivulets of sparkling liquid showered her throat and breasts.

"Ah, nothing like icy water on a hot day," she purred huskily as she put the T-shirt back into the pool and dripped more fluid diamonds over her body. "I was burning up."

The dog was panting hard. Cole was burning up, too, but his condition wasn't entirely due to the heat.

Erect, spellbound, he watched as the blade of grass got caught in the currents of water tracing down her smooth, gleaming belly before sliding down to her navel. When a slender fingertip plucked it off her skin, heat shot through Cole. His sex, hot and hard, swelled painfully against tight denim. When Cinnamon walked onto the dam and shook water all over Maddie, she screamed even as she giggled.

"You are all dog," she said huskily, but she laughed, teasing the mongrel rather than chastising him.

Damn her to hell and back for being so gorgeous and unnervingly sexy. She seemed sweet, too, just as she always had—the very essence of everything feminine.

But looks could deceive.

Even though he knew what she was, memories of the first time she'd lain with him struck him full force.

She'd been flushed and naked as she'd whispered she loved him and always would. She had begged him to take her.

He'd kissed her throat and stroked her hair. "Are you sure about this?"

"No matter what happens, I want it to be you…who's first, I mean."

For a long time, his hands had skimmed over her body, touching her, caressing her. She'd been so innocent and so infinitely precious to him.

Determined not to hurt her, he'd been gentle and patient even though his youthful hormones had been raging. Hell, he'd even told her he loved her, too. Worse—he'd meant it.

Don't think about it.

But how could he forget how tight she'd been, or how she'd held her breath so long after he'd entered her, she'd scared the hell out of him?

"Are you okay?" he'd whispered.

"Better than okay." When she'd pressed her soft mouth to his throat she'd sent him over the edge. He'd apologized, but she'd begun to kiss him again, and he'd hardened inside her almost instantly.

"I've had a crush on you for years," she'd said. "I just never thought you could care for someone like me."

"Well, I do."

"Sometimes I still have to pinch myself so I know I'm not dreaming."

Now, determined to push the bittersweet memories aside and regain control, he counted slowly…backward from one hundred to zero. Long before he reached zero, more memories bombarded him, each one sweeter than the last. Then he couldn't count, couldn't think, couldn't do anything but feel his testosterone-engorged body thicken.

More than anything, he wanted to touch her warm, velvet skin, to taste her sweet lips…just one more time. Maybe once he was sated, he would be rational enough to remember how shabbily she'd treated him.

As if she sensed him, she slid into the water, screaming because it was so cold, and then swam away from the dam, leaving a trail of graceful ripples flashing in her wake.

Instead of listening to the voice of reason that told him

not to play with fire, he strode down to the bank and stood above her in the long shadows of the cypress trees, watching her swim, willing her to turn and face him.

When she did, her face whitened with shock. "Cole! What are you doing here?"

The alarm in her slanting blue-violet eyes cut him to the quick. But still his tone was hard when he said, "I heard you were chasing Cinnamon on my land, so I came looking for you."

When her exotic face went even whiter, his own craven desire made his gut clench.

Without another word, she dived underneath the water and swam as far away from him as she could. When she finally came up, she crossed her hands over her breasts and scrambled behind the nearest rock. "I—I didn't mean to bother you!" she began, blushing furiously as she gasped for breath. "If I'd known you were in town—I would never have come here! Your brother, Adam… He told me you wouldn't be back anytime soon. I swear he did!"

"Didn't you see the No Swimming signs? A kid nearly drowned here a couple of years ago, after a flood. Cinnamon is not worth risking your pretty neck by swimming here alone."

"Okay. I won't do it again. If you'll just leave, I'll dress and go."

"The last thing I want is you dressed and gone."

The stark look of terror reappeared in her eyes. "Don't start!" she whispered. "Please—"

The shame and fear in her frantic gaze tore at his heart. He remembered how sensitive she'd been on the subject of her mother and how shy she'd always been about sexual matters, especially in the beginning. But she'd never been this skittish. Suddenly he wished he could take back the suggestive comment.

"Somebody told me a while back that you're a mother now...that you have a little boy..."

Her violet-blue eyes widened with even more fear. Why?

"I just meant that as a mother, you shouldn't take unnecessary risks—like swimming here alone."

"My son is no concern of yours!" Her voice was high and thin. "You made that very clear—"

"When did we ever discuss your son?"

"What?" She seemed to catch herself. "You're right. Of course you're right. I saw your signs. It's just that I'm upset because you startled me. I shouldn't have gotten in the water without a buddy. If you'll just leave, I'll get out, dress and go. Like I said." She had begun to shiver, and her lips were blue.

"You can swim as long as you like...now that I'm here to watch over you."

"I don't want you here watching over me." Her teeth were chattering.

"Right." He set his hot, insolent gaze on her.

"Cole, I'm...I'm freezing. If...you won't go, would you please turn your back so I...can get out and dress?"

"Okay, already." Halfheartedly, he turned his back.

Not trusting him, she hesitated. A moment or two later, he heard water splash on limestone, followed by the whisper of damp feet on grass and the breaking of twigs as she scampered across the rocks to retrieve her clothes.

When a low curse escaped her lips, he turned out of concern and was rewarded with another glimpse of her tantalizing breasts and thighs. His breath hitched as she struggled to push her slim arms through the knotted sleeves of her wet, tangled T-shirt. Absorbed in pulling on her jeans, she didn't look up and see that he couldn't take his tortured eyes off her.

When she'd fastened her cutoffs, she looked up. "You cheated," she said.

"Sorry."

"I guess I shouldn't wonder, since you'll always think I'm the kind of girl who doesn't deserve your respect." With an indignant frown she leaned down and secured the now-docile Cinnamon with a leash.

"Damn," he muttered, feeling guilty as well as angry.

That she could chastise *him,* for anything, when she'd jilted him for Turner, was gallingly unfair.

"Don't worry. I won't presume to trespass on your land again," she said almost haughtily.

"You can swim here anytime," he said coldly. "It's just that I'd prefer that you bring a friend with you the next time."

"Who? With the exception of Miss Jennie, people here don't really like my mother or me much. If you'll recall, I...I never had any real friends in this town."

"I hear eight men stopped by to check on Miss Jennie this mornin'."

"For your information, I wasn't ever who you thought I was or who they probably think I am. It's taken me a long time to believe in myself...after...after the way you and the town treated me."

"Oh, really? I find that surprising. For someone so sensitive and romantic, you sure as hell slept with me and then ran off with Turner without so much as a goodbye."

When her skin went as pale as the bleached limestone bank, he felt as if someone had kicked him in the gut. But even as she began to tremble, her eyes blazed.

"Believe what you want about me!" she whispered as she hugged her arms around herself. "I'm glad I don't have to care anymore." But her eyes belied her indifference.

When he'd left the rig today he'd sworn he wouldn't re-hash the past, but now he had to ask. "Tell me why you ran off with him. You owe me an explanation."

"Once...I foolishly thought...maybe I did owe you. So, before I left, I called you to explain, remember?"

Fury that she would lie so carelessly swelled inside him. "The hell you did! You called me eighteen months later—when it was a little late, since I was already married to Lizzie!"

"No! I called you the night I left. But your mother answered the phone. She told me exactly what you told her to tell me, that she didn't want my kind in your life. So, excuse me if I didn't call you back. I had a lot on my plate. But my problems then are none of your business now."

"My mother? You talked to my mother that night?"

She nodded.

"I don't believe you! There's no way she could have resisted throwing such a call from you in my face!"

"I don't care what you believe. Do you deny that when I called you again, a year and a half later, you were even less receptive than she'd been that night? If you do, let me refresh your memory. You answered the phone and told me you never wanted to talk to me again! Then you slammed the phone down. At least your mother had the guts to talk to me!"

Her beautiful violet eyes shimmered with remembered pain, making a muscle in his gut pull. Her accusation about his mother didn't play. His mother, who had rigid views of social order, would have skinned him alive if she'd found out he had anything to do with Jesse Ray's daughter.

"The truth is—you waited a whole year and a half after you'd run off to call. Like I said, it was too late."

"Well, then let's leave it at that! You got married to a nice, respectable girl. Maybe I moved on, too. Okay?"

But it wasn't okay. Why were feelings that he'd suppressed for years suddenly so important to him?

"I told myself to leave it at that! And I did, as long as Lizzie was alive—for her sake. But now that she's gone and you're here, damn it, I want to know why you left me for Vernon without any explanation. All I knew was what your mother told everybody—that you'd flaunted yourself around Vernon to spite her and had run off with him for the same reason."

She whitened. Although she tried to hide her fear, he saw that her hands were shaking. What was she so scared of?

Then she drew herself up straighter, and her beautiful lips thinned with determination. It was as if she found some inner strength that enabled her to face him down.

"I—I wasn't myself when I left. After talking to your mother, I believed you were relieved to be rid of me."

Relieved? He'd been in so much agony he'd thought he was dying. When he couldn't get in touch with her, he'd been wild to find her, to talk to her. Wanting to hurt her now, as she'd hurt him then, he said, "I should have been relieved. Any sane guy would've been. You *were* your mother's daughter, in the end."

"Well, there you go," she whispered in a small voice. "Lucky you...to escape my clutches."

Her casually tossed comment pushed him over the edge. "Well, damn it, what if I wasn't smart enough to be relieved?" he growled, hating himself for not hiding that she'd held such power over him. Hell, she *still* held power over him as she stood there looking pretty and wounded and sexy as hell in the wet T-shirt that clung to her breasts. "When you ran off, I was worried sick about you."

"You were?" She bit her lip and looked away in confusion, as if what he'd said made no sense.

"I thought about you all the time. I didn't want to believe what your mother was saying without hearing your side," he said. "Every night I'd come out here and wonder how you could just disappear like that. I missed you, damn it! I wanted to know you were okay, at least, even if you were with Turner."

"Did you ever try to find me?"

"I wanted to. But, hell, my father got sick a week after you left. I was forced to take over the family businesses. On his deathbed he confessed to having another son…Adam. Mother couldn't accept him. I had a lot on my plate, too."

Something in his low tone got through to her because she whispered in a raspy, broken voice, "I'm sorry about your father. I didn't know. I was upset when I left…and too ashamed to call you again after your mother had so soundly rejected me."

"You sure as hell should have been ashamed."

"It took me a while to get over…what happened." Her eyes darkened with pain. "But when I finally called you again, you didn't want to talk to me. No—you were cold and arrogant."

Because he'd been afraid he'd break if he spoke to her, because he'd been trying to be faithful to Lizzie, damn it.

"I don't see why you're dredging all this up now, Cole."

Maybe because nearly a year had passed since Lizzie's death, and he finally felt free to pursue whatever the hell he wanted. Because Maddie was here, looking even lovelier and more vulnerable than before. His reaction wasn't logical. He knew that. But somehow his involvement with Maddie wasn't over. Seeing her again had thoroughly convinced him of that.

"So, what was in those letters you wrote me after I refused to talk to you?" he asked. He remembered too well signing for those two certified envelopes and then angrily tossing them in a drawer and telling himself he had to forget them.

Maddie gasped and lost even more color. "Didn't you read my letters?"

"No. I signed for them, but I couldn't read them, for the same reason I couldn't talk to you on the phone—because of Lizzie. Maybe someone like you can't understand this—but I would have felt like I was cheating on her if anything you said tempted me. Then she died, and I couldn't read them out of loyalty to her. She'd been my wife. What had you ever done—except jilt me for Turner?"

Maddie drew in a sharp, anguished breath. Licking her lips,

she swallowed hard. "Okay," she finally said. "You just signed for them.... Well, whatever I said in those letters can't matter now," she said. "You owe me nothing. And I owe you nothing."

"I'm beginning to see they're a piece in a puzzle I need to explore in more depth."

"No! The past, which includes you, doesn't matter now!" But her voice shook. "I—I was nothing to you."

"How can you say that and act like I mistreated you—when you ran off with Turner?"

"You should thank me. I set you free so you could marry your precious Lizzie and have everyone in Yella think the best of you. And that's exactly what happened."

He remembered resenting how anxious his mother had been to push Lizzie on him after Maddie ran off and his father died. Maybe marrying Lizzie because he'd been sad and lonely and overwhelmed, and because his mother and the whole town had thought they'd make a perfect couple, hadn't been the smartest thing he'd ever done. Not that he could tell Maddie that he'd made bigger mistakes than sleeping with her.

"What did you write in those damn letters?" he demanded, really curious.

"Nothing that could possibly matter now," she said, too casually. "I was young and foolish. Money was tight. My girlhood fantasy got the best of my better judgment. You know, poor girl wins rich boyfriend after all...lives happily ever after with him in his big, white, legendary ranch house... and then everybody in Yella looks up to her. Some foolishness like that."

"I think it's high time I finally read them. I'll be the judge of what's foolish."

Her brows flew together. "You still have them?"

"I threw them in a desk drawer, in my office, up at my big, white house, as you put it. They should be there...that is, if Lizzie put them back."

"Lizzie?"

"On her deathbed, Lizzie confessed she'd found them when she was tidying up in my office and had steamed them open and read them. She said she resealed them and put them back. She made me promise to read them after she was gone, said I owed you that. And then she said she was sorry, truly sorry, she hadn't told me about reading them before…but that she'd been too jealous to do so, too afraid of losing me. Imagine what a heel I felt like for having made her jealous over some-one like you. Out of respect for her, I haven't looked for them since her death."

Maddie's gaze was fixed on Cinnamon. "Well, there's no need to read them now," she said softly. "I'll go…."

"I'm not finished," he said. "I told Lizzie those letters didn't matter, that they never had mattered, because I'd married her, and she'd been the most wonderful wife a man could wish for."

"You were lucky then," Maddie said wistfully. "I hope to be as lucky…someday soon."

He hadn't felt lucky. He'd felt guilt-stricken and low for never having loved Lizzie as she'd deserved because of Mad-die.

"She always loved you. From the time she first saw you," Maddie said softly.

"Yes," he muttered, familiar guilt washing over him. He'd broken Lizzie's heart to pursue Maddie in secret. After that first kiss in the barn, he'd burned for the town's bad girl so fiercely, he hadn't been able to help himself.

And now Maddie was back, as beautiful as ever. He still wanted her.

"Maybe it's good we saw each other today, so we can face the fact that the past is over," she said. "I'm sorry I ran off without saying goodbye. I was young, immature…" Her voice was even and polite, the voice she would use to console or dismiss a stranger. "It's nice knowing you had a wonderful marriage, and I'm truly sorry for your loss. It can't be easy... even now. Cole, I wish you well. I truly want you to be happy."

"Thank you," he muttered ungraciously.

"Someday you'll find another woman. Maybe she'll remind you of Lizzie. You'll have children, build a family together...." Her voice grew choked and then trailed off awkwardly.

He didn't want to be reminded of Lizzie, who had been the bride everyone else had believed would be perfect for him. They'd made each other very unhappy. He'd remained lonely even in marriage.

"Goodbye, Cole."

When Maddie turned to walk away, he watched her slim, denim-clad hips swing and noted the way her damp T-shirt clung to her back.

Just watching her move with liquid grace as she vanished into the woods had his blood surging like fire in his veins. His breathing felt shallow. He wanted to strip her, to hold her, to kiss her. He wanted her naked and writhing with her legs wrapped around his waist.

He wanted *her*—period. Longed for her.

He'd stay crazy if he let her walk out of his life a second time. At the very least she still owed him some answers.

Four

The past, all her secrets, were supposed to be dead and buried. But Cole had her letters! And he'd never read them! He didn't know about Noah!

Cole hadn't rejected Noah as she'd believed. Instead, he hadn't read her letters because he'd wanted to stay true to his new bride.

All these years, everything Maddie had thought about him had been wrong.

She'd hurt him when she'd left him. Imagine that. As she fought her way through the woods, back to Miss Jennie's house, she wondered why it had never occurred to her that he might have felt that same shredding of the soul that leaving had caused her?

Because she'd had zero self-esteem. Because she'd been Jesse Ray's daughter and he'd been a Coleman, and she'd told herself he would believe the worst of her as her mother had.

Even so, she had tried to call him and explain before leaving Yella. She'd been so hysterical she had called his home, no longer concerned with revealing their relationship. His mother's cruel words would be forever branded into her heart and soul.

"You've got your nerve, Miss Gray. How do you know my son?"

"We dated. This summer. I need to talk to him."

"You dated?" Hester's voice had been shrill. "I don't believe you. Maybe…he felt some cheap sexual attraction, but if he'd had any respect for you, he would have brought you home to meet his family. My son loves Lizzie. And I thank God for that! John doesn't care about you any more than any of the men who've slept with your trashy mother have ever cared about her. You're so far beneath him, all you'd ever do is drag him down into the gutter where your kind lives. I warn you, if you don't let him go, my husband and I will do everything in our power to destroy you."

"That won't be necessary. Somebody else already did that," Maddie had whispered.

She blinked at the blinding white light sparkling through the trees and came back to the present. She didn't want to remember. It shouldn't matter that Cole hadn't known what Vernon had done to her or that he hadn't known about Noah. It was too late to include Cole in Noah's life because any contact with her son's father was too dangerous to her own well-being.

Still, as Maddie walked away from Cole, the pain in her heart was so great she barely felt Cinnamon twisting and tugging against the leash. Even though the woods were dappled with golden sunlight, she felt that she was stumbling through a dark void.

She couldn't afford to feel sympathy for Cole. No way could she let herself care about the young man she'd walked out on six years ago, or the wounded man he was now. Not when long-suppressed fears concerning her son gripped her.

Her work had taught her that lives were fragile, especially the lives of the ill, the elderly, the young, the learning disabled and the people like herself who'd experienced severe trauma and didn't have wealth or a supportive family. One false step, one stroke of bad luck, could lead to ruin. That was why she had to marry Greg, who had a good job and a stable, loving family. Together, if they worked hard, they would build a respectable life. The kind of life she'd always wanted.

The Colemans were rich and powerful. They could do a lot for Noah. But they considered her inferior. What if they decided to use their money and connections against her—to prove her unfit and take Noah away?

Maybe she didn't have their kind of money, but she had character and determination and a mother's fierce love. If she followed her plan, she could give Noah the wonderful childhood and bright future she'd never had. Then Noah wouldn't need the Colemans' money or their name.

But if Cole found out about Noah now, she might never be free of his family and the past. And she *had* to be free of him…because he too easily aroused all her foolish dreams of love and romance. It wasn't her fault he'd believed the worst of her and hadn't cared enough to read her letters. She'd made a life for her son without him, a life that would soon include Greg.

Even though she was more mature now, just seeing Cole today had her heart racing in a torment of confusion that included hurt, loss and hope, which was the most dangerous emotion of all. She couldn't let herself listen to his side and believe in those dreams again.

But what if he wasn't like his mother? What if he had loved her when they'd been together?

And she couldn't help feeling sympathy for Noah, who would never know his father, and for Cole, who wouldn't know his son.

Maddie's mind warred with her emotions.

She'd spent her whole life trying to prove she wasn't like her mother, but she couldn't deny the surge of excitement she'd felt in Cole's presence this afternoon. She still wanted him.

If he learned about Noah and became a part of their lives, would Cole tempt her to cheat on Greg, the very best of men, whose appeal paled in comparison to the virile and charismatic Cole?

Bottom line—for Noah's sake she needed to maintain a stable relationship with Greg. And that would be more easily achieved if she closed the door firmly on her past, and on Cole.

If only she could get her letters back before Cole read them. But how? She didn't dare mention them again because that would just intrigue him all the more.

Suddenly she heard his heavy boots crashing through the brush behind her.

"Maddie!" he yelled in that deep, possessive baritone that instantly made her blood buzz with a fierce, hot need that both thrilled and terrified her.

Stunned by the urgency in her own heart, she whirled, her gaze widening when his green eyes caught and held hers. She should keep walking, but somehow she couldn't when his desperately intent gaze refused to release her.

The past and its new truths couldn't matter.

But they did.

Stirred too deeply to deny her true feelings, she felt herself in a time warp. A warm breeze swirled the emerald trees around them, and she remembered all the times she'd seen him looking just like this before she'd run into his arms in these very woods as a girl. Back then she'd trusted him completely. Back then he'd been hers to hold and love, at least in secret.

Now, instead of the hurt and rejection she'd felt for so long, she was remembering brighter moments, remembering how he'd picked her up and spun her around, remembering how he'd spread a blanket across the lush grasses beside the river before drawing her down beside him, remembering how he'd stripped her slowly so he could make love to her. Always, always he'd been infinitely patient and tender. And so dear.

At the happy memories, blood pounded in her temples, bringing tumultuous excitement and the kind of wicked delight she'd never once felt for Greg, not even when he kissed her. Six years were washed away in bursting sensations of breathless joy and hot carnal needs that exploded in every one of her nerve endings.

She hadn't slept with anyone since she'd left Yella. It was as if she'd been frozen—until this afternoon…with Cole.

Why him? How could she still want him when he brought back the past and all the ugliness of her life here? Why couldn't it be Greg? She wanted to look forward, not back.

What was happening to her? How could she feel so powerless to fight her feelings for Cole when she knew she could never trust him with her heart or with her son?

"I'll always be Jesse Ray Gray's daughter."

"I don't care."

He looked as conflicted as she felt when he grabbed her by the wrists and spun her into his arms, hard against his body.

"I'll get you all wet," she cried.

"Feels good," he rasped. "What could be better than a wet woman on a hot day?"

She felt herself blushing. When she clumsily dropped Cinnamon's leash, the little dog yelped and dashed away. Not that she cared. How could she concentrate on the dog when Cole was holding her so close she was trembling? How could she resist the burning need in Cole's eyes, even though some tiny, sensible voice in her head pleaded with her to be more intelligent?

Greg. Marriage. Stability. Noah's future.

Greg will protect you.

Cole's mother promised to destroy you.

"Cole," Maddie begged as her breasts lodged snugly against his muscular chest. "Cinnamon… He'll get away."

Cole tugged her nearer so that her nipples peaked against the violent thudding of his heart in his warm chest. "He knows his way home."

For no special reason her gaze lingered on Cole's sculptured, sensual mouth.

Reluctantly, she laid her head on his shoulder and inhaled his dizzying, clean male scent and the lemony flavor of his aftershave. "Oh, Cole," she whispered on a rush of longing.

He needed no further invitation. Pressing his warm lips against her earlobe, he sighed. "Baby, you feel so good."

A delicious current raced in her blood. His mouth nibbling her flesh set off sparks even as the memory of his mother's words ate into her soul.

You're so far beneath him, all you'd ever do is drag him down into the gutter where your kind lives.

For a long moment, Cole simply held her tightly against his long, hard body. "You smell good, like the woods and the creek…like everything I love best."

Feeling cherished, she closed her eyes and fought to forget his mother's cruel assessment, fought to forget that he'd let her go when he'd promised to love her forever.

Stroking her fingers through his thick ebony hair, Maddie felt herself in a sensual dream. He was so tall and solid and hot. He felt so right. For the first time in years, everything seemed perfect. Had she been striving for all the wrong things, when all she'd ever wanted was Cole?

He's the enemy, the man who threw you and Noah away.

No. That wasn't how it was. His father died right after you left. You were gone. He was so sad and lost, he turned to

Lizzie. He'd wanted to be faithful to his wife. She could see that, understand it.

When Cole lightly brushed his mouth across hers, his sweet kiss scorched.

When she clung instead of resisting, his lips became hot and hard and punishing. Fire raced in her veins. Another girl, without her mother's genes, might have felt shame to part her lips and give herself so easily. But Maddie gloried in the wildness of his touch and the sweetness of his taste as he made a thorough exploration of her mouth.

When he held her and kissed her like this, she couldn't deny what she'd really wanted these past six years: him.

Grabbing her bottom, he thrust himself closer and rotated his hips against hers so that she could be in no doubt of his state of arousal.

"I want you," he whispered possessively. "You know that, don't you?" He sounded angry about it. "Damn it, I still want you! I couldn't stop, no matter how hard I tried! Not even when I was married!" he raged. "I wanted you even then."

She could empathize with his anger. Oh, boy, could she ever. Yet his anger hurt, too. He'd wanted to forget her, had married to forget her.

"I tried to forget you, too."

Her fingers twined around his warm neck and caressed his damp hair even as she pressed herself into him as wantonly as he was pushing against her. His body felt like strong, sun-blasted rock, and she was melting in his heat.

In an instant, the past merged with the present. She was no longer an inexperienced girl. This was now, and she wanted him as a mature woman craved her one true mate. She couldn't deny it any more than she could deny her next breath.

Six years and all the battles she'd fought to become a new, respectable, brave person, the kind of young woman who could be a proper wife to a professional man like Greg, were nothing compared to this primal need she felt for Cole.

But what did Cole truly think of her?

Would he always see her as the trampy daughter of Jesse Ray Gray? Did he merely lust for her in a raw, animalistic way? Wasn't that why he'd rejected her and married Lizzie?

Because of her doubts, she found the inner strength to spread her fingertips wide against his chest. Shoving lightly, she stumbled back a step. With a growl, he caught her and steadied her by slowly pushing her against the thick trunk of an oak tree. With the tree supporting their weight, he began to kiss her lips, her throat and her breasts, which were still slick and damp. Feelings of desire swamped her all over again.

When his greedy, exploring mouth followed a silky path from her breasts to her lips, he plunged his tongue inside. Once more everything was softening and melting inside her. All too soon, passion blurred her doubts, many though they were, and she was ablaze and needy for more of his loving, which felt true and right despite everything. Nobody but him had ever kissed her like this, made her feel like this. There was an honesty in such feelings, wasn't there?

Sensing her response and riding it, his kisses grew harder and longer and infinitely sweeter, and she drank deeply of him, stroking his tongue with hers, feeling as if she could never get enough. When he brushed his mouth over hers again, she kissed him back, and with every kiss her soul-devouring desire built.

He began to murmur to her in soft, mesmerizing tones, his love words both passionate and tender. She felt his erection jammed hard against her belly.

Oh, she wanted to tear off her clothes and his, too.

But when he pushed her wet T-shirt up and began to fumble with the fastenings of her bra, a rush of cool air against her naked belly and Cinnamon's wild barks made her shiver and push his hands away.

This is happening too fast. You're not good enough for him. His mother hates you. He married Lizzie. No matter what he says, he rejected you—and Noah, too. By not talking to you and by not reading your letters, he rejected you both.

His pointed red ears cocked, Cinnamon stood five feet away, quivering as he watched her intently. She fought to concentrate on the eager little dog instead of on Cole, because if she didn't quit thinking about all the things she wanted to do with Cole, she was going to be naked and lying flat on her back underneath him, her legs spread wide, writhing like a wanton. No doubt, when he finished his business he would blame her and think her as cheap as her mother.

"We have to stop," she whispered, feeling miserable because she ached from wanting him. "Or we'll go too far... and regret it."

"I won't regret it."

He popped her bra loose with a snap. Lifting her breasts to his lips, his warm mouth licked each of her nipples until they beaded like a pair of ripe berries, causing tremors to race down her spine. Had she ever felt so weak and feverish and needy?

She pushed at him in earnest. "We have to stop this—now."

"What?" he muttered. "You can't be serious."

"I am!"

She felt desperately close to the edge. She shook her head even as her arms clung to him fiercely. "We have to stop," she whispered brokenly. "I'm begging you."

His eyes closed for a long moment as if he were trying to shut out her demand.

"Cole!"

"All right, then," he said at last. Giving her a dark, tortured look, he yanked his large, tanned hands from her body as well as his gorgeous lips from her breast. "You win."

Never in her whole life had she wanted anything more than she wanted him. She ached everywhere and all her nerves felt raw. Because her limp knees would not have supported her otherwise, she sighed heavily and leaned back against the tree. He looked so dark and bereft and handsome as he finger-combed his black hair, she had to sag against the tree for fear she would hurl herself back into his arms and beg him to take her.

Breathing hard, he turned his broad back on her and stared with weary frustration at Cinnamon and then at the sparkling river. For her part, she continued to lean against the tree trunk while she fought a losing battle to steady her breathing. After a long time, she pushed away from the tree and refastened her bra.

When she'd rearranged her clothes and smoothed her wet hair and was almost able to speak in a normal tone, she said, "I'm sorry about what nearly happened. I shouldn't have let things get so out of hand."

"It was my fault as much as yours," he growled moodily. "So, how long do you figure on being in town?"

"Why should that matter? This proves we need to steer clear of each other."

"I don't see it that way. I'd like to see you again. The sooner, the better."

"Not a good idea."

"Why?"

She just shook her head. "That's pretty obvious."

"What if I give you my word that I won't touch you? At least, not unless you ask me to."

Too aware of her own burning hunger, she stared at him.

"Look, there are things about our past I'd like to resolve," he said. "Maybe then we could both forget about each other. That's what we both want—right?"

She was so out of control, she didn't know what she wanted anymore. No. That wasn't correct. She wanted the life she'd planned, didn't she? So, why did denying him hurt so much she ached?

It was dangerous sport looking at man like Cole, a man who was still as wrong for her as he'd been in the past, especially when she was wet and trembling from his kisses. His stormy green eyes and tousled black hair made him look hot and turned on even while his uncanny resemblance to their precious son tugged at her heart...and her conscience.

At the thought of Noah, she flushed guiltily and shook her head. "We need to avoid each other."

"I swear I won't touch you." Cole's angular face was set, his low tone sincere. "Please—I really think we should see each other again. Do you think it's going to be easy for us to forget, if we walk away—after that kiss—when what we need is closure? We need to talk."

Even though she didn't feel at all sure of herself, she agreed with him. "Maybe you have a point."

"So let's ride and then have dinner at my house or have a picnic somewhere later this afternoon. You still like to ride, right?"

She'd always *loved* to ride. "You mean horses?"

"What else?"

In spite of herself, she brightened. "I'm afraid I haven't ridden much since I left Yella."

"Some things you don't forget." His eyes were on her lips as his words lingered in the charged air that separated them. "You always said you wanted to see my house and horse barn, but that wasn't possible...when my mother lived there."

"She's moved?"

"Yes. When my dad was dying, he told me about my

brother, Adam. I felt betrayed at first, of less importance to my father somehow. But I hid my feelings and drove to where he lived and met him. I asked him to come to Yella to help me manage the ranch so I could devote more time to the oil business. Mother didn't want me to have anything to do with Adam. She felt betrayed even though Adam had been conceived before she met Dad and without Dad's knowledge. She blamed Adam for the whole mess, and then me for accepting him. That's when she moved out of the house."

Maddie could understand Hester's feelings, but the mention of Cole's mother's intolerance dampened her spirits—and reminded her of what was at stake. If she went to his house, maybe she'd find a way to get back her letters, which he'd said were in his desk in his home office, without him ever having read them. Maybe she could secure her future.

Be honest. Really, you just want to see his house and spend a little more time with him. "Okay," she whispered faintly. "You win."

"How early can you get away?" he asked.

"I'll have to check with Miss Jennie."

"Good. Mind if I tag along?"

"If you do, Bessie will tell everybody. Your mother will probably know in five minutes flat that we were in the woods together."

"So what?" Smiling, he called to Cinnamon, and the maddening dog ran right up to him.

"He never does that when I call him!"

Casually Cole grabbed the leash and then laid the leather strap in her outstretched hand. His fingers brushed hers, causing a familiar jolt of heat that had her jumping back.

When he laughed, she scowled and kept a wary distance from him the whole way to Miss Jennie's. Even so, his striding grandly beside her in his boots and Stetson made her tension build.

Inside the house with him, it was even worse. Just knowing that he was lounging indolently in the parlor waiting for her to figure out a schedule had Maddie unable to settle, much less focus on her routine chores. She dropped things, and forgot what she was doing in the middle of a task.

The lean male figure sprawled on Miss Jennie's spindly ottoman was turning her life upside down, and she was powerless to stop him.

When her cell rang and she saw it was Greg, she declined his call.

"Who was that?" Cole demanded in a steely tone.

"Nobody important," she said, blushing.

"You're dating someone?"

"I don't want to talk about him."

He frowned as if the mere thought of another man in her life made him feel possessive, which, of course, he had no right to be.

"What about you? Are you dating?" she asked.

"No. When Lizzie died I told myself I wouldn't date for a year…which is nearly up, by the way."

"Oh…."

She was so mixed up. Usually she looked forward to Greg's calls. Usually she loved having him tell her about his morning and sharing her own with him.

Guiltily she remembered Cole's kisses on her mouth and breasts. Just thinking about them brought the butterflies back to her tummy and made her feel as wildly alive as an infatuated teenager.

Her pleasure in Cole's possessiveness and her disloyalty to Greg only increased the confusion she'd been feeling earlier.

What was happening to her?

Five

There was no telling what the neighbors had made of her wet hair and wet T-shirt when she'd returned to Miss Jennie's with Cole. So Maddie felt both light-headed and mortified when she left Miss Jennie's on Cole's arm later that afternoon. Not that he seemed to care what Bessie and her ilk thought about them being seen together.

He'd insisted on returning to Miss Jennie's in his truck to pick her up, after he'd taken his horse back to his house. And now, while he strode confidently to his truck, she kept her eyes glued to the sidewalk. They were almost to his big, white pickup when she saw Bessie's window shade move.

In a deliberate attempt to downplay her looks, Maddie had coiled her glossy black hair into a severe knot at her nape. She'd buttoned her white blouse to her neck and had secured its cuffs at her wrists. Her lips were pale because she hadn't bothered to freshen her lipstick. Her jeans were tight, but she'd brought only one pair.

"Bessie's watching us," she murmured.

Without bothering to so much as glance in Bessie's direction, he opened Maddie's door.

"She's probably already told everybody we went skinny-dipping," Maddie said.

His dark eyes traced her curves. "I wish you'd suggested that when we had the chance."

"No sexual innuendo. You promised!"

"No, I promised not to touch you."

"Innuendo leads to touching…."

He smiled. "You're saying there's hope."

"I'm saying don't!"

"Then stop tempting me by blushing so charmingly."

"There you go again!"

"Look, you're not committing a crime…just because you're beautiful. You could dress sexier. That wouldn't be a crime either. Hell, it's a bigger crime that you don't."

Her breath caught. Did he want to kiss her again as much as she wanted his mouth on hers?

Don't even think about it, or look at his lips, because he'll see how much you want him.

When he climbed inside and started the truck, she snapped on her seat belt. The nearness of him and the faint scent of his lemony aftershave made her blood quicken and her hands tremble. As they sped toward his ranch, her pulse beat unsteadily just because he was beside her.

When he sucked in a long breath, she realized he was on edge, too.

"It's really hot," she said.

"It's July."

They made a few more inane remarks about the weather and climate change before lapsing into a silence that lasted until they reached his house.

The Colemans had long been a respected family in Texas,

so naturally, like everybody else in town, she'd always wanted to see his grand yet informal house up close. But since he'd never considered her part of his world, he'd never issued an invitation.

As a girl, all she'd managed to catch were glimpses of his big, white house with its columns and wide verandas from her secret hiding place in the brush. How she'd admired the house and the barn and the swimming pool and tennis courts where she'd watched him play tennis with Lizzie. A paved road wound past grassy paddocks where horses sometimes grazed.

How different today was now that she was formally invited. How excited she felt when he parked at his front door and let her out in full view of his wiry foreman, Joe Pena. Not that some of her high spirits weren't dashed when the older man's weathered face blanched after Cole asked him to saddle Raider and a suitable mare for them to ride later.

"Miss Gray hasn't ridden in six years, so maybe Lily would be perfect," Cole said.

Joe smiled affably enough at Cole, but his jaw hardened whenever he looked at her. "Thank you," she said to Joe.

Without a word to her or a glance in her direction, the man turned his back on her and marched stiffly toward the barn.

Her mother had slept with Joe once or twice, and that had caused a rift in his marriage.

Cole took Maddie's arm gently. "Don't mind Joe," he murmured as he swept her up the stairs and inside his house.

"It's hard to forget that here I'll always be Jesse Ray Gray's daughter."

"It's way past time you grew a thicker hide."

"How—when all it takes is a dark look or a remark to bring it all back?"

"If you want me to follow him to the barn and invite him to a boxing match, I will."

"No."

"Good, because it's too hot for a boxing match. So forget about Joe and his stupid prejudices."

It was difficult when she knew his prejudices were well-founded.

The minute Cole shut the front door behind them, she felt as if she were in another, more privileged world. He pointed to a low table near a window and said she could set her purse down.

After doing so, she smiled in appreciation as he led her through a series of pleasant, oak-paneled rooms with tall ceilings, rooms that generations of women in his family had filled with antiques, Texas memorabilia and family history that included many pictures of the Colemans socializing with famous Texans and various presidents.

How did it feel to have a family you could be proud of?

She felt nothing but shame as she remembered the stench of her mother's trailer and the garbage-strewn lot it had shared with another even sorrier trailer on the edge of town. Had her mother ever taken a single photograph of her? The only pictures she had of herself were tattered school pictures that Miss Jennie had given her.

Here photographs of friends and family were abundantly displayed on walls and shelves. When his mother's likeness glowered at her from a beige wall, Maddie flushed with guilt. Did his mother already know he'd stopped by Miss Jennie's to see her?

"As you can see, Colemans aren't good at throwing stuff away," he said.

"Because you have a history to be proud of."

When his cell phone rang, he pulled it out and frowned. Instead of answering it, he said, "I'm turning this off. Damn thing rings all the time."

"Who was it?"

"My mother."

"Go ahead. Talk to her. I don't care," she lied.

"Later." He punched a button or two and slid it back into his pocket. "There—for now it's off."

Maddie couldn't help grinning a little triumphantly at his mother's stern picture before she began a study of the formal photographs and the painted portraits of his ancestors that filled his den. These were Noah's ancestors, too. She felt a pang of guilt that her son would never know about them.

Pushing Noah to the back of her mind, she imagined Cole spending his free time in this masculine room with its dark carpets and huge reddish-brown leather sofas and matching armchairs. How often had he brought other women here? Women he'd respected? Women he'd introduced to his mother?

He joined her, telling her again what she already knew, that the ranch had been put together shortly after Texas had won its independence from Mexico, and that during the Civil War, Yankees had burned the first house.

"This second, much grander structure was built after the family recovered. It faces due south just like our state capitol in Austin—for the same reason, to spurn the north and the 'damn' Yankees."

She managed to laugh lightly. "I hadn't heard that before."

"Like most Texans, we're a stubborn, proud bunch," Cole said, not bothering to hide his pride in his family and his state.

Cole's ranch house was lovely, classy. Once when she'd lain in his arms she'd foolishly dreamed of living here, of being accepted because she was his wife.

But the town and his mother would never have approved, so he'd turned his back on Maddie and had married Lizzie. As proof of his brief, joyous union with his wife, he kept several informal photographs of her on the tables and shelves. And in every one of them, sweet, blonde Lizzie was looking up at Cole's rugged, tanned face with adoring blue eyes.

Maddie lifted one of the photographs. "She looks so happy and in love."

Without a word, he took the picture from her and placed it facedown.

"She's gone now."

Maddie winced at the rejection she felt in his icy tone. She couldn't help remembering Miss Jennie telling her how worried the whole town had been because Cole had stayed drunk for six months straight after Lizzie's death.

"His mother says he'll never get over her," Miss Jennie had said. "They were high school sweethearts, you know."

Until a stolen kiss in a barn had temporarily awakened his lust for the town's bad girl.

In spite of everything, Maddie had felt genuine sympathy for him in his time of loss.

"She always loved you so much," Maddie said gently, knowing now that all he'd ever felt for her was lust. "Since she was a little girl."

"Yes," he muttered coldly.

"The whole town wanted you to marry her and give them their happy ending. And you did."

"Can we talk about something else?" Again his expression was grimly forbidding. "Look, I didn't bring you here to talk about Lizzie." A nerve jerked in his cheek. "All that's over now." He took her arm and led her toward the open door of what was obviously his office. "You haven't seen the rest of the house yet."

Forgetting his promise not to touch her, he took her hand and led her inside the room. Her quick shiver brought a wicked glint to his eyes, but he let her go without teasing her.

"This is where I work. Sloppily, as you can see."

Stacks of papers littered the top of his massive mahogany desk and spilled out of its drawers.

Her mind on the letters now, she gazed at the drawers, barely listening as he explained his various businesses to her.

There was the ranching operation to run, he told her, the other heirs who didn't live on the ranch to satisfy, several farms to deal with, his mother to cater to, his ongoing oil and gas business, which was booming and kept him away from the ranch, his beloved horses, and several other income streams to keep track of. Ranching, he said, was a difficult business due to the unpredictable nature of so many important variables such as the weather and the price of feed and cattle. His father had been on the brink of bankruptcy when Cole had taken over. He was still in the process of streamlining the cattle operation and diversifying into other, more lucrative businesses.

"We got lucky with this new oil and gas play," he said. "I've hired geologists and drillers, and am constantly expanding. There's so much exploration going on in Texas, I can't get the men or the parts I need. Or even the frac water to drill…"

Her gaze skimming the drawers, she listened absently while he told her about a greedy water-well driller. All but the bottom one were open.

"But I've been rambling, and you're studying my messiness instead of listening," he said, reaching for her and then dropping her hand when she jumped, startled at his touch.

"Sorry—I keep forgetting about the no-touching rule!"

Caught off guard and feeling slightly ashamed because she imagined he still saw her as an easy woman, Maddie jammed her hands into her pockets. "It's all very interesting," she murmured.

That was when she saw his arrowheads, which were framed and mounted above his desk. Much to her surprise, the ones she'd found near their secret pool and had given him were in the center of a collection he'd arranged in the shape of the state of Texas.

"Your arrowheads. You even framed the ones I gave you."

"Yes. You were always so patient and observant when we searched those old Indian mounds. I was too easily distracted."

He was staring so intently at her lips that she blushed.

"So, what do you feel like doing?" he said too abruptly, glancing outside. "Are you hungry?"

"Not yet," she whispered, suddenly feeling ill at ease and shy around him.

"Do you want to ride now? Take a picnic along for later?"

Riding was a rare treat since she couldn't afford her own horse. Thrilled at the thought of riding anywhere again, much less with him, she nodded. She'd worry about the future and what was best later. Later she'd find an opportunity to search for her letters.

She helped Cole pack ham sandwiches, chips, fruit, cookies and canned drinks before they headed out to his barn. As they approached the tall, red building, an Australian shepherd bounded out of it, wheeling between them, greeting them with exuberant barks. The dog jumped, licking her hands, sniffing her jeans. Laughing, Maddie knelt and let it lick her cheek, too.

"Why does Bendi get all the kisses?" Cole asked when she remained at the dog's level.

"Bendi, is that your name, fella? Bendi may be my only friend in Yella…besides Miss Jennie," she said, stroking the dog.

"What about me?"

"We weren't really friends, now were we?"

"I always liked you," he whispered.

"You never brought me here…the way you brought all the rest of your real friends."

"My mother and dad lived here then."

"See what I mean. I was always Jesse Ray Gray's daughter, so you were ashamed of me."

His face darkened. "With my mother, it was difficult. She was always so critical, and she had about a hundred rules she lived by. Maybe I wasn't ready to tell her about you. About us. Maybe I was too afraid she'd spoil it, or drive you away. Maybe I didn't realize how you'd see it and feel about it." He paused. "I never meant to hurt you."

"Look, I don't want to quarrel about the past. We have our own lives now, don't we? Let's just ride and enjoy what's left of the afternoon."

She rose from the ground and headed toward the barn in silence with the dog racing circles around her.

"If coming here was so important to you, you could have asked me to show you the house," he said defensively behind her.

Since she didn't want to argue, she just kept silent.

Except for Bendi's toenails scraping the concrete inside the barn as he trotted happily beside her and the sounds of horses munching grain and corn in their stalls, the shadowy barn was silent. In the tack room, saddles, bridles and halters hung from whitewashed walls. Everything—the sink, the desk that held a telephone, the floor—was immaculate.

The two horses that Cole had ordered to be saddled nickered as he opened the first stall door. Horseshoes rang on the concrete as he took the reins of a lovely palomino mare with brown eyes and led her out.

"Meet Lily. She's gentle and likes everybody."

"She's lovely."

At the compliments, Lily lowered her golden head and let Maddie stroke her.

"Good girl." Maddie held out the apple she'd brought and enjoyed the feel of the mare's lips and nose as she eagerly took a bite.

Horses—they'd been her salvation as a girl. If it hadn't been for horses and Miss Jennie, where would she be now?

Maybe in some shabby trailer enduring some awful man's abuse. Or worse, abusing her own child.

Cole opened another stall and led out a tall bay gelding. "And this is Raider. He and I go way back. He's half Arab and half quarter horse and pretty challenging to ride."

"In what way?"

"He doesn't like white rocks. And he insists on bossing all the other horses. He thinks he should decide which hay pile the horses can eat, and if they don't agree, he lays his ears back and charges them."

"Oh, dear." She began to stroke him. "A big boy who doesn't play well with others. In my line of work I meet a lot of people with your problem."

"Lily is so agreeable that he isn't threatened, so he doesn't get up to many of his bad tricks when he's around her."

Outside, the wind rustled in the trees. Raider stomped, snorted and tossed his head, eagerly anticipating their ride.

Cole gave Maddie another moment to stroke and talk to Lily. Then they mounted and headed for the narrow, shady trail that wound through the brush. "I keep the trail groomed in the summers, just for riding," Cole said.

"Do you ride often?" she asked wistfully, unable to imagine such a luxury.

"I've been away a lot overseeing my rigs and haven't had time when I'm here, so getting out today will be fun, especially since you'll be with me." His words, warm and seductive, sang along her nerve edges.

Don't say things like that. Don't make me long for what I can never have.

"Riding will be a special treat for me, too. As a single mom, I don't take off much time for myself."

The sky was a deep blue, and the clouds against the horizon looked as soft as huge tufts of cotton. The light breeze curling the grasses made the late afternoon cooler than expected.

Maddie, who rode behind Cole, found herself enjoying the ride more than she'd enjoyed anything besides Noah in years.

He set off on a gallop. Laughing aloud, she raced after him across one of his endless pastures with her hair streaming behind her. Her blood tingling from the thrill of it, she felt like a girl again with the big animal beneath her. When Cole turned and their eyes met, excitement charged through her in a white-hot jolt. Later, when he pulled up on his reins and headed in the direction of the river, she followed.

"The ground is not firm enough here to gallop," he said as he waited for her to come alongside him.

She wasn't surprised when Cole chose the pool where he'd discovered her earlier that day as their destination to water their horses and picnic.

When Cole helped her dismount, she stood beside Lily, stroking the horse, pretending she felt as calm as the mare, who dipped her mouth into the pool and drank through golden lips.

Cole opened a cold beer can and offered it to Maddie. When she accepted it, he popped the top off a tonic water and lifted it to his sculpted mouth. Studying his dark, angular face, especially his mouth, and the reflections of the trees and sky in the green water, she fought to pretend she felt nothing for him. But her blood was buzzing even before she drank deeply.

"So, who are you now, Maddie Gray?" he whispered as he led her to a limestone rock that served as a bench. "Now that you're all grown up and educated? What have you made of yourself?"

"My story is probably pretty ordinary."

"Not to me."

"I don't have your lineage of famous pioneer Texans. I was just a child here, going hungry on occasion and feeling trapped in that awful trailer with Mother when she was there.

And when she wasn't, I was always too scared of the neighbors in the next trailer to play outside."

He frowned as if he genuinely empathized with the child she'd been. "You don't have to talk about it."

"You asked," she said, touched by his response. She'd never talked about these things with him before. Or with Greg, she thought. Greg knew next to nothing about her past, and she didn't want him to. For some reason that she didn't understand, she felt like talking to Cole this afternoon. Since they both needed closure, maybe telling him as much of the truth as she dared would help.

"Yes. Maybe it's time I did talk about it. Mother didn't come home lots of nights—sometimes she'd be gone several nights in a row. Out on dates, I suppose. Dates that lasted all night…and sometimes several days. I would hide in the closet even though I was scared of the dark."

"Did you ever tell a teacher that you were so scared you locked yourself in a dark closet?"

"Only Miss Jennie, when I was in high school. She took me home with her one afternoon. Everything was so clean and bright and nice in her house, and she was so gentle and kind that I started to cry because I wanted to live in a place like hers, with no smudges on the walls, a place with tablecloths and clean sheets on the beds, a place where I felt safe and where people were kind. Mother, you see, always screamed and cursed at me. Most people in Yella treated me like they hated me, too, though not Liam or Lizzie, who were always nice to me. So, I never imagined that I might achieve a decent kind of life.

"But Miss Jennie gave me hope. Until I started spending afternoons at her house in high school, my only friends had been horses."

"What was the name of your first horse pal?"

"Remember how our trailer was next to Jasper Bower's

property? Well, Mr. Bower noticed that I used to bring his two horses apples after school. He was the one who gave me my first job mucking stalls in exchange for riding lessons. He let me take care of Pico and his other horses and gave me a good reference and that led to other jobs. I loved being in barns and working with horses, but until Miss Jennie saw how lost I was and befriended me, the human world mostly seemed big and unfriendly. And I felt helpless to ever change anything. She made me realize that if I didn't want to be despised my whole life, I couldn't hide out in barns. It was up to me to make something of myself. She'd been poor, too, you see, and she told me how she'd changed her life. She set out a very specific path to follow, with steps and options. We made a plan for what I'd do after graduation. I swore that if I ever succeeded, I wouldn't forget that there were other little girls like me who didn't have anyone to turn to, and that I'd help them…just like she helped me."

"And? Have you?"

"I try so hard. I try every day. I got my bachelor's degree in sociology and psychology so I could work at the same homeless shelter that took me in when I left Yella. Now, on cold days, I have coats to give shivering children and diapers for wet, dirty babies and bus tokens for poor mothers who need transportation to get to work. I run a day care for children and a shelter for women and children. And one for disabled men, as well. We feed lunch to three hundred people a day. I feel like the shelter I work for makes a difference."

"You make the difference." His gaze was so intense with interest and admiration, it caused a warm rush of pleasure and pride to swamp her.

"Working with these people requires many of the same skill sets I acquired training horses. Only you're dealing with people. With rules, patience, determination, compassion and a plan, you can sometimes work miracles." She paused. "When

Noah's older, I need to go back to school for my master's so I can do more. But right now I need to be with him as much as I can. Children grow up fast. You don't want to waste a moment."

"If I had a son I'd feel the same way."

Her head jerked. When her eyes met his, his warm, thoughtful gaze unnerved her.

"I'm sure you would," she whispered haltingly.

For a second or two she was so connected to him she felt she had to tell him about Noah—because it was the right thing to do. She caught a panicky breath. Thankfully, he looked away, and in doing so, broke the spell. Squeezing herself, she let out a sigh. She had to be careful. Confiding in him had made her feel closer to him, and that closeness was dangerous.

As the sun turned golden-red and the sky blazed, he continued asking her questions. So eager was she to answer them she barely noticed the lengthening shadows as the sun sank lower.

After she finished her second beer, he unpacked their sandwiches and chips, which were delicious. Since they were there, she ate too many cookies, which he teased her about after she lamented having done so.

"Lighten up on yourself," he said. "It's easy to know what you should eat, but not always so easy to eat what you should. Besides, what would the world be coming to if Yella's number one bad girl lived up to her virtuous ideals one hundred percent of the time?"

As she laughed, she found it amazing and scary that she could feel so easy opening up to him. It was as if he were a true friend of the heart, instead of what he really was to her— the rich college boy who'd once lusted for her body and the powerful man who could threaten her future if he discovered her secret.

"Do you ever save any adults?"

"A few. We are connected to all the agencies in town that

can help them with their special problems. If you're a person who's down and out, and you want to change, we can teach you how to get your medications, how to fill out a job application or an application for an apartment. But a person has to be fiercely determined to succeed. There are so many basic skills functioning adults require...like money management and taking care of health issues."

In his turn, Cole talked about his oil and gas company and his ranch. She got a little lost when he tried to explain a modern drilling technique called hydraulic fracturing. Fracking, he explained, involved using pressurized water, sand and chemicals to extract more gas and oil from rock formations than had previously been possible. "But I'm not saving lives," he said. "I'm just making money."

"The modern world can't survive without energy. You saved the ranch, your family's heritage."

"There's that." He smiled. "Hey, the sun's going down fast. We better ride back to the house before it gets totally dark."

When he helped her remount Lily, her spirits rocketed at his nearness and his casual touch. As she stared down at his handsome face, which was half in shadow, she felt her stomach flutter. His intent gaze lingered on her, as well, increasing her nervousness. He didn't have to touch her to be dangerous.

For years, she'd been crushed by loneliness and the hard work required to pull herself up from nothing. Even now that she'd found Greg, she often felt lonely. Why did she never feel as connected to Greg as she felt right now to Cole?

How can you think that when you know Greg wants you as a person and Cole wants you for only one thing?

Instead of feeling outrage over Cole's lust for her, a delicious shiver of excitement coursed through her. Was she as shameless as her mother?

She had to stop this. She had to get back to his house and find her letters and go.

Not long after they remounted and headed back to his home, a full moon rose, painting the landscape with shimmering silver. Beside Cole, her blood began to pulse in ever-deepening awareness of him. When they reached the barn, which loomed in the dark, and he lifted her down, she was already so hot for him that she couldn't prevent herself from trembling when her body slid briefly against his.

No sooner were her feet on the ground than she sprang free of him.

Not that she felt much safer standing several feet away. How could she when all she wanted was for him to wrap her in his arms again and kiss her?

Breathing hard, he stared down at her so hungrily her own mouth watered. "You said not to touch you."

"Yes...."

"Then don't look at me like that."

When she didn't stop, he closed his eyes on a groan. His massive chest swelled, and he rasped in a harsh breath. "We'd better put the horses up," he said, his voice biting as he heaved out another violent breath.

For no reason at all she was too shy and tongue-tied to utter a coherent thought.

She should never have come out with him today or talked to him so openly, baring her soul, so to speak. Maybe then she wouldn't have reawakened all those dangerous yearnings and unrealistic hopes that had haunted her for years. She'd always wanted more from him—so much more than he'd ever been able to give to a girl he'd considered beneath him.

She knew too well that theirs was an impossible relationship.

But tonight he'd brought her to his house, talked to her about his family and work, listened to her with respect.

None of that should matter. She should stick to her decision and marry Greg and have nothing more to do with Cole.

But that was a difficult plan when Cole made her feel so alive.

Six

Since her heart was in shreds just from spending a pleasant evening with Cole, she wished she could forget her letters and demand that he drive her home. But when Cole turned on the lights in the barn and neither Joe nor a groom appeared, the smell of hay and the soft nickering of the horses seduced her into offering to help him put both horses to bed.

Together they removed the saddles and bridles and carried them to the tack room. Together they hosed down the horses, rubbing their long, narrow faces with big puffy sponges, squeezing the sponges repeatedly so that the water ran down their great bodies and legs and gurgled in the drain.

"I've missed working with horses," she said. "Horses don't lie to you, so they don't break your heart as often as people do."

His eyes studied her face for a long moment. He'd hurt her, made her feel cheap and unimportant to him. Maybe he hadn't done it deliberately, but he'd hurt her just the same. For six long years she'd carried those scars.

"I'm sorry you had such a rough start in life. But you've certainly risen above it."

She smiled warily as he turned back to Lily, but the work was a pleasant distraction, causing her to relax in Cole's company. All sensual tension vanished. She simply enjoyed being with him and his horses. Soon they were laughing and talking easily.

"Would you like a cup of coffee before I drive you home?" he asked after he secured Raider in his stall.

She wondered if he was merely being polite, but his gaze was so intense, she couldn't resist.

"I'd love one," she lied, even though she never drank the bitter stuff.

Side by side they walked down the road to his house in the moonlight, each so wrapped up in their lighthearted banter they failed to see the Lincoln parked in the shadows of the huge live oak beside his house. He opened the front door as they were laughing at a joke he'd made.

"John, is that you—at last?" His mother's biting tone cut Maddie to the quick.

"Mother?"

"I was beginning to wonder if you'd ever come home."

"You should have called before coming if you don't like being inconvenienced."

"I did call. Your phone was off, or you didn't bother to answer."

Black silk rustled as his tall, elegantly slim mother stood up. Her flawless features held no warmth. She kept her thin nose high and angled away from Maddie.

"You should have let me know you were coming home, dear," she said. "I would have had Angelica make dinner."

"I had other plans. You remember Maddie Gray, don't you?"

His mother's lips pursed as her icy stare flicked briefly to Maddie. "Vaguely," she lied in a voice that made Maddie feel small.

"Hello," Maddie said.

His mother's nose arched higher. "I'd prefer to talk to my son in private."

Feeling like a child unjustly put into time-out, Maddie nodded. Her first impulse was to leave, but she couldn't since Cole had driven her here. Then she remembered her letters. Maybe this was the perfect opportunity to search for them. "Cole, why don't I wait in your office?" Maddie said.

"Because the den is larger and much more comfortable," he replied.

"I'll be just fine in there. You and your mother should take the den." Before he could object, she hurried toward his office.

He followed her. "Why did you have to choose the messiest room in the house?" he whispered as she sank down in his big leather desk chair.

"Cole!" his mother snapped. "I said I've been waiting for over an hour!"

At his mother's command he frowned. "There are a few magazines on the desk. I won't be long," he said gently to Maddie.

When he closed the door, Maddie faced his messy desk. She wasn't happy that his mother despised her, but she refused to dwell on something she couldn't change. This might be her only chance to search for her letters.

Knowing that she probably didn't have much time, she leaned down and tugged at the bottom drawer. Just as she'd suspected, it was locked.

"Okay—so, I'll look through the top drawers first!" she whispered.

While she riffled through the other drawers, which was slow going because they were stuffed with so many papers, she heard raised voices.

Not wishing to eavesdrop, but not being able to stop herself, Maddie's ears pricked to attention even as she continued her rummaging.

"I know you've been lonely, dear. But this pathetic girl—Jesse Ray Gray's daughter, of all people?"

"You don't even know her."

"I know she probably came back here deliberately to flaunt herself the minute she heard Lizzie died."

Maddie gasped.

"Lizzie has been gone nearly a year."

"Well, the whole town's talking about Maddie skinny-dipping on our land this afternoon just to lure you."

Maddie's hands shook with such outrage she nearly slammed a drawer.

"You're wrong about everything, Mother."

When Maddie had searched all the drawers but the locked one, she angrily grabbed the keys she'd noticed earlier, lying on his desk.

"You're too gullible," his mother said. "This cheap girl has set her sights on you."

Cheap.... The word stung.

"Mother, your voice is too loud. She's my guest." He lowered his voice and must have persuaded his mother to do the same because Maddie couldn't hear them for a while.

Furiously, Maddie began trying different keys. Naturally, it was the last one that worked.

Suddenly the voices in the other room rose again.

"Mother, I have a question. Did Maddie try to call me six years ago before she left Yella? Did you talk to her?"

Maddie's heart began to beat very fast.

His mother didn't answer immediately. "Do you think I

can remember every call from six years ago? I can tell you one thing, though—*if* she'd called, you'd remember me giving you a piece of my mind."

"All right. Look, I need to take Maddie back to Miss Jennie's. Maybe you and I can have lunch before I go tomorrow."

A sob caught in Maddie's throat. She *had* to find her letters. She did not want his formidable mother threatening her, or Noah, especially since Cole seemed to believe everything his mother said.

With unsteady fingers, Maddie sifted through the endless stack of deeds and contracts in the bottom drawer. When she heard footsteps approaching the office, she jumped back.

"Have you forgotten your manners completely?" his mother said. "Are you going to show me out or not?"

His heavy footsteps retreated. The front door opened and slammed shut.

If only his mother had insisted he walk her to her car. But she hadn't. Once again, Maddie heard his brisk footsteps heading toward his office.

In a panic, Maddie nudged the bottom drawer shut with her foot, only to let out a little cry when it jammed.

Grabbing a magazine, she whirled around in his chair and pretended to read an incomprehensible article about how irrigation affected hay yield.

"Sorry about that," he said in a world-weary tone from the doorway.

Maddie looked up. When she saw him glance at his keys, which were still dangling from the lock of his bottom drawer, her heart began to knock.

Then his concerned gaze refocused on her. "You're white as a sheet, and shaking, too."

Ashamed that the woman could still intimidate her, Maddie leaped up so that she could stand between him and the drawer. "I'm fine."

"I'm sorry you had to hear all that."

"I know she doesn't approve of me," Maddie said, hoping she sounded braver than she felt.

"Well, I think you're a wonderful person," he said.

"You do?"

"After what you told me? Of course!"

"You believed the worst of me when I left."

"Even that didn't stop me from caring about you."

Too bad he'd never made that fact known to her.

As he led her out of his office toward the kitchen, she thought he was being awfully nice even if he was a little more reserved after his mother's visit. He caught her hand in his and pressed it reassuringly in his larger palm. "Forget about her, okay?"

"She's right. The whole town's probably talking about me skinny-dipping to lure you by now."

"They're just jealous."

"Don't joke."

"Forget about her...and the town."

"Can you?"

"Look, she's my mother. I'm used to her trying to control every second of my life. I thought I'd learned how to handle her a long time ago, but then Lizzie died, and I went through a dark patch. Guilt, grief, regrets—I was pretty messed up. Mother wanted to move in with me, to take over. Fighting her helped snap me out of my funk. I know she loves me in her way, but I can't allow her to get too close. She's needy and critical."

"I'm sorry about Lizzie," she said again. "She was sweet. Even to me. She used to sneak down to the barn and watch me take care of the horses."

"Yes, she was sweet to everybody. But there's something I need to tell you. I didn't deserve her, and I'm not sure I made her happy. It's not always easy to be married to the town saint, you know."

Because he looked so troubled by this admission, and she thought he was going to say more, she didn't reply.

"She's gone," he said simply. "It's too late to change anything. Except there is one thing I can say for sure—she wouldn't mind you being here. She would have wanted me to see you and sort my feelings out. She loved me—in spite of the many ways I disappointed her."

He looked more at ease after he said that, less tense, and Maddie couldn't help but wonder if Lizzie had known all about Cole's desire for her and sensed his guilt. Maybe her sweet, forgiving nature had made him feel that he was a worse person than he really was.

But what did his marriage to Lizzie have to do with his feelings for Maddie now? Did he or did he not agree with his mother's low assessment of her? Could he ever respect her?

What if he could? What if he *did*?

Suddenly Maddie knew she couldn't leave; she couldn't return to Austin and marry Greg without finding out what Cole meant to her and what she meant to him. Greg was a good man. It would be unfair to risk hurting him as Cole believed he'd hurt Lizzie. She couldn't marry Greg until she came to terms with her feelings for Cole or purged him from her system.

"So—do you still feel like a cup of coffee?" he asked.

"I'm not much of a coffee drinker."

When his face darkened with disappointment, her own heart brimmed with wild, illogical joy.

He wants me to stay! Despite his mother's disapproval and the risk of more gossip!

No doubt his mother had come to warn them off each other. But Maddie was no longer a teenager who could be easily bullied. She had to know how Cole felt. His opinion mattered.

Not his mother's. It was time she stood up for herself, time she showed his mother and the gossips of Yella that she wasn't who they'd thought she was.

"I think I'd like a glass of wine," she said.

His brilliant smile made her tummy flip.

"White or red?"

She laughed, feeling warm and flushed from just looking at him. "You pick. What we drink is not my top priority tonight."

"Then what is?" An electric current charged the air between them. Looking charmingly baffled, he stared into her sparkling eyes.

"I can see I'll have to give you a great big hint." Because she simply couldn't resist, she reached up on her tiptoes and put both arms around his neck. When he made no move, she arched her body into his.

His black brows lifted quizzically, and for a few more seconds he hesitated. Then his strong hands at the back of her waist locked and pulled her closer. "You did say no touching," he whispered huskily.

"You know what they say about women being allowed to change their minds?"

His eyes blazed as he ran his knuckles up the gentle curve of her throat, causing her to shiver. Staring at her mouth, he cupped her chin, his thumb caressing the sensual fullness of her bottom lip. "I've been wanting to kiss you all night—and very badly." When she licked her lips, he groaned and snugged her against his hips more tightly. Without further invitation, his mouth came down on hers, hard. She opened her lips, sighing in soft pleasure when his tongue moved inside, probing the soft interior of her mouth so erotically he took her breath away.

Sensing her surrender, his pelvis crushed hers, communicating his blatant arousal.

"Oh, my," she said. "Is that for me?"

When she kissed him even more hungrily than before, he swung her up in his arms. "Baby, I can't believe you've finally come home...to me."

"I didn't intend to. But I'm kinda glad I did."

"Just kinda?"

"Way more than kinda," she whispered, nuzzling her cheek against his.

Still kissing her, he carried her to the kitchen where he grabbed a bottle of wine and a can of tonic water, his drink of choice ever since he'd pulled himself out of the booze hole he'd fallen into after Lizzie's death. Holding Maddie tightly, he mounted the stairs, taking them easily. Then he strode down the darkened hall toward his vast bedroom.

Laughing, feeling like a bride, she reached out and twisted the doorknob and pushed the door ajar for him.

"If you're going to say no again, say it now," he whispered in a low, urgent tone.

"I want you," she said. "And I'm weak. I've always been weak where you're concerned. But then, what do you expect from the bad girl of Yella, Texas?"

"I expect wild, wanton sex," he murmured as he kicked the bedroom door shut. "Lots of it."

Seven

She was lying under Cole in his dark bedroom writhing against his hot, hard, naked length. She was in his arms again after six years of abstinence, and he was doing all the wickedly delicious things she'd dreamed of for years. He was skimming his fingers over her everywhere, loving her with his lips and his exploring tongue.

Then, in the next moment, the horror of the past intruded on the sweetness of their fragile present.

She was a frightened, young girl again, trapped beneath another man, a vicious man she hated, whose rough hands and foul-smelling mouth tore at her body.

Suddenly, all the dark memories she'd worked so hard to suppress overpowered her.

With her hair still damp from a final afternoon swim and her heart full of love for Cole, she'd rushed home to the trailer fresh from having made love to him on the grassy bank beside the pool. Thinking herself alone, she'd let herself in, only to find her mother's boyfriend, Vernon, sprawled on the sofa in dirty, ripped jeans and a T-shirt. With his huge, tattooed arms, he'd seemed like a spider waiting for her in that tangled web of darkness as he'd squashed out his cigarette.

He'd come on to her before, and she was usually able to avoid being alone with him. "Why aren't you at work?" she'd asked.

An ugly, drunken snarl had distorted his scarred face as he lunged toward her. "What's it to you if I got fired? Bet I know who you've been with. The whole town knows about Prince Coleman Charming." When she'd tried to squeeze out the door again, he'd grabbed her arm, wrenching it behind her and dragging her back inside, locking the door.

"I know where you spend your time. You won't let me touch you because I'm not good enough. Then you chase Coleman like a bitch in heat. Who do you think you are, girl? Well, I'll tell you! You're Jesse Ray's girl, that's who! You're nobody! Worse! You're trailer trash, just like me! Hell, you're lucky to get me!"

Vernon had reeked of beer and cigarettes and worse as he'd slammed her against the wall and pressed his pelvis against her as she'd fought desperately to escape. How she'd reeked of those things, too, later, when he'd finished with her.

Afterward she'd felt so dirty and scared and ashamed. Most of all she'd felt powerless. Sore and battered, she'd cried and cried, but what good had her tears been? Vernon had laughed and said nobody would believe her if she ratted on him, not even her mother. And he'd been right.

When her mother had thrown them both out, Maddie had known she couldn't tell the authorities. If her mother hadn't believed her, there was no way the cold-eyed sheriff would. Nor would anyone else. Hadn't they always thought the worst of her?

Even before Vernon had hurt her, she'd always been afraid

Cole thought he was too good for her. Still, she'd gathered her courage and called him. Only that was when his mother had answered. In Maddie's broken emotional state, Mrs. Coleman's harsh words had compounded Vernon's injuries tenfold. She had crushed Maddie's spirit and her sweetest hope of love and happiness.

Don't think about the past! Don't!

Cole shifted his weight beside her, staring at her in the dark. Gently, his hands brushed her cheeks. "Your eyes are glassy and wild, and you're shivering and crying. Why?"

"Am I?" In shock, she traced her cheeks with her fingertips and realized they were wet. Thinking about Vernon could do this to her.

"No reason," she lied. All the secrets that had driven her from Yella still lay like a stone on her heart.

Cole drew her closer and bent his head to nuzzle her hair. "I've dreamed of this," he whispered. "All through my marriage to Lizzie, you were there between us. I wanted you even then. And I felt horrible about it."

"I know. I'm sorry," she said, empathizing more than was wise. His breath against her ear made her tremble.

"I felt so guilty. But I would lie in bed, with her beside me, thinking about you—about your lips, about how your nipples used to peak when I kissed them, about your silky black hair and how I loved to play with it. I think I hated you for that… more even than I hated you for Vernon."

At the mention of Vernon, Maddie sobbed hoarsely. "You don't know what you're saying. Or what happened. You don't know anything."

"Because you ran away with Vernon without ever telling me anything. So all I had to go on was what your mother said."

After his mother had been so cruel and Maddie had run from Yella, she hadn't let herself think about Cole because it had been too painful. Then she'd been afraid she was pregnant with Vernon's child. It was only when she'd realized how much Noah looked like Cole that she'd worked up the nerve to call him, but he'd hung up on her. So, she'd had to write it all down in those letters he hadn't bothered to read.

"I don't care about Vernon anymore," he said.

"You don't?"

"That was six years ago. You were young. I was your first. Maybe I was coming on too strong. Maybe you had to get away and be on your own to grow up. I only know that your coming back here is the best thing that's ever happened to me," he said. "I like who you seem to be now, and I don't want to ruin our reunion by blaming you for what's past. Don't cry. Please. Because I can't bear it if you do."

He kissed her brow and then her temples with warm lips that soothed. He'd always been so nice to her when they'd been lovers. While growing up, she'd hated feeling that she was condemned for her mother's sins. In his arms, she'd found an escape. Cole had made her feel as though she could change her life—before Vernon's vicious act had nearly destroyed her.

Cole seemed as wonderful tonight as he'd been that long-ago summer. His gentle voice and kind words made her swallow her salty tears. Hadn't Vernon ruined enough of her life? Because of him, she'd been afraid. She'd kept to herself and lived an impossibly lonely life until she'd met Greg.

"I won't cry," she said, rubbing her eyes with the backs of her hands. "My tears are all gone. See? So kiss me. Love me. Please, just love me again."

She needed new memories, beautiful memories with Cole, to make the bad ones lose their power.

"All right." He kissed her, but tenderly, sweetly, undemanding. His lips fell onto her brow, onto the pert tip of her upturned nose and then lightly onto her lips. Running his tongue over her breasts, he caressed her nipples with his hands while he held her close, slowly persuading her to put aside the past and all the pain and shame Vernon had inflicted on her for the pleasure that Cole alone could give her.

Soon his touches and kisses had her so dizzy with desire she forgot everything except her need to be with him. When he finally put on a condom and slid into her, she wrapped her arms and legs around him, moaning, clinging, so that he could sink deeper—oh, so much deeper—before he rode her. Then she clung to him and wept, but this time her tears came from joy…and the rush of new hope.

When his passion made him drive into her harder, his need to claim her primitive and demanding, she reveled in it, bracing herself for the power of his thrusts, for the pleasure of them, arching her hips to meet them, needing this forceful mating as much as he did. She circled his strong shoulders with her arms and surrendered with a completeness that stunned her, that wiped her clean of everything but her fierce desire to belong to him.

When finally he shuddered as he found his release, he cried out her name as if she were everything to him, and the sound of it made her sizzle and come in a blazingly glorious explosion of her own. For a long time after that, she held on to him, their hands locked, their damp brows touching. After six lonely years she wanted to prolong the moment of togetherness. Even when he pulled away, she murmured, clinging to him. Only in his arms and in his all-consuming passion had the dark shadow of Vernon briefly vanished.

Not that Cole seemed to mind her clinginess. No, he held her tightly and brushed his fingers through her hair, murmuring that she smelled of flowers and of her.

"You're so sweet. You're everything to me," he whispered. "Everything…. You always were. I don't care who your mother was or what my mother thinks. Those things don't matter."

Drowsily she lay in his arms, content, feeling utterly complete and happier than she'd felt in years.

He pulled her closer. For the first time in ages she wasn't afraid as she closed her eyes. Though she wasn't ready to contemplate telling him about Noah, she knew that tonight, if she woke up screaming as she sometimes did, he'd be there. What a wonderful feeling of security it was to know that.

When they awoke, he made love to her again. Afterward she felt an even greater sense of belonging only to him. The feeling wasn't based on anything more than the sensual pleasure of sex. But each time he made love to her, she felt happier, if that were possible. She snuggled closer against his warmth because he made her feel safe. Wrapped in his arms, she fell asleep.

Hours later, when she came awake with a start as she often did after one of her nightmares, Cole's strong arms no longer held her. As always, she'd been running from some unknown black terror. Just when she was nearly to safety, a strong male hand reached out of the darkness and pulled her down roughly. No matter how hard she fought the faceless figure, she couldn't free herself. Trapped and helpless underneath him, she opened her eyes.

Only the monster wasn't there. He never was. She was all alone in the hot darkness of Cole's bedroom, drenched with perspiration from her nightmare. Her fingers played across the nightstand searching for her flashlight, but it wasn't there. Then she remembered she was at Cole's, not in her own room where she kept a flashlight by the bed. But she did have a small one in her purse, which she'd left on that little table downstairs near the front door.

"Cole?" she whispered in a panic. "Cole!"

When he didn't answer, she moved toward his side of the bed. If only he would wake up and take her in his arms, she wouldn't feel afraid. But his side of the bed was empty. She pushed free of the cool tangles of sheets and sat up in the dark.

Shakily, she grabbed his pillow, which was cool although it held his scent, and pressed it against her lips. Because of her nightmare, all the newfound confidence Cole's lovemaking had instilled in her deserted her.

Where was he? Why had he left? He'd made her feel so safe and cherished, but was their night together just rebound sex for him after losing Lizzie?

Desolation swamped her. The distrustful mindset she'd experienced ever since Vernon's attack slid back into place. Suddenly she was filled with doubts about everything. About her feelings, about having given herself with such abandon to Cole when she barely knew the man he now was or what his true intentions toward her might be.

Did he believe what his mother had said, that Maddie was as low as ever and after him for his money? Did he regret sleeping with her? Or was she just a sexual outlet? Would she never be free of the stigma of her childhood in his eyes?

Made more anxious by her nightmare, she felt increasingly disconcerted by his absence as she stared at the flickering shadows on the ceiling. When he didn't return after a lengthy interval, her doubts built to a terrifying level. She grabbed a sheet and pulled it around herself. Determined to reassure him that he owed her nothing, she stood up and padded out of the room to search for him in his vast, shadowy house.

When Cole switched on the overhead lamp in his office, his gaze zeroed in on the keys dangling from the lock of his bottom drawer.

"Son of a..." Cole cursed vividly under his breath. He would never have left his keys there. He remembered Maddie's look of alarm when he'd entered the office earlier in the evening. She'd been pale, and her hands had shaken as she'd read that boring magazine article he hadn't been able to get through about hay. He'd thought she was upset because of the hateful things his mother had said. Now he wondered.

Had Maddie played him?

The vague impression that something was not quite right in his office had niggled worrisomely at the back of his mind even after he'd collected Maddie, but he'd been so focused on trying to make up to her for his mother's rudeness that he'd dismissed any suspicions he might have had.

Then they'd slept together, and their hot sex had distracted him further. Had she intended that? When he'd awakened, as he often did in the middle of the night, and had begun to ruminate on the various ongoing challenges in his life, he'd replayed in his mind Juan's message concerning the driller who'd failed to show after cashing the advance check. Since Cole couldn't do anything about the driller until morning, he'd decided to come down to his office to see what could be done.

Now he remembered thinking there had been something furtive in Maddie's manner after his mother had left. He remembered that she'd insisted on waiting in his office even when he'd tried to talk her out of it.

More suspicious than ever, Cole knelt and touched the keys. Then he yanked the drawer open wider. He'd intended to read the letters the first chance he had after Maddie had mentioned them. They'd been on his mind when he'd gotten home with Raider, but Juan had called. After that, Joe had wanted to discuss what the vet had to say about a sick bull. Then the roofer who hadn't shown up to reroof the barn had called with a litany of excuses. Cole had hung up from that call furious. One thing had led to another, and he hadn't thought of the letters again until he'd been driving back to Miss Jennie's to pick up Maddie.

Had Maddie chosen to wait in his office so she could search for her letters?

What the hell was in those damn letters anyway?

Curious now, he grabbed the piles of deeds and mortgages he stored in the fireproof lower drawer and tossed them carelessly onto the floor. Then he riffled through the remaining documents until he got to the bottom, where he found the two yellowed envelopes exactly where he'd placed them five years ago. Exactly where Lizzie must have dutifully replaced them.

Whistling, he sank back into his chair and held them up so he could study the postmarks. Then he grabbed his bronze letter opener and ripped into the first letter. After the first sentence, he sat forward, his heart thudding with a vengeance.

When I left Yella, I was pregnant.

Pregnant. He whistled again. He knew the kid was Vernon's. Why should the word slam him? It was the way she put it somehow, right in the beginning of a letter she'd addressed to *him*.

Her mother had a reputation for getting her lovers to pay for stuff. Had Maddie been trying to stick him with Vernon's kid?

Not that I realized I was pregnant that final day in Yella. And later, I admit I thought the baby had to be Vernon's since you were always so careful to protect me.

Anger ate through him like acid at her admission that she'd slept with Vernon. Which was ridiculous, since her mother had told everybody Maddie had run off with Turner years ago.

But Noah has your dark hair and green eyes and your widow's peak.... And he is like you, Cole. He collects arrowheads just like you did as a little boy. He is just so bone-deep good, in all the ways a person, even a little, mischievous person, can be good. He's so good,

Cole, that I know now he's yours. You're welcome to do
a DNA screening of course.

Noah? His? Good?

Through his shock, Cole felt her gladness in that final word. Obviously, she'd seen through Turner even back then. But she'd slept with the nasty creep anyway; she'd thought she was pregnant by him. For more than a year of Noah's life, she'd believed Vernon to be the father, so she hadn't told Cole when he'd been free and able to claim his son.

Cole thought he'd forgiven her for leaving with Turner, but there was a roar in his ears. Tonight, when Cole had made her his again, he'd wanted to erase their past, to erase Turner, to forgive all. But the letter made the past and all its pain feel fresh again, made him hot at the thought of her ever having been with that man, even for one night.

Unable to forget her sweetness and her total surrender in his bed a few hours earlier, Cole clenched his fist, seething as he fought for control.

What did his anger matter, if she was right about Noah being his son?

Cole thought of all her struggles and achievements. No matter what she'd done, if she was right about Noah being his, she was the mother of his son.

Cole's big hands shook as he slashed into her second letter.

I know you received my first letter because you signed
for it, and if I don't hear from you after this one, I'll
know for sure that you want nothing to do with Noah—
or me—ever again. I understand why you would feel
that way, and I promise, you don't need to worry that I'll
hound you any further. If I don't hear from you in two
weeks, I will consider you free of all obligations toward
our son and me, and I'll go on with my life.

Cole sank back in his chair and buried his face in his hands as he remembered how coldly he'd rejected her over the phone, how coldly he'd tossed her letters into his bottom drawer.

Free? She'd really believed he would knowingly cast his son aside! How could she have ever believed that of him?

*But...*he had signed for the letters. And he hadn't answered her. Was it really fair to blame her for drawing that conclusion when he'd drawn his own hellish conclusions about her?

How had she raised their son alone? With no money? While struggling to educate herself?

Worst of all, what had Noah done without because of his father's blind arrogance? At the very least, Noah had never known he had a father who would have cared about him.

Cole knew too well how such a revelation could tear up lives. His own father had had a secret son by his first love, Marilyn. That son was his older brother, Adam. Neither Marilyn nor his dad had known she was pregnant when they'd broken up. By the time she'd found out, his father had been in the military overseas. When she'd finally located him, he'd already married Cole's mother. Although his father hadn't openly claimed Adam, he'd assumed full responsibility and had secretly supported Marilyn and Adam. He'd even gone to see them as often as he could. It wasn't until Cole's dad was gray-faced on his deathbed that he'd confessed everything to Cole and had begged him to go and see Adam in West Texas.

"I always felt I had to protect your mother from knowing about Marilyn and Adam. You know how she is, so fine and proper...and so unyielding and self-righteous. For her sake, I never told you about your brother. I want you to go to him now. Try...to be a brother to him. And please ask your mother to forgive me."

Cole had asked her, all right, but his mother was still very bitter about Adam. Against her wishes, Cole had taken Adam into the family business as his father had wished. They'd even become close, considering they hadn't grown up together and still didn't totally trust each other.

Cole's hand dug into his scalp as recriminating emotions tore at him.

Damn it, you thought you were protecting your marriage and Lizzie when you refused to take Maddie's calls or read her letters.

No, you were a selfish, arrogant coward...just like your father.

That's not true! Dad did the best he could.

What is your own arrogance compared to Maddie running off with Turner?

Forget Turner. Forget what she did. You have a son—Noah. He has to come first.

Eight

Cole got up and turned off the light. Unable to face returning to the bed where Maddie slept when he didn't know if her warmth and sweetness were real, he remained in his dark office and shut his eyes.

What was the truth?

Were the people in Yella right about her after all?

Unsavory as the subject was, Cole had to dig the whole story out of her. Why the hell had she run away with Turner? Why did she turn white and look scared every time his name was mentioned? Had her mother lied?

Not that the answers to any of those questions mattered nearly as much as Noah.

What the hell was he going to do? How would he ever make up for six lost years?

Cole must have fallen asleep because he jumped when he heard a soft footfall in the den. When a woman's slim hand

90   HIS FOR THE TAKING

pushed the door ajar, and the narrow beam of a tiny flashlight fell on his dangling keys, he froze.

Where the hell had she gotten a flashlight?

Swiftly, Maddie, who was swathed in white from head to toe, entered the office and knelt beside the drawer. She'd been as silent as a ghost until she found the drawer open... and empty. Then she let out a strangled scream.

He snapped on the lamp beside him with a hard jerk of his wrist. "Looking for these?"

When he held up her letters, her slanting eyes widened. Then she dropped her flashlight and it rolled under his desk.

"Give them to me," she whispered, her exotic face going even whiter as she leaned down to retrieve her flashlight.

"Sure!" When he laid them on his desk, she snatched them away. "Why not? I already read them," he said.

"You had no right."

"Really? You claim we have a son together, and I have no right? Tell me something. Did you come over here today just to get these letters? When you failed to find them while my mother was here, did you stay and sleep with me just so you could stay a little longer and sneak back down here and try to get these letters?"

"You can believe that if you want to. You've believed worse of me."

His dark eyes were probably as lethally fierce as he felt, because she quickly averted her gaze.

"I wonder why?" he asked, hating it when she paled further. "I want the truth this time, damn it."

"No, you don't. Nobody in this town has ever wanted that from me. All of you want to despise me. So go ahead! I should be used to it by now." But her eyes were wild and her voice caught on a raw sob.

"I want to know if my mother's right, if you used your beauty to play me for a fool! And I want to know if you used your beauty when we were kids. Did you chase me because you thought I was rich and you'd be bettering yourself? You are, obviously, by your own admission, ambitious."

"I never chased you, if you'll remember! You chased *me*. And then…when I realized you'd never really wanted me for more than sex, I walked away."

"With Vernon?" he snarled.

She gasped. "I let you go." She paused. "But yes, I am ambitious. Yes, I want to give my child a better start in life than I had back then. And not only my child…but to give other children a better start. I don't want any child to have to grow up like I did!"

Something earnest and heartbroken in her eyes tore at him, but he ignored it.

"Right—you're the saint now, and I'm some entitled, arrogant demon from hell who got you pregnant and then callously rejected you and our son after I married another woman!"

Despite her stricken expression, she notched her chin a fraction of an inch higher.

"All I know is that tonight…coming here…what we did… was a mistake," she whispered. "I should never have confided in you at the pool, or slept with you."

"Well, you did, damn it!"

"Can't we just please forget tonight ever happened?"

He stared at her pale, forlorn face in disbelief. *No!* he wanted to yell.

Forget he had a son? Forget how seeing her again, how having her in his arms again, had made him feel so complete and so connected to her on a soul-deep level that his loneliness of six years had fallen away? Forget that despite everything he knew about her and everything people said about her, she looked defenseless and stricken and so damn innocent he wanted to take care of her? Forget he'd begun to trust her again and she'd disappointed him? Hell, furious as he was, she had him crazy with desire. How could he feel this way about her even now, when he'd just learned they had a son she'd planned to conceal from him forever?

She was as unscrupulous and selfish as her mother, but, on some level, he didn't care.

Why the hell did his heart and body refuse to believe what his mind knew about her? Fool that he was, he still wanted her.

Not that he was about to let on how much power she had over him.

"Once I would have given anything to hear you say you wanted Noah, anything.... I couldn't believe it when your only response was my two self-addressed, green postcards that came back with your boldly scrawled signature. After that there was nothing. No phone call. No letter. No email. Nothing. I kept waiting to hear from you. I went through hell. So, no—I don't care how you feel now because I can't trust you. Don't you see? I can't let myself care. I'm a mother. I have to do what's best for Noah."

"Right," he growled. "You're the trustworthy one. You were going to keep your son from ever knowing his real father. How do you think he'd feel about that if he ever found out?"

Clutching her letters against her breasts, which were covered by a long sheet, she squared her shoulders and backed toward the door. "I'm going to get dressed. I want you to drive me back to Miss Jennie's."

The finality in her tone cut him like a blade. But he refused to react, refused to let her see how her indifference shredded him.

"Sure. But we talk tomorrow. Don't you dare even think about leaving Yella before we talk. Because if you do, I'll make things worse for you. I could come to Austin, meet the do-gooders who pay you, tell them what people here think about you."

"Why would you do that?"

"Noah is my son, too."

"Why are you doing this? Surely you can't want Noah!" she whispered.

"Wrong!" He sprang to his feet, truly infuriated now. "I didn't know about him! Now that I do, you're going to have to deal with it, the same as I am! I could do a lot for Noah, you know. And for you."

"I want you out of my life!"

Heat engulfed him.

Her words pushed him over some dangerous edge, because he wanted her in his life as much as he wanted Noah. Even now, knowing that she'd probably slept with him for the sole purpose of remaining in his house long enough to get her letters so he would never find out about Noah, he wanted her.

"Well, that's too damn bad! Noah has two parents!"

After she'd left him for Vernon, he'd felt dead. Even when he'd been married to Lizzie, he'd felt dead. For years, he'd buried himself in his work in an attempt to forget her. Lizzie had felt neglected, and rightfully so. When Lizzie had died, he'd chosen booze so he wouldn't have to face the guilt and the emptiness that ravaged him—or the insane need he'd felt to search for Maddie.

When he'd seen her at the pool this morning, the sun had seemed to brighten and the water to sparkle with a special blinding radiance. Because of her, the whole world had seemed new and fresh. He couldn't tell her any of that, though, because then she'd know her power and use it against him.

"I don't like this any better than you do!" he yelled as she ran out of the room and up the stairs with his sheet trailing behind her.

Angry as he was, the knowledge that her voluptuous body was soft and naked under his sheet had him brick-hard again.

When he tore after her, he intended to appease her at least a little before pulling her into his arms, but she turned on him at the top of the stairs. And the words she flung at him through her sobs slammed him like mortal blows.

"I'm engaged to be married! To a wonderful man, I'll have you know! He grew up poor like me, so he understands me. He's a teacher, so he's wonderful with kids. He would never reject and abandon me, the way you did, and he already considers Noah his son. He's everything that Noah needs in a father."

"Then why the hell did you just sleep with me?" he thundered.

"Hormones. It was a horrible mistake. Please, just drive me home, and stay out of our lives!"

"You ask the impossible," he whispered in a ravaged tone. "Where's his damn ring anyway?"

"We're…we're informally engaged."

She raced into his bedroom and slammed the door.

Moonlight flooded his bedroom as Maddie sank down on his big bed with its tumbled sheets where they'd made love such a short time ago, where she'd been so happy…so foolishly happy, she thought now.

When she'd awakened from her nightmare filled with doubts and insecurities, he hadn't been there, and she'd felt rejected and afraid of her own powerful emotions.

She'd felt afraid that he didn't care about her, that he never had and that he never could. She thought maybe to him she was just a carnal pleasure—and of no more consequence than a coveted toy a spoiled child might enjoy from time to time.

Had Cole come after her when Vernon had hurt her? Had Cole rescued her like a knight in shining armor? Not that she believed in fairy tales, but still… Had he even questioned her mother's sordid story? Or had he simply believed the worst, like everybody else? Had he ever tried to find her? Or had he already been chasing after Lizzie—a proper girl, Yella's sweetheart? If she'd mattered to him at all, if she'd had a background he'd approved of, wouldn't he have found a way to reach her?

All her old doubts and insecurities had torn at her as she'd lain in the dark. Then she'd gotten up the nerve to search for him to determine his true feelings.

The lower part of the house had been dark when she'd made it down the stairs, so she'd made her way to her purse on the little table by the window and pulled out her tiny flashlight, which she always carried.

Thinking maybe he'd fallen asleep on a sofa, she hadn't wanted to turn on the lights as she searched for him.

When she hadn't found him on any of his big sofas or easy chairs, she'd seen his office door ajar. The lower drawer had been open, and she'd let out a little scream after she'd sunk to her knees and realized he'd probably read her letters.

At the realization that he knew about Noah, that the knowledge was why he hadn't come back to bed, she'd felt confused and scared, crazy. She hadn't been ready to face him, to talk to him about Noah. No, she'd felt too vulnerable after the sex—sex that had revealed how much she still cared for him. So when she'd found herself suddenly backed into a corner about Noah, she'd reacted to Cole's righteous anger and accusations defensively. By becoming furious, she'd made a royal mess of everything.

But she wasn't about to let hot sex weaken her into agreeing to include him in her son's life when that might not be the best thing for her and Noah. Cole hadn't been there when she'd needed him the most—when she'd been scared and helpless.

Well, maybe she and Noah didn't need him now.

What the hell was she doing up there? Sulking? Plotting? Or just feeling as sick at heart and confused as he was?

With a heavy heart, Cole mounted the stairs and waited outside that closed door until Maddie dressed. When she came out, she rushed past him and down the stairs without looking at him or speaking to him. On the way downstairs he found a tiny red flashlight on a carpeted stair. He kneeled and closed his fist around it. Uttering a low animal sound, he jammed it in his pocket.

Neither of them spoke as his truck ripped through the suffocating darkness on their way to Miss Jennie's rambling house, but the atmosphere inside the cab felt as charged as one of his gas wells about to blow. When at last he slammed on the brakes in front of Miss Jennie's and the truck jerked to a standstill, he jumped out and raced around to open her door.

She stayed where she was. Then, without a word, she began rummaging in her purse.

"Looking for something?"

"My flashlight. I must have dropped it somewhere."

He yanked it out of his pocket and flashed the narrow beam inside her purse.

With a frown she flung herself out of the door and grabbed it from him. "I'm perfectly capable of seeing myself to the door," she snapped.

Turning her back on him, she aimed the tiny beam on the sidewalk and marched stiffly toward the porch.

She didn't give him so much as a backward glance as she let herself inside the dark house and bolted the door behind her. Miss Jennie wasn't one to keep her shades down, so he watched Maddie's flashlight bob as she made her way to the back, watched when her bedroom light went on. Then her door closed, and the front of the house was dark again.

"Baby, if you think this is finished, you're very wrong," he growled softly. "If Noah's mine, he's mine. Not Greg's! I'll use DNA and the whole damn legal system to get him."

Nine

Usually, challenges seemed less daunting to Cole the next morning. Not today. Too much was at stake.

As soon as the sun flamed like a red-hot ball of fire against a mauve horizon, Cole dragged himself out of bed and made coffee. Although he had a headache from hell and burned with impatience, he had called Juan about the well. Fortunately, the driller had just arrived, so Cole could vent some of his frustration by blasting that glib, overpaid shirker who thoroughly deserved it. After the call, he went for a run before he drove over to Miss Jennie's.

Morning doves cooed in the treetops above Miss Jennie's house. Shadows from her big oaks slanted across her overgrown lawn. The last traces of ground fog hovered at the fringes of the brush where his ranch bordered her property.

For a long moment Cole stayed in the cab of his truck and observed the single light burning in the kitchen window. Maybe Maddie hadn't been able to sleep very well. He knew *he* hadn't. No, after dropping Maddie off last night, he'd lain in his bed, tossing and turning, torturing himself with visions of her lying in her fiancé's arms.

Gathering his courage, he dragged himself out of the truck and walked up to the front door and knocked. He was about to raise his hand again when the door opened and Cinnamon wheeled around from the back porch, yapping.

Propped on crutches, Miss Jennie, whose wrinkled face was softened by her bright blue eyes, beamed up at him sweetly as Cinnamon rushed inside.

"Good mornin', Cole. I expect you're here to see my darlin' Maddie."

"You're right about that."

"Well, she's in the shower. The poor thing's as pale as a ghost this morning and seems plumb tuckered out. I don't think she slept much last night. I heard her pacing early this morning, but you come on in…that is, if you don't mind waitin' for her."

He removed his Stetson. "I don't mind," he said politely, feeling ashamed of his own violent emotions as he stepped inside Miss Jennie's quiet, orderly parlor, which was filled with faded carpets, well-used antiques and the scarred piano that every kid in town had hammered on, including him.

"I have a fresh pot of coffee in the kitchen. Or if you'd prefer a soda, there's several in the fridge. I think I'd like a soda myself. Maybe you could open one for me, and we could chat at the kitchen table while we wait for our girl. Or sit on the screened porch."

"Wherever it's cooler."

"That would be the kitchen. I've got the air on."

Cole poured himself a mug of coffee and set a chilled can of soda before Miss Jennie, who was quick to thank him.

"I can't manage these crutches and get a soda out of the fridge at the same time," she said. "Not enough hands. Maddie's been so good to come here and help me with little things like that. She's fed Cinnamon and chased him, watered the plants and done the laundry. Mainly, though, we've caught up on our visitin'. I'm mighty proud of how she turned out."

He nodded courteously. He had immense respect for Miss Jennie, who had been his senior English teacher as well as Maddie's, only Miss Jennie hadn't championed him. Quite the opposite. Once, when his grades had fallen, she'd kept him from playing football for six weeks even though his parents and the coaches had pressured her to relent.

"I never knew you were friends with Maddie back when she lived here, you being a Coleman and all. She never once mentioned you until that awful night when she came here and said she had to leave Yella for good. She told me plenty about you that night, though. Cried her heart out, she did, poor thing, because you were so high-and-mighty, so far out of her reach. I told her to call you and lay it all out—to give you a chance. But that only made her weep harder because she said she already had and that you'd made it clear you thought she was trash and didn't want her."

Cole clenched his hands into fists and then unclenched them.

"There was nothing I could say to cheer her after that. She just said, 'He doesn't want me. He never will. I'm scared. You've got to help me get out of this town, or I'll end up just like my mother.' So I did."

Whatever else Maddie might have been that night, he now knew she'd been scared, and he hadn't been there for her. He was going to find out what the hell had happened to her that had made her run. It might take a while, peeling through the layers of the truth, but he was determined. First, though, he had to deal with Noah.

"She turned out real nice, didn't she?" Miss Jennie's blue eyes drilled into him.

"She did turn out nice," he muttered, feeling defensive.

"Miss Jennie!" Maddie stood in the doorway. Her stern voice and her ashen face were enough to make Miss Jennie swallow whatever she'd been about to confide.

"Hello, Cole," Maddie said stonily.

He stood up awkwardly, having forgotten all he'd intended to say to her after Miss Jennie's startling revelation.

It didn't make sense that Maddie had come to see Miss Jennie, of all people, on the night she'd been so mad with love she'd supposedly run off with Vernon. And Miss Jennie had confirmed what Maddie had told him about having tried to call him. What did it mean that she'd been crying her heart out because of *him,* and yet she'd still left with Vernon?

"We have to talk," he muttered gloomily.

"I don't have long," Maddie said in a crisp tone. "Miss Jennie needs me."

"I'll be fine right here with my soda and my morning paper. You two take Cinnamon out into the back garden and talk. There's some shade, so it's not too hot at this hour with the breeze. But mind that you make Cinnamon leave Bessie's chickens alone, so George, her husband, doesn't take a notion to shoot him again. You take all the time you need. I'll be just fine in here."

Tension throbbed through Cole as he pushed the screen door open and called to Cinnamon. The dog wheeled between their legs, barking. Then, of course, the dog rushed straight for Bessie's chicken coop.

"I hope George doesn't take aim at Cinnamon and shoot you or me by mistake," Cole said to lighten the mood. "He's a lousy shot."

A tight-lipped Maddie whirled on him as soon as they were where Miss Jennie could neither see nor hear them. "We have nothing to say to each other!"

"Why don't we start with the fact that I've had a son I

haven't known about for six damn years." Deliberately, he kept his tone soft.

When she shut her eyes, he was sure it was to block him out, not because the sun slanting through the oaks was so brilliant.

"I want to see him," Cole said. "To know him. For him to know me. As soon as it can be arranged and you feel that Noah is prepared, I want to meet him. Is that so wrong?"

"This has all happened so fast, I can't think. All I know is that you weren't there when we needed you. We've built a life—apart from you. It wasn't easy, I'll admit. I know you said you could do a lot for Noah, but the man I'm going to marry, Greg, can take care of us. He'll work hard to make us happy."

"Noah's still my son," Cole said. "I want to meet this *other* man, who's going to have a big part in Noah's life."

Out of the corner of his eye, Cole saw Bessie's shade lift.

"Please, if you ever felt anything for me…just go on with your own life. I was doing just fine without you."

"Well, maybe I wasn't doing just fine—not even before I knew about Noah. Maybe I want some answers. For six damn years I believed you jilted me and ran off with Vernon. In your letters that I stupidly didn't open, you said that you believed Noah was Vernon's. You sounded glad that he wasn't, like you were glad to think I might be Noah's father. Why? Miss Jennie just told me that you came to her right before you left Yella."

"Miss Jennie shouldn't be talking to you."

"Well, she called it an awful night. She said you told her about us, that you were crying and that you were in some kind of trouble. If that's true, I hope you'll trust me enough someday to tell me what happened."

"It's too late." Her flat voice was so faint he could barely hear her.

"Why did you tell her all about me if you were going to run off with Vernon? What the hell really happened that night?"

Her eyes grew huge and filled with pain. "I'm going to marry Greg, so none of this matters."

"We have a son. I want to know what happened."

"I can't go back there."

"I'm not asking you to go back. I'm asking you to communicate…honestly."

Refusing to look at him, she bit her bottom lip.

"Why did you sleep with me yesterday?"

"Because I'm weak and cheap…like my mother."

Was she? Grimly, he studied her wan face. He wished she could trust him enough to level with him.

Feeling so frustrated he wanted to shake her, he balled his fists and slid them into his pockets. "Maybe I would have been fool enough to buy that story before yesterday, but not now. I think you ran away from Yella because something terrible happened to you. I think you were scared and helpless, and I wasn't there for you. I think the woman who put herself through college while she raised my son alone, the woman who has a decent job now and a schoolteacher fiancé who's reputedly a damned paragon—that woman is the last thing from weak and cheap. I want the truth!"

She caught her breath. "Okay…like I keep telling you, the truth is that last night—the sex, I mean—was a mistake that I deeply regret."

"Not for me, it wasn't! It's the first good, completely honest thing that's happened to me in six years!"

It was bad timing that he'd read her letters right after that and had been forced to confront her about Noah. It would have been so much better for both of them if they'd had time to grow their relationship before they'd gotten into anything so heavy. But here he was—in too deep—with a woman he wasn't sure of. It was either sink or swim. He, for one, was determined to swim.

"I can't believe that," she began. "You're a Coleman, and I'm Jesse Ray's no-good daughter."

"Will you stop using the way everybody abused you as a weapon to club me? You've always been way more than that, and you know it."

Hardly knowing what he intended, he spanned the distance that separated them. So what if Bessie's shade notched up another inch or two. Wrapping Maddie, who smelled of shampoo and soap and her own sweet self, in his arms, he pulled her close.

"Even though you don't want me right now, you feel perfect in my arms."

When she tried to push free, he tightened his grip. Freeing her hands, he slid his arms around her waist.

"Cole, don't make this more difficult than it has to be."

"Kiss me," he begged. "You're going to have to prove to me you regret the sex." He paused. "I now believe you tried to call me the night you ran away. I believe my mother said something terrible that hurt you very deeply when you were already upset and terrified. I don't know why she doesn't want to admit it. I can only imagine she sensed the depth of my feelings for you and was too scared to confront me because she was afraid I'd choose you. No doubt she thinks she was acting in my best interests. Baby, I want you to trust me enough to tell me what happened that night."

"It's too awful."

"Maybe it will be easier to bear if you tell me."

Her lovely face crumpled. "I don't think so."

"I let you down. Okay. I know. I'm so sorry," he whispered.

"I don't know who you'll really believe—me or the gossips."

"If you'd talk to me, it would give me more ammunition against the gossips, wouldn't it?"

When she sighed, he hoped that maybe he was getting through to her.

"I'm such a fool," she murmured as she laid her head upon his chest. "I always was where you were concerned. I shouldn't listen to anything you ever say…especially when you hold me. I can't think."

"I was the fool. I never should have married Lizzie just because you'd run off and my dad was dead and my mother was hounding me all the time about Adam. I should have left Yella, left them all, and tried to find you."

"Maybe it would have just made things worse. By then, I knew I was pregnant. My life was such a mess. I was needy and desperate and struggling to find myself and carve out a new life. I wouldn't be who I am now if anything had been different. But all that's over and done with."

Stroking her hair, he held her. "I hate it that you had to face all that alone. I'm here now, and what I want is for you to marry me instead of Greg."

"What? You don't know what you're saying. That's impossible."

"Why? Noah's my son."

"But you're a Coleman, and I'm who I am. Marriage would mean we'd have to make a life together. We've been apart for six years, so we don't even really know each other at this point. You had a three-month secret affair with a girl who was forbidden, and we had yesterday. What else do we have?"

"Noah. Last night. Chemistry."

She blushed. "My mother ruined her life because her libido led her to make so many terrible choices. And there's your mother, who hates me."

"She'll either change her mind, or she won't see much of me or her grandson."

"There's Noah and how his grandmother's condemnation of me might damage him. I don't want what she and other people here think about me to make him see me as cheap."

"He wouldn't."

"Other children, other people, can be so cruel. You don't know, since you never suffered the kind of cruelty I did while growing up here."

"I'd be giving him my name and my protection. That will count for a lot in the future, just as it counts for a lot to everybody in Yella."

"Other people would side with your mother, her friends, everyone in Yella, even Adam…. They'd make me feel like I used to feel. I want to forget the past—all of it."

"We don't have to live here. And you're wrong about Adam. He and I don't agree on a lot of things, but he likes you. When he told me how beautiful and classy you were, nothing could stop me from racing back to Yella."

"Really?"

"I was irresponsible as hell to leave my oil well. I came back solely to see you." He held her tightly. "I'm sorry about the past," he whispered.

Very gently, he leaned down and laved the back of her ear with his tongue, causing her to flush beguilingly.

"Stop! I can't think when you do that," she whispered, her voice soft and breathy. "And I have to think."

"No. You've been doing too much thinking. Feelings count, too, you know. I think we fell into bed last night because we both wanted each other so badly we couldn't resist."

"In my life, lust has been a destroyer."

Slowly his fingers tucked her hair behind her ear. "Okay. I'll admit to a tad of lust, but not to the destroying kind. I never got over you, Maddie Gray. Because I cared about you."

"I don't believe that."

"Only because, after what you've been through, you're

too afraid. I don't blame you. But if you'd only give me another chance—"

"You're just lonely…because of Lizzie."

"I was hellishly lonely after you left…even after I married Lizzie."

"You haven't had time to think this through. Don't you see that it would never work?" She brushed at her throat with her fingertips as if suddenly she was too hot. When she tried to remove his hand, he wove his fingers through hers and brought her knuckles against his warm lips, his gentle kisses causing her to shudder.

"We'll have to find a way to make it work," he said.

When she glanced up at him, her beautiful eyes were aglow with fear and a wild, desperate hope.

"Let me go!" she begged.

Lowering his head so fast she couldn't dodge his lips, he claimed the exquisite softness of her mouth. When his tongue slid inside, she rasped in a breath.

"You have to break up with Greg," Cole muttered hoarsely. "You have to know that such a marriage wouldn't stand a chance when it's me you really want…in bed anyway."

"I can't care about that."

"You must, if you marry him wanting me. I could tell you a thing or two about marrying for the wrong reasons. About trying to make the wrong relationship work."

"Your argument doesn't stand. You and I would be marrying for the wrong reasons. I had this perfect plan…."

"You don't think I had a few plans myself? Last night blew all our plans to bits."

"I won't be bullied into a loveless marriage."

"Put like that, my proposal stinks. But your assessment is inaccurate. We'd be marrying for love—for the mutual love of our son."

"You don't know him."

"He's mine. I want him to be legitimate. I'd think that would matter to you since your mother didn't marry your father and people looked down on you for it."

"Oh… You do play dirty." She stared at him, aghast.

"When I have to. It's very simple. Go back to Austin. Tell Greg about me. Say you're confused, that you need time. In the meantime, introduce me to Noah as a good friend of yours, so we can start preparing him to accept me as your husband and his father. Then slowly we'll sort this out…*together*."

"No."

"I want to give Noah a stable life," he said smoothly.

"Do you think I don't want that?"

"Good. We agree on the fundamentals. We both want what's best for our son, and we both want each other."

"You don't love me."

"You don't love me either, but I'm not whining about it. I'm asking you to marry me."

"You're impossible…arrogant…entitled…"

He smiled as he waited for her to finish cataloging his many faults.

"But I want to marry you. I want to take care of you. I want to make up for six years of neglecting you and my son. Surely that makes up for two or three of my sins."

"You don't love me," she repeated.

Maybe not, but no way was he letting her go again, not after last night. For better or worse, she was his. Just like Noah was his. She just didn't know it yet.

He didn't like it that she'd intended to keep him from ever finding out about Noah, and he didn't like that she'd planned to marry Greg, but he had to focus on what he wanted—Noah and her—if he was going to win her over to his point of view. He didn't want another man being a father to Noah now that Cole was free to marry and claim his son.

As he held her and stared down at her lovely face, his blood began to thrum as he remembered how she'd felt last night in his arms. Suddenly, he was tired of arguing. As always, he marveled that she could arouse him so easily, so quickly—and that he could do the same to her.

"Maybe I don't love you, but I like a lot of things about you. For one thing, you're too damn beautiful to argue with and you're making me unbearably hot," he said.

"What?"

"Since everybody already thinks you lured me to my pool to go skinny-dipping yesterday, why don't we go there now… and actually do it?"

Her luminous eyes went so dark and shot so many sparks at him, he was afraid she was about to pull back her hand and take a swing at him. When she didn't, when she simply stared at him with what became a charming, incredulous expression on her blushing face, he relaxed and grew even hotter for her.

"Now?" she demanded. "We're in the middle of an argument. You can't be serious!"

Relieved that she hadn't said no, his hands twisted in her hair. He pulled her head back and her body flush against his own so that she could feel his erection. She gasped and cast a frantic look toward Bessie's window.

"Feel what you do to me," he whispered, right before he kissed her long and passionately. "Believe me—I'm very serious."

"But we were arguing about getting married. You can't just switch gears—"

"Who's switching? Obviously, everything we do together turns me on, which proves how much fun marrying you would be."

"Bessie's probably watching," she murmured, struggling to free herself.

"So? If we're going to be talked about, Miss Gray, we might

as well give the old biddies an X-rated kiss or two to specu-
late about, don't you think?"

When he laughed, her lips quirked as she attempted to suppress her own smile. "Just because I can't stay mad at you
doesn't mean I intend to marry you."

"I can't stay mad at you either, which I take as a good sign
for two people considering marriage," he countered.

She smiled a little.

"Hey, do you have a picture of Noah?" Cole asked, feeling
vulnerable at his sudden need to see a snapshot.

She nodded slowly. Pulling her phone out of her pocket,
she scrolled to her pictures. "Here," she said, placing the de-
vice in his palm. "I can email any you like."

Noah appeared to be a normal, happy, rambunctious little
boy in every picture. His tumbled hair was coal-black. The
kid's lively green eyes grabbed Cole's soul and refused to let
it go. He looked just like Cole had at the same age.

He had a son who was everything a man could want in a
child.

In one shot, Noah raced exuberantly toward a swing set
with two other boys about his same size. The untied shoelaces
of his sneakers flying, he was clearly ahead.

Competitive, Cole thought, remembering his days as a star
quarterback in high school.

"Does he know how to tie his shoes?" he asked.

"Yes. But not all that well because too many of his shoes
have had other types of fasteners."

"Then we'll have to work on that," Cole said.

In another shot, Noah was on the yellow roof of a red play-
house with a smiling blonde girl who was missing a front
tooth. His goofy grin and wide-eyed look of adoration tugged
at Cole's heart.

"Somebody's got a crush," he whispered.

"Her name's Missy. And you're right. I couldn't believe it

when he told me he brushed a spider off of her. He hates spiders with such a passion I knew she was special."

In another, Noah hung upside down from a tree limb like an impishly grinning bat while an admiring Missy smiled up at him.

"Aren't you afraid he'll break something?" Cole asked.

"Oh, yes. He already has."

She took the phone from him and flipped through the pictures until she found the one she was looking for. Then she handed it back to him.

The picture was of Noah lying on a hospital bed. There were dark circles under his worried green eyes as he studied his suspended arm in its white cast.

"What happened?"

"He broke his arm at school while racing a kid down a hill on the playground. Not that a broken arm slowed him down. Within a day he'd learned to do everything one-handed. The only time he complained of pain was when the doctor twisted his arm before he set it. Oh, and he did wax philosophical when he was snuggling with me in bed one morning about how easy it was to break an arm."

"He sleeps with you?"

"No. But he comes in a lot of mornings to cuddle before my alarm goes off."

His son was tough. But he was affectionate, too. Pride swelled inside Cole, and so did another, less easily defined but fiercely possessive and all-consuming emotion.

His gaze locked on Maddie's face. She was the mother of his son. Was that why he felt a profound need to claim her?

"I've gotta go," she said.

"It's a nice day for a swim."

She shook her head. "There's Miss Jennie to see about. She *is* the reason I'm here."

"Well, you call me if you change your mind. Since we

never went skinny-dipping, I say it's time you earned your bad reputation."

"You're incorrigible," she whispered with a grin, lowering her lashes as if she hoped that would lessen the sexual charge of their nearness.

"Call me if you want to swim," he repeated. He touched her arm, running his knuckles down the smooth skin, which caused her to shiver.

"You come over here and try to bully me into a marriage. Then you have the gall to invite me to go skinny-dipping? Neither is going to happen!"

Ten

What was happening to her? What mysterious power did Cole have over her?

Maddie felt both wet and hot beneath Cole's devouring gaze as she slowly peeled her jeans and panties down the length of her legs.

Sunlight poured through the thick canopy of leaves that surrounded them. The blaze lit up the soft scarlet blanket Cole had carelessly tossed onto the grass beside the icy green pool; the blaze lit her up, as well.

How could she so easily succumb to whatever wanton suggestion he tossed at her? How could she do this when Noah's future hung in the balance? Had she no will of her own? Was he right about their marriage being the best thing for Noah? He was certainly right about her wanting him.

Quickly, Cole yanked off his own clothes and laid them on top of hers on a limestone rock. When he gathered her body in his arms, the exquisite shiver that went through her made her cling to him. His warm, rough hands slid down her shoulders and closed around her waist. Then he pulled her slowly down on the blanket and covered her with his powerful body so that his heat enveloped her.

Cole's hands stroked her gently until she was so hungry for him she lifted her legs and urged him to take her. Her whole body was tense and aching for release, but he made her wait, made her beg in throaty, pleading purrs while he stroked and kissed her. Finally, when she felt as though she might explode, he smiled as he slid his body lower down her length so that he could bury his face against her sex. She cried out in pleasure when his tongue caressed and then dipped inside those secret lips.

"Take me," she whispered. "Just take me."

"Patience, my love," he murmured.

Using his seeking mouth and velvet tongue as instruments of pleasure, he soon had her melting and yielding everything. Instead of feeling ravaged and abused, as she had for so many years, she felt cherished and adored.

"You are beautiful," he whispered. "The most beautiful woman I've ever known. You smell good, too."

She felt beautiful, vibrant and aglow.

With a slow, delicate rhythm he licked her, skimming across her velvety interior until she was a quivering mass of nerves ready to fly apart at the slightest flick of his tongue. Only when the pleasure was unbearable, only when she was burning up and on the brink of release, did he stop.

"Don't!"

"Don't what?" he murmured.

"Don't stop."

"Who's stopping?"

Easing his body over hers, he thrust deeply inside her. Arching to meet that one forceful stroke, she came, crying out his name as a sudden gust of wind made the leaves above them swirl in an emerald-green blaze.

"Mine," he growled fiercely. "You are mine."

He crushed her to him even more tightly. Then driven by his own feverish urgency, he began to move inside her, faster and faster, and with such force that he stole her breath. Strange how after his sweetness, she didn't mind his violence and passion. His breathing grew harsh and ragged, and he whispered wildly erotic things in her ear as he carried her to another explosion that was wild and glorious and satisfying on a soul-deep level.

Afterward, when he stared down at her, his green eyes were sensual and tender. Tears pricked against her lashes. How could she feel so safe in Cole's arms?

He ran light fingertips over her breasts, causing her nipples to peak again. Sated with sensual bliss, she smiled up at him as she snuggled closer.

This isn't reality, she told herself. *I can't seriously consider marrying him, especially since his proposal was only about sex and a desire to claim Noah legally. Austin, my job, Noah—they are my reality.* Even if Cole were offering her the life she'd once dreamed of, experience had taught her she couldn't count on him. Greg was steady…and real. He would be there for her. There was no disparity of wealth and social class dividing them. Cole was only a fantasy.

Still, it was nice to be steamy hot and erotically satisfied in Cole's hard arms as a warm summer breeze brushed her body. It was nice running her hands through his hair while she stared past a haze of greenery at the brilliant cobalt-blue sky. She hadn't felt this pleasantly sexy in years, and she probably never would again. But she knew all too well that sex could be a destructive force.

Later, she discovered he'd hidden her clothes and wouldn't let her dress until she went skinny-dipping with him.

"I'm determined to make you live up to your scandalous reputation," he teased.

As they swam in that crystal clear pool, the years seemed to fall away, as did the walls that had protected her heart. During the brief interlude when they splashed and cavorted in the stream, she felt young and carefree and completely happy— as she never had as a girl.

Years ago, some ancestral Coleman had nailed rungs onto the thick trunk of one of the tallest cypress trees. When Cole began to climb, her heart leaped into her throat.

Even though she begged him to come back down, he let out a war whoop and jumped, terrifying her until he hit the water and she knew he was safe. Laughing, he swam toward her from the deeper end to where she stood, her breasts floating above the surface of the water. Reaching for her, he stroked the curving sides of her breasts. The loverlike way he touched them and looked at them, as if he'd never seen anything so alluring, made her feel desirable beyond words.

She wished she could freeze time, but moments like this were as fleeting as the fragile bubbles that frothed below the dam. Smiling, she ran her hands down his body and circled his erection, which she eagerly guided into her own fluid interior, which was warmer and somehow wetter than the water.

She gasped when he circled her with his arms and pressed himself even more deeply inside her. They clung to each other tightly as he began to stroke in and out, faster and faster, until soon she felt she was glowing and pulsating with that all-too-familiar piercing yearning for release.

When she could breathe again, he kissed her brow and held her close. Not speaking, they floated side by side, staring up at the sun-bright clouds through the branches. Later, when they dressed, they walked to their favorite Indian mound and spent half an hour searching for arrowheads. Not that they found much more than a few broken bits of flint. Still, she enjoyed placing her finds in his palm so she could watch while he examined each one thoughtfully.

"Sassy gets here this afternoon," she said as they sat together in his truck in Miss Jennie's drive. "So this is goodbye, because I'll be going back to Austin as soon as I pack."

"Why didn't you tell me earlier?"

"Maybe because I was afraid you'd start pressuring me again."

He folded her slim hand in his much larger one. Turning it over, he brought her fingertips to his lips. "Will you tell Greg about us?"

She hesitated. "I need more time."

"When I want something, I'm not a patient man." He leaned across the seat and kissed her, hard. "Juan keeps calling me and texting me. I've got to leave for the rig in a few hours. If things go as I expect, I can pry myself loose in a week and drive to Austin."

"Not a good idea."

"No—you want to put this off forever." He kissed the tip of her nose and the corners of her eyes and then drew her close against his body. "The quicker we resolve Noah's future and ours, the better."

Reaching across the cab, she brushed her fingertips along his jawline. "I can't marry you."

"That's an unacceptable answer."

A brisk knock sounded on his trailer door. Cole, who'd made no forward progress with Maddie since she'd left Yella a few days ago, had a headache from hell. Clamping his mobile phone against his ear, he stood and strode to the door.

The minute he pushed it open the incessant roar of his rig and its petroleum odors slammed him.

Juan handed him the latest printout and signaled that he needed to talk to him, too.

"Two minutes," Cole promised as he shut the door. "When are you going to tell Greg about me?" Cole demanded of Maddie.

"The more I think about your proposal, the more I think we're not right for each other. I have a life here that doesn't include you," Maddie whispered. "I don't want anything to do with Yella or the past, and you're a part of all that."

"Noah's my son. I won't have another man playing father to him."

"But I can't do without him. We have our big annual fund-raiser this week. Greg offered to sit with Noah that night. And Noah's looking forward to having the evening with him, too."

Cole gritted his teeth. He wasn't getting anywhere over the phone.

After his long silence, she said, "So, how are things at the well?"

Since he had no interest in discussing work, it took him a minute to regroup. "Slow as hell. But there haven't been any injuries, and it's definitely going to produce."

"That sounds really good."

"We've had a few breakdowns. We've had to order parts—parts that had to be back-ordered. Nothing major, just the usual challenges. I need to bring this well in if I'm going to be able to get up to see you."

"I told you. That's not a good idea. The sooner we forget about what happened in Yella, the better."

"Are you out of your mind?" Forget how great sleeping with her had been? Forget Noah?

He hated not being able to see her and touch her. Hell, he was hard just from talking to her. He needed to hold her and make love to her again—if he was to convince her they had to marry.

"I'm getting another call. I've gotta go," she said.

"Greg?"

When she didn't deny it, a nasty green emotion flared hotly inside him. After she hung up, the drilling site seemed desolate and his trailer dreary. Opening a can of tonic water so fast it spewed fizz all over him, he stomped outside to find Juan.

He was losing her. He had to bring this well in fast. Only then could he go to Austin and convince her they had to marry for Noah's sake.

No, he didn't like that she'd slept with him and then had sneaked downstairs searching for her letters. Nor was he happy about the fact that she would never have told him about Noah if he hadn't beaten her to his office. After that stunt, he wouldn't be normal not to consider that maybe there was some truth in what the folks in Yella thought about her.

If there was, that was all the more reason he had to make an honest woman out of her and claim Noah as his son. And even though he had his own doubts, he was willing to ignore them and go up against his family and anybody else who objected to their marriage.

Cole did not want his son growing up the way Adam had, deeply resenting that he was illegitimate. Whether Maddie admitted it or not, by giving Noah his name, he would assure his son of what Maddie claimed was most precious to her—the kind of respectability and sense of belonging that she'd never had.

The sooner he got to Austin and convinced her he was right, the better.

Eleven

His eyes narrowing on the numbers of each house, Cole tensed as he drove up Maddie's shady street for the second time. Her East Austin neighborhood was working-class but decent. Two little girls wearing helmets, big T-shirts and pigtails rode their bikes on the sidewalk. A couple of boys about Noah's age threw a football back and forth to each other.

At least there were kids for Noah to play with.

Probably Cole should have called before coming, but he'd been too rushed. He wasn't happy about having left Juan in charge of the well again, but seeing Maddie sooner rather than later had taken precedence over his business concerns. Noah's future was at stake.

The two-bedroom houses were a scramble of crumbling fixer-uppers and newly gentrified dwellings. Guilt swamped him as he realized she and Noah had probably struggled to survive in far less pleasant neighborhoods before she'd been able to afford even this. If only he'd taken her calls or read her letters when she'd tried to contact him…but he couldn't change the past. All he could do was the right thing *now,* and he *would* do it.

A silver SUV with heavily tinted windows and an aluminum canoe on the rooftop luggage rack swung in front of him and parked in front of a charming white house with a wide front porch. He read the numbers and realized it was Maddie's house.

Damn, he thought as a tall man with broad shoulders, enviable posture and thick, disheveled blond hair jumped out of the SUV and raced up her sidewalk.

Greg? If so, Cole's timing was lousy.

Cole parked on the opposite side of the street and watched a slender, dark-haired boy throw open the door and grin. Rocking back on his bare feet, Noah eagerly grabbed Greg's hand and tugged him inside.

The sight of his son welcoming another man filled Cole with longing, causing his mood to worsen. Nor did his mood improve as he sat outside for another ten minutes studying her sparkling windowpanes and counting, and then recounting, her roses.

Her bright red porch swing made it easy to imagine her sitting outside while Noah played on a nice afternoon. A white picket fence enclosed the backyard. Obviously, she'd made sure Noah had a safe place to play when she couldn't watch him out front, more evidence of her determination to give her son a better childhood than she'd known.

Impatience began to gnaw at him. What the hell was Greg doing inside Maddie's house for so long?

Just when Cole was about to get out of his truck and stomp up the sidewalk and pound on her door, it opened. Maddie, who wore a tight red T-shirt, white shorts and high, strappy sandals, stepped outside clasping Noah's hand. Greg shut the door and then quickly followed behind them.

Cole willed her to glance his way, but she was concentrating too intently on whatever Noah was saying. When she finally saw Cole, she froze.

A wellspring of desire tinged with anger swept through him. Her gorgeous violet-blue eyes framed by thick inky spikes captivated him. She was so lovely, he ached. Somehow he forced himself to wave casually.

Maddie gripped Noah's hand and all but dragged the poor boy to Greg's SUV.

Greg unlocked the doors and everybody climbed inside. When the SUV lurched away from the curb, Cole shifted into Drive and followed.

His mobile phone pinged almost immediately.

Hell, she'd texted him.

On way to Town Lake. Will call u when we get home. Don't follow!

Since he didn't text when he was behind the wheel, he called her back. When her phone went to voice mail, his only option was to leave a message.

"Sorry I didn't call first." Feeling jealous as hell, he hung up.

What was wrong with him? He felt as out of control as a wildly infatuated teenager.

He should go to a hotel, check in, chill, wait for her call. He should call Juan and check in with a few of his engineers.

Since he wasn't feeling all that rational, he stayed glued to Greg's tail.

The threesome parked near the water. From a distance, Cole watched Greg and Maddie unload the canoe and carry it down to the lake while Noah tagged along happily. To get the life jackets, paddles, thermos and cooler, the three of them trooped back and forth, making several trips. Once or twice Maddie glanced toward Cole and flushed angrily.

While they loaded the canoe, Noah knelt on the limestone

bank and sifted through the rocks, stuffing his pockets until they bulged. As a kid, Cole had been equally fascinated by rocks and had spent hours looking for fossils and arrowheads. In college he'd taken several geology courses, a study that had proved useful when he'd gone into the oil and gas business.

He didn't even know his son, but already the boy reminded him of himself.

There was a wide gravel jogging trail along the water's edge, so Cole followed the canoe on foot as far as he could. They didn't stay out long, maybe because Noah's constant squirming caused the canoe to rock back and forth precariously. Not that Greg seemed the least bit put out when forced to return to shore. No, he was a gem, patiently reloading the canoe and repacking the gear into the vehicle. Once they were safely on land and the canoe was on the roof of his SUV, Greg bought birdseed so Noah could feed pigeons. When Noah spilled the first bag chasing the birds, Greg bought another. Growing bored with the pigeons before he was halfway into the second bag, Noah threw the seed down, causing a mad flutter of wings as the gray flock converged on the bag. Pointing at a playground not too far away, the boy raced to it.

Greg and Maddie gave chase and then sat on a nearby bench so they could watch Noah, who was now climbing the colorful equipment. Noah swung, climbed poles, clambered up rope ladders and slid down the slides. When he fell off a swinging bridge and bumped his head, Greg ran over and picked him up. Long after Noah had dried his tears, he was content to hang on to Greg's broad shoulders and watch the other children play.

Hell. Unable to watch Greg with his son any longer, Cole pivoted and strode back to his truck. Climbing inside, he yanked the door shut and jammed his key into the ignition. Gunning the engine, he roared out of the park and headed toward Sixth Street in search of a bar.

Dealing with Noah in the abstract had been easier than seeing him with Greg and realizing that the kid had had six years to form attachments to other people. Illogically, Cole felt angry at Maddie for not telling him and then angry at himself all over again for not being there for her and Noah when she'd first reached out to him.

Six years. Six damn years he'd missed. Would he ever be able to make up for that? One thing was for sure—he wasn't about to give up the years he had left with his son.

Inside the first shadowy pub he found, he ordered a double scotch on the rocks, which arrived before he remembered the vow he'd made not to drink after he'd pulled himself out of his guilt/funk over Lizzie. Sliding the glass angrily aside, he signaled the waiter and asked him to replace the drink with tonic water and a twist of lime. He knocked that back with abandon even though what he really craved was the kick of the double scotch.

Maddie called him while he was having dinner alone. The hotel restaurant's terrace had a view of Town Lake and the sparkling lights of downtown. If he grew bored with that view, there was a friendly blonde in a red sundress who was also alone, sitting at the table next to his, who kept smiling at him.

"I asked you not to follow me," Maddie said.

"Did you tell him about me?" Cole asked.

"I was going to, but I couldn't think clearly with Noah around and you watching us. Plus, Greg had a bad day at school, and I need him to babysit for me during my fund-raiser."

"We need to talk—soon."

"This is a difficult week for me. The fundraiser is impor-tant to the shelter's survival."

He worried that she was just making excuses. "After seeing Noah with Greg I realize how much I've missed. I don't want to miss any more. The sooner we get married, the better."

"Look…"

"What about lunch? Tomorrow?"

"Can't. I'm already booked."

"With Greg?"

"If you must know, yes. I didn't know you and I would re-connect or that you'd find out about Noah when I made the date."

"Later, then?"

"I've got a completely full schedule at work tomorrow… and the fundraiser is tomorrow evening. We're always under-staffed, and Casey, my coworker, has a doctor's appoint-ment tomorrow."

"I'm not taking no for an answer." He said goodbye.

After he hung up, he wondered what he could do to change her mind about his proposal.

If Nita Stark was a big talker and temperamental as all get-out, she was also a huge donor and the keynote speaker at the fundraiser, so Maddie didn't dare rush their call even though she needed to get off the phone.

When she finally managed to hang up, it was already ten minutes past noon. She was thirsty and needed to touch up her lipstick and her hair before she led the tour that she gave every two weeks. It was a way to inform the community about the mission of My Sister's House. After that, she had to meet Greg. Feeling rushed, she grabbed her purse off its hook and raced out of her office, her high heels clicking on the polished tile floor.

Even before she reached the door at the end of the hall, where George, her favorite young volunteer, scanned the area with fierce, earnest eyes while he stood guard for her, she heard exuberant laughter erupting from the room that was used for tours, church services on Sundays and other meetings.

Strange, she thought. Then George pushed the door open and she saw Cole.

"Okay, everybody, she's here," George announced to the clump of women who were gaily laughing at something Cole had said.

"This is Miss Gray. She's going to conduct your tour today," George said.

Cole clapped.

"Sorry I'm late," Maddie began, feeling flustered as she tapped her lectern with her pen while Cole's amused green gaze drilled into her.

Damn him. She'd told him she didn't have time to talk today.

Usually her tour groups were dominated by staid, upper-middle-class matrons who were considering volunteering. Today the women were more focused on Cole than her.

When Cole gave Maddie another slow, insolent grin, she ignored him and began her talk about the shelter. Because he was such an unnerving presence, Maddie spoke fast, too fast, forgetting entire topics she should have mentioned.

Cole, who must have researched My Sister's House on its webpage, asked lots of questions.

"I always thought that places like this just enable dope addicts and prostitutes," he murmured drily.

Smiling tightly, she gave a quick reply. "Anybody who stays in our shelters must agree to drug testing. We are associated with all the best agencies in the city. They can help our clients get jobs, get clean and get their lives back on track. We are not enablers."

"Good to hear. What percentage of your clients do you save? Surely, it's quite small."

It was infinitesimal; still, it was a start.

"Not nearly as many as we'd like," she was forced to admit. Annoyed, she glanced at her watch. "But since I seem to be running a little late, I can't take any more questions until I finish the tour!"

He laughed.

Furious, she raced through her tour while the women remained distracted by Cole. By the time Maddie had completed her talk, she was breathless with outrage.

Ignoring him, she said goodbye to the ladies before handing them off to George. Then she stormed down the hall to her office. Racing to catch up with her, Cole stepped inside the tiny room before she could slam the door on him.

"I'm at work here. I don't have time to play games," Maddie said.

"Who's playing games?" He pulled a check out of his pocket. "Your talk inspired me to write My Sister's House a sizable check."

When she saw the truly generous amount, she grew so hot under her collar she was sure she'd burst a blood vessel. "You don't care about My Sister's House."

"I care about you. And Noah."

"I'll have you know you can't just buy your way into my office because you want to bully me."

"I beg to differ."

"I think you're contemptible."

"Take the check. I'm sure you, as the director, can't afford to turn down a donation that large," he murmured as he placed the check in her trembling palm and folded her rigid fingers over it finger by finger. "Just as I'm sure you wouldn't want me to inform your board that you wouldn't make time for such a generous donor."

She pressed her lips together and took a deep breath. "I will have my board send you a letter formally thanking you."

"I'm sure you will, but I'd prefer a personal thank-you."

"Okay! Thank you." Straightening his check, she slid it into her top drawer. "You've had your fun. Now, would you please go?"

"No. I intend to meet Greg—and Noah—before I leave town. Greg's due here soon, I believe?" He looked at his watch. "Oh, dear, is he late?"

She kicked her desk, wishing it were him.

Grinning, he sat down to wait.

When he refused to budge no matter how hard she glared at him, she sank down into her own chair in weary defeat. In the tense silence that ensued, time dragged and her green walls felt as if they were pressing in on her.

"Okay," he said in a terse tone several minutes later. "You're short on time, so let's not waste it by sulking. I'm here for one thing—to convince you to agree to marry me."

"This is the twenty-first century. You can't force me into a shotgun marriage six years after the fact."

"We have a son. Giving him my name is valid enough reason for me."

"I don't want to involve him in our messy relationship."

"It wouldn't be like that."

"Really? You expect me to believe that after your caveman tactics today? You think because you're a Coleman and I was born a nobody, you can bulldoze over me? You have zero respect for me or my job."

"I attended a public tour. The website made it clear anybody could attend."

"You know what I mean."

"If you think I'm going to sit on the sidelines and let another man father my son, even if that man is a paragon, you don't know me very well. Noah's mine, and I intend to make sure everybody knows it. I'll fight you—until you agree."

She stared at him. His green eyes were as brilliant and stubborn as Noah's. She studied his black hair with its widow's peak and couldn't ignore his striking resemblance to her darling, if tenacious, little boy.

Cole was so handsome. Even now when she was at loggerheads with him, his virile male presence filled the space of her tiny office in an overpowering way that made her desire him. If she quit fighting him, could a marriage between them work? They *did* both want what was best for their son.

Sensing that he'd scored on some level, he reached across her desk and caught her fingers in his. Even that was enough to make her sizzle. When she felt her cheeks flush, she tried to will herself to tear her hand from his, but couldn't. So she shut her eyes and counted to ten before she reopened them and met his gaze—and felt the same overwhelming need to hold on to his hand. She'd been alone so long, fighting for Noah and herself without much help. It hadn't been easy.

"I was jealous during the tour," she whispered. "Of you and those women."

"Were you really?"

"Ridiculously so," she admitted in a raw whisper. "And I hate feeling that way…because that's how I felt a lot of the time when I was growing up. You had all those girlfriends from good families chasing you, and I was so low in your eyes, you didn't know I was alive."

He smiled sheepishly and his hand tightened around hers.

"Sorry," he whispered. "I was a beast today. So much was at stake I felt I had to come."

At his sincere tone, she looked at him in confusion, every bit as dazzled by his dark good looks as the five women had been. Oh—she was hopeless. What did he really feel for her? "Do you really think our marriage could work long-term?"

"If we both work at it." In his eyes, all she saw was tenderness and compassion mixed with a profound, burning need.

"I feel like I've built something solid at My Sister's House," she said.

"I was very impressed by your tour."

She snorted. "I was awful, and you were flirting."

"With you."

"I feel that I might be throwing it all away if I married you."

"Nobody's asking you to quit your job."

"I used to have this foolish dream of marrying someone who loved me. When I became a single mother, I knew I would have to be more practical. Greg came along, and because of our similar backgrounds, I thought our relationship could work. But you—you and I live in different worlds. You have this huge, legendary ranch, and you own oil fields. You wouldn't be the least bit interested in me if it weren't for Noah."

"Then why did I drive home to Yella when I heard you'd come home?"

"I hate feeling that I wouldn't contribute to your life in any way other than being Noah's mother. I would be a burden."

He leaned across the desk and whispered against her earlobe in his deep, musical baritone, both thrilling her and chilling her. "I want you in my bed. Doesn't that count?"

He lusted after her the way every man in Yella had wanted her mother.

But for how long? she wondered, remembering how easily he'd let her go. How would he see her when he no longer felt that way? It could happen soon, if the people in his life who mattered to him refused to accept her.

"You want Noah, so you'll take me, too?"

"If our situations were reversed, and I had him, would you marry me, to be closer to him?"

She would have married the devil to be with Noah.

He pressed her fingers and stared into her eyes. "So, enough of this. What do you say? Will you marry me?"

Before she could answer, she heard quick, determined footsteps outside her door and jerked her hand free a second before Greg burst through the door. The unruly lock of blond hair that usually fell across his brow was as unkempt as ever. Smiling bashfully, he handed her a vase of limp yellow roses.

"I'm afraid I left them in my car all morning in the heat." His soft brown eyes held genuine regret.

"Why, thank you, Greg," she said, feeling awkward since Cole was staring holes through her. "There's someone here...."

When Greg turned to Cole, she lifted the roses to her nose in an attempt to conceal her nervousness. "Mr. Coleman is just leaving after making a donation."

She glared at Cole frostily, willing him to leave. Greg held out his hand to Cole. "The mission welcomes all donors, large or small. I'm Greg Martin, Miss Gray's fiancé."

"John...Coleman. Most people call me Cole." They shook hands.

"The oilman I've been reading about, who owns Coleman's Landing, who played a hunch and discovered the Devine-Chalk oil play over in Devine County?"

Cole nodded. "The same. More importantly, I'm Noah's father."

Maddie's face flamed with a mixture of guilt and anger even before Greg whirled on her. "Noah's father?"

"He was just going," she said.

"Noah's father?" Greg repeated. "No wonder I had the impression I was interrupting something important."

"We ran into each other last week in Yella," Cole said.

"Now I see why you've been so tense and uncommunicative this week," Greg said, glancing at Maddie.

"I—I meant to tell you," Maddie whispered.

Greg turned to Cole. "Maddie told me you were out of the picture...that you wanted nothing to do with Noah."

"I didn't know about him—until she came to Yella last week and we reconnected."

"Reconnected?" Greg's soft eyes glanced at Cole before

settling on Maddie. "I see," he murmured at last, after reading her face.

She resented Cole for forcing this on her. The last thing she'd ever wanted to do was to stun Greg like this or to hurt him.

"Greg, it's too complicated to explain right now, but if you and I don't leave, we will lose our reservation."

"We're not that late. I think I'd like to hear what Mr. Coleman has to say about this complicated matter."

She placed a hand on Greg's sleeve. "No…."

"Maddie and I parted in a rather unpleasant way," Cole began. "I was unaware she was pregnant. When she called to tell me about Noah a year or so later, I was newly married, so I refused her calls…and her letters. Now that I know about Noah, I want to be part of his life full-time."

"Of course." Greg's hurt, thunderstruck tone intensified her guilt.

"While it may complicate things for the three of us, having his father in his life will be wonderful for Noah," Greg said.

Maddie's mouth went dry. She resented the way both men seemed to be making all the decisions as if her opinion didn't matter.

"So—are you free for lunch?" Greg demanded of Cole.

She shook her head. When Cole said he was, she could have kicked him.

"What do you say I bow out, and you take her instead?" Greg said to Cole. His firm tone held a schoolteacher-like edge that she'd never heard before.

"Greg?" she pleaded. "What are you doing?"

"Sounds to me like you and Cole have a lot to work out," Greg said.

"Let me explain!"

"Don't worry. If you still need me tonight, I'll babysit… like I promised."

Then, just like that, he was gone—seemingly out of her life—and she was alone with Cole, whose green eyes glittered with infuriating triumph.

"I'm glad that's settled. Now, will you agree to marry me?"

Twelve

The French bistro where Greg had made reservations was located in a discreet brick building just off Sixth Street in downtown Austin. The waitstaff was French, the food was fresh and authentic, and the softly lit, informal rooms with their lace curtains and their cut flowers in old French liquor bottles had a sweetly romantic air.

Not that Maddie felt the least bit romantic. What she felt was a burning fury that Cole was so determined to have his way that he didn't care who he crushed to get it.

Since the restaurant was so popular, the small rooms were crowded, even at one-thirty, and the two of them were jammed so tightly into a tiny corner booth that every time she moved her thigh brushed Cole's. Despite her anger, she blushed in response.

Sulkily, she ordered her usual *salade verte* while Cole cheerfully ordered a *croque-monsieur* for himself. When their food came, they ate in silence. Only after she'd finished chewing her last scrap of lettuce did Cole speak.

"What time's your all-important fundraiser?"

"Seven," she said, her voice low, tense and sullen.

"What time does Noah get out of his camp?"

"That's none—"

"What time?" His tone was harsh and deliberately calculated to intimidate her.

"Four. But I'm going to leave him in aftercare until nearly six because I've got a lot of work…"

"I want to meet him—before the fundraiser—so change your plans," Cole said. "You're going to pick him up at four and bring him to the house. I'll be waiting for you there."

"That would mean I'd have to leave the office at three-thirty."

"Then do it."

She met his eyes, intending to argue, but his face appeared to be carved in stone. "I have a meeting with a board member at three," she said.

"I suggest you show him my check. Then tell him there'll be more, a whole lot more, tonight at the fundraiser, but only if you keep me happy."

"I'm not letting you take over—"

"I'm not sure you have a choice," he said smoothly. "I can assure you that if you make me happy, you'll have the most successful fundraiser in My Sister's House's history, which you've indicated is crucial this year. Then you'll be able to keep your position for as long as you wish. But if you continue to fight me, not only will you risk losing your precious job, you could end up in an expensive custody battle that you might not win."

She flinched.

"So, back to this afternoon," he continued pleasantly. "If you're smart, and I think you are, you'll tell your board member I'm demanding another meeting with you after four. If you take off early, I promise you, my generosity will more than make up for those lost two hours in your office."

I mustn't let him do this to me! But for the life of her she couldn't figure out a way to stop him.

"I...I'll never marry you after this," she whispered defiantly.

"That's a battle for another day...or night," he said, smiling. "One I don't intend to lose."

Ignoring the way she tensed, he held up his hand and signaled the waiter for the check.

Thirteen

"Oh, man!" Noah shouted from the backseat of her car.

Filled with dread at the thought of Cole waiting for them at her house, Maddie took her eyes off the silver, tanklike SUV ahead of her to study Noah in her rearview mirror. His black head was lowered as he concentrated fiercely on the game he was playing on her cell phone. Glancing back at the SUV, she turned on the radio so she wouldn't dwell on Cole.

Five minutes later, when she turned onto their street, Noah let out a war whoop. "Cops! Oh, boy!" he shouted. "How come they're at our house? Hey, and there's Tristan!"

Tristan, who had carrot-red hair and Harry Potter glasses, was their new next-door neighbor and Noah's new best friend.

When she jerked the wheel toward the curb, Cole and Tristan, who'd obviously had time to bond, rushed toward them.

"Who's that?" Noah demanded as he eyed Cole suspiciously.

Standing tall beneath the flickering shade and brilliance of her huge oaks, Cole's carved features resembled those of a pagan god, harsh and ruthless but dangerously compelling.

"Just an old friend," she whispered in panic.

His hard eyes on Noah, Cole's large, tanned hands were clenched as he waited for them to get out.

She stared past him to the uniformed officers on her porch with false bravado. "What's going on here?"

"There's been a break-in. According to the police, there have been several in your neighborhood. Whoever did it broke a back window."

Just what she needed, she thought wearily as Cole knelt to Noah's level.

"Maybe when the officers finish, you and your friend Tristan here can help me board up the window," Cole said.

"To keep the bad guys out?" Noah said, beaming up at Cole with immense excitement.

"Yes."

"Cool," Noah said.

"I'm Cole. What's your name?"

"Noah. This is Tristan."

"I already met Tristan. In fact, he and I are planning to play some football later."

"Cool! Can I play, too?"

"You'd better believe it!"

"Cool!"

Introductions over, Noah and Tristan dashed up to the porch to watch the police do their work.

Cole stood up. "Good thing I was here to deal with the cops. You look exhausted. How can I help?"

She felt exhausted, both mentally and physically.

"I have the fundraiser to get through, as you well know," she said. "Not to mention whatever ordeal you intend to put me through tonight. Now on top of all that—a break-in."

"All I want is to marry you and take care of you and our son. That doesn't have to be an ordeal, you know. It could be a mutual pleasure."

She shook her head. "I don't see how."

"Looks like I'll have to show you," he said.

Before she knew what he intended or had time to steel herself not to respond, he pulled her to him and kissed her hard.

As always when in his embrace, she lost the ability to control herself or think coherently. His muscular body was rockhard and her softer figure melted against him. Her wanton pulse raced while flames lit her nerve endings with a hunger that reduced her to a primal, craven creature.

She knew what he wanted—what she wanted—but she was determined to fight it. She wouldn't let him break her heart as he'd done six years ago.

"Stop," she pleaded, even as her body trembled beneath his onslaught. His caressing fingers on her flesh made her blood run hot. "Not in front of Noah!"

He tensed, and she sensed his reluctance to do as she asked.

"For now," he whispered roughly, letting her go.

Shaken, too aware of Noah watching them, she hugged herself tightly.

For his part, Cole stepped back a few feet, as if removing himself from temptation.

Hell, Cole was stunned by how much fun he'd had tossing the football to his son and Tristan while Maddie dealt with the cops. He'd enjoyed helping the kids nail a board over her window, as well, while a flock of grackles fought noisy battles in the highest limbs of her oak trees.

How long had he spent hanging out with the boys while Maddie got ready for the fundraiser—a mere hour and twenty minutes? And already paternal pride swelled inside him. He'd liked Maddie watching them from the windows; he'd liked making himself useful to her while enjoying the boys. Even in this brief time he'd had with his son and the mother of his son, he was surer than ever that he wanted to be a permanent part of their lives, all the time, not just for weekends and holidays.

Noah, who was as bright as a new copper penny, was quirky and cute. He'd shown Cole the Shining Star medal he'd won at school and had liked it when Cole had teasingly started calling him Shining Star.

The boy had a good arm. He could catch passes, too, and run like the wind. Funny how in such a short time, Cole already felt like his father.

He had to find a way to make Maddie see they could be a family.

The fundraiser was under way in the ballroom of one of Austin's fanciest hotels overlooking Town Lake. Shifting masses of elegantly dressed people danced, drank and chattered as Maddie seized the opportunity to slip outside while Cole was surrounded by board members.

Maddie wanted to stay furious at him forever for the high-handed way he'd treated her ever since he'd stormed into Austin. In one afternoon, he had rid her of Greg and made significant advances toward winning his son's affections. Tonight, with her on his arm, he'd easily worked the crowd, seducing most of the shelter's board members and important donors with smiles and witty remarks.

Maybe she hadn't sold as many tickets this year, but Cole had dazzled everybody who mattered when he'd produced a second check that was more than enough to pay the shelter's expenses for a year...and ensure her job.

Leaning against the railing, she stared at the shimmering reflections in the dark lake. He was outmaneuvering her by making himself useful. He'd helped straighten her house; he'd called her alarm company and arranged for them to rewire the window as soon as she had the glass replaced.

The music stopped. When Cole's voice came from behind her, she shivered.

"There you are," he said. "I've been looking for you everywhere."

"It's the first minute I've had to myself all day."

The music in the ballroom started again.

"Dance with me," he whispered against her ear.

When his arm slid around her waist, her heart began to beat to the seductive pulse of the music. Then he swept her around and around in a series of expertly executed turns. As they whirled, the brilliantly lit buildings of downtown Austin flashed by. Soon, she was breathless and feeling lightheartedly reckless.

He made her feel young and almost happy. She'd never gone to prom or done much dancing. She wanted the music to go on forever, to dance with him always.

Was he good at everything? Oh, why did it have to feel so treacherously wonderful to be in his arms?

"You look fabulous," he murmured even as his hot eyes scorched her skin.

His gaze admired her body in her tight red dress before he snugged her closer. Then the hard feel of his muscular body rocked her senses.

"Don't hold me so close," she whispered as she fought a losing battle against physical arousal.

"I want you," he murmured, ravaging the softness of her mouth. "Just as you want me. Why did you wear a dress that skims your body like a second skin if you didn't want to tempt me?"

She flushed guiltily. When she'd selected the dress tonight, she'd known she should have chosen something less revealing, but yes, she'd wanted to entice him.

At some point, they stopped dancing. When he lowered his mouth to devour hers, she didn't fight because she didn't have the strength. She wanted him, more than she'd ever wanted anything in her life. Within dizzying seconds, he had her weak and clinging breathlessly.

"We're going home, baby," he said.

"The fundraiser isn't over. I'm still on duty."

"I'll make your excuses," he said in that supremely confident male way that could so annoy her when she wasn't melting with desire.

Five minutes later, he'd made their excuses and they had exited the ballroom. Arms linked, he rushed her to his truck, which he drove with one hand while his other closed over hers with a fierce urgency that had her blood tingling.

Only when they were standing beneath the glare of her porch light did she come back to her senses.

"Good night," she said without unlocking her door. "And thank you—for the check." When he didn't kiss her goodnight and go, she said, "I can't ask you to come in. Greg's here, and Noah...wouldn't understand."

"No way am I letting you and Noah stay here alone after that break-in. I can sleep on the couch."

"No!"

Then Greg opened the front door, and Cole stepped past her into the living room.

"Noah's awake," Greg said. "He had a dream about some witches in his closet, so I've been reading to him."

"I'll take over from here," Cole said.

"No," she began, but she was talking to his back. He was already striding down the hall.

Too tired to fight him, she thanked Greg. After he left, she went to the closet and pulled out a set of sheets and towels and two pillows and tossed them onto the couch.

Determined not to surrender to Cole, at least not tonight,

she went to Noah and kissed his brow, promising that her kisses were magic and would keep the witches away.

Feeling too flustered to look at Cole, she crossed the hall to her own room and closed herself inside.

"One more story! Please! Please!"

"Good night, Shining Star," Cole said as he closed their third book. "Sleep tight." He leaned down and kissed Noah gently on the top of his head.

"If I close my eyes, would you stay here and guard the closet?"

"There aren't any witches in that closet. Remember how we just checked."

"The green one's not there all the time. Just sometimes," Noah stated matter-of-factly. "She looks sort of like an ugly, mean frog. She has snaky hair and big orange eyes. She comes up through a little hole in the floor. Then she grows bigger and bigger, while I grow smaller and smaller. When she's crazy huge, she sneaks out...." Noah broke off, but his enormous eyes remained fixed on his closet.

"It was just a dream. Try not to think about her, okay?"

Cole lay down beside his son and put his arm around him. Shining Star's black lashes lowered heavily to his tanned cheeks. It was amazing how calm and peaceful he looked when he was sleepy.

"Do you think my mommy's pretty?" Noah whispered drowsily.

"Yes," Cole admitted. "I do."

But Noah didn't hear him because he had succumbed to sleep.

Intending to stay with Noah for only a few minutes, Cole loosened his tie and the top button of his shirt. But the bed was soft and Noah was warm and cuddly. Within seconds, he was asleep, too.

Fourteen

In her own room, Maddie unzipped her sparkly red dress and stepped out of it. Naked, she stood in the moonlight, a strange restlessness consuming her. Burning for Cole despite her better judgment, she willed him to come to her. Even as her heart thundered, the house remained silent. Finally, she grew tired of standing all by herself in the silvery light and lay down.

Cole was everything she shouldn't want. He was part of the miserable past she wanted to forget. He was arrogant and determined to force her to agree to his terms. How could a marriage to such a man succeed once their physical attraction died?

Slowly, her eyelids fluttered and she drifted uneasily to sleep. At some point she began to dream.

She was a little girl again, riding horses, happy she could roam far from the trailer and her mother. The trees were emerald-green, the sky a vivid blue. But no matter how glorious her ride, eventually she had to go home, and when she did, the faceless monster was there, barring the door when she entered, grabbing her wrists when she tried to run. She knew that if she didn't get away, he would do the same horrible things to her he'd done before, so she clawed and kicked, but as always he bore her to the ground, and she began to scream.

Her own ear-splitting cries dragged her unhappily to consciousness. When she opened her eyes, moonlight and shadow played tricks on her imagination, causing her to sense a presence in her house even before she heard heavy footsteps in the hall.

Vernon? Was he here?

A mind-numbing fear gripped her. Scrambling across her bed toward the window, she searched for the lock while screaming for all she was worth.

Cole leaped to his feet at Maddie's first piercing scream and was sprinting down the dark hall before her second. When he opened her door, she threw herself behind her bed, where she crouched in the moonlight.

"Vernon?"

Cole's heart shredded. "No! It's just me—Cole."

"Cole?" Her dull, glazed eyes stared at him uncomprehendingly.

"I was with Noah, asleep down the hall," he said. "You're safe. There's nothing to be afraid of."

"You don't know him. You don't know what he's capable of!"

As Cole crossed the room and sank down beside her, he was afraid he did. A terrible understanding took hold even before he pulled her shaking body into his arms. Had that bastard raped her?

"There, there," he murmured.

"Hold me!" she whispered, her intake of breath sharp as she clutched handfuls of his shirt to draw him closer.

"Hey, hey, everything's okay." But it wasn't. Not if his worst fears were correct. He wasn't blameless if what he feared had happened. Far from it.

"No…"

He brushed her hair out of her face. "You've had a bad dream. That's all." He continued to murmur to her soothingly even as he cradled her in his arms, stroking her face and neck while his own conscience attacked him.

Instead of being so hell-bent on protecting his own reputation, he should have protected her.

"Just hold me, please," she breathed, sensing none of his inner conflict. She hung on to him with a desperation that made him ache for what she must have suffered at Vernon's hands.

Why hadn't he seen that he should have done more to protect her? Why hadn't the town seen that she was young and vulnerable and living in a dangerous situation? Suddenly he hated Yella, hated every individual who lived there who'd played a part in this, himself most of all. They'd sat in judgment of her and thus had left her defenseless. She'd hardly been more than a child.

"When…I heard you, I thought Vernon was really here. My dream was so real…I could almost smell him." She began to shudder uncontrollably.

Cole caressed the nape of her neck. "He's in prison, right?"

"Huntsville," she murmured thankfully.

"So, it's okay. You're safe. You're with me. I swear I won't let him or anybody else hurt you ever again."

"You promise?"

"Promise." And he meant it. With every fiber of his being, he meant it. If only she'd give him a second chance, he wouldn't let her down again.

His brow grazed hers affectionately. Then he pressed his nose to her nose, but somehow when he did it, their lips clumsily touched. His blood flamed. And because he felt so guilty, he hated the lust that drove him. But when he tried to pull away, she clutched him even closer.

She was so damn sexy with her huge eyes, her voluptuous breasts crushed against his chest. He inhaled the mingled scents of her shampoo and perfume and grew even harder. She was so soft and feminine, so ripe. When he felt her nipples tighten against his chest, he caught his breath.

It would be easy to slide her nightgown up and strip off his slacks, easy to take her when she was so open to him like this. But he hated himself too much for what he'd let happen, for what he'd willingly ignored. He didn't deserve her trust or her love. He had to process what had happened and deal with his guilt. Somehow he had to get it all straight in his mind.

But when he would have withdrawn his mouth from hers, she clung, kissing him desperately.

"Stay with me?" she begged in such a seductive tone that his whole body jerked with fresh need.

"Not tonight," he said hoarsely.

"Please...."

"Not after your nightmare about Vernon."

Not after he'd bullied her all day, not when she was scared and vulnerable. "You go back to sleep," he murmured gently. "I'll be right down the hall—if you need me."

Even as his heart pounded, he forced himself to push her away and stand up.

"Cole?" Her quick, sharp breaths sounded truly panicked at the thought of being alone.

"I'll be on the couch," he rasped.

Unable to sleep without Cole holding her close, Maddie counted sheep. Then she counted her rushing heartbeats.

When she still couldn't sleep, she got up, paced awhile and then went to the bathroom where she filled a glass with water. Not that any of it helped still her clamoring senses. More restless than ever, she lay back down in the dark.

She remembered Cole's flushed cheeks, the heavy glint of desire in his eyes. He'd wanted her, too; she was sure of it. But he'd been conflicted.

Curious, and feeling shamelessly needy, she arose and padded down the hall to her living room where she found him sprawled on the couch, his dark eyes wide and glued to the ceiling.

"Can't sleep?" she teased.

"Out!" he growled huskily.

"Don't make me beg."

"Can't a guy ever say no?"

Bending over him, she slid her hands under his shirt, feathering her fingertips through the crisp, dark curls that covered the broad expanse of his chest. At his quick gasp of excitement, she seized her advantage, tracing her hands blindly down the muscular length of him, kneading him until she worked her way to the huge bulge of denim between his muscular thighs.

"I thought so," she murmured, closing her fingers over him and stroking purposefully. "I want you naked," she growled into his ear.

He groaned savagely in protest. "Maddie!"

"I want you," she whispered. "But not here." She waited a beat. "My room." She shot him a flirtatious wink and then bolted, flying down the hall, only to be terrified when he did not follow her immediately. She needn't have worried. Two seconds later, they were naked on her bed with her door locked. He had her flat on her back underneath him while he kissed her lips with hot, urgent passion that tore her soul. In an equal frenzy, she kissed him back.

"We've got to slow it down," he whispered.

"No! I need you! Everything you have to give me! Quick. Fast. Hard. I don't want to wait. I need it. I want to erase all the ugliness." She had to erase Vernon for good.

"Then we're at cross-purposes."

With softer kisses and featherlight touches, he slowed the pace and changed the mood. With each tender kiss that he placed on her mouth, on her throat, on each of her nipples and in the center of that damp nest of dark curls between her legs, he made love to her with a reverence she'd never imagined possible.

"Next time I'll protect you," he promised.

"I know."

She wanted him to take her so she could feel his strength and possessive power in every cell of her being, to know that she was safe in his arms. But he lingered over her, loving her slowly, which caused her passion to build to a frenzy.

He placed his lips between her thighs and caressed her with his tongue until her whole body felt on fire.

"My turn," she teased when he would have taken her, "to torture you with my lips and tongue."

She took him into her mouth, sucking gently, teasing him at first and then adoring him. In the blaze of his building rapture, the last vestiges of her nightmare were consumed. There was only Cole and the exquisite, mind-numbing delight she found in his arms.

Suddenly there was a ferocity in them both as he tore free of her mouth and pulled her underneath him and slid inside her.

"Yes," she whispered. "Yes!"

He thrust and she arched, their bodies moving in perfect accord as the world tipped like a crazy top and spun faster. Then they tensed as passion washed over them.

After the explosion, she lay in his arms and wondered if two people like them, from such different worlds, had a chance together.

She awoke to a rosy dawn and noisy grackles, to Cole's hard arms wrapping her with a fierce possessiveness. She felt new and different and yet unable to trust her emotions.

"You look like a little girl when you sleep—a little girl who's every bit as innocent as Noah."

"Not Yella's wanton, wicked bad girl?"

"Don't ever call yourself that again," he muttered fiercely, pulling her closer. "You're the mother of my child. You're going to be my wife."

"Oh, really? What's got you so cocky this morning?"

"How quickly we forget," he said.

"I don't remember accepting any of your arrogant proposals."

"Do you remember the great sex?"

"And that gave you all sorts of ideas about our relationship?"

"If the sex didn't put you in the mood to accept my proposal, maybe I'll have to give you a repeat performance."

"That would be lovely, under different circumstances, but I've got work."

"It's early yet."

"Noah's going to wake up any minute. I don't want to have to explain you."

Instead of arguing, he got up and strode into the bathroom while she lay back and admired his muscular body. After he turned on the shower, he stuck his dark, sleep-tousled head out the door and shot her a grin. "Water's warm. Feels good. I could use some company."

"I really shouldn't. I'm tender as all get-out."

"And we took it so slowly…"

"But we did it so many times."

"We did, didn't we? No wonder I woke up in such a cocky mood. What if I promise to be gentle?"

When she joined him, she kissed him so fiercely he grabbed her hands and held them over her head. Pushing her back against the slick, wet tile he took her hard and fast as the steaming water blasted her. When it was over, she clung to him breathlessly, thinking herself a worse wanton than her mother.

The man didn't love her. He probably never would. And still she wanted him.

Stepping out of the shower, he left her to ponder all the reasons he was wrong for her.

While she dressed, he scrambled eggs and made coffee for them in her kitchen.

"I'm impressed. I didn't know you could cook," she said when she entered the kitchen.

"It's called survival. I can do eggs. I can do toast, bacon, burgers, steaks. I'm afraid that's about it."

She laughed.

After they finished eating, she cleared the plates. "I can't believe Noah's sleeping this late. What did you do to wear him out?"

"Worrying about that witch in his closet wore him out." He paused. "About your nightmare—"

She whitened. "I don't want to talk about it."

"I know." His hand closed over her wrist. "But I need you to sit down and tell me all about Vernon." Something dark in his voice made her suspect he'd already guessed the worst.

The last thing she wanted was to mar the beauty of their first shared morning together by reliving what Vernon had done to her.

"I've got to go to work," she pleaded. "Lots of threads are

hanging loose after the fundraiser. I still have checks in my purse, including yours."

"Sit down, Maddie."

At his fierce expression, she slowly sank back into her chair.

"What did he do to you? I want the truth, the whole truth, and if you don't tell me, I'll find your mother and so help me, I'll force it out of her. If that doesn't work I'll go to Huntsville…"

"No."

"Then why don't you make it easy for me?" He paused. "I don't believe you ever intended to leave me for him. He hurt you, didn't he? You weren't ever in love with him. You left because he hurt you? And because I wasn't there for you when you tried to call me?"

Barely able to breathe because of the fist clamped around her heart, she looked away.

He leaned closer. "Tell me, damn it. Did he do what I think?"

When hot tears of shame leaked out of her eyes, she brushed at them frantically. "I told myself I'd never cry because of him again."

"Just tell me!"

"My mother didn't believe me, so why should you?"

"Did that bastard rape you?"

A desperate sob rose in her throat. She wanted to deny it. If only she could reclaim her innocence somehow, but he saw; he knew.

"My mother said it was all my fault."

"The hell it was."

"I—I tried to stop him. I really did."

"I know, sweetheart. I believe you," he whispered, his voice as agonized as hers. "Go on…."

"But he was so strong. Even though I had a black eye and

a cut lip, my mother refused to believe me. She said I seduced him to be mean to her. When she threw me out, I didn't know who to turn to or where to go, so I called you...and got your mother, who told me how cheap I was."

He shuddered. After an endless pause, he managed, "And then you went to Miss Jennie?"

"Yes. She was wonderful."

"Thank God." He reached across the table and took her hand, pressing her slim fingers hard. "I should have guessed the truth."

"How could you?"

"I don't know, but I shouldn't have been so wrapped up in my own damn ego and pain, so furious and hurt that you could leave me for Vernon that I didn't question your mother or the gossip. I drove you away. I was as bad as everybody else in Yella—worse, because I should have known better since I really knew you."

"I felt so ashamed..."

"I'm the one who should be ashamed. It's a good thing he's locked up, or I'd have to find him and make him pay."

"No." She began to shake. "Then they'd lock you in a cage, too. I don't want that." She paused. "When Noah was around one, Vernon came to Austin. He told me that if I ever went to the police and told them the truth, he'd kill me. You see, he was on parole at the time. He said any infraction could put him away for good. He put his hands around my neck and squeezed so tightly I couldn't breathe...just for a few seconds, just to give me a taste of what it would be like to die, he said. He said Noah would be raised by foster mothers who'd be worse than my mother. After that, I was scared of everything, of my own shadow. Even after he went back to prison for raping another girl, I was still scared. That's when the nightmares started."

"If only you'd called me."

"I did," she reminded him. "You hung up on me because you'd just married Lizzie."

"Oh, God. My sorry treatment of you…"

"It doesn't matter."

"The hell it doesn't! It will always matter. In my own way I was worse than Vernon. If I'd claimed you as my girlfriend from the beginning, maybe he would have been afraid to touch you because of the high-and-mighty Coleman name. Did I ever go to your home once? Take an interest in what you had to deal with there? Warn him to leave you alone or he'd have to deal with me? No, I left you powerless, defenseless. *Oh, it matters.* It damn sure matters."

She looked into his eyes and saw everything she needed to see. He believed her.

"You were in college."

"I was old enough to know better," he said, his low tone filled with self-loathing.

"I blamed myself, too. My mother said I'd been asking for it for weeks, dressing sexily to put her down and make her feel old…but I'd only been trying to be pretty for you. I should have been more aware of how I affected Vernon."

"It wasn't your fault. Get that through your head."

"It wasn't yours either," she said, rising from her chair because she wanted to touch him and to be held.

Slowly she slid her hands across his broad chest and laid her head against his shoulder. When his lips brushed her forehead and he pulled her even closer, happiness filled her. His dark head bent over hers. Then he lifted her chin and kissed her gently on the lips. Wrapping her arms around his neck, she inhaled his scent and savored the muscular texture of his body.

She was sighing when the door behind them banged, and Noah hurled himself into the kitchen.

"Can I have pancakes for break—" When he saw his

mother wrapped in Cole's arms, his eyes widened and his bottom lip stuck out.

Stunned, she sprang free of Cole and rushed to her son. Kneeling beside him, she said, "Darling. Mommy's late for work, so we need to get you dressed and ready for school."

Noah stared at Cole. "What's he still doing here? Why was he kissing you?"

"I said we have to get you dressed and ready for—"

"How come you let him sleep over and you never let Greg?"

"Honey, Greg and I broke up yesterday."

"Because of him?" Noah waited. Then he tore free of her and crossed his arms over his thin chest.

"We'll...we'll have to talk about all this later."

"I don't want to talk about it. I don't want to go to school." Noah turned and marched huffily back to his room.

"Do you want me to try to talk to him?" Cole asked.

She shook her head. "I'm afraid everything's happened too fast. I should have prepared him. I think you'd better go," she whispered. "He and I need some time, just the two of us, to work this out. I'll call you."

"No. We've got to tell him who I am—now."

"Not this morning!"

"The sooner we tell him the less confused he'll be."

"You never stop."

"Not when I know what has to be done." He turned and walked down the hall after Noah.

"Cole—no!" By the time she caught him, he was already inside Noah's room.

"I know how you feel," he was saying to their son, "because this is all happening so fast."

"I—I don't understand," Noah said sulkily.

"I'm here because I'm your father. I know it's a shock because I just learned that fact myself."

When Noah's huge eyes glanced at her for confirmation, she nodded.

"I want to take care of you and your mother. I want to marry your mother. I want us to be a family."

When Noah stared at him, Maddie wondered what was going on in his head.

"You could have waited," she said when Cole came back out of Noah's room.

"No. I couldn't. I've already lost six years, and so has he. I want to go to bed with you every night knowing he's in the house and to wake up beside you every morning like we did today."

At the memory of how sweet he'd been last night and this morning, she let out a long sigh. In spite of his pushing so hard, a part of her wanted those things, too.

"So, I've made a little progress?"

"Maybe a little," she admitted.

"Good." Cole pulled her into his arms and gave her a quick kiss. "Go see Noah in case he's more upset than he seemed," he whispered. "I'll see myself out."

Noah, however, was dressed and ready for school. He'd taken the news in stride and was willing to talk to Cole when he called later that night. And because he was, her own objections and doubts lessened.

Maybe Cole was right. Maybe their marriage could work.

Fifteen

One long week later, Cole checked his watch as he rushed up Maddie's sidewalk. He'd made it. It was 5:30 on the dot. He'd even managed to buy her a long-stemmed yellow rose from a homeless vendor on a busy street corner.

As soon as he'd completed his well, Cole had jumped in his truck and driven straight back to Austin.

Not that he was sure he'd find Maddie home yet. The traffic had been so bad on the south side of the city, it seemed very likely she'd be stuck somewhere. But before he was half-way up her sidewalk, her front door opened and she ran toward him.

God, she was beautiful in her sexy blue sundress. When he swept her into his arms, her brilliant smile warmed him as nothing else could. He caught the sweet fragrance of gardenias before he crushed her close.

"My well came in."

"Congratulations!"

"How'd your week go?" he murmured, handing her the rose that was a little worse for wear due to the Texas heat.

Taking the golden blossom, she clung to him. "I missed you," she admitted huskily. "Craving you is beginning to feel like an addiction."

He sighed. "I'm just as hooked as you are."

Even though they'd spoken over the phone, being away from her hadn't been easy. She'd tentatively accepted his proposal, and they were trying to figure out how to share their lives. For some reason she was determined that he shouldn't cut himself off from everybody in Yella because of her, and she'd offered to come back to Yella to face both the gossips and her demons.

"You've been through enough there," he'd said.

"We need to give your community a chance to accept me now," she'd said bravely.

"I don't care whether they do or not."

"But I do—not only for your sake, but for Noah's. Your mother lives in Yella. It would be nice if Noah had at least one grandmother."

Because of Maddie's insistence, Cole had already told friends and family the truth about their relationship and the truth about Noah's paternity. They had understood his being infatuated with her in the past and getting her pregnant, but they didn't approve of him being seriously involved with her again. Everybody except Adam warned him to stay away from her.

Not wanting to think about other people's prejudices, Cole pushed a long strand of black hair back from Maddie's face. "Where's Noah?"

"At Tristan's. Watching a movie. Which means we have a little time alone. He'll be home soon, but then they're doing a sleepover, which I planned so we could enjoy—"

"Our own sleepover," Cole finished.

"Exactly." Blue flames lit her violet eyes as he nipped her bottom lip seductively. When he kissed her harder, he felt her body heat against his. He loved how responsive she was.

"Here. I've got something special for you," he said, pulling a little black velvet box from his shirt pocket. Feeling embarrassed, he sank to one knee. "I'm afraid I should have thought of a more original and romantic way to propose."

Taking the box and opening it, she laughed, gasping with awed pleasure when she saw the huge diamond. "Wow!"

"So, will you marry me?" he whispered, looking up at her.

She knelt to his level, her fingertips skimming his cheek. "Yes. *Yes!*"

He took her hand and slid his ring onto her finger.

When she turned her hand to admire it, the diamond flashed. "I definitely can't wear this to work. I'd blind everybody. Or get my finger cut off walking across the parking lot."

"Well, wear it whenever you feel like it."

"Like when I come back to Yella."

"I've been thinking that maybe people there need a little more time to adjust to the idea of you and me."

"So, you've told them about us and they warned you away."

He was silent.

She studied his grave expression. "Have they said things to make you ashamed of me?"

"No. I just don't like giving them the chance to hurt you again."

"I need to go back and face the past, for myself as much as for us. I've been running from shadows for far too long. I gave one incident too much power over me. Since I told you about Vernon, I haven't had another nightmare. It's like this huge emotional weight just lifted off me. I don't understand it. For the first time in years I feel free. And good about myself. I think that if I faced other demons, I might feel even better."

"I'm so glad."

"Maybe I need to convince myself you'll really stand up for me, as well. So, I've made arrangements to get off work and come to Yella for a week or two. I guess we'll find out if we both have the guts to take this thing to the next level. Only you have to promise me that if it turns out one of us doesn't think it'll work, you'll let me go."

He wasn't about to do that. "What about Noah?"

"You'll always be his father. No matter what, I want you to play an active role in his life. It's just that we might not marry…"

"I can't go there."

"What if we both realize marriage isn't the best solution?"

"I refuse to believe that."

It was nearly noon, and Maddie's brow was wrinkled from so much paperwork. She was looking forward to taking a break before her lunch meeting when her phone buzzed. Hoping it was Cole phoning to say he'd arrived safely back in Yella, she blushed as memories of the wild sex they'd indulged in the night before bombarded her. He'd possessed her in every possible way, in every possible position—on her bed, on the floor, against her wall. On her bedroom desk. And she'd reveled in it like the wanton she was reputed to be.

"Hello," she whispered a little too huskily.

"I have a lady in the waiting area to see you, Miss Gray," Lucy, her secretary, said.

"Oh."

"I can't place her, and she refuses to give her name. She looks important."

Maddie smoothed her hair and glanced at her watch. Maddie understood wealthy donors. So much for taking a quick break.

"Show her in."

Seconds later, Hester Coleman, her black silk suit as severe as her face, stood before Maddie's desk. Gloved hands knotted, Hester stared down the length of her long, aquiline nose, her gaze sweeping both Maddie and her tiny office with its stacks of papers and folders on the floor.

In her rush to stand, Maddie knocked over the bud vase with Cole's single yellow rose in it, spilling water onto the stack of envelopes she'd just sealed for mailing.

"Oh, dear." Quickly she set the vase and the rose upright and lifted dripping envelopes out of a puddle of water. Mopping at her desk with one of the paper towels she kept nearby, she attempted a smile.

"May I sit down?" Hester said.

"Why…of course." Nodding nervously in the direction of the chair opposite her desk, Maddie sank back down in her own.

"I know about the child you're using to blackmail Cole."

Maddie went hot with indignation. "I would never use Noah in such a way!"

"How effective to tell Cole now…when he's free again. How else could a girl like you get him to consider marrying you? You don't care what you cost him, do you?"

Maddie did care. "Does Cole know you're here?"

"That's hardly the point. He may be a fool, but I'm not. I'm here to offer you a generous settlement, in cash, if you refuse to marry him."

With her rage and hurt simmering just beneath the surface, Maddie stood up. "This interview is over. I want you to leave my office."

"What? You can't throw *me* out!" Outraged, Hester arose. "When you've cut him off from everybody he's known and loved his entire life, how long do you think you'll continue to fascinate him? He'll resent you," Hester cried. "Eventually he'll leave you."

"Maybe." Maddie picked up her purse. "But you're risking as much as I am. You have a grandson. Do you want to lose him? Do you want to be cut out of his life forever? Is that what you really want?"

Color flamed in Hester's cheeks. "No, but whatever sorrows I might be experiencing as a grandmother, my real distress has to do with my son for becoming involved with a woman who will ruin his life. If you were any kind of mother, you would understand."

Maddie, who hadn't been able to eat more than a couple of saltine crackers after Hester left, had felt so weak and shaken she'd barely been able to function for the rest of the afternoon. Her anger and sense of injustice ate at her. Indeed, she was so upset she made a mess of every project she touched. Finally, she grew so frustrated with herself for letting the woman's words get to her, she went home early.

Once home, she took her phone off the hook and tortured herself by replaying the older woman's vicious looks and cruel slights in her mind. Was Hester right about Maddie's background making her unfit to be Cole's wife? Would their marriage cut him off from everybody he knew and loved? He had said he thought they should live in Austin, so the past wouldn't cloud their future. But she knew what Coleman's Landing meant to him.

After a miserable hour spent beating up on herself for no crime other than having been born who she was, she dragged herself out of the depths and reconnected her telephone. When Cole called five minutes later to ask about her day, she didn't mention Hester's visit. Instead, she gave him the dates for her upcoming visit to Yella.

"Maybe we should put that off and just enjoy each other for a while."

She sensed his hesitation and doubt. He'd been sweet and

understanding when she'd told him about Vernon. But would he fight for her? Did he truly believe in her?

Or did he just want Noah?

Sixteen

Cole looked up from his desk just as his mother's Lincoln pulled up to Coleman's Landing in a cloud of dust. He got up slowly and strode outside to greet her, letting the screen door bang behind him. She'd been on a tear ever since Maddie and Noah had moved in with Miss Jennie for Maddie's visit. When his mother frowned, he knew he was in for it.

"It's hot. I could do with an iced soda," she said coolly when he met her at the door holding a cup of coffee.

He led her inside and brought a soda to the den where she waited for him. "Why did you drive over here when you could have called more easily?" he asked.

"Because I can't stand the way you flaunt your relationship with Jesse Ray's girl so publicly, Cole."

"Maddie's my fiancée, Mother."

"I'm sick of everybody telling me where they've seen her and that gaudy ring you gave her. Sick of the way people are laughing behind your back."

"You've got a lot of influence on the women in this town. Tell them you won't listen to another bad thing about Maddie, and a lot of them will shut up."

Cole hated the way his mother and the people in the town acted toward Maddie, lifting their noses and staring at her coldly, even when she was on his arm and Noah was with them. It was as if they were more against her than ever—just because he planned to marry her. He'd had words with nearly everybody in town. "Maddie is an educated woman who spends her life trying to help the less fortunate."

"I have no doubt about her ability to relate to such people. After all, she's an inferior herself."

"Adam likes her."

"Because he's jealous of you and wants to bring you down to his level. He sees that by marrying her, you'll do just that." Her eyes narrowed. "Besides, Adam's a man."

"What's that supposed to mean?"

"It means he probably finds her attractive…in that base sort of way men find women like her attractive. If you don't watch them, they'll end up in bed together."

Bright, hot anger flared inside him. "I respect her more than I respect the people who are gossiping about her—and that includes you!"

"Because she's using sex and that child to hook you. She'll use the same appeal on Adam and on every other man she meets. Did you know he drops by Miss Jennie's nearly every afternoon to see her?"

"He's doing that to show his support for me." But Cole's gut clenched as he remembered how Maddie had slept with him and then sneaked downstairs to get her letters. How far could he really trust her? Trust either of them?

"Be careful what you say about her, Mother." His doubts made his voice harsh.

"I saw Adam's truck at Miss Jennie's when I drove over

here." She arose. "Enough. I've done my duty. Don't come running to me when you find her in some other man's bed."

"If that's all, I've got work."

He hated himself when he didn't go back to the stack of papers on his desk after she stormed out his front door. Instead, he drove straight to Miss Jennie's, where the sight of Adam's truck parked out front made him go hot with fury. Instead of knocking on the front door, he stomped around to the back where he found Maddie, her face rapt as she stared up at Adam. Not caring that Bessie Mueller was probably watching, Maddie leaned forward to catch whatever Adam was telling her.

"Maddie! Adam!" Cole called.

As the pair sprang apart, Bessie's window shade fell.

Maddie smiled guilelessly as she ran toward Cole. "Adam's been playing football with Noah," she said.

"Noah sure can pass a mean football," Adam said. "But hey, I've got to get back to work—so I can rest from all the running outside in the heat. Your kid's fast." With an easy grin, he tipped his Stetson and strode past Cole.

Maddie watched him until he vanished behind the house. "Your brother's so nice."

Tension made a muscle tick in Cole's jaw. "I hear he comes by nearly every day."

"Noah looks forward to his visits. At least he's on our side and trying to show people he supports us."

Cole was careful to keep his voice neutral. "I'm not sure that's how the town sees it."

"What do you mean?"

"Never mind. Where is Noah?"

"Inside. Playing a computer game." She paused. "What's the matter? Did something happen?"

"My mother came over to tell me people are talking about you and Adam."

Her expression darkened. "And she made you doubt me. So you came over here because…because you thought maybe I was as bad as they say I am?"

"No!"

Her brows knitted. "You still don't trust me, do you?"

"I didn't like hearing about you spending time with somebody else, even my brother. He and I haven't had the easiest relationship. He resents being the bastard son, so that makes him resent *me* at times."

"You don't trust him either?"

"No, that's not what I'm saying." Then why was it suddenly so hard to meet her gaze as she studied him?

"Cole, let's get something clear. I enjoy your brother's company…as a friend. He's the only person besides Miss Jennie and a few of her elderly friends who've been at all supportive of me while I've been here. Several men have dropped by but…they—"

"They hit on you?" She didn't deny it. "Damn it. Tell me who they are, so I can deal with them." He let out a low curse. "For the life of me I can't see why it is so all-fired important to you to stay here and expose yourself to more unjustified criticism by a bunch of dirty-minded gossips."

"Maybe you're right. Maybe I was wrong to come back here. As a kid, I had a fantasy. I used to hope that if people here saw that you cared about me, well, they'd finally accept me."

"When are you going to figure out they don't matter? You're kind and hardworking. You've accomplished a lot. All that matters is that you and I are trying to make a life together for the sake of Noah. We can live in Austin."

"I know. And we will. But Coleman's Landing is your ranch. I want you to be able to come here whenever you like or need to and enjoy it without worrying about me. I want you to be able to bring Noah here, and for Noah to feel safe and accepted."

"The ranch is just a place." He wrapped his arms around her and kissed her hard. She turned into him and clung with a desperation that drove out his doubts, at least temporarily.

"All my life I've wanted to be accepted and loved. Even here. I'm just so afraid that the past and these people will find a way to make you regret marrying me."

"That's not going to happen. I'm not going to let it happen. When are you ever going to learn that other people's opinions don't matter all that much?"

"That's easy for you to say, since you've always enjoyed their good opinions."

Holding her close made his breath quicken. She'd been baring her soul, and suddenly all he wanted was her naked. He needed to make love to her so he could focus on what mattered instead of the town's vicious lies about her. "Hey," he murmured, "I was wondering if you think we could sneak off for a swim? Just the two of us?"

Her sparkling gaze lifted teasingly to his. "I'd have to ask Miss Jennie to watch Noah."

"Do it."

"Can we please get chocolate pudding for our picnic with Cole?" Noah asked as Maddie pushed their grocery cart down the aisle past a row of boxes of instant pudding.

"Pudding is not on Cole's list."

Noah scowled as he struggled to read a label on a box.

"However...he did put down chocolate chip cookies."

"But can we have pudding, too? Please, can we?" Noah's bright green eyes pleaded.

"Okay," she said, smiling. "One. Just pick one."

"Oh, boy!" Noah leaned closer to the puddings so he could concentrate on the words and pictures.

Maddie caught a whiff of all-too-familiar whiskey breath and looked up in alarm.

"Is that your brat?"

The woman who'd spoken was shuffling clumsily toward them. When she burst into rough laughter, Maddie felt an icy chill race down her spine. Kneeling, Maddie clutched Noah closer.

Caught off balance, he dropped a box of pudding and sent it sliding down the aisle straight at the woman.

"Hey, my pudding!" he cried and would have run after it if Maddie hadn't held him fast.

"You're a bad child!" the woman scolded. "Just like your mother was."

"Pick another pudding," Maddie ordered through clenched teeth even as she stood up and whirled her cart around to escape.

But the woman, who was faster, lurched toward Maddie and seized her cart. "You think you're too good to speak to your own mother, do you? Because that fool Coleman gave you a big rock and says he's marryin' you? Well, you're not, girlie. You're no different than me. You should hear what people around here are saying about you. They say you snuck around…chasing him when you were a girl 'cause he was rich. They say you lucked out…havin' 'is baby, keeping it a secret, so as you could make him pay for it later. If they play, make them pay. That's what I taught you, baby girl, didn't I?"

Maddie was desperate to get Noah away from this woman, who was kin to her biologically but in no other way. Several shoppers, who had frozen to watch their embarrassing exchange, were standing together in a tight little clump, their mouths hanging open. No doubt they'd heard every ugly word and believed every ugly lie and would repeat them to anyone who would listen.

Feeling the weight of their contemptuous gazes, Maddie's

mouth went dry. But it was her mother she most wanted to escape. Feeling queasy, it was all she could do not to abandon her grocery cart, grab Noah and race out of the store.

But she wouldn't cower or give any of them the satisfaction of seeing how devastated she was, so, instead, she notched her chin higher and drew herself up straighter. Shoulders back, she marched toward the checkout counter where she waited patiently while Noah tugged at her jeans, begging for candy while the teenage checker with multiple piercings took forever to scan their groceries.

Seventeen

Tears streaming down his cheeks, Noah burst into Miss Jennie's kitchen like a tornado.

"Don't stomp or run in the house," Maddie said to Noah as Cole, who was drinking coffee at the table, looked up from an agricultural journal.

"I hate Bobby Mueller! I hate him!"

"Remember now, we don't hate people. We may get angry at them," she said. "We may not like what they do, but we don't hate them. And what did I tell you about slamming doors?" Noah's chest rose and fell with impotent fury as he struggled to process what must have seemed like very ill-founded advice.

Cole's dark brows drew together. "What's wrong, son?"

"Mueller called me bad names." Warily Noah approached the table where they sat. Then his face contorted with misery as he stared up at his mother. "He called you a bad name, too, Mommy. He's always calling you bad names. Then Luke and him laughed. They say you're a bad lady because I don't have a daddy."

"That's bull," Cole thundered. "Why didn't you tell them I'm your father?"

"Easy," Maddie murmured.

"Easy? No way! You want me to go easy on the morons in this town who attack you?" His carved face fierce, Cole turned to Noah. "Listen to me. The next time you see that big-mouthed brat, you tell him who I am."

"But you're not married to Mommy!"

"Okay, you're right. I should have married her a long time ago. Before you were born. But do you see that ring on her finger? It's called an engagement ring. I gave it to your mother because I love you and because I'm going to marry her. Soon. But we don't have to be married for you to know you have a daddy."

"Really?" Noah asked, his eyes brightening ever so slightly. "Can I tell Mueller?"

Cole and Maddie both spoke at once.

"No," she said very firmly. "Stay away from him."

"Yes," Cole said. "Tell him if he says any more bad things about your mother, you're going to tell me, and I'll go over there. Then he'll have to deal with me."

"Will you beat him up? Oh, boy! Can I tell him right now?" Noah demanded eagerly.

Maddie felt her collar tighten. "I don't think..."

"Sure," Cole said, meeting her gaze. "Why not? If you don't fight for what's important to you, you don't have a chance in hell of getting it."

Noah leaped for the door and raced out of the house, banging the screen behind him even harder than before.

Maddie turned on Cole, but he spoke first. "I think we've given everybody in this town long enough to get used to the idea that we're getting married. And where has it gotten us? Brats are attacking Noah. I say we move on to the next step."

"But they don't accept us as a couple."

"Who says they ever will? I know their acceptance is important to you, but I say to hell with them. What matters is being a family for Noah."

How did he feel? she wondered. He wanted Noah, and he liked to sleep with her. But what kind of person did he believe her to be? Could he ever feel close enough to her to share his soul, to love her? Would she always feel this guarded and defensive around him because she wasn't sure he thought she was good enough for him?

"Let's have our engagement party," he said. "We'll invite everybody you're so set on impressing out to the ranch for the best barbecue in the county. I'll hire the best band. They can come or not—whatever. We'll get married a week later and move to Austin. Then they can gossip all they want to."

When she would have protested, he arose and pulled her into his arms. "I'm tired of sleeping at the ranch and you and Noah sleeping here. Every night just seems to get longer and lonelier."

At his words, Maddie felt something hot and wanton flicker to life inside her.

"Don't make me wait any longer," he demanded, his low, hoarse tone holding more impatience than ever.

"All right," she finally agreed. "All right." Not that she felt completely sure of him. Still, she repeated, "All right."

The ranch house exploded with music and people, people who were making it obvious they didn't want her in Cole's life.

Maddie needed to get a grip, to relax, so that she could at least pretend to enjoy herself at her engagement party. Not easy, since she was in an overly sensitive mood that had her feeling everything was false, even the few smiles tossed her way. She could think only about one thing: Would Cole have considered marrying her if Noah hadn't been in the picture?

If only he respected her as much as he lusted after her. If only he'd let her wear something she'd picked out instead of the sexy blue number that shimmered and clung to her body like a second skin.

"I want them to eat their hearts out because you are so beautiful," he'd said.

Apparently curiosity trumped disapproval in Yella, Texas, because nearly everybody who'd been invited had come. Or else, like most Texans, they were all addicted to barbecue.

Exhausted from having worked so hard to put a party together on such short notice and from standing in three-inch heels in the receiving line for nearly an hour, she roamed the throng jamming the rooms of Cole's brilliantly lit ranch house. Her stomach growled, reminding her she hadn't eaten in a while, but she felt too nervous to eat spicy barbecue. She considered going outside where a tent had been set up and a second band played, but decided that maybe she needed a drink to settle her nerves first.

Four young women she'd gone to high school with brushed past her on their way to the bar without even looking at her while several men she'd known her entire life stared at her with lewd frankness. When she glared back at one of them, he smirked. The only friendly faces belonged to Cole's employees.

Halfway to the bar she saw Hester, so Maddie ducked into a shadowy corner to search for Cole. Finally she found him in the middle of a group, talking to Becky Weber, a beautiful brunette who'd been Lizzie's best friend. Just as Maddie was about to move out of the shadows and go after her drink, leaving Cole to his conversation, a deep, friendly voice behind her said, "There you are. I've been looking everywhere for you."

She whirled. "Adam!"

"Would you care for a drink?"

"I'd love one."

"What would you like?"

"Pinot grigio."

He vanished, returning with it almost immediately.

"That's some dress," he said, his friendly brown eyes skimming her figure. "You look stunning."

She blushed self-consciously. "Cole bought it for me and wanted me to wear it." She smiled. "I'm so glad you showed up. At least now there's one friendly face."

"Wouldn't have missed it. I know what it's like to have Hester Coleman against you. Cole doesn't. His mother's relentless. In her opinion, I'm the bastard brother who doesn't belong, and you're the wrong girl for Cole. She thinks she's protecting Cole and the family, but in truth, she's so insecure she's easily threatened and excessively territorial. Bottom line, we've both got to fight to win any sort of acceptance here. I've made a little headway, but it's slow going."

When his dark face began to spin against the sea of people, she realized she shouldn't have drunk the wine before she ate.

"I should be used to it," she said with a pretense of bravery, but her voice quavered a little. "I shouldn't care so much about her opinion at this point in my life. Mainly, I just want to know how Cole truly feels about me."

"He's marrying you, isn't he? He plans to move for your sake, doesn't he? Since I grew up without seeing much of my father, I can speak from experience. His marrying you will be good for Noah."

"I know."

"You feel like getting some air…or maybe dancing?" he asked.

Since Cole was still engaged with Becky, she nodded. "Maybe the fresh air will clear my head." Smiling, she took his arm.

* * *

The whole time Cole had been surrounded by Becky and several of Lizzie's dearest friends, he'd been aware of Maddie, who looked vulnerable standing all alone in her dark corner. Before the party, he had imagined her triumphant, dazzling everyone in her blue dress. She was being very brave, but he could tell she was struggling to hold her own.

Thus, at first, he was grateful when his handsome brother brought her a drink. Then his friend Lyle, who'd been watching Maddie the whole night, jabbed Cole and shot him a lewd smile.

"Knowing who she is and what she's capable of, I'd be afraid to leave her alone for long…even with my brother. They look pretty chummy, don't they?"

"Would you lay off?" But Cole couldn't help glaring at the pair.

"If they're that friendly in public, what do you suppose they'd do behind your back? I hear he's been dropping by Miss Jennie's a lot lately."

"To play ball with my kid."

"Right." Lyle chuckled.

Cole watched Maddie incline her head toward Adam, saw Adam lean down to catch what she was saying, saw him smile as he put his big, tanned hand under her arm to lead her out of the room.

Why the hell was Adam taking her outside? Surely they weren't leaving together? What about Maddie? Didn't she know she was making a spectacle of herself?

Suddenly doubt had white-hot jealousy boiling to the surface. Clenching his hands, he fought for control.

He trusted Adam. And Maddie…

Then he saw his mother eyeing him triumphantly.

Misreading Cole's silence as tacit agreement with his insulting comment, Lyle elaborated. "Nobody says you and your brother shouldn't enjoy her, Cole. We just don't think either of you should marry her."

Suddenly Cole's fist shot into Lyle's smug jaw with such force he sent the man stumbling backward onto the hardwood floor where he lay spread-eagled, staring up at the ceiling as he rubbed his jaw.

"Damn it, Lyle, don't you ever say another word about Maddie! Do you hear me? I'm marrying her, and I don't care what you or anyone else in this room thinks!"

"But what do *you* think about her, Cole?"

Cole started, aghast at his behavior. Lyle had struck a nerve. Yes, he wanted Noah, and he wanted Maddie in his bed. But would he ever feel sure of her?

As his guests watched in shock, Cole leaned down and yanked Lyle to his feet. "Get the hell out of my house!"

Lyle scrambled for the door. When he was safely out of Cole's reach, he said, "Did you see that? He hit me! He's crazy! She's made him crazy! You're a damn fool to marry her, Coleman, and you know it!"

Cole raked a hand through his black hair. "Sorry about the disturbance," he muttered before he plunged out of his house in search of Maddie.

He must have looked upset because when Maddie saw him, she got up from the chair where she'd been sitting beside Adam and ran to him.

"Are you all right?" she cried.

"We're leaving," he said.

"Okay, but since this is our engagement party, are you going to tell me why?"

"Because I just lost it in there."

"He hit me—because I told him the truth about you and Adam. And I told him that he'd be a fool to marry you just so he could sleep with you, and he knows I'm right," Lyle yelled at her as he roared past the porch in his truck before driving away in whorls of dust.

"Is that true?"

Cole flushed darkly.

"Because of me? And Adam?"

"He said something I didn't like."

"And you believed him? You thought that your brother and I…that we were flirting or worse?"

"No, I just didn't like him saying it. I couldn't let him get away with talking about you like that."

"Because you don't trust me."

"I do trust you. It's just that…"

"No, *you don't*. You don't respect me. You're just like they are, ready to believe the worst of me at the slightest provocation—because you believed him, just a little. Or more than just a little."

"No, I got mad. I lost it. I'm not feeling too good about it either."

"You'll always be the high-and-mighty Coleman, and I'll never be anything but Jesse Ray's daughter."

"That's unfair. You're blowing this out of proportion… just like I blew what he said out of proportion."

"Maybe, but there's a grain of truth. For your information, your brother was just being nice to me…*because* everyone else was ignoring me. He was explaining how he understands how I feel, because sometimes he sort of feels like an outcast here, too."

When she looked up, she saw that Cole's mother, and everybody else, was staring at her.

"I've never felt so absolutely cheap and humiliated in my whole life as you made me feel tonight," she whispered. "You believed what Lyle said—instead of having faith in me."

"No! I got jealous!"

"I hate to say it, but your mother was right. She said you were attracted to me solely for the sex."

"That's not true."

"It is. It's all you see in my friendship with your brother—who's a really sweet guy, by the way—who's also having a rough time in this town."

"I know his problems a helluva lot better than you do."

"Sex is not enough to hold a marriage together. So, if you'll be so kind as to lend me your truck, I'll drive myself home to Miss Jennie's. Then I'll pack and return to Austin. Miss Jennie will call when I'm gone so you can pick up your truck."

"Damn it. I'm not letting you go."

"This isn't going to work, Cole! You need a woman you and your friends can respect, a woman you can trust and be proud of."

"You're that woman."

"I wish I was, but I'm not. Not if you found it that easy to believe I could hit on your brother at our engagement party!"

"I got jealous, damn it!"

"Well, I don't want you marrying me because you feel obligated, because we have a son. I want my husband to love and trust me. I grew up without love, so maybe I've wanted that my whole life!" She paused. "Look, I told you—you can see Noah whenever you like. But we can't marry because you don't respect me, and I need your respect more than I need anything else. Added to that, I don't want our marriage to cut you off from everybody you're close to."

"I don't care about them! I want to live in Austin. With you."

"You cared enough to hit Lyle. No matter what you say, you'll come to resent me in time. If I let you go, you'll find someone else, someone who fits in the way Lizzie did, who's really right for you."

"And you'll go back to Austin and settle for Greg?"

"No. Being with you has taught me what it's like to feel passion. You've helped me grow stronger. I'm not going to settle again because now I know I deserve someone who loves me and who respects me, too."

"But I love you and respect you."

"I wish you did, but you don't. You're just saying you do to get your way."

"I was a fool. I made a mistake."

"You're right about one thing. We both nearly made a terrible mistake."

Slowly she slid her engagement ring off her finger and handed it to him. "I'm feeling very tired, Cole. I need to lie down. Will you please give me the keys to your truck so I can go home?"

When he reluctantly dropped the keys in her hand, she walked away, stumbling on the first stair of his porch, maybe because the tears that had been threatening to fall were blinding her.

Cole rushed forward to help her, but she cried out when his fingers grazed her elbow. When she turned, and he saw the raw anguish in her luminous eyes, he realized how profoundly he'd hurt her.

Struggling to push him away as the whole town of Yella gaped, she said, "Don't touch me! I won't allow you to treat me like I'm something low and despised."

"I don't despise you. *I love you!* I swear I do!"

"I don't believe you," she whispered on a heartbroken sob as she hurried past him toward his truck.

Eighteen

Cole felt as though his soul was shattering into a million pieces. He stood in the barn outside Raider's stall listening to the music drifting from the ranch house, where his engagement party remained in full swing.

He loved Maddie, but like a fool he'd never told her until tonight. He'd probably loved her for years.

A pain as terrible as what he'd felt when he'd believed Maddie had left him six years ago fisted around his heart and squeezed hard. Only when she'd run from Yella had he learned how much she'd meant to him—that he couldn't live without her.

For six years, he'd endured, breaking Lizzie's heart in the process. He didn't want to suffer like that for the rest of his life, or make some other unlucky rebound lover suffer as he'd made Lizzie suffer.

How could he have gone on believing that maybe the gossips were right about Maddie? "How did I screw it all up so fast, Raider, old boy? What the hell can I do to get her back?"

The gelding rasped in a breath. Then he snorted.

"I have to get her back."

Raider's ears pricked forward. Then Cole heard a footstep behind him and turned to see Adam striding into the barn.

"You didn't totally kill your engagement party. There's still a few diehards. Your mother just left."

"At least someone's happy."

"I don't think so. Surprisingly she seemed a little chagrined. In fact she asked me to find you. So, do you wanna punch me, too?"

"I think I've made enough of an ass of myself for one night."

"For once, you admit it," Adam said.

"For once, I won't resent you throwing it in my face. Look, I know you had it harder than I did growing up without our dad. But that wasn't my fault!"

Adam smiled. "Who else can I blame? Dad's dead, and you're here. But I want to talk about Maddie. I don't resent you so much that I'd try to come between you two. I was just trying to be your brother and her friend."

"I know. I just let a stupid remark get to me."

"I like Maddie. I like Noah. I think you and she are right for each other."

"Like it matters now. Don't you get it? I crushed her. In public. In front of the idiots she was trying so hard to impress. Worse, I made her feel like she has to apologize for who she is. She left me."

"Good for her. By the way, you look like hell—which means you've probably already figured out how precious she is to you. You're not going to let her go back to Austin, are you?"

"How the hell am I going to stop her?"

"Why don't you go over to Miss Jennie's and throw yourself on her mercy? *Crawl. Grovel.* She's not like the hardhearted gossips who despise her. Unlike them, she's got the softest heart in the universe. You love her. And she loves you. What else really matters?"

Maddie felt like throwing the phone at the wall.

"What? I can't believe you sent him over here! Well, I don't want to talk to him, Adam!" Maddie cried. "I'm packing, so I'm going to hang up!"

"No, you're not! Because I'm your future brother-in-law. And you're not that rude."

Through her tears Maddie stared at the brightly colored T-shirts spilling out of the suitcases on her bed.

"What part of 'I broke it off with him' don't you understand? He'll never respect me! So, no, I don't want to talk to him. If you send him over here, I won't answer the door."

"He looks terrible," Adam said.

"That's not my fault."

"He loves you."

"No, he doesn't. Not if he thinks I'm capable of the same sort of low, despicable tricks my mother's capable of."

"You're wrong. I'm not saying he didn't behave like a fool. Or that he didn't totally embarrass you. He did. He messed up *because* he loves you. Guys only screw up big-time with the women they love. Lyle hit a nerve, and Cole lost it."

"Look, I have to go. I'm throwing things in my suitcases as we speak."

"Now you're being an even bigger fool than he was. You two are good for each other. You know it. Have you ever been this mad at anybody else before? Or felt this hurt?"

"No!"

"See there!"

"You're crazy! I'm hanging up!"

"Don't throw it all away. Relationships always require some give along with the take. He's Noah's father. You grew up without a father just like I did. Do you want to do that to Noah?"

"That last was a low blow."

"He hurt you. Get over it."

No sooner had she hung up the phone than Miss Jennie appeared at the door. "Who was that, dear?"

"Cole's interfering brother. Adam was trying to talk me into forgiving Cole."

"But you're much too angry to even consider that, aren't you?"

"This has nothing to do with anger. It has to do with the fact that Cole will always see me as Jesse Ray's daughter. And I've always tried so hard to be more than that."

"You've always been more than that."

"You see it. You always saw it. But Cole isn't capable of seeing it."

"He is a man with a man's blindness, but I believe he loves you, and that no matter what his failings, he's always loved you. Maybe tonight made him realize who you really are."

"And snakes can fly."

"Horrid thought," Miss Jennie said, causing Maddie to smile. Miss Jennie paused. "You know that I lost my darling Raymond in the Korean War, and I never found anybody else."

"I know."

"Think about that. You could go your whole life and never find anyone you love half as much as you love Cole. Or find a man who loves you as much."

Maddie was silent as she considered the long, lonely years that would stretch ahead. For no reason at all, she thought of the intense way Cole looked at her sometimes.

"Raymond's dead, so I could place him on a pedestal. I can always think of him as absolutely perfect. I've conveniently forgotten all our silly squabbles and his many faults. It's really quite nice to have this perfect fantasy lover who never disappoints you. But life can be so messy. I think all men, however desirable, are the messiest of creatures. They have such limitations. Cole fell back into old habits, old thought patterns. Look at his mother, the woman who raised him. I never told anyone in Yella this, but she and I grew up in the same town. Did you know she grew up poor? That she was abandoned in a Dumpster as a baby by a teenage mother who was sent to prison? That she wasn't adopted by the wealthy family who raised her until she was six years old?"

"No."

"She's very insecure and has worked hard to keep those secrets. No doubt she worked just as hard to try to instill all sorts of extremely silly ideas and prejudices into her son. He got jealous and suffered a momentary lapse of judgment and hurt you, which I'm sure he profoundly regrets."

"But—"

"I'm not finished. Unfortunately, at the party, you fell back into the old pattern of feeling left out. And you reacted defensively by lashing out at Cole. Self-worth comes from the inside, Maddie, and you have plenty of it…most of the time. But we all have our weak moments, and find ourselves filled with self-doubt. That's all that happened. He got jealous at the wrong moment. You weren't your best self either, and you took it out on each other. It was bad timing. Don't throw away something as precious as the love of a lifetime without being sure it's the right thing to do."

"Oh, Miss Jennie, will he always see me as an easy, untrustworthy sort?"

"You won't be the first woman ever to face the challenge of convincing a man how lucky he is to have you. Trust me, if he doesn't know your true worth now, he will."

* * *

Maddie stood in the open doorway of Miss Jennie's house as she anxiously waited for Cole to drive up. After he cut the engine, she took a faltering step across the porch toward him, and then another. He got out of Adam's truck and walked toward her just as slowly, as if he felt as unsure as she did.

"I…was waiting out here for you because Adam called me and told me you would come," she said breathlessly. "I was so hoping you wouldn't change your mind about coming… about me…about us."

"Forgive me," he whispered.

"I was every bit as much at fault as you."

"No, I knew how important it was to you to make a good impression on everybody, and what did I do? I made you wear that sexy dress that you didn't feel comfortable in."

"Because I have hang-ups."

"Because you're you. I'm sorry for what I did. For what I said. I need to respect your feelings. Then that lout insulted you—I should have defended you instead of behaving like a perfect ass."

"I should have been more understanding. But I'd been feeling sort of abandoned and isolated while you talked to Becky, so when you accused me…"

"You felt violated," he said.

"I don't want to rehash everything," she whispered. "It was painful enough the first time around."

"Yes. But there is one more thing. Lyle just called me on my cell, after drinking several cups of coffee, and apologized. He said he was out of line…about everything. He said you were the loveliest woman there in that sexy blue dress, and he was drunk and jealous of me. He said I was lucky you'd have me. He said he was going to call my mother and tell her it was high time she quit bad-mouthing you to everybody in town. He said he was going to call you and apologize."

"That's…that's kind of nice."

"I thought maybe you'd like it."

She smiled. "Yes, but I see now that it's what I think about myself that matters."

"So, what about it—will you still have me?"

She caught her breath and pulled him close. "I love you so much, I'd be crazy not to. I overreacted, too. I was feeling scared at the party surrounded by all those people, imagining them thinking the worst of me. Maybe I was looking for an excuse not to face up to the past and simply let it go. So what if I had a lousy childhood? I'm a success now. You're more important than the past. I love you too much to let you go so easily."

"You sure scared the hell out of me."

"I scared myself, too."

He laughed. "I love you. I've always loved you. I was just too big an idiot to see it."

"I love you more."

"I guess we have the rest of our lives to argue about that."

"You're forgetting something," she whispered.

"What?"

"My engagement ring. I want it back!"

He laughed. Reaching into his pocket, he pulled it out. She held up her hand, and he slid it on. Then his lips found hers, and she forgot about the ring, forgot about everything but how much she loved and wanted him.

He loved her, too. Imagine that.

He'd always loved her.

Epilogue

The ballroom where their glittering reception in Austin was held had sparkling views of Town Lake. Not too many people from Yella had come to celebrate her marriage to Cole, but she didn't care all that much because her dear friends from Austin were there.

Somebody tapped a knife on a crystal glass to silence the throng.

"A toast to the bride," rang Hester Coleman's imperious voice.

"Oh, no," Cole muttered as he took Maddie's hand. "Mother, I don't think—"

Maddie squeezed his fingers. "No, she's been nice to me lately. Maybe she's turning over a new leaf. Let her say whatever she has to say. It's enough that she's here. Whatever she says, I promise you that I'll be okay."

"But this is your day, not hers," he said. "I want it to be perfect for you."

"Life is messy," she said, winking at Miss Jennie when she caught her eye.

"In a long life, people make mistakes," Hester began. "I've made my share. Today, I wish to toast to the happiness of my son and grandson and daughter-in-law. I wish them all joy and long lives!"

"Well, that wasn't too bad," Cole muttered, clutching his bride close. "Maybe she's coming around."

"Maybe," Maddie whispered. "Until she does, we have each other again. That's all that really matters."

Noah went up to Hester, and the older woman's face lit up as she knelt to chat. Maddie thought of her own mother, whom she hadn't invited, whom she wasn't ready to forgive and maybe never would be. At least with Hester there was the hope of a better relationship in the future.

Cole pulled her close and kissed her, not caring if his mother and everybody watched. Her groom's kiss swept her away, and she was only dimly aware of the joyous applause that surrounded them, only dimly aware that his mother was clapping, too.

Then Noah left Hester and ran to them. Leaning down, Cole lifted his son into his arms.

"Are we married now?" Noah asked joyously. "Are you my daddy for real?"

"Yes," Cole said, hugging Maddie to him with his other arm. "For real and forever."

* * * * *

THE SECRET HEIR
OF SUNSET RANCH

CHARLENE SANDS

This book is dedicated to my late father Charles, who proudly served in the army during World War II, and to all the other brave military men and women, both past and present, who have served or do serve our country with honor.

One

Justin Slade was home. It'd been three days now.

His Ford F-150 truck barreled down the highway with enough horsepower to match the equine force of Sunset Ranch's best thoroughbreds, radio blasting Luke Bryan's latest country hit. It was beat-tapping music. At any other time, Justin would be pounding the dashboard in sync with the rhythm.

But today, he wasn't enjoying the music, the blue Nevada sky or the morning weather, which was clear and crisp enough to remind him winter was on the distant horizon. His gut churned in half a dozen ways as he faced what he was about to do. The marine in him hadn't a doubt he was doing the right thing. He had to come clean for Matilda Applegate's sake and for…Brett.

He punched the off button on the radio and Luke's voice disappeared.

Appropriate silence filled the air.

A cold shiver of dread hung around him like an invisible cloak, refusing to be shrugged off with upbeat music or good weather. Brett Applegate was dead. It was Justin's fault, and Brett's aunt, his only living relative, needed to know the truth.

He pressed his foot to the pedal and glanced around the outskirts of Silver Springs as a sultry female voice on his GPS gave him the coordinates. Gravel spit under his tires.

The deserted road narrowed and a knot in the pit of his stomach begged for this to be over. He'd been on dangerous missions in Afghanistan that hadn't caused him this much anxiety. Guilt and apprehension sucked as constant companions.

Justin popped two antacids into his mouth. He'd been living on the darn things lately.

"In fifty feet, turn right," the GPS voice instructed.

Justin made the turn and drove his truck down a dusty dirt path that wound its way toward a one-story ranch house matured by frigid winters, hotter-than-hell summers and a string of bad months in between. Seeing Brett's home in such a state of neglect was a sharp shot of reality, testament to the economic misery the Applegates had suffered over the years. Brett had always said his uncle Ralph would've gotten heartsick seeing what had happened to his once-proud home.

As the truck ambled closer, Justin caught a glimpse of a disabled car near the house, the back tire flatter than a flapjack, and a woman bending over, her head deep in the bowels of the trunk. Her jewel-pocketed derriere pointed skyward, drawing his immediate gaze. Hell, it was a beacon for any man in his right mind to stop and help out.

Justin pressed on the brake, keeping his eyes trained on a sight he hadn't seen in a long time: a gorgeous, perfectly shaped female ass. It was enough to get his juices flowing. Heck, after nine years in the marines, it didn't take much. But hot damn, the view was fine.

He swallowed and climbed down from the cab of his truck. His boots ate gravel as he neared the back of her car. The woman's silky blouse climbed her waist while she continued to search the trunk, and his eyes locked on to five inches of soft-as-butter, creamy skin.

"Sweet heaven, what else is going to go wrong?" Her

voice flowed over him like smooth bourbon. He grabbed a peek of that exposed skin again.

Man, oh, man.

He cleared his throat. Darn his mama for teaching him gentlemanly manners. Forcing his gaze away from her beautiful bottom, he focused on her curly, platinum-blond hair.

"Excuse me, miss. Can I lend a hand?"

She jerked up and hit her head on the inside of the trunk. "Ow."

She scowled as her hand went to her head, rubbing away the pain. "Oh, I didn't see you—"

Their gazes locked. Her hand froze in her shoulder-length platinum locks. Her brows pulled tight and her lips rounded. "Oh."

She was a stunner.

A twinge of recollection jarred him out of his lusty thoughts.

He remembered those deep jade eyes, that pouty mouth and Marilyn Monroe hair only a few women could pull off. He would've bet his last dollar he'd never see her again. And now, here she was…in the flesh.

On Matilda Applegate's homestead, no less.

He didn't much believe in coincidences. And this one was too big to ignore. His gut churned again, begging for another antacid.

Maybe he was wrong. It had been over a year and a half ago. Maybe she only looked like the woman he'd met in New York City that one weekend.

Justin removed his Stetson and her eyes flickered at the gesture.

"Sorry if I startled you, miss."

Seconds ticked by as she took note of his shiny black boots, new jeans, silver belt buckle and tan shirt opened at the collar. She studied his face and gazed deeply into his eyes. With her hand in her hair, her fingers wove through the silver-blond strands as if she was fashioning some new upswept hairdo. With her arm raised and bent at the elbow, she tilted her head to one side and gave him thoughtful consideration. The move exposed the delicate softness of her throat. A breathless sigh escaped from her mouth.

That bit of body language was unique to the woman he'd known. Sexy. Not forced. Genuine. A jolt hit him smack between the eyes.

It had to be her. He thought back to that night at the Golden Palace Bar.

"I don't date soldiers," she'd said as he stood by her table.

He'd taken a seat and smiled anyway. "But you'll make an exception for me."

"B-Brett? Is that really you?" The hope in her voice confused him and then another jolt hit. Oh, man, this wasn't possible. "I don't understand," she was saying. "We were told…we were told you were dead. Killed in a gun battle. Oh, my God, your aunt Mattie will be so happy. Was there a mix-up? What happened?"

He pulled oxygen into his lungs, then looked away from her puzzled face and squinted against the bright afternoon sunshine. *Jerk.* He hated himself for the lie, and for the hurt he'd cause when he told her the truth.

"I'm not Brett Applegate," he told the blonde.

She pursed her lips and inclined her head, studying him. "But I remember you. Don't you remember me? I'm Katherine Grady. I go by Kat."

Hell, yeah. He remembered her. But he didn't have a clue why the heck Kat was here, looking gorgeous, in front of the Applegate home.

Silently, he cursed the bet he'd made with Brett Applegate. Justin never thought he'd lose an arm-wrestling match to his buddy. He never had before. But damn if Brett hadn't bested him three out of five times right before they'd been selected to accompany a high-powered general to a three-day summit in Washington, D.C. After they served out their mission, the general granted them weekend leave in New York, before they were to head back to their forward operating base in Afghanistan.

The price of the bet? Reversing roles for the weekend.

They'd emptied the contents of their pockets, and good ole Brett had jumped at the chance to live in Justin's skin for a few days. He'd waved Justin's gold credit card in his face and scooped up all seven hundred-dollar bills Justin had dumped onto the bunk. "Gonna have me some fun being you," he'd said, grinning like a fool.

For his part, Justin had blown Brett's spending cash on a bottle of house wine at the hotel and afterward Kat had taken him to her tiny fourth-story walk-up. He'd been looking for a good time. He thought she was, too. They'd clicked. And then things got complicated.

"I remember you, *sugar.*"

Her eyes softened. "No one else has ever called me that."

Justin winced at the sweet tone in her voice. "My name isn't Brett. I'm Justin Slade and I live about twenty miles north of here. Brett and I served together on a tour of duty in the marines."

Her voice dropped off. "You're Justin…*Slade?*"

He nodded.

"*Sunset Ranch,* Justin Slade?"

He nodded again.

"But, we… You told me your name was Brett Apple-gate. You were a marine heading back overseas. You told me all about this place…. You—"

He grimaced. He was the worst kind of heel. He'd taken advantage of a woman's trust, something he'd never done before. He swallowed down regret and then softened his voice. "I lied."

She condemned him with her eyes. He didn't blame her. It was an idiotic bet and a fool thing to do.

Slowly, her hand went to her mouth. Slender fingers covered her lips. She began shaking her head. "Oh…no. No, it's not true."

"Maybe we should go inside the house and talk. I'll try to explain. Is Matilda Applegate home?"

She closed her eyes and kept them closed as if she were silently praying.

He spoke firmly. "Kat."

Her eyes popped open and she blinked a few times. She spoke quietly. "We can't go inside."

"Why not?"

The front door creaked open and an older woman with hair the color of a sunburst stepped onto the front porch, holding a baby boy dressed in brown corduroy in her arms. The woman moved slowly, but with precision as if she calculated each step she took. Her light blue eyes were the most vital thing about her, painted with black eyeliner and deep-sea blue eye shadow. Blotchy face powder accented rather than hid the wrinkles on her face. But the kindness in her eyes was authentic and aimed straight at him.

"I thought I heard voices. Who have we here?"

The baby took a peek at him and then whipped around to grab at her neck with a death grip, his little legs kicking at her hips. She squeezed him tight, and whispered reassurances in his ear. "Now, now, Connor baby. Don't be afraid."

Kat cleared her throat. "Aunt Mattie, this is Justin Slade."

The woman's brows drew together as she tried to place him. "Slade? The name sounds familiar."

"I was a friend of Brett's. I came here to talk to you."

* * *

Katherine Grady knew how to handle a lot of tough situations. She'd grown up the only daughter in an abusive household. She'd moved from one women's shelter to another with her mom, running from a belligerent father and trying her darnedest to keep her mother from falling apart. There was nothing pretty or heroic about living hand to mouth. About never knowing if they'd have to pick up and run or have enough food and shelter for the month.

Kat learned how to survive from early on.

What rattled her more than anything was fear of the unknown. How could she fight something she couldn't see coming?

This was one of those times.

Usually she hid her emotions well—thanks to all that training from her youth—but right now fear tightened her throat and sped up her heart. Her body shook so hard her knees wobbled. Could it be possible? The man she thought was Brett for all this time was really Justin Slade. *Gracious.* She couldn't wrap her head around the bald-faced lie she'd been told. It was a lot to absorb all at once. But Kat's emotions didn't matter at the moment. Her concern was for Mattie. The older woman couldn't afford a setback in her recovery.

Mattie invited Justin inside and he didn't hesitate to approach the front door. He held the screen open and allowed them to step inside first and then followed behind. The door slammed shut as it was prone to do and Kat jerked, her nerves worn thin by something much bigger than that familiar sound. Funny, how just a few minutes ago, her biggest problem was a tire that needed changing.

But the scene that was about to play out in the parlor of Aunt Mattie's modest home could very well kill her with grief. Kat didn't know how to stop it or protect her from the truth.

"Have yourself a seat, son," Aunt Mattie said. "I'll take a seat, too, if you don't mind. Little Connor here is quite a handful, tiring me out. He's weighing nearly twenty pounds now, isn't that right, Kat?"

Kat's stomach ached. She gave a hesitant nod. Justin waited for both of them to take a seat. Kat perched uneasily on a colorful floral chair and Aunt Mattie lowered herself onto her brushed suede recliner that must have once been a lemony yellow. Justin finally sat on the sofa and set his tan felt hat next to him. He kept darting glances at Connor.

"Pardon the mess," Aunt Mattie said. "Kat here is doing wonders fixing the place up on a scant budget. She's got quite a flair for it, wouldn't you say?"

Justin scanned the room politely. Kat wondered if a man's eye would notice things like handmade pillows in contrasting colors, small scatter rugs that tied the room together and flower vases and pictures placed strategically to enhance the modest three-bedroom home. When Kat had first arrived, with Mattie's illness sapping her strength, the place had been a wreck. In the two months she'd lived here, she'd managed to stage the living spaces to bring new life to the house. Her arrival, or rather Connor's arrival, had brought new life to Matilda Applegate, as well.

"Looks nice and homey," Justin said.

She still couldn't believe this man sitting here being polite to Mattie had lied to her about who he was. Why?

She understood lies to some extent. She'd had to lie her way out of a few tight spots in her life. She could abide them, if it meant keeping your nose clean or protecting someone you loved. But why would Justin Slade lie to her about who he was back then?

Her teeth clamped down so hard, pain shot to her head. Any second now...

"You say you knew my nephew Brett?"

"Yes, ma'am. We met in the marines. When we found

out we were practically neighbors, coming from this part of Nevada and all, we got friendly."

Connor was beginning to relax. He turned around in Mattie's arms and plunked his little bottom down in her lap. Tears welled in Kat's eyes. This was a special moment, a brief but monumental span of time when Connor's sweet brown eyes locked onto Justin's for the first time. The gravity of the moment sent Kat's mind spinning.

Her son meeting his father.

"Oh, look, Connor's warming up to you. This is Brett's boy. Going to have his first birthday before you know it."

Kat lowered her eyes, the weight of the situation crashing down on her shoulders. She had to think fast. To find a way to protect Mattie.

"He's your boy?" Justin asked her.

"Yes." Kat rose quickly and moved over to Mattie. "Let me take him, Aunt Mattie. Your arms must be tired from holding him most of the morning."

"Kat was trying to fix the flat," Aunt Mattie explained to Justin. "The roads here are murder on the tires, you know. My arms are getting a bit tweaked. I'm not as young as I used to be," she said as she handed Connor over carefully. "Though there's nothing in this world better than holding our little Connor."

The baby was on his best behavior, not fidgeting as he was prone to do when he was around strangers. Connor clung to Kat's neck and she kissed his soft little cheek before turning to face Justin. "Aunt Mattie is recovering from a heart attack. She took the news of Brett's death *very hard*."

Aunt Mattie interjected, "I think I would've died, if it hadn't been for Kat and Connor showing up when they did. That little boy was like an angel coming down from heaven to save my life."

Justin rose. His gaze switched back and forth from Connor to Kat. The suspicion she'd known would come lit up his eyes. "Brett never said he had a son."

Aunt Mattie chimed in. "That's because Brett never knew about Connor. Kat came here looking for Brett, to finally tell him about his baby. But it was too late for Connor to meet his daddy. Kat's been living here, taking care of me ever since."

Justin's eyes rounded on her. "You never told *Brett* he had a son."

The lines around Aunt Mattie's eyes crinkled with worry. "Oh, dear. Did I say something wrong?"

"No, it's okay, Aunt Mattie," Kat told her softly. "Justin was a friend of Brett's. He might as well know the truth." She stared at Justin, hoping to get her point across. Now that it had sunk in that she'd been deceived, she didn't want to transfer the damage to Mattie. Her emotions rolled through her like a tornado, but she kept up appearances rather than hurt Mattie Applegate any further. "I met *Brett* in New York and we spent time together. After I learned I was pregnant, I tried to reach him overseas. But I never heard back from him. So, I stayed in the city and worked, raising my son until…well, until the day I decided to come to Nevada to try to find Brett here."

Justin glanced at the little boy in her arms and then focused back on her.

Kat stilled her frustration at the man who'd deliberately lied to her. She continued quickly, "I didn't find Brett, but I found Aunt Mattie." Kat turned to face the older woman. "Meeting Connor was the best medicine for her. Her health has improved so much even her doctors can't believe it. Isn't that right, Aunt Mattie?"

Aunt Mattie leaned forward in her recliner, nodding and making the sign of the cross across her chest. "It's a miracle, is what it is. Connor is a gift from God."

Justin squeezed his eyes shut for a second and then

glanced at Connor with a proprietary look that curdled Kat's stomach. "He is at that."

The older woman began to rise. "Where are my manners? Would you like some pie? I can my own peaches and Kat made peach pie this morning. We'll put on a pot of coffee, too. And then we can talk more about Brett."

"Sorry, I can't," Justin said firmly. "Please don't get up. Thanks for the offer, but I'm short on time today."

Mattie's face crumpled with disappointment. "You'll come back, though. I'd like to hear about your friendship with Brett."

Justin stared at Kat, condemning her with a solemn look. At least he caught the gravity of Mattie's situation and kept his lips buttoned. Kat was thankful for that. "I promise I'll come back." He walked over to Aunt Mattie and lowered down on one knee to gently take her hand. He focused his full attention on the seventy-year-old woman who had raised Brett Applegate since the age of five, after his folks were tragically killed by a deadly storm.

"That's good." Mattie's blue eyes glowed with warmth. She looked twenty years younger with that twinkle. "I'm very happy to meet one of Brett's friends."

"Nice to meet you, too, ma'am. Brett always went on and on about his aunt Mattie. Why, I'd say Brett's talk about your peach pie got all the men in our unit longing for a piece of that pie."

"Oh, that's nice to hear, son. Next time you come, I'll be sure to serve some up to you."

"Will do. I'll be by again before you know it. We'll have that talk about Brett." Justin grabbed his hat and walked to the door, glancing Kat's way with a pointed look. "Kat, if you come outside to lend a hand, I'll change that tire for you."

"Isn't that nice," Mattie said, settling back in the recliner.

Kat forced a smile. The authority in his voice told her the marine sergeant wasn't one to mess with. But the more she thought about Justin Slade lying to her, the more she couldn't tamp down a surge of anger. She wanted answers. "I'll be right there."

Once Justin left the room, she kissed Connor's cheek and placed him in the play yard that sat three feet away from Mattie's chair. Connor sank his butt down and immediately picked up a Baby Einstein musical toy. He pushed the button, something he'd just learned to do, and "Twinkle, Twinkle, Little Star" rang out to placate him.

"I'll watch him," Aunt Mattie said.

"Thanks. I shouldn't be long."

Mattie peered outside the window with a thoughtful expression. "He seems like a nice young man."

Kat practically choked out her agreement. "He does seem so."

Then she walked outside to confront Justin Slade.

She had no doubt in her mind the fudge was about to hit the fan.

Justin set the jack on the ground and began hoisting up the underbelly of Kat's ten-year-old Chevy. Kat kept a safe distance away, watching him work with rolled-up sleeves, his face tight, sweat beading on his forehead.

Looking at him now, she took a subjective view of what had happened in New York and understood why she'd broken her rule with him. Normally, she didn't date soldiers or any other man who might drag her down to the ditch she'd clawed her way out of. She was heading to the top and nothing would stop her. She'd gone the poor man's route once before with a young man, and that had gotten her nothing but grief. But Brett…or rather Justin, had had enough charm to persuade her to make an exception. She'd been so lonely, so desperate for a true friend. And he'd been that for two solid days. She'd opened up to him about her life and the recent loss of her mother. He'd listened. He'd understood. He hadn't pressured her for sex. He hadn't made a move on her that first night. He'd slept on her tiny living room sofa without complaint. They'd toured the city on a dime, and had laughs. The whole time, Kat knew the weekend was going nowhere. There wasn't enough charm in the world to get her to give up her dream. She wasn't going to fall for some down-on-his-luck and out-of-money hog farmer.

With the jack in place, Justin fastened the wrench he'd found in the trunk over a lug nut on the wheel. The nut refused to budge and Justin dug his heels in, determined. Corded muscles in his forearms strained and bunched with each powerful jerk he gave the wrench. A vein popped from his neck as he put the full force of his body behind each counter-clockwise turn. After he managed to loosen the first lug nut, he sat back on his heels, wincing against the afternoon sunshine, and then shot her a glare. "Is Connor my son?"

"Shh," she said, glancing at the front door. Hopefully, Mattie was dozing. "Don't let Aunt Mattie hear you."

Justin fastened the wrench to the next lug nut and turned it sharply to the left. The nut released. "How many men did you sleep with before and after you met me?"

One other, but she wasn't going to tell him that. She was certain Brett Applegate was Connor's father…or at least the man she'd thought to be Brett. "You lied to me. You told me you were Brett."

Justin finished removing the nuts from the wheel and rose, his grim expression aimed straight at her. He approached, taking slow predatory steps. "Just how hard did you try to reach Brett Applegate after you got pregnant?"

Kat visibly shook at his tone. He was determined to get to the truth. She wanted that, too, but protecting Aunt

Mattie came first. "We can't talk about this here. You saw Aunt Mattie. That woman has been through enough heartache in her life. Her heart is frail. I'm convinced she'll have another setback if she overhears any of this conversation."

He stared at her with the full force of his dark brown eyes. *Connor's eyes.* As if reading her thoughts, he spoke with a rasp in his voice. "That baby has my eyes and dark hair."

It was true. Connor looked enough like Justin to make those comparisons.

"Shh, Aunt Mattie loves Connor. He's given her new life. We can't…we can't have this conversation right now. If you're truly a friend of Brett's you know how much he loved her. He wouldn't want her getting hurt. And that's exactly what would happen if you—"

Justin took the hint and spoke more quietly now. "I don't plan on hurting Brett's aunt. But if that boy is my son I have—"

"Please…" Her nerves raw, she glanced at the door again. "Don't you get it? I'm not going to talk to you about this here."

"We're gonna have this conversation, Kat. Meet me at seven at my house at Sunset Ranch. It's twenty miles west of here."

Kat's body shook. She couldn't go to the Slade house. Showing up on Sunset Ranch would only complicate matters. And she wasn't going to tell Justin why just now. "I can't."

A vein throbbed against the side of his throat, looking ready to burst. "Why not?"

"I'll meet you somewhere else. Someplace neutral."

He folded his arms across his chest. "I'm listening."

"There's a little café in Silver Springs called Blossom. Do you know it?"

"I'll find it. I'll meet you there at seven."

"Eight. I have to put Connor to bed first. I read to him every night and we have a routine. He's a pretty good sleeper. It'll be easier on Aunt Mattie if he's already in bed when I leave."

Justin's eyes softened at the mention of Connor's sleep habits and for a second or two, she felt a sense of relief that her son's daddy wasn't lost to him forever. Then, Justin turned a sharp eye on her once again. "If you're not there, I'll come looking for you."

Really? Did he think she'd run out on him? "I'll be there. I want answers, too."

"You'll get them." Dismissing her, he turned around and walked back to repair the flat.

Her heart beating like crazy, she walked into the house. Mattie was indeed dozing. Thank goodness. Little Connor took one look at his mommy, rose onto his knees and then hoisted himself up by the wall of the play yard. He stood on planted feet, holding on tight to keep his balance. His eyes sparkled with pride over his newest accomplishment and Kat beamed with love and that same sense of pride.

Your daddy is alive, Connor.

He's also rich and powerful.

The implication made her dizzy. But Kat couldn't think about all of that now. She had Mattie's welfare to consider. There wasn't a doubt in her mind that Matilda Applegate would suffer heart failure if she learned the truth about Connor. Kat couldn't let that happen. Mattie didn't deserve any more heartache in her life. There was a tipping point, and this was it. Kat would do everything in her power to protect her. With her flamboyant red hair, and sweetly feisty spirit, the older woman had touched something fierce and protective in Kat.

She picked up Connor from the play yard and hugged him to her chest, stroking his soft dark curls.

It was only minutes later, after she heard Justin drive off, that she could finally breathe evenly again.

Two

Justin ground his teeth together as he drove off the Apple-gate property. Shell-shocked wasn't a strong enough term for what he was feeling right now. He'd come to spill his heart and guts out to Matilda about how Brett had died, and instead discovered he had a son—an adorable dark-haired, brown-eyed boy.

His son.

His mouth twisted. He had to be careful. He didn't know anything for sure right now. The boy may or may not be his child.

But he did remember Kat. So many things about her. He remembered her beauty, her creamy skin, her pretty green eyes and the way she accepted him inside her body with tight, wet, welcoming heat. Though he'd spent the weekend with her, they only had one night of sex. That one night made up for the prior eight months he'd gone without. Once they got going, there was no stopping them. She'd had no boundaries, no fussy little complaints, no inhibitions when they were together. Her only rule was that she didn't want any entanglements afterward.

She'd spelled it right out.

She didn't want a relationship with a soldier or a farmer.

In other words, he was good enough to bed, but that's where it would end.

Justin had gotten the message loud and clear and after

leaving her without so much as exchanging phone numbers or addresses, he'd also understood better what Brett Applegate was up against with the fairer sex.

Eight o'clock couldn't come fast enough for him.

He downed two more antacids and pushed the button to lower the windows. Damn that fool bet. Reversing roles hadn't been one of his wisest moves, but now a child's life was at stake. If Connor was his, then he would move heaven and earth to make up for lost time with his son.

Stepping on the gas pedal, he peeled down the road. During scorching hot summers in Afghanistan he'd picture himself whipping down the highway with the sun at his back and the cool wind blowing his hair in ten different directions. Like now. He'd daydreamed about coming home to Sunset Ranch and working alongside his brothers, too. He'd clung to those thoughts as he battled both enemy and unyielding climate.

Justin pulled into the parking lot of the Amber Pail, a hot spot for Douglas County locals and a place he probably should avoid. But it was early yet and he needed to kill some time and think without his family around. He climbed out of his truck, plopped his hat on his head and kept his sunglasses on. He strode toward the entrance to the bar and had nearly made it inside, when a man's voice boomed out behind him.

"Justin Slade…tell me you're not planning on drinking alone."

Justin turned to find Sheriff Robbie Dunphy striding in his direction. Justin had gone to high school with the sheriff's younger sister, Tiffany. "Hey, Robbie. How's it going?"

Robbie strode up to face him on the sidewalk. He filled out his tan uniform, the buttons on his shirt ready to pop. He stood head to head with Justin, and as usual had a smile on his face. He hardly fit the bill for a stereotypical hard-nosed lawman. "I got no complaints. How about you? You acclimatin' to being home again?"

"I'm getting there. Nine years is a long time to be away."

"I got to thinkin' you might just make a career of soldiering, with you getting the Congressional Medal of Honor and all."

Justin clamped his teeth together. The medal was a source of pride to him but at the same time, it reminded him of his failures. He didn't think of himself as a hero, but as a soldier who'd done his job. Brett's death had hit him hard, and he'd decided when his last tour of duty was up that he was through with the military. "At one time, I thought the same thing. But looks like I'm home to stay now."

"Well, good." Robbie gave him a congenial slap on the back. "Come on, then, and let me buy you a welcome home drink. Amber's still here, working her ass off and brewing the best ale in the state. You gotta try her latest concoction, something she calls Nevada Punch."

What the hell. He couldn't very well insult the sheriff and tell him he wanted to drink alone. Maybe some hometown company would keep his mind off of troubling thoughts and help him pass the time. "Sure thing, Sheriff."

They sat at a table right smack in the middle of the darkened tavern. It was a throwback to the sixties, with dim yellow lights reflecting off a long mahogany bar. The second his butt hit the padded vinyl seat, Amber came striding over, her teased brown hair as big as ever, swept up in the back with bobby pins and a little black bow.

"You're a sight for sore eyes, Justin Slade." She gave him a motherly kiss on the cheek.

"Hi, Amber."

"I do believe this is the first time you've been in my bar legitimately."

"Wasn't old enough before I left for boot camp."

"I know it, but you've been here dozens of times. I used to open the back room up for my son and the rest of you boys to play pool. You remember that, don't you?"

He nodded, thinking back on that time. "I'll never forget that trusty old pool table." He'd lost his virginity on that pool table with Betsy Ann Stankowski when he was sixteen.

"I'm not hearing any of this," the sheriff said, leaning way back in his chair.

Amber waved him off. "Robbie, don't tell me you didn't know about the boys coming here. You didn't make any noise about it because your little sis would tag along with them sometimes, so don't you get all high and mighty now. For pity's sake, I never gave any of the kids liquor."

The sheriff shrugged off her reprimand. "Who's getting high and mighty? I'm here to buy Justin a drink. What'll you have, boy? Want to try you some Nevada Punch?"

"Sure do."

"It's on the house," Amber said. Then she pointed at the sheriff. "And your favorite iced coffee since you had the good sense to bring Justin in."

"Thank you, kindly," Justin said.

"You got a heart of gold, Amber Louise." Robbie sent her a grin.

She lifted her brows at the sheriff dubiously before she turned to focus on Justin. "It's the least I can do for you. Why, you're a hero, saving five lives like you did. You make us all proud."

Though he was uncomfortable with the praise she lavished on him, Justin thanked her. She meant well. Everyone meant well, but he didn't want free drinks, or meals on the house, or reporters poking around Sunset Ranch, hoping to get an interview with the hometown hero.

What he wanted was time to adjust to being home.

Kat Grady had thrown a wrench into those plans, pronto.

Amber served the coffee to the sheriff and her specialty beer in a tall pilsner glass. Justin brought the glass to his lips and took a gulp of the dark, rich ale. "This is pretty good," he said to the sheriff.

"Hits the spot, doesn't it? So what are your plans now that you're back home? Planning on working on the horse farm with your brothers?"

"Don't rightly know yet. Those two have the ranch running smooth as silk."

While overseas, he'd given it a lot of thought. He loved the land and raising horses, but when he'd returned home three days ago, he wasn't sure where he fit in the well-oiled machine Sunset Ranch had become. Logan and Luke had been at it a long time, and they had the running of Sunset Ranch, the lucrative Slade horse farm, and Sunset Lodge, an upscale version of a dude ranch, down to a science. Sure, Justin could work with them but not out of necessity. They didn't really need him.

And since Brett's death, Justin had been bouncing something around in his head that wouldn't roll away. The more he thought about it, the more it made sense to him.

But first, he had to deal with fatherhood.

He glanced at his watch. He had four more hours before his meeting with Kat.

"Well, if you're of a mind at all for public service, let me toss this suggestion out at you," the sheriff said. "There's a county commissioner's seat opening up next month. You'd be perfect for the job. Why, with your background, you'd have pull and influence enough to get a lot of things accomplished. Could do a lot of good for the citizens of Douglas County."

Justin couldn't believe his ears. "What?"

Sheriff Dunphy's eyes shone bright as he nodded encouragement. "Jeff Washington, our county assessor, well…he and I were talking about the vacancy and the upcoming special election yesterday. Your name came up first thing."

Justin began shaking his head. "I've been home three days, Robbie, and my name's coming up for a special election?"

"Well, no, not exactly. Your name came up because we've got to clear a date on our calendar. The county's planning on throwing a parade in your honor."

Caught off guard, Justin felt the blood drain from his face. He kept his mouth from dropping open, just barely, as humbling astonishment rolled through his gut, making him ready to pop a few more antacids. "I...don't know what to say. A parade?"

Wasn't that sort of thing reserved for Olympic champions and, well...Santa?

The last thing Justin wanted was a parade. He didn't deserve the adoration of the entire county. He'd barely made it home in one piece mentally, and the word *hero* was reserved for soldiers much braver than he'd ever been.

"Yes, we're all excited about it. But it's gonna take a while to pull it off. Douglas County wants to welcome their hero home in style. We've got three high school bands practicing, a news crew alerted and the county's Women's Association and the Boy Scouts working together to build you a float."

Holy crap.

A thought flitted into his head and he turned a suspicious eye on the sheriff. "You didn't just bump into me today, did you, Robbie?"

"Of course I did. I would never abuse my authority by having patrol cars give me your location or anything." The sheriff's wry smile said the exact opposite.

Robbie was a sly one, not as Gomer Pyle–ignorant as he had people believing.

Amber strolled over, carrying a tray with two dishes

of fried chicken, potatoes and gravy. She set the plates down on the table and smiled at him. "Here you go, Justin. Meal's on the house, too. It's my way of saying thank you for your service to the country."

Robbie Dunphy rubbed his hands together, peering at his plate with boyish glee. "Looks delicious, doesn't it, Justin?"

Justin stared at the food for a second and then raised his eyes to Amber, who patiently waited for his approval. "Sure does, Amber. Thank you."

"And while we're eating," Robbie said to Amber, "Justin's gonna think about becoming Douglas County's new district commissioner."

"That's wonderful. Well, you two take all the time you need."

After Amber walked off, Justin finished his ale and leaned forward in his chair. "Robbie, I know you mean well, but I'm not ready to make any decisions about my future just yet. The one thing I do know is that I'm not a politician. No way. No how."

He didn't want a parade in his honor, either, but Justin couldn't bring himself to call it off. There were already too many people involved. Douglas County had been good to the Slades over the years, and Justin wouldn't insult the citizens by telling them he'd rather be face-to-face with a rattlesnake than sitting on a float, waving to people who'd come out to pay him tribute.

It wasn't until he pulled through the gates of Sunset Ranch that Justin's muscles began to relax. Spirited mares and stallions dotted the pastures along the drive toward the house. The acreage was fertile here, the soil nurtured by runoff from the Sierra Nevadas and rain plentiful enough to keep the pastures green most of the year. Justin inhaled the scent of alfalfa and manure, of leather and earth, as he approached the one-story Slade house and parked the truck.

He'd always loved his childhood home and since returning he felt a greater appreciation for the freedoms and privileges life brought to him. He'd been in hellholes, seen danger and atrocity at its worst and survived, though not without some painful internal scars. The place he'd come from in the Middle East seemed far removed from life on Sunset Ranch.

Off in the distance he spotted two riders and immediately recognized one as his brother Luke. The woman riding beside him was his new fiancée, Audrey. The two had recently become engaged and were due to have a child of their own.

With Luke engaged and Logan's wedding fast approaching, Justin felt like a fifth wheel already. And he'd only been home three days.

He climbed down from the cab and gave a wave to Ward Halliday, who was standing next to his car over by the main corral. The ranch foreman had welcomed Justin on his first day home with a manly hug, making no mention of his war hero status. He'd only wished him well and told him he'd missed him. Justin appreciated how perceptive the man was not to make too big a deal out of things. "How's it going, Ward?"

"No complaints," he called out. "Molly's got beef empanadas waiting for me at home."

"Sounds good. Tell her hello."

Ward nodded. "Stop on by sometime. Molly would love to see you."

"I will."

Justin climbed the steps of the house and walked inside. From the foyer, he could see Logan leaning against his office door down the long hallway. He was drinking liquor from a tumbler and nodded for Justin to join him.

"About time you showed up, little bro. I've been fielding your calls all day. Come take a look."

Justin's boots clanged against the stone floor as he made his way toward the office where Logan conducted Sunset Ranch business. Logan worked at the house, while his fiancée, Sophia, worked at Sunset Lodge. The two were planning a big blowout of a wedding. But they'd waited for him to come home; Logan had asked him to be his best man on his first day back.

Luke, too, had decided to wait so that Justin could be in attendance before tying the knot with Audrey.

"Want a drink?" Logan asked.

"No, I'm good." He glanced around. Today, just like the other days since his arrival, he felt his father's presence in the room despite Logan's efforts to remove all traces of Randall Slade. Some things just died hard, he thought as he plunked down into a black leather armchair.

Logan sat down and faced him from across his desk. "You might, after you see these. You have seven phone messages flashing on the machine, and Ellie took all of these from the house phone." Logan handed over a stack of notes. "Looks like you have at least three messages from Betsy Ann Stankowski alone."

Justin's head shot up. "You don't say."

Logan gave him a knowing smile. "Maybe she wants to pick up where you left off before you enlisted."

Justin balked at that. Logan had caught them fooling around behind the barn once and when questioned, Justin had confessed Betsy Ann had been his first. His older brother had told him point-blank not to mess around with girls on the ranch or anywhere else. He was too young to know what he was doing and there could be consequences to pay. Yeah, well, years later, he hadn't taken that advice with Kat, and as a result, he'd fathered a child. *Maybe.*

"Betsy Ann and I were over way before I left town."

"You mean, you actually listened to me?"

Justin clucked his tongue. "Now why would I do that?"

A smile spread across Logan's face. "I didn't think so. Betsy Ann teaches grammar school and I hear her students love her. She's also made a name for herself as the president of the Douglas County Women's Association."

"Seriously?" Betsy Ann would always be stamped in his memory for granting him those painfully awkward, profound and awe-inspiring sixty seconds on the pool table. "She always did like school."

"Three messages in one day," Logan said. "She sure wants you for something."

Justin didn't think Betsy Ann had any lingering feelings for him. She'd dumped him like a hot potato in their junior year for some older guy. He'd bet fifty bucks that he knew what she wanted from him. If she was president of the Women's Association, then she was calling about the parade. Justin didn't want to open up that can of worms with his brother now. He had enough to contend with.

He scanned over all the messages scribbled down on notepaper, tossing them down one after another onto the desk. At some point he'd have to call these people back, but he wasn't going to do that today.

Logan spoke up. "Let me know if I can help. You shouldn't be bombarded by everyone you've ever known in a fifty-mile radius on your first week back."

"Thanks, but I'll take care of it."

"I also gotta tell you Luke shooed two reporters off the property this morning after you left. They want interviews with Sergeant Slade."

Justin jerked his head back and forth. "Man, I didn't think my homecoming would cause such a stir."

"Be patient," Logan said, leaning back in his chair. "You coming home a war hero is big news around here. Everyone wants a piece of you."

"Tell me about it. Robbie Dunphy cornered me today. He's got some wild ideas about my future. Don't even ask."

Logan's eyes lit with understanding. "Okay. Listen, Sophia wants to have you over to the cottage for dinner tonight. It'll be quiet with just us, Luke and Audrey. No phone calls. No one barging in or cornering you."

The cottage had been Sophia's home when they were growing up. She'd lived there with her mother, Louisa, who managed the lodge. But when it came out that Louisa and Randall Slade had been lovers, the whole thing went bad and Louisa packed up Sophia and left Sunset Ranch. Recently, because Randall had put Sophia in his will, she'd returned to the ranch for her inheritance and Logan had fallen in love with her. "Sounds good, but I can't make it. Tell Sophia I'm sorry. I have a…something to do tonight."

Logan's brows lifted. "A female…something to do?"

Justin glanced away. His brother was too damn perceptive. "Let's just say, it's important. I'll tell you about it once I figure it all out myself."

"All right, but you know that Luke and I are here if you need us. We have your back."

"I appreciate that."

Justin left Logan's office and walked to his bedroom in the opposite wing of the house. Baseball trophies from his Little League days sat next to a smattering of CDs and DVDs from his teen years on a bookshelf. Textbooks were stacked one on top of the other, and his old dial-up computer that deserved a spot on *Antiques Roadshow* was stored on the lower shelf. Justin grinned at the old thing, thinking how far technology had progressed since his childhood. When he'd arrived home, he made a vow to tackle this room and get it up to speed ASAP. But he hadn't brought order to the chaos yet. There was something mildly comforting in having things as they were… at least for a little while longer.

His brother Luke had seen fit to order the only new item in the room, a king-size bed to replace the single he'd had since he was a boy. When he sat down, the firm mattress supported his weight and he smiled as he stared directly across the room at the walk-in closet that had once doubled as a fort, a secret hideaway and an imaginary campground.

For the past nine years, he'd gotten used to close quarters with only the essentials of everyday life. Just a short time ago, his entire personal space on the outpost could fit inside that walk-in closet.

He closed his eyes for a moment. An image of Brett appeared. He couldn't force it from his mind.

He was holding Brett's limp body. His face was streaked with blood, clear blue eyes suddenly wild in the face of death. Crimson puddles pooled over Brett's belly. Justin's hand pressed down on the bloody seepage.

"Get out of here. I've lost this bet."

"Hang on, buddy. Stay with me, Brett. Brett."

Eyes devoid of life stared back at him. His friend's warmth turned to ice.

Justin lay there with him, clinging to his body.

Shedding tears.

Justin snapped his eyes open. His body jerked involuntarily and he bounded from the bed. He paced, pounding the floor with his boots, back and forth, back and forth, with his head down. Tremors made it hard to breathe. His heart raced.

Brett's bloody face remained.

He'd died four months ago and for all those months, the grief and guilt had been eating at Justin.

He forced his mind to turn to something else.

Connor's chubby cheeks and vivid dark eyes filled his thoughts. Images of the little boy, so small yet so mighty, slowed his racing pulse. His breaths came easier now.

Connor.

Justin thought of the boy with proprietary pride.

He had to find out for sure if the boy was truly his son.

"I'm going in to kiss Connor good-night," Kat whispered to Aunt Mattie from outside the bedroom door. "He'll most likely sleep through the night. Thank you again for watching him."

Aunt Mattie gestured with a wave of the hand. "Don't you worry about a thing. You have a nice visit with Cecelia now. Doris is coming for a cup of tea. We'll watch out for our little boy."

Kat tiptoed into Brett's old room—which she now shared with her son—and made her way to the snow-white crib on loan from one of Matilda's neighbors. She smiled at the sight of Connor asleep atop baby-blue sheets with cartoon monkeys printed on them. "You be a good baby now. Sleep tight," she murmured, placing an air kiss over Connor's cheek. "Mama loves you."

She lingered there a few extra moments, watching him breathe, in and out, his plump baby chest rising and falling. This little person, cozy in a terry-cloth sleeper decorated with brown footballs, filled her world with joy. She'd never get over the miracle of her unexpected but cherished son. It was hard to leave him, if even for a short while, but this meeting tonight had to happen.

Kat hated lying to Aunt Mattie. But she couldn't think of any way around it. At least a lie didn't feel so much like a lie if there was some truth in it. So Kat had told Matilda she was picking up a check from Cecelia Tilton for the baby clothes she'd put on consignment at her boutique. A month ago, when Kat had mentioned Babylicious, her budding online store featuring the fashionable and affordable baby clothes she designed, a very gracious Cecelia had offered her a place in her shop to help promote her work. Cecelia's home wasn't far from Blossom and this afternoon Kat had phoned the woman to make the arrangements.

Her conscience continued to nag her as she left the house and headed to Cecilia's. But half an hour later, as she drove away from the shop owner's home with a small check in hand, she felt a little better. Three hundred and forty dollars would go a long way in helping Mattie pay for her medications.

Kat shelved thoughts of business as soon as she pulled up to Blossom. Her heart in her throat, she shook off tremors of doubt, straightened her frame, held her head high and walked into the deserted café. Blossom was known more for their savory hot breakfasts and so-so lunch salads. Not too many patrons dared their blue plate specials at this hour of the evening.

Kat spotted Justin sitting in a corner booth with his head down, looking impatiently at his phone. Her tremors took on a different character as memories rushed in of that weekend she'd spent with him. She'd let down her guard for two days with a hot, charming, understanding man, who'd left his indelible stamp on her. She'd thought about him for weeks afterward but had convinced herself he wasn't right for her. *He* hadn't been enough. She'd wanted more out of life than he could offer. They'd ended things civilly with no illusions of anything else developing between them.

On a steadying breath, Kat lifted her chin and ventured farther into the café. But a piece of broken grout between the floor tiles trapped her four-inch heel, throwing her off balance. Flailing her arms, she managed not to fall flat on her face. But darn if the perfectly dignified entrance she'd plotted in her head wasn't shot to hell.

Justin saw the whole thing.

As she walked closer, he took in her clothes with his piercing gaze. She wore stretch blue jeans and a billowy white top tucked under a cropped jacket. A sterling silver rope chain made of entwined oblong circles dangled from her neck. On her wrist she wore a matching bracelet.

The clothes were her own designs and had been rejected by every major fashion house in New York City.

"You're late," Justin said, rising from his seat.

"Babies aren't predicable. It always seems to take longer than you think to put them down to sleep."

He gave her excuse some thought. Then his lips thinned. "I wouldn't know."

Oh, boy. Kat got it. He wasn't happy about the circumstances, but then neither was she. If they were going to accomplish anything, they would have to agree to civility. By this time of night, after a day of taking care of a baby and an aging woman, Kat was pooped and not up to verbal sparring. "I can leave and we can do this another time...when your attitude is better."

Justin swore under his breath. His mouth clamped down and he sent her a long thoughtful look. Then like magic, his demeanor changed before her eyes. His body visibly loosened up, as if on command, and he gave her a reluctant but gracious smile. "You're right. I apologize. Please sit down so we can talk."

Accepting his apology, she dropped into a cushioned seat facing him and set her purse down beside her. As she looked across the café table, a quick zip of awareness caught her off guard as she really, really studied Justin's handsome face.

My God...Connor looks exactly like him.

Yes, their hair and eyes were the same color, but Connor shared Justin's wide full mouth, too, and a deep dimple that popped out on the left side when they smiled. She couldn't begin to count how many times she'd kissed that disappearing dimple on her baby's face. Their skin tones were smooth and olive and she imagined Connor would easily tan golden-brown just like Justin when he got older. They shared the same hairline that cut a neat straight line across their forehead. Connor would have the same arrow-sharp nose, too, when he grew up.

Her son's adorable baby features were a precursor to Justin Slade's adult appearance.

His brows furrowed. "Who's watching the baby?"

"Aunt Mattie and Doris Brubaker are with Connor."

She went on to explain, "Doris is a neighbor. We're friends, and I asked her to stay with Aunt Mattie until I got back. They're having tea and I don't want to impose on them any longer than necessary."

"Okay. Let's get on with it, then. Ladies first."

"You told me you were Brett Applegate. I want to know why you lied to me." Then she added, "I would appreciate the truth."

"Just remember that when it's my turn to ask questions."

A waitress wearing a snappy blue outfit and white tights showed up at the table with a notepad. "Hi, I'm Toni, and I'll be serving you tonight. Have you looked at the menu yet? Just so you know, the blue plate special is—"

"Decaf coffee for me," Kat said. Her stomach knotted at the thought of food. "That's all I'd like."

"I'll have the same," Justin said, nodding to the young girl. "Thank you."

"No cherry pie or apple cobbler?"

They both shook their heads. "Okay, I'll be back with your coffee in a sec."

Kat watched the waitress walk away and then turned to Justin. "You were about to tell me why you lied to me that weekend."

The muscles in Justin's face pinched tight, a distant look in his eyes hinting at regret. "I lost a bet."

Kat blinked. "You lost a bet? What does that mean?"

He leaned forward, his elbows flat on the table. The material of his navy shirt pulled taut across his broad shoulders, and it wasn't hard to remember what he'd looked like with a shirt off. She could almost feel the sensation of touching his golden skin and ripped muscles under her fingertips now. "It means Brett beat me at arm wrestling. Best of five."

Kat didn't like where this was going. "So?"

"So, I made this stupid bet with him, because I never thought I'd have to pay up. He was egging me on in front of my men until I finally thought, what the hell. I'd never lost a match to Brett before. If he won, I'd have to trade places with him the next time we had time off. We'd switch wallets—and the cash and credit cards inside—and assume each other's identity with…" Justin's lips snapped shut. He ran his fingers over his mouth and winced.

Kat caught on. "With women?"

He gave her a slow nod.

"So, the weekend you spent with me was to pay off a bet? You used me…lied to me…had no intention of ever telling me the truth?"

Something hard flickered in his eyes. "I didn't use you. If you remember correctly, I didn't pressure you for anything. And you made it clear you wanted no ties to a hick from a small town, remember? We didn't exchange so much as cell phone numbers when I walked out your door."

That was beside the point. He'd been amazing that weekend and by the time the second night rolled around, Kat couldn't imagine not sharing her bed with him. He'd been compassionate and kind and patient and just what she'd needed at that moment in her life.

Maybe he'd assumed more than Brett's identity that weekend; maybe Justin had taken on Brett's personality, as well. That weekend helped heal some of her old wounds. She'd needed a strong shoulder and an understanding heart. It hadn't been all fun and games between them, it had been unexpectedly more. "I'd put it a little gentler than that, Justin. But yes, it's true. I couldn't get romantically involved with a man that wouldn't—"

"Serve your purposes?"

She tried harder to explain. "Didn't fit into the life I wanted. Don't forget, you lied about who you were and that might have altered my decision about the weekend."

"You mean if you'd known I was a loaded Nevada rancher, you might have taken me to bed one night sooner?"

Her cheeks burned. His accusation was a hard slap to her face. He wasn't going to get away with it. "You have no right to judge me. You have no idea who I am and what I've been through. I didn't ask you to come over to me at that hotel bar."

"Why wouldn't I want to meet a beautiful woman? It was obvious you were waiting for someone. You kept checking your watch. I figured some jerk stood you up. And I was right. He didn't give a crap that your mother had recently passed away, did he?"

That jerk had been Michael Golden, the heir to the entire Golden Hotel chain. It was a blind date. Later, she'd found out from her friend that he'd been called out of town suddenly and hadn't gotten word to her. She'd been waiting for him more than an hour when Justin strolled up to her table.

The waitress walked over and set their coffee cups down. Taking one look at the intense discussion at the table, she lowered her voice. "I'll be in the back if you need anything else."

Justin gave her a sharp nod and she strode away.

Steam wafted up from Kat's ceramic mug of decaf and she moved it out of her line of vision. "I told you that night, I didn't date soldiers."

"We told each other a lot of things."

"But what I said to you, what I confessed during those

two days that we were together was the truth. You can't say the same, can you?"

He pursed his lips and hung his shoulders. "No."

She leaned back in her seat and stared at him.

He stared back. "I'd like to know something. How hard did you try to find Brett?"

Her lids lowered. "I wrote to him and he never answered back. I don't know if he ever received my letter."

"*One* letter was all he was worth to you?"

"I didn't say that."

"We were stationed in a forward operating base in Delaram, the third battalion of the 4th Marines. I know I mentioned that."

"All I heard you say was Afghanistan. I didn't want to know the details. I didn't remember anything else. It doesn't really matter now. Clearly, it wasn't Brett I slept with that night. It was you. But I didn't know that because you lied about your identity."

Justin shook his head. "I didn't know we'd conceived a child."

"Obviously," she said. "I wasn't planning on having a child, either, but I wouldn't trade having Connor in my life for anything." A surge of emotion brought tears to her eyes. "My son is everything to me."

When she'd finally looked Brett's family up and come to Silver Springs to do the right thing, Aunt Mattie had given her the news of Brett's death. Brett had died in action, and Kat couldn't help but think if she'd tried harder to find him, he wouldn't have taken chances. Maybe he wouldn't have died at all and maybe Mattie Applegate's heart wouldn't have been broken. Now Kat understood that wasn't the case at all because if her letter had reached Brett, he would've put two and two together and shown it to his buddy. He would've known the baby she carried wasn't his but Justin's.

It was a sad set of circumstances and she'd lived with the guilt of not trying to find Brett sooner. But in the end, she had done the right thing. "I know there were some things I could have done differently. I…didn't." She shrugged a shoulder, not knowing what else to say. "I just didn't."

Justin peered deep into her eyes. "There are things I would've done differently, too, had I known. Tell me one thing. Do you believe that Connor is my son?"

She didn't hesitate. She'd always known exactly when she conceived her little boy. "I know he is."

For a moment tears welled in Justin's eyes. The hard planes of his face softened and his shoulders fell with relief. As he took it all in, he began nodding and Kat saw his expression transform suddenly. Determination set his jaw. "It's been a year and a half."

"Yes. Almost."

He blinked and then blew breath from his lungs.

Just then the waitress walked into the room and said, "I've got to start closing up, but you can finish your coffee. Don't mind me."

She glanced at the two cups that had gone untouched and then looked away.

Justin pulled a twenty out of his wallet and set it down on the table. Then he rose to his full six-foot-two height and reached for Kat's hand. "Let's get out of here."

"Where?"

"Doesn't matter. We need to finish this conversation."

Reluctantly, she took his hand and let him lead her out of the café.

Three

His hand across her lower back, Justin guided Kat out of the café. Darkness and the chilly night air surrounded them and Kat shivered. "Get your coat," Justin said.

"I didn't bring one. Why, where are we going?"

"For a walk. Give me a second." He marched to his truck, ducked inside the front cab and came up with a leather bomber jacket. It was worn, its soft leather cracking a bit and the lambswool lining thick enough to warm a body in a snowstorm. "This will do," he said. "You gotta know these nights get cold."

"I didn't think I'd be spending a lot of time outside this late."

"It's not late and we've hardly gotten started."

He wrapped the jacket around her shoulders and she fit her arms through the sleeves. The jacket was two sizes too big for her, the shoulder seams going partway down her arms and the hem nearly touching her knees. Watching her platinum curls bounce off the collar, he gripped the lapels and drew her closer. Her eyes, big and green and surprised, snapped up to his. She was unique, a throwback to a classic fifties movie starlet with that ice-blond hair, an innocent expression that proved deadly and a luscious mouth painted pink and rosy.

"Warm enough?"

She glanced at his mouth for a split second, a tempting little look that pulled his groin taut.

"Uh-huh."

He hesitated to let her go.

Moments ticked by as they stared into each other's eyes. His grip tightened on the fabric, his knuckles grazing her torso just an inch from the two full ripe breasts that had given him a sliver of heaven once. He hadn't forgotten.

He heaved a big sigh and let go. Immediately, she tugged the jacket tight across her chest and crossed her arms.

Justin put a hand on her back again, guiding her down the street. "When I drove up, I saw a town square. There's a gazebo we can use. Or we can just sit in my truck with the motor running and the heater on."

She shook her head at that notion and he was glad of it. Kat warm and comfy in the cab of his truck wouldn't serve either of them well. The last time they'd been alone together in close quarters they'd had a marathon of combustible sex. Justin still felt the pull of attraction to her, but the stakes were too high now for any wrong move.

They walked south with light from the streetlamps leading the way. A few people were out for a brisk stroll, and Justin and Kat both smiled cordially or nodded their heads in greeting while they pressed on. The gazebo was visible in the distance, marking the center of the town square. They walked past park benches and down a garden path until they reached it. Luckily, they had it all to themselves.

Justin led her to a wooden bench that was painted white and she sat down. Behind her, past the lattice, flood lamps lit the surrounding shrubs, giving off enough faint light so that they could see each other's faces. Justin paced for a second, pulling in his scattered emotions.

"Tell me about Connor."

Kat's face beamed immediately and her voice took on

a whimsical, loving tone. "He's an amazing little boy. He was born healthy and strong. His Apgar rating was ten."

"What's an Apgar rating?"

"It's a test they do at birth, named after the doctor who invented it. It measures things like heart rate and breathing and muscle tone. Ten is the highest score a baby can get."

Justin nodded. Unfamiliar pride pierced his heart.

"When I brought him home from the hospital, he took to breast-feeding right away. He's a good eater and a pretty sound sleeper. You have to know a few little Connor tricks to get him to take a nap and I'm learning just like he is, every day."

"What kind of tricks?"

"Well, first I give him a bottle. And then I sing to him. If that doesn't work, I show him a *Sesame Street* video clip on my phone. He's crazy about some of the characters. And once he's mellow, I hum to him, some of his favorite baby tunes. When I get him to sleep, sometimes I just watch him breathe and thank my blessings for him every minute of every—"

Kat stopped talking abruptly. "I'm…sorry."

Regret pumped through his veins. "So am I."

"It's done, Justin. We can't change the past."

"I'll never get those months back, Kat. I lost all that time with Connor."

Sympathy settled in her eyes. "I know that. I can't imagine what that's like. But if you had known, it's not like you would've seen Connor that much. You were serving in the military."

"That's not the point. He has a family here and I would've done what I could to spend time with him. To acknowledge him, even if I couldn't watch him grow. But that's all going to change starting right this second. I'm going to be a major part of his life now. He's going to know I'm his father."

"No, Justin." Kat's green eyes sharpened. "You can't do that to Mattie. It'll kill her. If you take that baby away from her, she'll die. I swear to you, she'll go into cardiac arrest."

Justin took a step back, noting the warning in her voice. Was she serious or overstating the facts?

"You have no idea," she continued. "When I got here two months ago, she'd just been released from the hospital. She'd had a major heart attack after she learned of Brett's death. She had no reason to live. She'd lost fifteen pounds, and as you can see, she's a small woman to begin with, and she didn't want any part of rehab. She was living in the house alone. I saw the hopelessness in her eyes, Justin. It reminded me, of…well, of my own mother. When I told her my story, about how I met Brett and conceived his child, she…she made a remarkable comeback. In just the few months I've been here, she's put on weight and her whole outlook has changed. Her heart is still damaged and she has to take it easy, but the doctor has told her over and over that our little Connor is her antidote to heart disease. You have to believe me. You *cannot* tell that woman that Connor isn't Brett's son."

"That's hardly fair, Kat. I've already missed out on so much with Connor. And it's not fair to the boy to deprive him of his real father."

"Do you want to be responsible for putting Aunt Mattie back in the hospital…or worse?"

Damn it. His gut told him Kat was telling the truth. The blow was hard to take. He didn't want to deny his son a father a second longer. But he'd seen Matilda Applegate with his own eyes. She was frail and weakened. She certainly looked older than her seventy years in body, but when her gaze lit on Connor, it had a youthful spirited glow. He hated to admit it but that woman's life revolved around that little boy.

Every day of Justin's life, Brett's death gnawed at him.

He'd vowed that once he returned home, he'd come clean and speak with Brett's aunt. Telling Mattie the truth about Brett's death would go a long way in clearing his conscience. It had taken Justin three days to build up the courage to visit the woman and he'd been prepared to lay it all on the line. But now, as he studied Kat's determined expression, the set of her delicate jaw and the plea in her eyes, he was boxed into a corner. "I don't want to hurt Mattie Applegate."

"Then…don't."

"I want to know my son."

"You will. I promise." Her voice held conviction.

Justin stared at her. A promise from Katherine Grady? Could he trust her? The fool in him, who saw her as a beautiful, sexy, desirable woman, wanted so badly to believe her, but he couldn't chance it. The stakes were just too high. He had every right to know his son, to learn Connor tricks and comfort him when he was tired and grumpy. He wanted to bond with him and give him fatherly love.

Justin stepped closer to her. She smelled like gardenias, fresh and fragrant and distinct. Her light springtime scent contrasted sharply with the time of year, the chill in the air. "What are you suggesting?"

Kat's lashes fell to her cheeks, blond curls bouncing as she shook her head. "I don't know, Justin. We'll have to work it out secretly. I do know I won't stop you from seeing Connor. I'll make every effort to make it easy for you to be with him, as long as you don't tell Aunt Mattie the truth. Please."

Whether Matilda Applegate would truly die of a coronary or not upon learning the truth, no one would ever know, but Kat sure believed it as fact. And that's all he could go on right now. He couldn't chance it, but he damn well didn't have to like it.

He'd had a plan in mind for Mattie Applegate from the

start, to honor Brett and his late uncle Ralph, who had also been a war veteran. He wanted to help the Applegate family. Maybe now was the time to implement that plan.

He didn't want to deny his son's birth but what choice did he have? "All right. I won't tell her."

Gratitude filled her eyes as a broad smile graced her face. "Thank you, Justin. Thank you."

Swallowing hard, Justin couldn't look away. Her glowing appreciation and gleam in her pretty green eyes was a little too hard to take. He wondered if his good sense had taken a joy ride. Was he remembering too much about the leave he'd spent with Kat, or had he just been without a woman for too long?

He gathered the lapels of the bomber jacket in both hands and gently drew her onto her feet and close to him.

"Oh."

He focused on her tempting pouty mouth. She didn't pull away and that was good enough for him. He reached behind her neck and tugged her mouth to his.

"What are you doing?" she whispered over the seam of his lips.

He brushed his mouth over hers, once, twice. Testing and tasting her.

From down deep in her throat, she purred.

What the hell *was* he doing? It was already too complicated between them, but that didn't stop him from delving deep into her mouth with strokes of his tongue. From bracing his hands inside the jacket and absorbing the heat of her skin burning through her clothes.

He held her hips, nestled her closer yet, and drew out sweet nectar from her inviting mouth. From the first touch of their lips, everything had come back to him. During those cold lonely nights overseas, how often he'd think of the time he'd spent with her like this. Holding her, tasting her and making love to her. She hadn't been the only woman he'd been with during his time in the military, but she'd definitely been the most memorable.

From under the warmth of the jacket, he lifted her blouse and splayed his fingers across her belly. His fingertips touched where she'd carried his baby. Her skin now was firm and flat and silky smooth.

A whimper rose from her throat and she leaned into him. She smelled like heaven. Strands of silky hair fell across his cheek. From his gut, a low moan climbed up his throat as he slid his hand to the warm flesh around her waist. Raw, powerful desire zipped through his body.

Flashing lights from an oncoming car brightened the square for a second and touched on where they stood in the gazebo. Kat startled and backed away, her hand going to her mouth and her eyes lifting to his. In them, he saw longing, surprise and condemnation all at once.

Her lipstick was smeared, her hair ruffled, but none of that mattered on Kat. She was gorgeous no matter what. Drop-dead gorgeous. She wrapped the jacket tight around her torso and hugged herself as if summoning courage to say something. Then, her eyes flickered and she blurted, "I dated your brother a couple of times."

Justin snapped to attention. "What?"

"I thought it'd be better if you found out from me. Luke and I…"

"What about you and Luke?"

"It was nothing…. I was lonely and worried sick about Mattie. We saw each other briefly. You might as well know now, I've met your whole family."

A shudder wracked his body. Justin couldn't tear his gaze away from the woman who'd just dropped a bombshell on him. Kat and Luke? Her confession ripped right through him. His pride suffered and he gnashed his teeth at the thought of Kat with his brother. What other bombs

would she drop on him? It served to remind him that he
didn't really know Kat Grady at all.

"Do you want to know about what happened between—?"

"I'll get my information from Luke. But I do want something else from you."

She blinked then, her lips trembling. "What would that
be?"

"A paternity test."

Justin followed her home and waited until she was
safely in the house before revving the engine and speed-
ing off. Kat sighed quietly. She wasn't thrilled about Justin doubting her word about the baby's parenthood and
demanding a paternity test, but if it was necessary to ease
his mind in order to keep the secret a little while longer,
she had to agree for Mattie's sake.

Kat moved through the house she thought of as home,
realizing that all this could come crashing down around
her. She'd made some boner mistakes in her day, but protecting Mattie Applegate from the truth wasn't one of
them. She felt it deep down in her core, that she was doing
the right thing by keeping the truth from her.

She peeked in on Connor first, and the gentle beam
of love she carried inside brightened when she looked at
him cozy and warm in his crib. There weren't any words
strong enough to explain the unconditional love she had
for her son. There were no borders, no boundaries or limits in her adoration. She'd only wished she hadn't tried so
hard to make it work with Michael Golden in New York.
He was all wrong for Connor. She realized that now and
she chalked up her bad decision to survival.

Next, she moved to Mattie's room and tiptoed two steps
inside to peer at the patchwork quilt nestled around Mattie's slender shoulders.

"I'm still breathing," the older woman said.

Kat laughed softly. "I would hope so."

"Keeping awake, just in case Connor needs me."

"He's sound asleep, Aunt Mattie."

"That's good, sweetheart. Not a peep out of him tonight."

"You can go to sleep now," Kat said, backing out of the room.

"I think I will."

"Good night, Aunt Mattie," Kat said from the doorway. "Thank you."

"Good night, sweetheart."

The glow inside Kat's heart got a shade brighter with Mattie's affection. Kat may be saving her life, but Matilda Applegate might just be saving hers, too.

Kat walked quietly into the spare bedroom Mattie had used to store all of Ralph's clothing and fishing gear. He'd been gone for years, but Mattie said she liked to have his things surrounding her to keep him close. Kat thought it sweet and romantic. She'd never had that kind of relationship with anyone. But she had Connor now and he was enough.

Mattie had cleared out half of the closet and four dresser drawers for Kat's business. Kat had found an old pine desk in the barn, then sanded and lathered it with walnut stain to make it useful for her purposes. Now it housed a printer and her laptop computer. Fishing rods held up one corner of the room and tackle boxes were stacked up three high in another, with Aunt Mattie's sewing machine in between. Luckily it wasn't a relic and Kat had been able to update some parts to make it run more efficiently. Kat saw it as her salvation, a way to put her talent to good use.

She sat down at the machine and picked up the dress pattern she'd designed last month. Then she started poking pins into the yellow dotted Swiss material of the garment she'd started working on early this morning, before Justin Slade had turned her world upside down.

Her lips tasted of him and his rugged musky scent filled her nostrils still. A steady low hum like a gentle spring breeze whispered through her body, invading her good sense. She could easily fall into those sensations again. Pitiful female that she was, she missed the strength of a man's arms around her and a strong shoulder to rely on when the strife of the day got to be too much. So sue her for responding to that kiss, for letting herself fall prey to Justin Slade's advances tonight.

She may have been guilty of some things, but he'd lied to her in the first place, causing this whole mess. Justin Slade was no saint.

Except that he was. He'd received the Medal of Honor for saving five soldiers' lives. She'd looked him up on the internet after he left this morning. She faintly recalled Luke mentioning once that his brother was a decorated soldier. At the time, she hadn't made any connection, but then, why would she? She'd had no idea Luke was related to her son's father. The paternity test, a mere swabbing of the baby's and father's mouths, would prove Justin's paternity, she had no doubt.

She fed material into the Singer and guided the fabric through. Her shoulders relaxed with each perfect stitch, her heart warming with the steady automatic buzzing of the machine. Kat let nimble fingers work their magic on cloth that would soon become a sunny Easter dress for one lucky little girl. With her prototype designs shipped to fashion houses and orders coming in now from local towns, Kat ran her small-time business, Babylicious, from Mattie Applegate's spare bedroom. But for right now, tonight, sewing this dress, losing herself in work she loved, helped bank her rising fear that somehow Justin Slade could make life extremely difficult for her.

* * *

Justin thought his time hiding behind corners and being suspicious of everything around him was over. He was wrong. Keeping a paternity test under wraps in Douglas County wasn't possible. He couldn't trust anyone within earshot of his doctor's office to keep a secret this big. Not now, when every acquaintance he'd ever known was stopping him on the street to shake his hand and friends he hadn't seen since high school were coming to pay him a visit on the ranch.

Justin had called in a favor from a family friend, a doctor who'd gotten a pretty sweet deal on a thoroughbred stallion from the Slade horse farm. Dr. Barrington practiced two towns over in another county, and promised discretion.

The next morning, he arranged to meet Kat in a minimall parking lot in Silver Springs. Then, with Connor strapped into the car seat, he drove Kat's car to Dr. Barrington's office for the appointment. It actually took longer to boil water than to give the test, and afterward Justin wasted no time driving them back to where he'd parked his truck.

The boy had fallen asleep, his little head propped against one side of the car seat, his hair damp with sleep sweat, breathing quietly. Justin's heart lurched. He'd experienced anger and regret and bitterness from this situation, but right now, all he felt was a magnetic pull to the child he might have fathered. Already, he was thinking of the future and of all the things he wanted to teach his son.

"That didn't take long," Kat said with quiet relief.

"Connor didn't seem to mind." Justin already felt protective about the boy. He was glad the swab test was just as accurate as a blood test. No needles. DNA was DNA, no matter how they acquired it, Dr. Barrington had assured them.

"It was painless, thank goodness," Kat said, glancing in the rearview mirror to check on Connor as they drove on.

Justin's chest filled with pride. "He seems like a good baby."

Kat's smile was bright as sunshine. "He has his moments. I suppose all babies do, but he's wonderful. He loves to laugh. We play giggle games. And he loves to eat. I don't think I've ever seen him refuse food." The look in her eyes when she spoke of Connor was something to see.

They stared at each other for several seconds.

Justin wanted to spend the day together, to take them to lunch and watch Connor eat his meal. To walk the baby around town in his stroller, just like a real family, and to do all the things he'd missed out on. But Justin stood to lose too much in the off chance the paternity test came back negative.

He'd learned patience in the marines. Wait for the right moment. And this wasn't it.

Justin just couldn't trust Kat. She was aware of the Slade wealth. She knew Justin's background. She'd seen Sunset Ranch and had already tried to get her foot in the door by dating Luke. Was passing her son off as a Slade just another ploy? When he returned home from war, he thought he'd never experience the type of suspicion that crept up his spine now. But how could he believe anything she had to say?

Waiting for the paternity test and finding out whether that little cherub-faced boy with the inky curls and big dark eyes was truly his son would make for the longest three days of his life.

He wanted Connor to be his for the boy's sake, so he wouldn't go through life fatherless.

But if the baby was his son, the peace and solitude he'd craved since Brett's death wouldn't come. The situation with Aunt Mattie would complicate matters.

Justin drove into the parking lot in the minimall and parked Kat's car next to his. With his hands draped on the steering wheel, he turned to her. She glanced at her wristwatch and sighed. "I'd better get going. When he wakes up, he'll want to eat. He howls when he's hungry."

"That I'd like to see."

"You will," she said softly, assuring him. "He's yours, Justin. But you'll have your proof in a few days."

Justin got out of the car and waited until Kat drove away before he climbed into his truck. Then he pulled out of the parking lot, and headed toward Silver Haven Cemetery where Brett's body had been laid to rest. After driving for twenty minutes, he passed through a four-way stop and slowed his truck when the stately iron gates of the cemetery came into view. They were opened wide like welcoming arms to the mourners who were there to pay their respects. He stared at the ivy-covered brick columns at the entrance as his heart pumped hard inside his chest.

Turn the wheel. Go in. Make your peace.

His hands were frozen in the ten and two position on the steering wheel as he sat in his truck, numbly staring at those gates. Closing his eyes, he said a silent prayer for Brett. But a car approaching from behind helped him make his decision. He touched his foot to the gas pedal and the truck limped along the road as Silver Haven vanished in his rearview mirror.

He'd lost his nerve. He wasn't ready to travel through those gates. He didn't know when he'd ever be ready. With trepidation in his heart, he changed direction and made the necessary turns that would lead him home, to Sunset Ranch.

He'd tried.

It would have to be enough for now.

It was late in the afternoon by the time Justin parked in front of his house. He sat there for a long while, studying the dashboard with eyes that only saw the past: things he couldn't change and mistakes he'd made along the way.

Rap. Rap. Rap.

Justin jerked to attention, brought out of his deep thoughts. When he was an on-duty marine, daydreaming like that could get a man killed.

Luke's voice penetrated the front window of the truck. "You having a party in there all by yourself?"

Justin rolled his eyes. "Yeah, and you just crashed it."

"Didn't anyone tell you a party has to involve at least two people and one of them should be female?"

Despite his teasing grin, Luke's eyes shone with understanding. Luke was the sensitive type, under all that blond brawn and bulk. He was Justin's go-to man when he had a problem. Except that now Luke could conceivably *be* the problem.

As Luke stepped back, Justin exited the truck. "We need to talk."

"Sounds serious." Luke lost the grin.

Justin squinted against sunlight, gazing across acres of Slade land. "You have time for a ride?"

Luke gave him a nod. "If it's important, I'll make time."

Justin squared him a look. "It's important."

Luke tipped his hat brim farther down on his forehead and spoke with a Clint Eastwood rasp. "Okay, then, let's saddle up and leave this ole ranch in the dust."

Justin appreciated Luke's attempt to lighten the moment, but not even an exaggerated cowboy drawl was going to make him smile until he found out the truth about Kat and his brother.

Four

"It's nice of you to visit again so soon, Justin," Mattie said, sitting across from him on the recliner in her parlor. "Are you sure you don't want any peach pie?"

"Not right now, ma'am." He was seated in the same spot on the sofa as the other day. "I'll have some later."

"Pie will keep. Just about everything keeps when you get to be my age."

Justin smiled. Aunt Mattie wore a housecoat with bright red, turquoise and orange flowers. Her hair was up in a do—straight back, then curling at the nape—that reminded him of his mother. He could almost see through Aunt Mattie's years to the attractive, flamboyant young girl she must have been once. "My grandma used to say age is just a number in your head. It's how you feel inside that matters."

She leaned forward in her seat and the smile she gave him took two decades off her face. "Well, then if that's true, I'm sixteen."

Justin nodded. "That's what my grandma used to say, too."

"'Course when your body breaks down, you tend to forget that."

"Yes, ma'am."

"So, you came to tell me about Brett. How nice. Did you know him very well?"

"Yes, ma'am, I did. He enlisted a few years after I did.

He was deployed to my unit at Delaram about two years ago. We served together and got on as friends."

Matilda leaned back in the chair and a distant, almost tragic smile spread across her thin cheeks. "He was like a son to me. Ralph and I raised him, you know. Now, my Ralph and Brett are serving the Lord up above. Tell me about your time with Brett."

Justin launched into story after story about his friendship with Brett. He told her about the barracks, how they lived in close quarters, the blazing heat and the frigid cold, and about how much friendship came to mean to the soldiers serving over there. They had little contact with the outside world—no television, no internet access most of the time. Justin told her about the poker games they'd play and how they would swap rations and break out pictures and talk about home. Always home. It got to be that they knew each other's home lives just as well as they knew their own. He told Aunt Mattie how much Brett talked about his uncle Ralph and about how much he'd loved her. He told her how Brett felt bad, leaving her alone, but hoped to come home one day to build Applegate Farms back to its original glory. Brett had every intention of doing that very thing.

He told her how Brett was as fine a soldier as there was.

He told her everything there was to tell, except the one thing that she needed to hear the most. How Brett died. The words were on his lips, begging to come forth, but they failed, time and again, either because Justin had just made her smile, or she'd gotten a faraway nostalgic look on her face, or she'd gather her hands to her chest as if holding his words near to her heart with such hope that it tore Justin up inside.

He'd come ready to purge his guilt and lay down the heavy burden he'd been carrying around for months. His memories haunted him. His dreams had turned nightmarish. He thought that today he could finally own up to his part in Brett's death, knowing that Aunt Mattie deserved the truth, and then he'd be able to deal with all the rest.

But he couldn't do it.

The time was never right. He didn't want to blurt out something that would hurt the older woman. A battle raged in his head, and he was glad that Kat and Connor were out this morning shopping in town. Glad that he'd had this time to speak with Mattie alone.

At first, when Mattie had answered the door to his knock, he'd been disappointed. He'd wanted to see Connor. He'd gotten his expectations up and had been anxious to see the child again, anxious to look upon his chubby cheeks and glimpse the spark of intelligence in his eyes.

He'd wanted to see Kat, too.

She hadn't lied to him about Luke. They'd dated briefly and had shared nothing more than a kiss or two. Luke had sworn on his unborn baby's life that nothing had happened between him and Kat other than friendship, and that was more than good enough for Justin to hear. His relief was as powerful as anything he'd ever experienced.

Luke had been stunned when Justin then told him the entire story of his involvement with Kat. It wasn't the kind of thing that happened every day. Mostly, Justin hated admitting to his brother about making and following through on such a fool bet.

"Guess that makes you far from perfect," Luke had said. "Something I've always known."

Justin appreciated his brother's frank assessment. It was hard living up to war-hero status. Luke always knew the right thing to say.

Unlike Justin, who now couldn't summon the words he'd practiced saying a dozen times over: *Brett is dead because of me.*

And Aunt Mattie had the good grace not to ask about

Brett's death. The older woman was as wise as her years. He suspected she knew the pain it would cause both of them.

So Justin moved onto another subject. "Aunt Mattie," he said. "Is it all right if I call you that?"

The woman's eyes brightened. "I'd be honored."

"I have an idea and I need your okay first. I've been thinking on this for a few months. And I hope you don't mind me saying, the land around here has gone to ruin."

"I won't fault anyone the truth," she said, nodding. "The place is a weed trap, full of gopher holes and snakes, and out beyond the dilapidated barn, there's nothing but hard dirt and cactus. Ralph tried and tried, but when the dog-gone contracts dried up around here, he couldn't keep the place right as rain like he wanted. He was a good man, my Ralph."

"I know that, ma'am. Brett was always singing his praises. He said the hog farmers lost out to big companies and then the place sort of shriveled up along with those contracts. Brett wanted so much to bring this farm back to life when he got home."

Tears misted in her eyes. "I know it. Brett's heart was as big as this house and then some."

"Well, I'm hoping to honor both Brett and your Ralph along with other war veterans. Ralph served in Vietnam and Brett gave his…his life in the Middle East. There's a whole lot of men out there wounded on the inside and out who need help. I'm hoping you'll sell your outer land to me. There's got to be at least six hundred acres here that could be—"

"Six hundred and thirty-five," she added.

Justin nodded. "With that acreage, I hope to build a retreat for wounded soldiers. We'd have horses here, and we'd build a facility, away from your house, that could be used for temporary lodging for the men. Young and old could come to work with horses. Sunset Ranch can provide mares and geldings that need some tender loving care of their own. It'd be an equine horse retreat. If you're willing to sell, I'll make sure this house gets the repairs it needs, too. It was Brett's dream to restore this place, and I'd like to see that happen."

Mattie's teary eyes spilled over. "Why…I don't know… oh, my goodness. That's about the darnedest idea I've ever heard. My land…a retreat for soldiers?" Her voice broke to a frail whisper of awe. "Wouldn't my Ralph and Brett love a notion like that?"

"Don't cry, Aunt Mattie." Justin slid down the sofa and plucked a tissue from a table by her recliner. He offered it to her and she thanked him as she dabbed at her tears. "I'd make you a fair offer for the land," Justin assured her.

She waved him off with the hand holding the tissue. Sniffing, she spoke quietly. "I don't have a doubt about it."

Such blind faith. Justin took a hard swallow. Stabbed with guilt, a nagging voice in his head urged him on. This was the absolute right thing to do to honor Brett and Ralph and all soldiers who'd sacrificed their bodies as well as their souls for their country. They needed some TLC of their own. In a small way, he could make up for Mattie's loss.

"If you agree to it, we can call the place the Gateway Equine Retreat."

"Oh, my…" Joyful light beamed from her eyes, even though wet eyes. "I don't know what I did to deserve all this," she whispered, clearly astonished. "First Connor and Kat come into my life and now you, with an offer like this. I don't see how I can refuse such a wonderful thing."

"I think Brett would approve," Justin said softly.

She began nodding. "Yes, he would."

The front door swung open and Kat entered with a grocery bag on one hip and the baby flat up against her chest. Connor faced forward, his legs dangling from two openings in the sling that kept him plastered against her. Justin's heart tumbled, seeing the two of them again. He rose from his seat and looked the boy straight in the eye. Connor didn't turn away like he had before and his sweet inquisitive gaze nearly knocked Justin off his ass.

Baby mortar. More explosive and deadly than any IED he'd come across in Afghanistan.

He took hold of his emotions and walked over to help Kat with the bag, but before he could get close enough, she moved and let the grocery bag slip from her arm onto a maple end table.

Ignoring him, her gaze flew to Mattie's teary face and a quick gasp escaped her throat. She turned accusing eyes toward him. "Justin, why are you here?"

"Kat, dear, Justin's just told me something so—"

"What did you tell her?" Her face pinched tight with panic.

"Hold on," he said quietly.

"I won't hold on. You didn't tell me you were coming by today."

"I told Mattie I'd come by to talk about Brett."

"He doesn't need an invitation, dear. He told me the nicest stories, Kat. I'm sure you'd like to hear them, too."

Kat's shoulders slumped in relief, although Justin noted her annoyance, as well. She worked the latches on the baby sling and undid the contraption, wrapping her arms tight around Connor as she pulled him free. "Nice stories?" She raised her eyebrows. "Then why is Aunt Mattie crying?"

He pointed to the grocery bag. "You have any more of those in the car?"

She nodded.

"I'll get them while Aunt Mattie tells you why I'm here."

"Sit down with Connor, Kat," the older woman said

sweetly, dabbing at her eyes. "Justin's come up with such a wonderful idea."

Kat, in tight jeans and a soft pink sweater that revealed all her curves without revealing an inch of skin, did crazy things to him. The baby she held in her arms only added to the beautiful picture that stirred all of his emotions.

Baby mortar *and* blonde bombshell.

Pummeled by unexpected combative forces, he walked outside, climbed down the steps and leaned against the porch column to catch his breath.

Closing his eyes, he let go a few choice cuss words, then pushed off from the wall to unload the grocery bags from the car.

Coming home wasn't supposed to be this hard.

Kat made the gravy, scraping at the crusted drippings from the pot roast she'd just removed from the pan. The gravy popped with bubbles as she stirred the rich brown sauce with the wooden spoon. Justin worked directly beside her, slicing the roast.

"Don't need a knife for this," he said. "The meat's just falling away. I guess that's what they mean by fork tender."

Darn Aunt Mattie for inviting Justin to dinner.

He'd been hanging around all afternoon, helping her put groceries away, talking up his idea for the equine retreat to Aunt Mattie and now assisting in the dinner preparation while Connor and Aunt Mattie both napped.

"Didn't get anything fork tender at the base."

They bumped hips. It seized her breath, being so close to him. "I don't imagine so."

"The cooks wouldn't win the first round in the *Top Chef* competition, that's for sure."

"Was it awful being there?" she asked as she focused her attention on the gravy. She didn't want lumps to form in the sauce because she was distracted by the sexy man beside her. But he smelled so good. Woodsy and fresh.

It hurt to know he'd used her. She'd been running from abusive men all her life, but when Justin had pretended to be Brett, she'd poured her heart out to him. She'd told him things she hadn't shared with anyone else, about her young life, about her dreams. Maybe it was because she knew he'd be leaving and she'd never have to face him again or maybe she just felt she could trust him. Could've been a little of both.

"Awful? It was kinda hard being isolated from the world. Makes a man feel out of touch with himself, his life, everything he's ever known. All that's up ahead is the mission and seeing that it turns out successful." He put his head down, staring at the platter. "Losing Brett was the awful part."

She turned and looked into eyes that couldn't hide pain.

"You saved lives, Justin."

"You've done some homework."

She shrugged. "You're a hero. Douglas County is throwing a parade in your honor. It's been in the news."

"Not my idea."

"But you can't deny that you saved five men. They would have died if you hadn't been there."

"I didn't save Brett," he whispered, taking a swallow, staring at the kitchen wall, "and I could have."

Kat didn't know about that. Nothing she'd read about Justin Slade mentioned his connection to Brett Applegate. Justin had been honored with the Congressional Medal of Honor and that wasn't something to sneeze at. Five men were alive today because of his bravery.

"I'm sorry Brett died," Kat found herself saying. "The retreat is a good way to honor him."

Justin's lips twisted and he shook his head. "I wanted to do something."

"You are," she said, turning off the burner. She faced him with a direct look and lowered her voice. "You're keeping a secret that will protect his aunt's life."

"A few hours ago, you thought I'd gone back on that promise."

"Aunt Mattie was crying. I didn't know what to think."

"You really care about her?"

His question unnerved her. Didn't he think she was capable of caring for a woman who had shown her nothing but kindness? Didn't he think her capable of putting someone else's needs above her own? Not that Aunt Mattie could replace the mother she'd lost, but she felt a kinship with the older woman, a bond that was brought on by their mutual love of Connor. "Of course I care about her."

Justin braced his hand on the kitchen counter and leaned in close, until his handsome face was all she could see in her line of vision. He touched a wisp of her hair, so gently, so tenderly. Her body reacted with warmth and a tingle that went down to her toes. He traced the line of her jaw with his index finger and shifted his gaze to her mouth. "I don't go back on my promises, Kat."

She swallowed. Aware they were alone in the small kitchen for the time being, she couldn't muster the strength to back away. Tempted by his dark eyes and sensual memories, she spoke quietly. "But you lied to me over an entire weekend."

"I wanted you."

His hands came out to rest on her waist. Through her soft sweater, she felt the urgency of his touch, the potent pull as he gathered her closer. Their legs meshed together, her breasts crushed his chest. He groaned softly, letting her know what he intended. Their lips were inches apart.

"I still want you," he whispered, right before his mouth claimed hers.

Kat fell into the kiss, the power of his sensual words

and touch too much to fend off. She wanted him close. She wanted to feel his mouth on hers, to feel his body's urgency and know she was the cause of his desire. She kissed him back, throwing her arms around his neck and feeling immeasurable heat between them.

He plunged his tongue into her mouth and she welcomed him with a soft moan. His kiss deepened and awakened her lust for the opposite sex. She hadn't felt a need this powerful since before Connor was born. She needed Justin's lips on hers, needed his body close, and reveled in the sensations he stirred in her.

He trailed away from her mouth to drizzle tiny biting nibbles on her throat. She craned her neck, allowing his lips to drift down to the base of her shoulders. His hands inched their way up the material of her sweater. Caressing the soft cashmere, he found her breasts and rubbed them with his palms. Between her legs, she throbbed with sparks of delight. She pulled his mouth to hers once again. She wanted more from him, now. Right now.

It was impossible. Connor and Aunt Mattie slept in the next room.

It was dangerous, and normally, she enjoyed sexy games, but not now. Not with her son so close. It was madness. Justin tugged at her sweater, yanking the material away from her body. His hands found her skin and hot needy fingers pulled the underside of her bra down. He caressed her breasts, flesh to flesh, his firm rough palms teasing her soft nipples. Steam rose up, swamping her with heat.

"You feel just like I remember," he whispered. "Do you know how hard it was not sleeping with you that first night? Do you know how much I wanted you?"

Kat's mind filled with memories. She'd almost fallen for a hog farmer, a man with empty pockets, the kind of man Kat didn't want in her life ever again. Dirt-poor and earnest. But now, it was different. Justin wasn't Brett Applegate. And he was driving her crazy.

"We…can't, Justin."

His hands froze as he stared into her eyes. She could relate to the disappointment on his face. She felt it, too. With a reluctant nod and taking a deep breath, Justin removed his hands from her body. "You're right. We can't do this here."

Trembling, she wrapped her arms around her waist, still tingling from the places Justin had ignited on her body. "It's complicated enough."

"It's not that complicated between you and me. With us, everything's pretty clear."

They locked gazes for beats of a minute. "I know," she admitted quietly and then her mind drifted to Mattie and Connor and all the lies she'd told in the past for her own survival. And to insure a good life for her son. "I've got to check on Connor, would you mind putting out the—"

"I'll go with you. Then I'll help you with the meal."

Kat couldn't refuse him. He had a right to see Connor. While he wasn't sure of it, Kat was certain that Connor was his son. She'd conceived him that weekend before she took up with Michael Golden. She gave him a small smile. "All right."

He followed her into the bedroom. Connor was just rousing. When he saw her, he rolled to a sit-up position in his crib. His eyes still drugged from sleep, his hair curling at his nape, the baby just looked around as if trying to get his bearings. "Hi, sweet baby."

His little face contorted as he rubbed his eyes with the full force of his palms, up and down, stretching the skin. Kat gently removed his hands from his face before he poked himself in the eye. "Takes him a few minutes to fully wake up," she said to Justin.

"Okay by me. I could watch him all day long."

She glanced at this tough soldier, this hero standing beside her, his eyes full of pride and warmth. How quickly he'd fallen under Connor's spell. It wasn't hard. Kat would move heaven and earth for her child. She had a feeling that Justin would do the same. A shiver of dread rode down her spine, but this time, she wouldn't cave to those feelings. "Yeah, me, too."

She turned to Justin. "I have to change his diaper. You can leave if you'd like."

He gave her an are-you-kidding squint and shook his head. "I've seen worse in my day."

"Okay, but remember you asked for it. Smell that? It's gonna be a good one."

A resounding chuckle rose from Justin's throat and both she and Connor glanced at him. "You're not scaring me. Diaper away."

Later, with all of them seated at the kitchen table, Connor in his high chair, the pot roast and potatoes served, Justin began talking business about the sale of Aunt Mattie's outer land and how he wanted to get the ball rolling as quickly as possible with the equine retreat.

The change in his demeanor gave Kat some breathing room. Up until that point, he'd been watching her every move, darting quick glances at her mouth and sending sexy secretive smiles her way. Worse yet, the adoring, yet cautious look in his eyes when he studied Connor was hard to miss. Aunt Mattie wasn't born yesterday; Kat saw her watching them and wondered just what the older woman was thinking.

"I'm having the papers drawn up and will bring them by in a few days," he said to Aunt Mattie. "If you're sure about this?"

The money from the sale of the land would help pay Aunt Mattie's medical expenses and give her a nice cushion for her old age. Aunt Mattie had no use for the neglected land anyway, and no one could've come up with a better plan than Justin's to restore the land and do some good along the way.

Aunt Mattie glanced at Connor in his high chair, eating vegetable puffs that looked suspiciously like Cheetos, and her eyes narrowed to thin slits. Her face fell short of the contented expression she usually wore. "I don't think I realized up until this moment," she said, easing the words out slowly, "that I might be robbing the boy of his birthright."

Justin shot Kat a sharp look.

Kat's cheeks burned.

No one had thought of this before and of course, Aunt Mattie wouldn't be robbing Connor of anything, since he wasn't really her great-nephew. "Oh…but Aunt Mattie, we don't want anything from you. You've already done too much, putting a roof over our head."

"Nonsense, girl. You came here and immediately took over my care. You've brought joy to this old woman's life. You're doing more for me than I could ever do for you."

"But Aunt Mattie, I told you when we arrived here, we didn't expect anything."

"But the boy's my kin. He deserves—"

"Not run-down parched land that won't do anybody any good," Justin said gently. "Remember, I'm giving you a fair price for the land. It's like trading one thing for another. Connor's not losing out. And you'll still have this house, fully refurbished as I promised."

Aunt Mattie leaned back in the kitchen chair, her wrinkles bunching up as she nodded. "I suppose you're right. It's hard making these decisions at my age." She looked at Kat with such trust that Kat's heart swelled. "If you think it's a good idea, Kat. I'll take your advice."

Kat drew a deep breath. She had no right making decisions for Mattie, but the look on her face said otherwise. She was banking on her advice. "Connor won't know the difference. And the equine retreat would help heal a lot of good men."

"I suppose you're right. It's a good thing."

"It is a good thing." Kat rose from her seat and drew open the box of weekly pills she had sorted out for Mattie's care. She plucked two out, one to regulate her heart, the other a blood thinner. "Here you go," she said, placing the pills on the tablecloth, "time for your medicine."

"Thank you, dear."

Justin was back to watching her every move again.

"So then, it's settled?" Kat asked.

"Yes," Aunt Mattie said, swallowing her medicine. "I'll sell Justin the land."

After the dishes were cleaned, Justin bid Aunt Mattie good-night. Kat, with Connor in her arms, walked him outside. They stood on the porch, the moonlight and chilly air casting a momentary spell. Connor was warming up to Justin now. He no longer shied away and he'd begun to recognize the sound of his deep voice.

"This works out in your favor, doesn't it?" he asked Kat.

"What are you talking about?"

"You'd stand to win, no matter what. If that woman dies, you'd get everything she owned. A quarter of a million dollars for dried-up acreage would serve you well, wouldn't it?"

"That's not why I'm keeping the secret, Justin. I came here—"

"Yeah, I know the story. What I can't figure is what took you so long to decide to find Brett's family. Connor was what…nine months old when you came to Silver Springs? What were you doing for all that time?"

I lived with Michael Golden, who'd promised to raise my son in the lap of luxury.

Kat would lose all credibility if she confessed the truth.

She kept her lips buttoned tight. With the mood Justin was in, she wasn't going to win this argument.

"If he's my boy, he'd be worth eighty times the sale of the land, but you know that, as well, being that you dated Luke."

"I told you, Luke and I were…just friends."

Justin's lips pursed, but she noticed a hint of relief in his eyes. "He confirmed it. Wouldn't have kissed you in the kitchen the way I did if it turned out otherwise."

"You wouldn't believe me when I told you that very thing," Kat said, hoisting her chin up.

"Sugar, I don't know what to believe."

His eyes softened when he looked at the baby. Slowly, he put his hand out to touch Connor's ruddy little cheek. His fingers lingered there. "Better get him inside. It's cold out here."

Then he turned around and climbed down the steps, leaving Kat to wonder at the conflicting emotions stirred up inside her belly.

The next morning, Justin clicked off his cell phone and stared at the darn thing for a full minute, before striding behind the bar in the corner of the parlor. He pulled out a bottle of fifty-year-old whiskey and glanced at the label.

"The good stuff," he mumbled and then grabbed a tumbler. Placing it on the polished surface, he poured himself two inches of liquor and raised his glass. "To fatherhood."

The first sip he swallowed slid down his throat easily. Unfamiliar tears wet his lashes and he blinked them away. "And to Connor. My son."

Taking a steady breath, he absorbed the truth and grinned like a silly old fool. He was Connor's father. Man, it felt good to know for certain about the boy.

Images of his own father popped into his mind. He'd had a good relationship with Randall Slade. The man was stern in some ways, but Justin always knew where he stood with him. He always knew his father had his back. He wanted that for Connor, too. He wanted his boy to know that no matter what, Justin would be there for him.

Love—that had probably surfaced since the first day he'd met the little guy—filled his heart. The strong emotion stifled him a bit with its powerful intensity.

Connor had to be his son. He looked just like him. Had the same eyes, hair and skin coloring. But hearing it confirmed by Dr. Barrington sent a string of emotions barreling through his system. He was happy. No denying that. He wanted that beautiful boy to be his son. Through a twisted set of circumstances they'd been kept apart and there was no going back to make up for the time lost. It was a convoluted mess, more complicated than anything he could've imagined.

He couldn't do a darn thing about it now, what was done was done. But now that he knew about Connor, he'd damn well change the things he had the power to change.

"I want my son to know his family."

Kat had shuddered at the demand when Justin called this morning and told her to make it happen. He would come pick her and Connor up. She'd begged him not to, and made a compromise to drive to Sunset Ranch this afternoon. She'd wanted at least that much on her terms. If things got too weird and awkward or if Aunt Mattie needed her, she could leave anytime she wanted.

Justin had balked at that solution, but finally agreed. It wasn't as easy as Justin thought to come up with a viable excuse to leave Aunt Mattie at dinnertime and to make arrangements for one of the neighbors to drop in on her at a moment's notice.

Aunt Mattie always assured her she was fine when left alone, and Kat didn't argue, but she also didn't leave her for more than an hour or two at a time and rarely in the evening. She liked knowing Aunt Mattie and Connor were sleeping before she headed into the sewing room to work on her designs for Babylicious.

When she'd come to Silver Springs, she'd vowed her lying days were over. She'd done enough of that in her early years to last a lifetime. She hated that she'd broken her vow not to lie to Matilda Applegate about anything else. And to add to her problems, today Connor's paternity would come to light, at least among the Slades now that Justin knew the truth. His prideful tone and the proprietary way he spoke to her this morning still rang in her ears. She'd begged for secrecy and Justin promised that his family could be trusted with the truth.

But she'd learned the hard way that no one could be trusted.

It was five o'clock when she pulled up in front of the main house at Sunset Ranch. The sun dipped low, nearly hidden behind the rocky mountain wall surrounding the property. "Okay, sweet baby, let's get you out of the car."

She leaned into the back and unfastened the car seat straps. Connor flung his arms out, eager to be lifted from the contraption. He wrapped his arms around her neck and she nuzzled him as she straightened with him in her arms. His sweet baby smells filled her nostrils, blocking out the pungent sent of manure, earth and straw. She slung the loaded diaper bag down next.

The ranch was grand, with stately buildings, corrals, barns and a sprawling one-story main house. She'd been here once before, on Luke's arm. But that had never taken off and it was a good thing.

Connor caught sight of movement in the corrals. He loved horses and he began pointing and grunting and bouncing in her arms, urging her in his own little way of communicating. "Okay, sweetie. We'll go see the horses."

She set the diaper bag down beside the car and walked the distance to the corrals. She stopped at the fence post and turned Connor so he could see, bracing him against her chest. His eyes rounded, filled with fascination as he studied three mares.

She enunciated slowly, "Hor...ses."

"Oh...sees." Connor mimicked.

"Yes, that's good, baby," she said, squeezing him tight. "Must be in his blood."

She turned to find Luke Slade coming up beside her. She froze. She'd dreaded facing him and the rest of the family. "Wh-what's that?"

"His love of horses."

She gave him a quick nod. "This is weird, Luke."

"I know, but don't feel strange around us. Me, in particular. I spoke with Justin and told him how it was between us."

"Thanks for that." Her nerves settled a little. Luke had always been fair to her. He was a nice man. "But the circumstances are pretty...extraordinary."

He smiled at Connor and ruffled his hair. "They're downright bizarre. But now, here you are and this little guy is my nephew."

"Crazy, isn't it?"

He shrugged. "I guess. But life's like that. It's not always neat and tidy."

"No, it's not. So, I hear you're marrying the fainter?"

Luke laughed. "I am. Pretty happy about it, too. And don't mention the fainting, okay? Audrey was embarrassed about that. She thought she'd never have to face you again. She's pregnant."

"It's a good reason to faint. I went through a lightheaded phase when I was pregnant. Some people might say I never got over that."

Luke shook his head, amused. "You'll keep my brother

on his toes. Good thing, too. I was afraid he'd be bored when he got home. Nothing's further from the truth."

She smiled. "Congratulations, Luke. I'm truly happy for you."

Out of the corner of her eye, she saw Justin approach. She swiveled halfway around, adjusting Connor in her arms.

Justin stared into her eyes.

Her body reacted, zinging with memories of the kiss that would've taken them to wicked places if there were opportunity. He looked handsome as ever, his military crew cut having grown out enough to drop a lock of dark hair onto his forehead. Dressed in faded jeans, a black shirt and a black hat, he looked like the villain in a spaghetti western.

The baby craned his neck and pointed his finger toward the corral.

His gaze softened the second it landed on Connor. "Likes horses, does he?"

Luke walked over to him, grinned and gave him a slap on the back. "Congratulations, Papa. He's a beautiful boy."

Justin nodded as Luke walked away. "See you at the house."

Justin moved closer to her. "I'm glad you brought him."

"You didn't give me much choice."

Justin could always hold the truth over her head, maybe even reveal it to Aunt Mattie, and it was a vulnerable place to be.

"You said you'd make sure I knew my son."

"You. Not your family. It's risky."

"No, it's not. They know the situation. They'll keep quiet."

Kat allowed her gaze to flow to the horses in the corral. Connor, still captivated by them, bounced in her arms, kicking his legs.

"I want to hold him. Do you think he'll come to me?"

The look of longing in Justin's eyes nearly did her in.

"We can try. Just keep him facing the horses. He's fascinated."

"I can see that," Justin said softly. "Come here, son."

Justin put out his arms and Kat did the transfer.

Kat had never had to share Connor with anyone before. Not like this. Not with knowing that Justin had every bit as much right to Connor as she had. But their son barely noticed that he was being held by Justin. Instead, the little boy's eyes honed in on one gray mare in particular that had ventured closer.

Justin stood stiff, his grip on the baby awkward. He was treating Connor like a delicate gem that would break if he made a wrong move. It was another monumental moment in her life, watching father and son bond for the first time.

"That's Starlight," he said to Connor. There was awe in his voice, and a gentleness that Kat understood, as well. "She's about as old as you are, son."

Connor lifted his eyes to his father. "When you get older, I'll teach you to ride."

The baby looked a little confused, and turned to her, his lower lip quivering. His arms jutted out, reaching for her at the same time his body lurched in her direction. "He wants his mommy."

Justin slid Connor back into her arms and Connor squeezed her neck as tight as he ever had. Rocking him prevented his tears. She swayed back and forth. "He'll warm up to you. It's just been him and me for so long."

Justin's stare lingered on Connor for a few seconds more. Then he inhaled a sharp breath. "The family's waiting. Are you ready to come inside with me?"

Mustering her courage and burying her dread, she gave him a nod. "As ready as I'll ever be."

With a hand to her waist, he guided her toward the

house. She clung to the warmth of his touch, taking what little comfort she could grab.

This was going to be awkward with a capital *A*.

Five

Connor banged the keys on the LeapFrog piano, making dogs bark, ducks quack and the letters of the alphabet sing out in the middle of the parlor floor. He was surrounded by stacking cups, a plastic giraffe teething toy and a Baby Elmo, along with half a dozen other gifts. Sophia and Audrey, women Kat had already met before any of them had known the truth, made her feel comfortable right away. Logan was equally charming, offering her a hug when she'd walked into the house, and Luke gave her a friendly smile. Connor received unconditional love from the entire Slade clan immediately. He was a sweet little boy, so she wouldn't expect any less, but it was strange to say the least, knowing that these people were his family. For the longest time, she'd thought he would never have a family other than Aunt Mattie.

Despite the cordial reception by the Slades, Kat's stomach twisted and she felt out of place. She didn't have a clue where all of this was leading. Justin made her nervous, period. Seated next to him on the sofa, she was aware of his every move, his every breath, the scent of his lime aftershave wafting by her nose. The kiss they'd shared the other day was embedded in her mind so forcefully, she couldn't recall any other man's touch. It was bad. She wanted more kisses, his hands on her and all the things that went along with it, but she couldn't forget that they had to tread carefully. One wrong move, one bad decision and Connor could get hurt in the long run.

Seeing the look of adoration in Justin's eyes as he leaned forward on the sofa, his elbows braced on his knees, fully smitten with Connor's symphony of noise, should've made her feel better about things. Yet a string of nerves kept her on the edge of her seat. Her entire life had been turned upside down. She'd come to Silver Springs to make a fresh start. And look how well that had turned out! Now, the Slade family was entwined in a web of lies, too.

"He loves making music," Luke's pregnant fiancée said. Audrey's small baby bump was high and round. She stood behind the sofa, her hand on her belly, watching Connor poke at all the knobs and buttons on the toy.

"If you can call it that," Luke said, a glint in his eyes. "Sounds like a racket to me."

"Baby sounds," Kat offered. "I don't even hear it anymore. It all blends into the background."

Audrey nibbled on her lower lip. "Oh, boy. I have a lot to learn for when our baby arrives."

"It kind of comes at you in small doses. You don't have to know it all, right away. A lot of it is instinct," Kat reassured her.

Audrey glanced at Luke. "That's good to know. I can handle anything in small doses."

Luke gave her a quizzical look and Logan burst out laughing. "I'm sure you've had to deal with a lot of *small* things, with Luke."

Audrey rolled her eyes and pointed her finger at him. "Don't start with me, Logan. You know I didn't mean it like that."

"I didn't take offense," Luke said. "It's your pregnancy brain talking."

She whirled on him. "I do not have pregnancy brain!"

Luke's expression faltered and he glanced at the women in the room for help. "I thought that was a good thing."

Slowly, Kat and Sophia shook their heads. Luke sent Logan an I'll-get-back-at-you glare, but Logan continued grinning and switched his attention to Connor and the piano.

Kat watched the Slades in action with sweeping sadness. She'd never had a family surrounding her with love, teasing her mercilessly, offering her advice or giving support when she was pregnant. She'd had no one to rely on. It was pretty much how she'd lived her life after her mother died. Alone. Fending for herself.

Now Connor's every whim would be granted and Kat didn't know how she felt about that. Justin had mentioned giving him a filly for his first birthday, a thoroughbred he'd already handpicked for his son, so that child and horse could grow up together.

It was too early for such a gift. Connor was still a baby. Justin couldn't make up for lost time with lavish gifts, and she would have that discussion privately with him at some point. She had to be careful how she broached the subject, though.

Justin's fatherhood had been thrust upon him instantly, with no preparation, and now he wanted to give Connor the world, but some of that eagerness and enthusiasm had to be tempered. It was hard for Kat to share the decision-making regarding Connor. It was something she'd never had to do before.

Lately, she'd begun to really wonder if things might've turned out differently had she known the hog farmer she'd gotten involved with was really Justin Slade, wealthy rancher. Would she have wanted a long-distance relationship with Justin, even though he was a soldier? She wasn't going to delve into what that said about her. She'd heard it all and most of it had come from her own father when she was a child.

"You whorin' little bitch, you mind me now, or that stupid smile will be minus two front teeth."

From the age of five, she'd learned how to let the bad words slide off of her.

The Slades' housekeeper, Ellie, walked in. "Dinner's ready. The dining room's all set up with the good dishes and everything."

Logan raised his eyebrows. "We rated the good dishes?"

"I made Justin's favorite. It's a good way to celebrate his homecoming," Ellie said. The housekeeper's eyes filled with a warm glow as she looked at Connor.

"We're having macaroni and cheese?" Logan asked.

Ellie nodded. "Your mama's recipe. It's by Justin's request. But don't you worry, I've made a roasted pork and sweet potato pie, too."

"Hey, I love your mac and cheese, Ellie," Logan said.

"So do I," Luke added. "We haven't had it in a long time."

Justin looked Kat's way and explained, "It's gourmet mac and cheese. I can pretty much guarantee you've never tasted anything better. I think the boy will like it, too."

"He usually eats mac and cheese out of a box," Kat said softly, "but I'm sure he'll love it."

Kat wondered how much the housekeeper knew about Connor. Justin's expression didn't give anything away as he rose to his feet and offered her his hand. She took it, whispering, "Connor will make a mess in the dining room. Good dishes? I hope they're not heirlooms."

"There's a new high chair waiting for him in there. He'll be fine. And there's nothing in this house he can break that's worth more than me having him here with all of us."

She understood. The Slades were rich. Items could be replaced easily. Connor couldn't do anything wrong at this point. Kat held her thoughts close as she scooped Connor up and carried him into the dining room with Justin at her side.

"Of course, you and Connor are invited to our wedding," Sophia said, three minutes into the meal. "Logan and I would love to have you join us."

Kat looked up from her plate. Struggling to keep her composure, she had to think fast. Unfortunately, she'd lost some of her moxie when motherhood came along. "Oh…I, uh."

Seated next to her, Justin nodded. "Of course. I want Connor at the wedding."

"It's next week," Sophia said. "On Saturday in Reno. Justin is the best man."

"I don't think…it's…a good idea."

She sent Justin a pleading look. He had to know how it would look if she attended the wedding on his arm. "It's not because we don't want to, but, well, with the situation with Mattie and all, it'd be hard to explain our presence."

"Justin's explained it all to us," Audrey said quietly. "And personally, I think it's wonderful how loyal you are to her. It's a tough situation, but we all have agreed to keep the secret."

"Yes," Sophia added, "we know the woman's health might be jeopardized. We'll be careful."

Justin stiffened. On a heavy sigh, he reached for her hand under the table and gave it a gentle squeeze, letting her know he had more to say on the subject. "We'll talk about it later, after dinner."

As he let her go, he pushed the material of her skirt away to give her thigh a gentle, sensual stroke. Her eyes rounded in shock, as his hand skimmed over her sensitive skin and glided farther up her leg. She squirmed in her seat, praying that no one noticed. "O-kay."

She turned her attention toward Connor, who had been

a perfect angel sitting in his new high chair gnawing on the giraffe teether. "Want to try the mac and cheese, sweet boy?"

He let the giraffe fall from his mouth, his eyes trained on the food. "Oh, that means that you do, don't you?"

Kat lifted the spoon to his lips and he gobbled down the cut-up morsels of mac and cheese and mashed sweet potato. Justin's gaze never left him and Kat got a sinking feeling in the pit of her stomach.

For better or worse, through Connor, she would be tied to Justin Slade for the rest of her life.

With his belly full and after all the attention from the Slades, Connor conked out in Kat's arms right after the meal.

Justin walked her to a guest room in the spacious estate and busied himself making up a little bed for him on the floor with blankets and a paisley blue-and-gray quilt.

"That's fine," she whispered. "He'll be comfy here."

She kneeled and laid him down carefully. As he nestled in, he automatically rolled onto his side. Then she folded the quilt so that it covered him up to the waist and bent low to brush a kiss over his cheek.

"You sure he can't sleep on the bed?" Justin asked quietly.

"I'm sure. He might roll off it in his sleep."

Fear entered Justin's eyes. His Adam's apple bobbed up and down when he took a big swallow. "I guess I should know things like that."

He got down on his knees and cradled the back of Connor's head in his hand, ever so gently, wisps of the baby's hair filtering through Justin's fingertips. With obvious love shining in his eyes, Justin's gaze stayed on Connor a long time, and a pang of guilt wedged its way into Kay's mind, making her question her decisions.

Justin rose and walked over to the queen bed, leaving Kat to follow. His gaze flowed over the room, with its wooden shutters instead of curtains, hardwood flooring and dark walnut furniture. It spelled out masculine without going overboard. In a lowered voice, he said, "This will be Connor's room. I'll have the room decorated any way you like. You just tell me what he needs. The bed is yours, too, for those times that Connor stays overnight."

Immediately struck by Justin's assumptions, Kat put up a hand to stop him. "Whoa, Justin. You're getting way ahead of me here." She kept her voice low enough not to wake her sleeping baby.

"I'm not ahead of you. I'm behind. By about eleven months."

Wow, she'd walked right into that one. While Justin had deceived her, he wasn't about to let her forget what he'd missed in not knowing Connor. She could understand his impatience to create a bond with his son, yet she struggled with how to make all of this work. "I can't guarantee that Connor's going to spend a lot of time here. As for me…" Her traitorous eyes darted to the bed.

Justin must've seen something in her moment of hesitation. A glint entered his eyes.

"Never mind," she said.

"Can we leave him for a few minutes?" he whispered. "We need to talk and I don't want to risk waking him."

Kat glanced at her baby sleeping cozily on the bank of blankets. Then she picked up pillows from the bed and secured them around Connor's precious little body, creating a barrier of protection for him. "He should be fine now. He's a sound sleeper."

Justin clasped her hand. "My room's next door. If he cries, we'll hear him."

Kat let him lead her to the next room. She was immediately struck by the boyish theme of this former soldier's bedroom. Old computers, stacks of videos and sports trophies littered the room in a homey, lived-in way. She pictured what life was like for Justin Slade growing up here on Sunset Ranch. Envy stabbed at the hollow places in her heart. Justin could give Connor this. Justin could provide a better life for Connor than she could.

"Have a seat, Kat." His voice was soothing as he gestured toward his bed.

She took a seat and he settled down beside her in the middle of the bed. The subtle hint of lime cologne sweetened her senses and drew her to him. His nearness was a force she couldn't combat. Why did Justin Slade have this effect on her? She rebelled against the endorphins racing through her body.

Right now, Justin held all the cards. He had legal rights to her son. With one word, he could injure Mattie and make her whole world come crashing down around her.

Her thoughts scattered as soon as he spoke. "I want to know my son. That's a given. I won't tell anyone else about him, you have my word. And my family will do the same, but I do want a few things. Connor will have a place here on Sunset Ranch. Secondly, I really do want him at my brother's wedding. He's missed out on so much family time already."

Kat immediately saw the problems in that. "It won't be easy. What will I say to people?"

"I'll introduce you as a family friend. You don't have to explain yourself. And if some nosey person asks, you'll stick to the story you've been telling all along."

Kat took a sharp breath. "You may not believe this, but I don't like lying, and when I came to Silver Springs I believed all those things to be true."

"I know you did. We'll work through this, Kat. We have to for Aunt Mattie's sake, right?"

Kat nodded slowly. What choice did she have? She

struggled with the situation, wanting to do what was right by giving Justin the time he craved with his son. Going to the wedding was just the beginning of the concessions she'd have to make.

"Listen, I know nothing about this is easy," he said. "I'm asking you to come to Logan and Sophia's wedding with me. We'll stay overnight in Reno. You'll have your own room, don't worry."

"I sure will have my own room," she said, her voice curt to her own ears.

"So then you'll go?"

She shrugged. She didn't want to go. She didn't want to be placed in this position, but she saw no way out. "I'll go. I just have to figure out what to tell Aunt Mattie."

He gave her a nod and then his lips curled into a big warm smile. It was devastating—and so appealing—when he let down his guard like that. "Then it's settled. I'll get back to you with the details. But I do have one more request. I want to hire you to work with me."

"What?" Kat blinked several times. "Why? I don't know anything about developing a retreat for soldiers or horses."

"Ah, but you know about design and decorating. I promised Mattie to refurbish the house and I need help. That's where you come in. I don't know anything about style, color schemes, appliances and flooring. That's not my thing. But apparently it's yours. And there's no denying that you put yourself together pretty well. You've got style."

Heat bubbled up at the way his gaze softened and traveled over her body. He took in her clothes, but it felt more like he was remembering her naked. She thought back to when he'd touched her under the table tonight. She'd nearly melted. He had good hands and he knew what to do with them. If she wasn't careful she could get suckered in and fall for the guy in a big way. "Why hire me? You know I'd do it for free."

"I don't know that. There's very little I really know about you. Once the ball gets rolling, it's going to get very hectic and chaotic, very fast. I'll need a commitment and I'd rather hire someone that Mattie trusts than a complete stranger."

She began nodding. "Okay…I'll do it. For Aunt Mattie. And to prove to you that I'm not going anyplace anytime soon."

Justin blinked. "I never said that you were."

Kat raised her chin. "But that's part of the reason. You want me invested in a project as insurance that I won't pick up and leave town. Admit it."

Justin's lips thinned to a fine line and his gaze shifted away. He was battling with something, and more than a few seconds passed before he said, "Maybe I want to work with you for selfish reasons."

"Like what?"

"Like this." He wrapped his arms around her waist and drew her tight against his chest.

Heat flamed between their bodies. Her nipples pebbled and she willed the sensual sensation away. Justin drew a sharp breath and tugged her into his lap. Her skirt slid up her thighs, baring her legs to his gaze. The force between them pulled at her. It had been this way in New York, too. She'd been hopelessly drawn to him, even though he'd been all wrong for her. She still couldn't keep her distance, when it was more important than ever.

His hot palms caressed her thighs with sure and bold strokes. His gaze fastened on her mouth, and everything below her waist ignited. She bit back a curse at her own weakness, at the way Justin only had to look at her with desire before she caved to his caresses.

One hand left her thigh to move to the underside of her breast. His fingers teased and touched there, making her nipples pucker more and her belly squirm with desperate need. But he didn't stop there. He moved to the side of her throat, the tips of his fingers barely whispering over her. Goose bumps broke out on her neck and she shivered with anticipation of more touching, more temptation. Then he sank his hand into her hair and drew her head down to his lips. "No more teasing, sugar," he said right before his lips came over hers in a kiss that tasted like rich, heady wine.

Kat's breath caught. Heat flooded through her body and her skin tingled. Justin was giving her unbelievable pleasure. He smelled lime-fresh, but like the earth, too, his masculine scent bringing overwhelming memories to the front of her mind. "Straddle me, Kat," he whispered over her lips. "I'm gonna touch you."

Kat obeyed his command. She wrapped her legs around his waist and a groan came from deep in his throat. He plunged his tongue into her mouth, his teeth scraping with hers as he sought to go deeper and deeper. She was pliant, moving with him now, allowing him to pleasure her without question.

There were no thoughts beside the present—what was happening to her now and the growing need building up inside her. When his hand rode up her thigh this time, she welcomed him with a moan and an arch of her back. He shoved aside her panties and his thumb stroked over the sensitive folds of her womanhood. Her moan grew louder, still within the whispers of the night and darkness surrounding them.

She was vulnerable to him, in this position, allowing him to do what he would to her. But she trusted in him, trusted that he only sought to please her. He kissed her over and over as his fingers played a tune of their own on her body, slipping in and out of her womanhood, until she wanted to scream her joy. It was unbelievable. She rocked with him as he stroked her again and again, swaying with him and uttering low unintelligible things.

Justin's eyes widened with pleasure just as she closed her own. Her body pulsed, straining with release that was so needed, so necessary to her life, that she wanted to cry tears of joy and relief when it was all over.

Justin slipped his hand out from under her panties, straightened out her skirt then brought his lips to hers one more time, murmuring, "I've dreamed of doing this to you a thousand times in Afghanistan."

Sated, Kat swallowed the lump in her throat. She'd dreamed of him, too. But she never thought she'd ever be with him like this again. "Justin..."

She had no words and he seemed to understand.

He lowered her down on the bed and held her tightly in his arms. She saw his need, the strength of will he mustered to contain his lust.

Turning his body, he took her face into his hands. "This is how it is between us."

She searched his eyes for more, to find some hope. Something to show that he trusted her, something to show that she could trust him. There were lies between them, and a son and an old woman neither of them wanted to hurt.

"I'm not going to run out on Mattie...or on...you."

"Connor will be part of my life, Kat." Her heart tripped seeing such love in his eyes. She understood that love. The boy was the best thing about herself. "If I'm at all wary and cautious, it's because I'm not taking any chances when it comes to Connor."

Kat thought about that a few seconds. "I understand, and in a weird sort of way, I'm relieved that you feel protective about him. He deserves..."

"The best from both of us."

She stared at the deep emotions displayed in Justin's eyes and heard the little catch in his throat when he spoke Connor's name.

"Yes," she whispered. Then her gaze skimmed over Justin's taut, rigid body. He had yet to find any release or relief. With Connor sleeping in the room next door and the family still in the house, making love wasn't an option. Not that Kat was ready for that. The physical side of lovemaking wasn't the issue, but all the implications and complications that would follow would be too much for her right now. "Are you going to be okay?"

One corner of his mouth lifted in a smile as he gazed at the ceiling. "I learned a lot about self-discipline in the marines. They put us through mind-blowing tests of will. Lying here with you, on this bed, and not losing my head puts me at Level Four."

Kat couldn't keep her lips from curling up. "I take it that's bad?"

"It's no walk in the park."

"How far do the levels go?"

"Five."

"What would that be?"

"That would be if you stripped me naked and touched me in places that needed touching."

"And you couldn't respond?"

"Oh, I'd respond. There would be no stopping that, but I wouldn't be allowed to touch you back."

Kat thought that sounded intriguing. And sexy.

"You're a Level Five if I ever saw one," Justin whispered in a gentle caress.

He brought his hand to her hair and played with the tendrils, watching them slide through his fingers. Air filled his lungs and he gave her one last piercing look, then rose from the bed. Leaning close, he spoke in a tortured voice. "I've got to get out of here. Why don't you check in on the baby. The family will want to say good-night to both of you and then I'll follow you home."

She opened her mouth to protest. She didn't need a

chaperone, but Justin gave a firm shake of his head, declaring his intentions nonnegotiable.

She clamped off her words of refusal and nodded.

Some battles she was better off not fighting.

The next morning, Kat rose earlier than usual and checked on Connor, who was still sleeping in his crib. Then she peeked into Mattie's room. She was sitting up in her bed, reading her bible. "Morning, Kat."

"How are you feeling this morning?"

The older woman peered over her eyeglasses and gave a watery smile. "Excellent…I'm a new woman."

It was the same response she'd given Mattie for the past two months. "I'm glad you're feeling well. What would you like for breakfast?"

Mattie's lips twisted. "Well, since I can't have ham and eggs with biscuits and gravy, I guess I'll settle for one of those vegetarian sausage patties." She made a face. "Never heard of a hog farmer not being able to eat the hog."

"You don't have hogs anymore," Kat said with a smile. "And the doctor says those veggie sausages are good for you."

"I know, but my Ralph is turning over in his grave right about now."

Kat laughed. Dear old Aunt Mattie was no wilting flower. She had a lot of pep in her still.

"I'll get our breakfast…I'm feeling up to cooking this morning," Mattie continued. "I bet you've got some work to do today. You go on and do what you have to, I'll holler if I need help."

"Okay, thanks, Aunt Mattie. I'm working on a new design for a little boy's Christmas suit."

"Oh, that sounds lovely." Aunt Mattie closed her bible, removed her eyeglasses and folded herself out of bed.

Reaching for a terry-cloth robe lying across her bed, she put her arms through the sleeves and tied the belt.

"I've got some news," Kat said, lingering in the door-way.

"Did you get another rejection from those fool buyers?"

Kat had been receiving letters, almost weekly, rejecting her line of affordable baby clothing from major department stores. Those rejections were a big letdown. She believed in her work and knew it would be a hit judging by the success of her growing sales on the Babylicious website. She just needed a chance, yet her dream of becoming a professional fashion designer kept eluding her. "No, but I was offered a job from Justin Slade. He wants to pay me to refurbish the house."

"Oh?"

"He says he has to pay someone anyway and it would make your life easier if I did it. He wouldn't have to bring a designer into the house. We could work together, Aunt Mattie. We'll fix this place up and make it shine. What do you think? Want me to do it?"

"Well, sure...of course. Nobody knows me or this place better than you. You'll do a bang-up job." Aunt Mattie's expression grew serious. "But that's a lot to ask of you, isn't it? You're already so busy."

Kat shrugged. "Not really. I work on the designs, because I love to do it and I'm selling a little here and there, but that only takes a few hours in the evenings. This we can do together, and we'll work around Connor's schedule."

Aunt Mattie tilted her head slightly to one side. "It's what they call multitasking, isn't it? Back in our day, it was simply called chores. Doing what needed to get done, and if that meant fourteen-hour days, we did it."

Kat laughed. "You're right. The label is different, but it's the same thing."

"Well, all right, then."

A loud ruckus from outside the yard filtered into the house and Kat walked over to the parlor window. "What on earth?"

"Oh, it's the bulldozer," Aunt Mattie said, approaching the window. "The sale hasn't gone through yet, but I figured it was okay to let Justin start up the work. That boy is in a hurry to get things done before the cold weather sets in. Tractors are going to clear the acres beyond the house and the bulldozer's going to knock down the rotted barns and feed shacks on the grounds." Mattie's eyes sparkled with curiosity. "I'm surprised Justin didn't tell you, being that you saw him last night."

Kat immediately balked. "It wasn't a date or anything. We talked and he offered me the job."

Aunt Mattie gave a quick nod of her head. "Nice boy, that Justin."

"The Slades also invited Connor and I to Logan Slade's wedding. It was a very generous offer and all, but I don't want to go."

"I bet Justin wants you to go. He did the asking, didn't he?"

"Actually, no. Logan's fiancée, Sophia, did. I think they were just being nice."

Aunt Mattie's eyes narrowed in on her. "You don't want to go, or you don't want to leave me alone?"

Kat focused on the banged-up canary-yellow bulldozer rolling past the house. Two tractors followed behind. "Both. I'd have to spend the night in a hotel."

"Well, shoot, Kat. If you're invited to a fancy shindig with a good-looking man and asked to stay in a nice hotel, you're gonna do it. You know I don't want to stop you from living your life."

"You're not, Aunt Mattie." She turned her attention away from the bulldozer to look into her eyes. "You're not stopping me from anything."

"You know Ralph's sister Maisey's been wanting to come for a visit. You just tell me the date and I'll have Maisey come by and stay with me. You'll have time all to yourself."

"But the wedding's this Saturday. That's not much notice to make arrangements."

"Why, that's almost a week away. Maisey's got nothing on her dance card. She's a widow, just like me. I'm sure she'll come. You go on now. Accept that invitation. You deserve a little break from tending to me."

The bulldozer crawled past the house. Justin moved fast when he wanted something. The way he was stepping up the time frame for the retreat was just another reminder that she had to be on her toes around him.

He'd boxed her into a corner with this wedding invitation. Justin wanted Connor there. With Connor, he also got Kat. And now Aunt Mattie wasn't giving her a way to refuse the invitation.

Kat had no choice. She would go to Sophia and Logan's wedding and Connor would get to know his relatives a little better. She shuddered at the thought. Justin's prank, switching places with Brett and deceiving her, was a constant reminder not to believe in anyone but herself. Now Justin was asking her to trust him and his family to keep their secret.

How could she trust in anything, when she'd been let down so many times in the past?

She gazed into Aunt Mattie's aged blue eyes. "Go ahead and call Maisey."

"So then, you'll go?"

Kat let a sigh escape her throat. "I'll go."

Aunt Mattie reached out and clasped her hand. Her thin fingers gave a little encouraging squeeze. "I'm glad. You'll have fun."

Aunt Mattie's generosity only made Kat feel guilty

about everything. She was the one person she didn't want to lie to and yet the lie about Connor's paternity was the biggest lie of all.

Six

It figured the wedding was at a Golden Hotel.

Kat couldn't catch a break. The knot inside her belly twisted another turn when Justin made that announcement on the drive up to Reno. Logan wanted the very best for Sophia, to make up for all the grief he'd caused her in the past. And Golden Hotels, renowned for impeccable service, elegantly decorated rooms and culinary excellence, were at the top of the hotel food chain. The family-run hotels were located in every major American city from New York to Los Angeles. Kat was a walking encyclopedia on the subject.

She took a swallow and trembled.

"Come here, little man," Justin said, removing Connor from the car seat and securing him in one arm.

The valet helped Kat out of the front seat and took care of their luggage.

She kept the diaper bag and hung it over her shoulder. Connor gazed up at Justin with curiosity, and Kat smiled, her heart pounding in her chest as they entered the hotel together.

Check-in was quick. Justin had reserved adjoining suites that required taking a special elevator up to the fourteenth floor. As they approached her suite, Justin slid the plastic key card over the brass door plate. A light flashed green, the lock clicked open and he pulled the handle down to let them in. "After you," he said to Kat. "I think you'll like your room."

She took a few steps inside. "It's...beautiful." And it was. She knew the decorator, Amando Guerrero. They'd had lunch several times in New York. He was a man with an eye for location. A Reno hotel would have all the same Golden amenities, but would also include subtle changes that emphasized the feel of the West. Remington statues of cowboys astride horses, artful rustic trim and patterns that depicted Nevada history gave the entire hotel tasteful ambience.

Justin scanned the suite with a satisfied glance and nodded. He was more interested in the little guy in his arms. But Connor began squirming and reaching for her and Justin didn't push it. He handed Connor over. "He wants his mommy."

Connor hugged her neck tight and then turned, giving Justin his stink face, which consisted of narrowing his eyes and pursing his rosy lips. Kat chuckled.

Justin made a similar face back at him. "Hey, buddy. You don't know it yet, but I'm your best friend."

Connor whipped back around in her arms. She'd assured Justin several times in the past that Connor needed time to warm up to him. It would happen in time, so she kept her lips clamped this time. She could tell Justin was impatient to have his son's affection. He wanted Connor's acceptance and love...*now*.

Kat walked to the rectangular bay window that overlooked the Reno landscape. It wasn't New York with its towering buildings and mere slices of sky above. It was Nevada, sparse and dry, with rambling blue clouds visible for miles—white puffs that you could almost reach out and touch.

"Your luggage and baby gear should arrive shortly."

"We'll be fine."

"Do you think he'll nap?"

She glanced at the parlor sofa and then beyond to two French doors opening to a large bedroom. "Maybe. I'll give him a snack and a bottle and see if I can get him down."

"Okay, good. If you'll be needing anything, I'm in the next suite. Just knock on the adjoining door. I've got to clean up and get ready for a quick walk-through rehearsal downstairs. I'll be back for you in two hours."

She kissed the top of the baby's head and nodded.

Justin focused on where her lips had just touched Connor's baby-fine brown hair and smiled. He strode over to them and took the baby's cheek in his palm, his eyes filled with longing as Connor looked at him. With the pad of his thumb he stroked the baby's cheek. "It's pretty amazing, isn't it?"

Kat knew what he meant. One glimpse at her big-eyed, dark-haired little son was enough to make her believe in miracles. He was the only thing beautiful about her world. "It is," she said quietly.

Justin dropped his hand before the baby had a chance to turn away and focused his attention on her now. He cast soft caring eyes her way. "I'm glad he's here today."

She was reduced to mush when he turned on the charm. And she almost forgot how uncomfortable she was being here. But there was too much at stake. Too much to lose. She'd known hardship in her life and she'd known powerful men. Justin could hand her a world of hurt if he wanted to make her life difficult. She felt compelled to cooperate and attend this wedding but she wasn't fooled into thinking Justin cared about her. He was trying to make up for lost time with his son. He blamed her for missing out on the first year of Connor's life.

But he wasn't blameless, either.

She found no need to rehash all that.

"We'll be ready."

* * *

It was trickier than she thought getting them both dressed and ready for a wedding. She didn't know how long the little guy would hold up at the reception, although she had managed to get him down for a thirty-minute nap in a crib that was set up by the hotel staff. She'd brought along his monkey sheets, just in case, and Connor felt right at home when she'd laid him down on his own bedding. Room service had arrived shortly after with an array of lunch entrees that Justin had ordered.

The penniless soldier she'd met had turned into a man of privilege.

Odd how life sometimes turned out.

She dipped the mascara wand into the tube and gave her eyelashes one final upward stroke. "There," she said to the baby. "A diaper change for you and we're all set."

He watched her from a standing position in the crib, his head barely peeking over the slats. Dressed in a navy-blue suit with a miniature bow tie and hat, her little man was ready to attend his first wedding.

A light tapping on the door came five minutes early. Not a slow learner, Justin was already discovering the intricacies of fatherhood by deliberately knocking quietly in case the baby was sleeping. "That's your daddy," she whispered to Connor, leaving him in his crib to walk over and open the door.

Justin stood at the threshold in a charcoal suit, brocade vest and black tie, hat in hand. He made her palms sweat when he gave her a low whistle of approval.

"You're a little early."

He didn't wait for an invitation, but strolled in and walked right past her. "Looks to me like you're ready. You sure couldn't get any more gorgeous."

Her face flushed with heat. She closed the door and stared at it, taking a steadying breath. When she turned around, she found his eyes fastened on her. "You look nice, too."

"Isn't every day I stand up for my brother."

"It is a special day."

Another flick of his eyes told her he approved of her dress. Pride swelled in her chest. She'd designed it herself, with her bust size and curves in mind. Too tight, and she looked trashy. Too loose, and it was frump city. Kat's one-of-a-kind dress was deep violet with a high rounded sheer neckline, a lacy overlay and a scalloped hemline. The dress dipped low enough in the back to be provocative but not too dangerous. Petite rhinestone chandelier earrings and four-inch open-toed satin pumps finished off the look.

Connor uttered his baby sounds and Justin's gaze strayed to the crib. *Thank goodness.*

"I'll get him," she said, scurrying past Justin to the crib set up just inside her bedroom. "He needs a diaper change."

"Gawd, he looks cute," Justin said, walking over. The awe in his voice was another source of pride for Kat.

"I know, doesn't he?"

"Where'd he get that outfit? He looks like—"

"A little prince?" Kat asked.

"I was gonna say, a little dude. He just needs a miniature Stetson."

Kat smiled. "I'll be sure to remember that next time."

Justin eyes lifted to her. "You made that suit?"

Kat nodded. "I did. It's part of my line of baby clothes, but I made this one a bit more special since Connor was wearing it to his…his uncle's wedding."

Justin's expression didn't change, only now his awe was directed at her. "Talented."

"Thank you."

She made quick work of changing the baby's diaper while Justin looked on. Kat's stomach began to ache when they left and took the elevator down to the lobby. They exited the building through automatic doors that led to a private outdoor garden where the wedding would take place.

Trees and greenery draped with twinkle lights created a natural perimeter for the garden. Stone steps separated by patches of groomed green grass led to the raised altar. Sweet William adorned the archway over the altar and dozens of small candelabra twinkled alongside the adjoining wooden beams. As they approached, she noticed rows upon rows of Chiavari chairs lined up. And a lot of people milling around. Before they fully entered the garden, Kat stopped and put a hand on Justin's arm. "How many people are invited?"

Justin pursed his lips. "Does it matter?"

"Two hundred?" she guessed.

Justin shrugged.

"More?"

"Two hundred and fifty, give or take. Are you nervous?"

"Only about lying. People are going to look at the three of us and assume..."

"The truth?"

Kat squeezed her eyes closed. "No one could ever possibly guess the full truth. It's too bizarre."

"If it were up to me, and Mattie wouldn't get hurt, I'd tell the entire world about my boy."

His proprietary tone didn't help matters.

"You promised," she reminded him.

"I know what I said. I won't break that promise," he said quietly to reassure her. "So don't you worry. We'll stick to our story for now. It's believable enough."

It was about all she could do. And it only took two minutes before she had to put his theory to the test when a hulk of a man walked over to greet them. He took Justin's hand and pumped hard, giving Justin a quick look before staring at Kat and Connor. She tamped down her initial panic. She used to be a better liar, but somewhere along the line,

Kat had grown to hate lies and liars. Circumstances being what they were, Kat had no choice right now.

"Katherine, this is Sheriff Robbie Dunphy. You get outta line in Douglas County and Robbie here knows all about it."

She smiled. "Well, then I'd better be careful."

"Pleased to meet you, ma'am." He removed his hat and took her hand, giving it a surprisingly gentle shake before glancing at Connor. "And who's this cute little tyke?"

"This is my son, Connor," Kat said. "It's his first wedding."

"He looks like a well-behaved boy."

Kat grinned. "Thanks, but tell me that *after* the ceremony. I might have to dash out if he fusses."

"Aw, I'm sure he'll do fine."

Awkward silence ensued and just as the sheriff was about to ask Kat a question, Justin distracted him with talk of Douglas County politics. Connor began squirming in her arms and Kat focused her attention on him, only hearing snippets of the sheriff urging Justin to enter into the fray. Justin in politics? Of course, he was viewed as a hero and would win hearts and minds, but Kat couldn't quite put that square peg into the round hole. The man she was beginning to know wasn't cut out for the political arena.

A few more men approached Justin and the sheriff. There was a good deal of hand shaking and backslapping. Curious eyes drifted her way and Justin smoothly introduced her as a good friend of the Slade family.

An older gentleman with a handlebar moustache and gentle eyes put his hand on Justin's shoulder. "The parade is set to go as scheduled. Three weeks from today."

Justin looked like he wanted to jump out of his own skin, but simply smiled and nodded. As the circle around Justin grew larger, Kat felt someone touch her arm. She swiveled her head and was relieved to see Audrey beside her. Luke's new fiancée stared straight into her eyes and spoke slowly. "There's a little fishpond over behind the altar I think Connor would like to see."

Kat wasn't slow on the uptake. She thanked heaven for astute women like Audrey Thomas. "Connor would *love* to see the fish."

Audrey's blue eyes lit, silently saying *save succeeded* with her grin. "I thought so. Follow me."

Kat excused herself and strolled away from Justin's entourage, arm in arm with Audrey.

"Thank you," Kat said a few seconds later. "I owe you. You look fabulous, by the way."

"You think so? Sophia asked me to be in the wedding a few days ago and we picked out this dress. I look a little lumpy in it, don't I?"

Kat chuckled. "I remember feeling that way when I was pregnant, too. But actually, the empire fit is perfect for a woman with a baby bump. I love the deep lavender on you." The one-shoulder style gave Audrey a sultry look. "No reason you can't be sexy just because you're pregnant. Remember *bump,* not *lump,* and you'll be fine."

"Okay, got it. Do you think your little man will give me a dance later?"

"I'm sure he will. He loves music."

As they approached the tropical fishpond, Kat made one mistake. She swung her head around at the last minute to find Justin still encircled by the group, his focus fastened right on her and Connor, his incredible dark eyes filled with wishful longing.

Something squeezed tight in her heart.

She wished Justin could join them.

And she felt a twinge of guilt in abandoning him.

How crazy was that?

In a wedding gown of ivory satin with a sweetheart neckline and subtle folds cascading to the floor, Sophia made a stunning bride standing beside Logan. His eyes beamed with adoration for his soon-to-be wife. Justin and Luke stood beside him a few feet away. Little Edward Branford, a sweet boy who lived on the ranch with his grandma Connie, Sunset Lodge's head chef, balanced a ring bearer's pillow on the steps of the altar. Audrey was standing at the altar next to Sophia, and Kat thought she looked great, like a budding flower ready to blossom.

With Connor on her lap, she sat in the second row near the far aisle, just in case. It wouldn't be hard to make a clean getaway if Connor got loud or fidgety. But luckily her son was still captivated by the fishpond from minutes ago and was on his best behavior.

Tears filled her eyes when Logan spoke his vows. His devotion to his soon-to-be bride touched the very core of her. Kat didn't know too many people who were so desperately in love like Logan and Sophia. Or like Luke and Audrey for that matter.

Audrey and Luke had invited her to their courthouse wedding next month. It would be more of the same on a less grand scale. She couldn't refuse Audrey. She'd been a friend and an understanding presence when Kat needed her.

The Slade family stuck together. They were devoted to each other. Even some of their employees, like Ward Halliday, Sunset Ranch's head wrangler, and Constance Branford, the lodge's executive chef, were close-knit with the Slades.

Kat wasn't used to being surrounded by loved ones like this. Instead of family dinners and gatherings, she and her mother had spent their days trying to elude her father and his unholy harsh hand.

Sometimes Kat felt phantom pain on her cheeks where her father had struck so often. Sometimes Kat would dream of standing up to him when he'd vented his rage on her mother. Sometimes Kat wished her father had died twenty years ago, instead of two, and she wondered if that made her a horrible person.

Connor wrapped his little arms around her neck and laid his head on her shoulder. "That's my sweet baby," she whispered into his ear as she began to gently rock him. He tightened his grip on her and it was the best feeling in the world.

She'd never once regretted her pregnancy. She'd never once wished anything but good things for her son. He was her glue. He kept things in perspective. There wasn't anything she wouldn't do for him.

Sometimes that devotion got her into trouble.

She lifted her lashes at that moment and found Justin's eyes on her, the hard lines of his mouth softening just a bit.

She tilted her head and regarded him. It wasn't difficult to react to Justin. He swept her in with a magnetic force that she couldn't quite explain. She sensed he was more than a military hero, a man everyone wanted a piece of, a man hell-bent on doing right by Brett Applegate. At times a haunted look took over his expression. At times, he seemed distant and wary and Kat wasn't naive enough to think he'd had it easy overseas. On the drive up here, Justin had retreated into himself. She'd see him shake off a thought as if it tortured him. She'd wondered what he was remembering. Or what he was trying to forget.

He was a complicated man, who could complicate her life.

And he wanted Connor.

She fought off a wave of panic and focused on the vows being spoken. Minutes later, with love shining in their eyes, Logan and Sophia said "I do" to each other and the marriage ceremony concluded with a flourish of applause and a few hoots and hollers. The newlyweds marched arm in arm down the steps, sweeping past her, their smiles beaming from ear to ear.

Kat joined in the applause as tears welled in her eyes. She always got a little sappy at weddings. Images flashed in her head of when she was in the throes of despair, sleeping under a rickety roof at a women's shelter, wearing threadbare clothes, her mother's arms firmly around her. Kat would dream of her wedding day. She'd think of the handsomest boy at her school and pretend he was her fiancé. She'd wear a Cinderella dress of frothy lace—the design stayed in her mind even to this day—and she would be smiling. It was all pretend, a fantasy she knew, by the light of day, would never come true.

She banked her sentimental urges, burying them away for now. She vowed to never forget the hard times, but to never dwell on them either if she could help it.

Clasping Connor's hands in hers, she encouraged him to clap. He took his cue and put his palms together at an angle, his chubby fingers spread wide, and began to clap along with the other guests. "That's it, sweetheart," she said.

He bounced happily in her lap, eager to show off his talent and turned to her with a big four-tooth smile.

Her heart exploded with pride. She snuggled him close, kissing the top of his head. "You're such a good clapper, baby boy."

Lost in the moment, she slowly lifted her lashes to find Justin standing in front of her, watching them. Fatherly pride filled his eyes, a dead giveaway to anyone paying attention, but luckily, the guests were filing out of the garden, one row at a time behind the wedding party, and no one noticed Justin's display. Or that Justin had taken a detour to come get them.

She understood his adoring look, as dangerous as it

might be, because her love for Connor was so intense, she couldn't imagine anyone not loving this sweet little boy.

Kat stared at Justin and for a second forgot all about the predicament she was in.

"Ready to go inside?" he asked, offering his hand.

The sun took its final bow on the horizon, casting the garden in a soft crimson glow. It was peaceful and quiet now. She could sit out here all evening and watch the candles flicker. "Sure. We'll go in now."

"That's good, because my brother will never let me live it down if I neglect my best man duties."

She smiled and took his hand. His touch brought immediate warmth. "I wouldn't want you to disappoint Logan."

"I was talking about Luke. You know, the old favorite-brother thing." His wide grin and the firm grasp on her hand, shot her blood pressure up. "He'd never let me live it down."

Joking about sibling rivalry seemed so normal to the Slades.

Justin put his arm around her waist and they walked back into the hotel where the elaborate reception was just beginning.

There was no doubt in Justin's mind that he was dancing with the most beautiful woman in the room. There was also no doubt that he was going to make love to Kat tonight.

"He's fine with Audrey," he whispered for her ears only. Kat's mothering instincts kicked in as soon as he'd taken her onto the dance floor. She kept looking over his shoulder, swiveling her head to find the little guy.

"I know he's fine. It's just that, I'm…"

"Paranoid?"

She gathered her brows. "Cautious…with him."

His brothers had danced with Kat already, so he figured one turn around the dance floor with her wasn't out

of line. Hell, he'd watched her dance with a few other men
and it had been hard to take. He would've thought the baby
would be a deterrent instead of a magnet.

Yet baby or no baby, Kat was hot. She was unique. She
had a curvy body that could destroy lesser men.

"My family wouldn't let anything happen to him," he
assured her.

He drew Kat an inch closer. It was hard to keep a proper
distance from her, when all he wanted to do was feel every
soft morsel of her skin against his, to run his hands up and
down her arms and bring her close enough to sniff her
platinum hair and breathe in her female scent. But she'd
set limits when he'd asked her to dance. Katherine Grady
and Justin Slade were just supposed to be family friends.

God, he hated the lies. The pretense. He hated not being
able to claim Connor as his son.

"I know your family is good with him, Justin. But it's
been just me and him…and I'm…I'm overprotective."

Justin let that comment go. She was a good mother. He
liked that about her. But he wanted more from Kat tonight
than arguments or explanations.

"Are you having a good time?" he asked.

A hum purred from her throat. His groin tightened from
the breathy sound. "I haven't danced in a long time."

"You're a pretty good dancer, keeping up with my two
left feet."

Her eyes went dewy soft. "You're not so bad."

He wanted to tuck her in close and hold her to his chest.
"This isn't easy."

She snapped her head back and looked injured. "Dancing with me?"

Gently tugging her half an inch closer, he spoke with a
rasp in his voice. "Not being able to pull you into my arms
and slow dance with you the way I want to."

Her body trembled and he was glad he wasn't the only one feeling tense. "Oh."

He took a step back and then twirled her around in a smooth exchange of places in rhythm to the music, thanking high heaven he'd learned some basic dance moves from Betsy Ann Stankowski. That girl had given him lessons in more than a few things.

When he took hold of Kat's hands again, he brought her another inch closer. To anyone watching, it was an innocent move and that's the way it had to be for now.

But it was hard. Erotic perfume tickled his nose and he couldn't hold back a quietly executed groan. "You smell so damn good."

"Thank you."

He lowered his arm to her waist and splayed his hand over her back, drawing her a little bit closer into the circle of his arms. His fingers found the exposed part of her back, her skin the softest there, the flesh supple and silky smooth. Her pretty green eyes blazed in question. He answered her with unspoken words in the way he held her, the way he returned her gaze. Everything uniquely female about her pounded into his skull. He wasn't going to be denied tonight, but he was grateful when the music stopped.

"I'd better go," she whispered softly.

He stood still and nodded, releasing his hold on her.

He wasn't a good actor, not even close. Anyone watching him now would guess his intentions from the way he was looking at her. At the moment he didn't give a damn.

She turned from him, hips swaying as she walked off the dance floor. She stopped when she reached Logan and Sophia's sweetheart table where Audrey was standing with the baby. The entire family gathered around Connor, taking turns holding him.

So much for being discreet. Babies attracted attention.

And Connor certainly was doing that, not only with the Slades, but with many of the guests in attendance.

Audrey handed the baby over to Kat and she braced him tight to her chest. Peeking over the baby's shoulder, Kat found Justin again and the sensual glint in her eyes told him what he wanted to know.

A rare kind of emotion poured into his heart.

He glanced at his watch. The best man's speech came next and then a few more wedding day rituals. Logan deserved the happiness he was getting and Justin had every intention of being here for him. Both the bride and groom had waited for him to return home so that he could be a part of the ceremony and celebration, but as soon as the reception was over, Justin wouldn't delay in taking his family back up to the hotel room.

Seven

Standing over the crib in Kat's suite, they watched their son sleep. Justin's warm breath drifted over her throat, sending her mind in a direction it shouldn't be taking. Kat had always imagined being a family like this. As a young girl, she'd clung to her dreams when life pounded her from all sides. When all she had was her mother's distracted love and no real place to call home.

If only the circumstances for the three of them weren't so darn messy.

The wedding had been wonderful, and she was greatly relieved she hadn't been put on the spot. No one had asked her probing questions and she hadn't had to tell any lies. Thank goodness.

"I want to be here when the baby wakes up," Justin said.

Justin's request was reasonable. He'd never been around when Connor awakened; the baby was usually in his best mood at the first light of day, cackling and smiling and affectionate. "Okay, I'll knock on the adjoining door when he—"

Justin grabbed her hand and tugged her out of the room. She let him lead her, though she was a little surprised by his abrupt behavior. He brought her to the parlor just outside the bedroom and pinned her against the wall. He wasn't rough, but he wasn't gentle, either, and her heartbeats sped with delicious anticipation. "I meant, I want to be in bed with you, when the baby wakes up."

Her throat clamped. "Oh," she squeaked. "Do...do I have a choice in this?"

Justin yanked off his tie and unfastened the buttons on his white dress shirt with one hand, while he grasped both of her wrists with the other. He held them high above her head, slamming them up against the wall. A thrill raced through her body as his mouth hovered close to hers. "You always have a choice, sugar."

But then his lips closed over hers and she was completely swept up a bruising kiss that took all choice away. "Yes, yes," she uttered, as he kissed her once more.

Her back arched away from the wall, her body responding to him naturally as she pressed against him. Beautiful desperate groans spilled from his lips and he continued to kiss her. She had an urge to touch him, to rip his clothes off.

He might've read her mind, because in that instant, he yanked his shirt free, shifting to keep her hands pinned above her head. Her body heated like a furnace kicking on full steam. With nearly unquenchable need driving her wild, she moved her hips and bucked toward him. He plunged his tongue into her mouth, leaving her chest heaving, her nipples aching and her legs wobbly.

He was muscled, ripped like a man who'd had to be strong, not for vanity but for survival. She ached to touch him, to weave her fingers through the light cropping of hairs on his chest. To feel his muscles under her fingertips and run her tongue along his belly.

"Easy, sugar, easy," he said, his breaths labored. "Don't rush this."

But Kat needed him. She needed to feel the connection from something deep and lonely inside her. Justin was perfect, probably too good for her, and that made her want him all the more. She was from the gutter. He was bred to be a hero. None of this made sense. Except that the two of them, making love, always made sense.

She didn't have to deal with appearances right now. She could have this one moment, this one ounce of unabashed pleasure. It wasn't as if she and Justin were strangers. They knew each other well, sexually. She wanted him inside her. She wanted the release that came when you placed one hundred percent of your trust in another person. "Touch me, baby. Touch me."

She'd nearly shouted her plea and it surprised her, how desperate she sounded.

Justin broke the kiss, and she whimpered from the loss. His hand closed over her breast. "Like this?"

Through her clothes, she felt the scorching heat of his palm as he massaged her back and forth. Jolts of electricity traveled with lightning speed through her body. Her nipples puckered in response. "Yes, oh, yes."

He kept her pinned and it frustrated her not to touch him back. Every time she tried to loosen his grip, he tightened his hold on her.

His one hand did enough magic though, as he expertly rubbed the sensitive tips of her breasts. Heat puddled in her belly. Below that, she felt herself go suddenly taut. Tension built to extremes until Kat couldn't comprehend anything but the pleasure that was about to explode inside.

She felt her dress being hiked up, and Justin's fingers finding and caressing her oh-so-sensitive sweet spot.

It was enough to topple her.

Spasms wracked her body, everything went hot and tight. Quick, short gasps spurted from her mouth from the sudden, unexpected release.

It was crazy. It had only taken seconds for Justin to completely arouse her. Still fully clothed, and so surprised, she'd had one of the best orgasms of her life.

Thank you, Justin Slade.

Her eyes slowly opened as she came down to earth. Justin looked on in awe and spoke with reverence. "Amazing."

Somewhere along the line, he'd released her hands and she was now free to touch him, but before she could lay a hand on his chest, she found herself being lifted up and carried away.

She had the good sense to remember Connor. "The baby."

"We'll keep the door between the suites open. We'll hear him if he needs us and we'll check in on him later."

For the first time since she'd met Justin, she didn't mind hearing the "we" in Justin's command. "Okay," she said, leaning her head on his shoulder.

His bedroom was in shadow. Justin loosened his grip on her and she slid down his body, balancing on her high heels once her feet touched the carpeted floor. He took half a step back to look at her. Then she brought her fingertips to his toned, bronze chest.

He trembled from her touch and a fierce possessive gleam sparkled in his eyes. She stroked him more, laying the palm of her hands flat on his chest. He closed his eyes slowly with an expression of pure pleasure. Then she let her hands roam free, touching every cord, every ripple of muscle under his skin. It unnerved her how much she wanted to please him, to hear his soft groans, to see his arousal displayed in the veins popping in his neck and the breadth of his taut body tightening even more.

Then she rose up to run her tongue along the seam of his lips. He took her into his arms and kissed her thoroughly until her limbs went limp. A sexy thought entered her mind and Kat wasn't going to play shy. She whispered her desire over his tempting lips. "I want to touch you, Justin. But you can't touch me back yet."

His eyes narrowed on her cryptically. "You want to torture me?"

A throaty chuckle escaped her throat. She thought of all the reasons she might want to torture him, but that wasn't her intention at the moment. Tonight was about satisfying pleasure. The more she thought about it, the more she wanted Justin at her mercy. With a tilt of her head, she asked, "Would you consider it torture to have me touch you?"

He gave it one second of thought and the hot glint in his eyes told her he was ready for anything she might send his way. He pulled her close and kissed her again, whispering, "Hell yeah, if I couldn't touch you."

"You've already touched me plenty." She'd gone undone in his arms. "I want to reciprocate."

His brows arched. "I'm not gonna refuse an offer like that."

"Are you sure?"

He didn't hesitate to nod and smile. "Do your damage, Kat."

"Okay, then." With a keen sense of triumph, she spun around. "Will you unzip my dress?"

He stepped closer, his breath whispering over her shoulder. He planted tiny kisses there and up the back of her neck. Goose bumps erupted everywhere. "You're touching."

"We haven't started yet."

He eased the zipper down past her waist and his fingertips lingered on the curve of her spine just above her buttocks.

Kat's skin tingled in response. "I see I have a cheater on my hands."

"And they say cheaters never win." His fingers skimmed over the slope of her derriere.

She shuddered in response. "I'll get back at you for that," she said on a stifled breath.

"I'm hoping you do."

A gasp broke from her throat and she whirled around to face him. His eyes devoured her. She'd never seen hunger as strong or powerful before. If she wasn't careful, she'd lose her nerve. "Will you lie down on the bed?"

"What are you going to do?"

"Undress for you."

"I'm there," he said. And he was. In seconds, Justin was sprawled across the king-size bed, waiting for her. Memories rushed forth of making love with Justin before and she knew tonight would be equally satisfying.

She slipped her dress over her hips and gave a wiggle. Violet material pooled at her feet. She took a little step over it. Next came her bra and panties; as she hastily removed them, she suddenly felt less bold than a minute ago when she suggested this. She shot Justin a quick glance. He gave her an encouraging nod, his expression filled with patient, reverent awe.

Oh, how she wanted him.

There was no backing out now anyway. She stood naked in the shadows and came forth into a ray of light slicing through the window.

Justin rolled to his side, braced an elbow on the bed and watched Kat move toward him. If he wasn't so damn turned on, he'd be amused at her sudden shyness as she approached the bed. She was one hundred and fifteen pounds of creamy, smooth-skinned perfection. She had big breasts, a tiny waistline and curvy hips. Her hair was the color of rich French vanilla ice cream and her lips were as juicy as ripe apples.

When she put her knees on the bed, Justin rolled onto his back, giving her room to join him. He put his hands behind his head, lacing his fingers tight. The lady wanted to play this game and he wouldn't deny her.

"Close your eyes," she said as she lay down next to him.

"That's not part of the deal. I like watching you."

"You're going to like what I plan to do even more."

He shut his eyes. Immediately, the mattress dipped a little and he felt her presence. The aura that was Kat, along with her heady perfume, intoxicated him. For a minute, she said nothing. Did nothing. He was about to protest, until she moved a little closer and soft strands of her hair brushed over his face. He breathed in sunshine and freshness. Then her lips covered his.

Her kiss jerked his body to attention.

Instantly, he knew keeping his hands off would surely kill him.

Her slender delicate fingertips grazed over his skin, lightly, gently, and she removed her mouth from his to drizzle dozens of tiny kisses onto his throat. He took a deep swallow and maintained his position. Next she nipped at his earlobe, her teeth nibbling, her breath coming in short bursts as the fingers of one hand probed below his waist.

She worked at his belt buckle and then unzipped his dress pants.

What came next tempted him to reach for her and wind his hand in her hair, but he held firm, keeping both hands behind his head, his fingers entwined.

Kat worked magic on him, her mouth, her tongue making him crazy. He bucked and arched, feeling her hair caress his belly, her soft cheeks brush against his skin. He broke out in a sweat, beads of moisture pooling on his brow, his head thrashing back and forth on the pillow. She made mush of his resolve. He was ready to cave, ready to cry uncle, but he didn't want her brand of punishment to end. It was too good, too damn exciting even if it was killing him at the same time.

He loved the sexual being that she was. He loved that she was uninhibited. Every touch, every damn stroke of her tongue was meant to give them both pleasure. No wonder he hadn't forgotten that one night they'd had together in New York. While his memories of her appearance had begun to fade when he was stationed overseas, the memories of making love to Kat hadn't. They had kept him warm on many a cold night. Being Brett that weekend had had only one advantage…making love with Kat.

His groans filled the silence of the room. Every fiber of his being battled to claim her, to untie the imaginary bonds on his hands. His body was on high idle, ready to race toward the finish line. He wanted to take her…now.

He shook with uncontrollable force, trying to take his mind other places. But it wasn't working. All he could think about was fishing a condom out of his pants pocket and bringing them both to completion. "In my pants, get it," he managed to say, opening his eyes.

Kat didn't hesitate. She must've sensed he was on the brink. He watched her get the condom and rip the package open. When he was sheathed, she rose over him and straddled his legs. Lying on the bed, seeing Kat above him, blonde and beautiful and seductive, knocked him ten ways to Sunday. It was more than having great sex with her. It was more…so much more.

She went slow and easy, and he could tell it'd been a long time for her. She moved cautiously at first and Justin kept pace, aching to slam into her, to release the pressure that had built from a small tornado into a raging twister. But he wouldn't hurt Kat. He wouldn't do anything to ever harm her.

Her movements grew more frantic and she took him faster and faster until she breathed out, "Touch me, Justin. It's okay. Please…I need you to touch me."

Justin didn't need any more encouragement. He brought his hands to her hips and guided them both home.

Sated and drowsy-eyed, Kat lay on the bed nestled up to him. Justin ran a hand along her body, letting her warmth and softness sink in. He stroked the slope of her breast and brushed a kiss into her hairline.

"Do you think I should check on the baby again?" she asked.

"We just did ten minutes ago. He's out. Let's give it a few more minutes and we'll both go in again."

"Okay. Mmm, feels good."

"Me touching you? I'm trying to make up for lost time."

"That, too," she purred, snuggling closer under the covers. "But it feels good having someone else to rely on with Connor. I never thought I'd say that."

"You can always count on me."

"I know."

"You put me through hell, you know," he whispered, splaying his hand over her waist and giving it a squeeze.

"Really?"

"You've been killing me in small doses since I met you at Mattie's house. You're beautiful and talented and I've wanted to be like this with you since the second I caught sight of you bending over that old clunker when you were trying to fix that tire."

She chuckled. "That must've been a sight."

"You kidding?" He smoothed his hand over the curve of her hip and blew out a breath. "You don't see sights like that when you're overseas."

"But you're a civilian now."

"Yeah…feels weird in some ways. In other ways it's pretty much perfect." He gave her hip a little squeeze to prove his point.

"How is it weird for you?"

He didn't really want to talk about the weirdness of coming home. About people's perception of him, how everyone expected him to behave in a certain way because that's how they remembered him in the past. But because Kat had asked him in earnest and seemed to really want an answer, he offered, "Combat changes you. It puts life in a big ole glass bowl and makes you see what's really important. You bond with people you might never ordinarily associate with, and they become important to you on an everyday basis. Your life is contained in a small cylinder of space. Your focus, your mission, the friendships you develop are all a part of that cylinder. If that makes any sense?"

"Yeah, I think it does. And when you lose someone, the cylinder gets even smaller."

"Yeah," he said. "That's how it works."

"Justin, will you tell me a little bit about Brett? Not now, if you can't. But maybe in the future? I'm curious about him."

His chest constricted at her request. He cradled her closer in his arms as his thoughts turned somber.

"What do you want to know?"

She laid her palm on his cheek, her fingers soft against his beard stubble. "He was your good friend?"

"We were close. As close as two men could get in that kind of environment."

"Aunt Mattie says wonderful things about him. Was he a good guy?"

Justin tensed. He wasn't sure why the conversation had taken this turn. He had a sexy woman in bed with him and didn't know if they'd ever get the chance to have a repeat performance of tonight. Was he ruining the moment with talk of his soldiering days? Yet he found that talking to Kat came easy and maybe he needed to get some things off his chest.

He began in a quiet voice. "He was no saint by any means. Sometimes I thought the devil caught him by the tail. But he was real decent and a lotta fun to be around. He had this innocent charm about him and he'd…he'd do anything for the people he cared about."

"You've never grieved for him, have you?"

Her question came out of left field, shocking him. "I'm not sure I know how."

"Maybe talking about it will help, Justin."

"Maybe I don't want help. Maybe I need to suffer."

"You don't really mean that."

Justin drew a sharp breath. "I think I do. I'm responsible for Brett's death and I'll never forgive myself."

She stroked his face with a tenderness he didn't deserve. The comfort she offered almost brought him to tears. "You need to pour out your heart, Justin. You need to tell someone."

He grabbed her wrist and kissed her fingertips. "I don't want to let it go."

"Yes, you do. You want to tell me," she said gently. "And I want to listen."

He sat in silence for a few moments, fighting the emotion warring inside his head. Where were Connor's waking cries when he needed them? Why wasn't the phone ringing off the hook? Why wasn't room service knocking on their door by mistake?

One look at Kat's sweetly sympathetic face threw his world off kilter. Those reassuring eyes told him she would understand. That beautiful mouth would speak words of comfort. She was offering him a way out, a way to ease his conscience. She was cracking the fortress walls he'd built up. Maybe Kat was right. Maybe he did want to tell her. Maybe he needed to speak of it. Sure as anything, he had her rapt attention. Maybe he needed to let go of the part of him that caused all his nightmares.

He released a deep breath and started talking slowly. "I guess I was still reeling from the Qaisar mission in northern Afghanistan."

"That's when you saved five men from an ambush, right?"

"Right. I was just doing my job the way I was trained to do. The result was a good one and no one died that day. The praise started flowing from generals all the way down to privates and I appreciated it. I really did, but I didn't much like the label of hero. It's something I still don't embrace. Real soldiers don't think about being heroes, they think about staying alive and helping their buddies stay alive. It's grueling over there and there's no glory in it, just survival."

"But you have to feel good about saving so many," Kat said.

"Hell yeah, I do. I wouldn't change a thing about that day. But what happened with Brett came a few months later. I was thinking I had it all figured out. I was a little cocky, which is dangerous when you're over there. I was assigned to check out an abandoned schoolhouse in an Afghani village. We'd gotten tipped off that there was a cache of explosives and ammo hidden there.

"Brett had been battling pneumonia. He'd been laid up for two weeks and was eager to get his boots on the ground again. He'd been bored out of his mind in the infirmary and wanted in on this mission. Originally I told him no, it was too soon. But he'd gotten clearance for regular duty and he convinced me he was feeling up to it. 'I'm right as rain,' he'd said. 'C'mon, buddy. Let me in on this one.' He pulled the friendship card, and I caved. Against my better judgment, I changed my mind and allowed him on the mission.

"When we got to the village, we detached from our convoy and eight of us walked over some rugged terrain to get to the schoolhouse. On orders, our demolition guy would detonate the explosives if they were there. We took all the usual precautions and were careful going inside. The dust was heavy that day, blowing in from the west, and we were covered in it. Brett started coughing, loud, hard coughs that could split a gut. I knew then he wasn't fully recovered. Disgusted at my lack of judgment, I ordered him back to the convoy for his own safety. He was in no shape for the mission. Just as he stepped outside to obey my orders, shots were fired.

"Immediately I knew we'd been set up and ambushed by hostile forces. Three of the patrol guards I'd stationed around the school perimeter fired back and then dove for cover inside the schoolroom. But Brett never made it back inside. He'd been caught off guard from those damn coughing fits and shot to death. We called for backup from our convoy and the troops scared off our attackers. But it was too late for my friend."

Justin's lips quivered and he put his head in his hands. The memory fierce, his harsh words to Brett resounded in his head. "My last command to him was to get the hell back to the convoy and stay put.

"There wasn't anything I could do to save him. I held him, was covered in his blood when he took his last breaths. I made two mistakes that day. Letting him sweet-talk me into going on the mission was one. He wasn't fit for combat. But I should have left it alone once he was there. The truth was, I was pissed at myself for not standing firm."

Kat sat up on her knees. She touched his forearm and rubbed comforting circles on his skin. "No, Justin. No. It wasn't your fault he was shot."

He stared into her pretty green eyes, saw her adamant expression and turned away. "Don't give me a break on this. Don't tell me it wasn't my fault. I should've known better."

"You sent him back for his own good. You couldn't possibly have known about the ambush—"

"Ambushes are part of the deal over there. I needed my men to be one hundred percent healthy, for everyone's safety. Brett wasn't, not that day. And my bad judgment cost him his life, damn it."

"You did what you thought was best."

"Maybe I got too damn cocky, believing my own press. Maybe I wasn't careful enough with my men."

"You're punishing yourself for something that wasn't your fault. Maybe—and here's a revelation—it was Brett's fault. Did you ever think of that? That maybe Brett shouldn't have pushed so hard. That maybe the error in judgment was with him."

Justin refused to let Brett take the blame for his own death. "You don't know what you're talking about, Kat."

"Oh, I know. I've been there and I can tell you, blaming yourself for things out of your control doesn't work. The guilt you feel isn't going to bring Brett back. It isn't going to fix you, Justin. Just like it didn't fix me."

Justin turned partway toward her. "What do you mean, it didn't fix you?"

"I mean…I had a horrible childhood. About as horrible as you can imagine. My father was abusive. In the beginning, it was just to my mom. But then, he started in on me. He was a nasty drunk and he'd say awful things to me. I had very low self-esteem because of him. How could I be anything but insecure, when my own father told me a dozen times a day how stupid I was? How much he hated that I was born. How he wished I'd grow some brains. I'd go to bed at night and cry my eyes out, thinking I was to blame. If only I could do better, and not leave the milk cap off, or put away all my clothes, or get A's on all my tests, my father would love me more. Every time he took a hand to my mother because she defended me, I blamed myself. Over and over and over."

"Ah hell, Kat." Justin looked at the naked woman on his bed and saw more than her beautiful body—he saw into her soul. Into the heart of who Kat really was. He gently cupped her face in his hands and looked into her eyes. "That's rough for a kid."

"I'm not trying to outdo you in the sympathy department, Justin," she said softly. He let his hands drop away, completely captivated by the sincerity in her eyes. "I'm trying to help. Guilt isn't healthy. You have to come to terms with what happened to Brett."

"Did you? Did you finally come to terms with your father?"

"Yes. My mother ran away from my dad. She got a restraining order that didn't do much to stop him and we ended up living out of a suitcase, going from one women's shelter to another. We never had money, but we had each other. My mother…was amazing. She tried like crazy to make up for our sorry lives and to this day I think she was the best person I've ever known. I see my father for who he was now. I have no guilt about him."

"It's different with Brett," he whispered. "And someday I'm going to have to explain to Mattie Applegate my part in how he died."

Soft baby whimpers drew their attention. "It's Connor," Kat said. She rose from the bed and picked up Justin's shirt. She threw her arms through the sleeve, and the material fanned out like a cape, before gently settling against her body. That, and the wild, blond wisps around her head, made a beautiful disheveled picture as she waited for him to retrieve Connor. Something wonderful squeezed tight in his gut.

He got up and quickly put on his pants. Then he strode

toward her and offered his hand. With a sweet smile she clasped it.

"Let's go get our son," he said.

And together they walked hand in hand to ease the soft cries of their boy.

The Golden's luxurious columns blocked sunlight from beaming down on Connor as Kat held him in her arms outside the hotel. "Your daddy will be here soon," she whispered near his ear.

Connor played with the thin silver necklace around her neck. There was just something about shiny things and babies. His fascination with the tiny crystal beads on the links kept him occupied while they waited for Justin to say his goodbyes to his family. The baby's dark curly hair ruffled in the slight breeze and Kat rocked him gently, more out of habit than need.

A black Lincoln limousine pulled up and came to a stop ten feet away. Kat watched as a chauffeur got out and opened the door to the backseat. A handsome light-haired man climbed out, ducking his head and then standing to full height.

Kat froze. "Oh, no," she murmured. It was too late to make a hasty exit. Michael Golden's eyes were on her instantly. They locked gazes and Kat tightened her hold on Connor.

Up until four months ago, she'd been living in New York in a penthouse suite with him. They were engaged to be married until Kat had broken it off.

Memories flashed of her time with Michael. She'd begun dating him a few weeks after she'd been with Justin in New York. Michael was witty, charming and very attentive. When she discovered she was pregnant, she'd been honest with Michael, telling him up front that she would understand if he wanted to end their relationship. Michael couldn't have children, so they'd known the child wasn't his. He'd often thought of adopting, so news of Kat's pregnancy didn't throw him for a loop. Quite the opposite. He continued his healthy pursuit of her and had been overly kind during her pregnancy. She'd moved into his penthouse even as thoughts of Brett Applegate stayed in her mind.

"Kat?" he said, tilting his head as he approached. "Is that really you?"

The sound of his baritone voice made her nerves stand on end.

He strode toward them. His clear blue eyes sharpened on her before he directed his gaze to the baby. It lingered there and Kat nervously shifted Connor in her arms. "Yes, it's me. Hello, Michael."

The most eligible billionaire in New York City smiled a winning smile. "Hello, Kat. I never expected to see you in Reno. At one of my hotels, no less."

"There was a wedding." She didn't volunteer anything more. Michael looked like a zillion bucks. What else was new? He had a flare for fine clothes. He put himself together well, or rather his valet did. It was one of the first things she'd noticed about him when they'd met, his desire for fine fashion. She'd thought that his connections could get her foot in the fashion industry door. And he would have helped her after the big wedding he'd promised to give her.

He continued gazing at Connor but didn't reach out or try to touch him. Longing filled his eyes. For months, Michael had treated him as his own son. "He looks good. Healthy."

"He is. We're doing fine."

"I've spent a long time missing him."

Which said it all. Michael missed the idea of Connor as his son. He might have even loved him, but that was the problem. Michael didn't love her. She didn't love him.

They were using each other for what was missing in their lives. Michael wanted children, Kat wanted a career. New York society labeled Kat a gold digger, a woman who was after Michael for his money and the connections he had. In a sense, that had been true. She'd been alone after her mother died, and here was this man…an extremely rich man, who wanted a child and would provide an amazing life for both of them.

"It was a mutual agreement, Michael. We decided it was best to have a clean break."

"That's not how I remember it."

"No, I don't suppose you would." He'd been resistant to the idea of a breakup initially and it had gotten a little ugly before she finally left.

"I gave you everything." He ground the words out. "But it wasn't enough."

After Connor was born, Kat began seeing a different side to Michael Golden. He was a control freak and had to have a say in everything she did and everywhere she went with the baby. He questioned her every move. The walls began closing in on her. She was being suffocated, choking down Michael's manipulations until she couldn't take it anymore.

He'd been very much like her troublesome father, and it had taken Connor's birth to make her really see it. She shuddered as bad memories poured over her like hot oil. Michael Golden hadn't been abusive physically, but every day she'd borne the brunt of his caustic words. Every day she'd been slapped with his harsh demands. She'd vowed to never allow another man to control her or make her life hell like that.

"It's in the past, Michael. Let's leave it there."

He glanced at her son again and snarled with accusation. "You took Connor away from me."

She began shaking her head and glancing around, trying

to find a way to make a clean exit. "He was never yours, Michael. We've talked about this. I'm sorry it didn't work out between us."

He blinked. "Are you? Did you ever find the baby's real father?"

Kat wasn't going to answer that question. It was none of his business now. For months, he'd discouraged her from pursuing Connor's father and she'd allowed him to influence her. She certainly wasn't blameless, though. Her decision to initially not seek out Brett to tell him of her pregnancy rested fully on her shoulders. It was something she'd have to live with the rest of her life.

She did a quick inconspicuous scan of the surroundings, searching for Justin. The last thing she wanted was to see the two men face-to-face.

That wouldn't be good at all.

She was saved from answering his question as a leggy woman with platinum-blond waves and pouty red lips climbed out of Michael's limo behind him. Blood rushed to Kat's face. The woman was almost a mirror image of her...and Marilyn Monroe. The resemblance was uncanny. Kat recognized her as a soap opera star.

"Are you coming, Michael?" The woman's impatience cut through the warm Nevada air.

"I'll be right there, honey."

The smile he aimed at Kat was lopsided and cocky, as if to say *you're replaceable*. He began backing away. "Goodbye, Kat." Then his gaze roamed over Connor with genuine regret before he turned away and took hold of the starlet's hand.

Kat's body sagged. She'd dodged a bullet today. It wasn't too often that happened to her. Her luck wasn't always this good

Michael disappeared into the hotel lobby with his date and just seconds later, Justin walked up behind her wearing a big smile. He gave her a kiss on the cheek. "Sorry to keep you waiting."

"No problem."

He studied her face for a second and she hoped he hadn't noticed her distress. "Everything okay?"

Kat drew a breath and gave him a quick nod. "Everything's fine."

"You ready to head home to Silver Springs?"

"So ready." She smiled and squeezed Connor's little body tight. With Justin by her side and Connor in her arms, her life seemed perfect and...complete. She wasn't going to let running into Michael today ruin that. "You have no idea."

Eight

Kat leaned against her bedroom dresser and unfolded the letter she'd received yesterday from Lowery's Department Store. Her shoulders sagged with despair and she shook her head as she reread the words. Her future on the line, she stood there for a few seconds contemplating what she should do with the rest of her life before she refolded the paper and slipped it back into its envelope.

She pulled the dresser drawer open, lifted up her underpants and placed the letter on top of the pile of rejections she kept there. A nice neat stack had accumulated during the past weeks, and when she put her underwear back to cover the letters, it came to the very top of the drawer. She flattened the fabric with the palm of her hand and then used her hip to slide the drawer closed.

When Kat entered the kitchen, Aunt Mattie was at the table, feeding Connor breakfast in his high chair. The creamy concoction of oatmeal, bananas and blueberries warranted a fingertip taste test. "Yummy, Connor," Kat said, after taking a second taste. "Mommy likes it, too."

The baby smiled.

She kissed the top of his head and ruffled his dark hair.

Noise from the demolition crew working a short distance away drew her attention. Sheds, old feed shacks and outer buildings on the property were being torn down.

"Won't be long now before the sale will go through and

we'll see a building going up for the retreat," Aunt Mattie said matter-of-factly.

After the special night Kat had spent with Justin in Reno two days ago, she better understood his need and determination to get this project underway. Justin didn't waste time. He was used to acting and then reacting and she sensed that getting the Gateway Equine Retreat started quickly would help ease his tremendous guilt over Brett's death.

He'd let her inside, for a few stolen minutes, and allowed her to see his pain when he was most vulnerable. She'd like to think he'd trusted her—at least for that one night—with his innermost, deepest thoughts and secrets.

Sexually, they were compatible… Oh, boy, they were compatible. Justin was an amazing lover and Kat wasn't one to hold back with him. She gave and she took equally and they both enjoyed the consequences. But even she knew that great sex wasn't enough. And right now, that's about all that they had together.

Connor pointed to his oatmeal that was more blueberry and banana than oats.

"You want more?"

Aunt Mattie fed him another spoonful. "The boy certainly has an appetite this morning."

"He sure does."

"Brett loved breakfast the best. He'd eat a half a dozen eggs if I let him, then he'd start on pancakes and then of course about a pound of—"

"Bacon," they said in unison.

Aunt Mattie's eyes lit and they both chuckled. The laughter was loud enough and Kat's smile wide enough to conceal her own guilt over the lies she'd told and would continue to tell the older woman. It shook her resolve some, but not enough to open up to Mattie with the truth. That would have to come sometime in the future.

"Wouldn't expect anything less from a hog farmer, now would you?" the older woman asked.

"No, I wouldn't." But Kat refrained from adding to the lies by agreeing that Connor took after Brett.

Kat fixed Connor a bottle. When he'd finished his solid food, she lifted him out of his high chair and sat down next to Mattie to feed him the formula.

"Ah, I never do get over the sight of mama and baby like that."

"It's sweet," Kat said. "One of my favorite things to do."

She snuggled Connor a little tighter in her arms, loving him with every ounce of her being as he suckled on the bottle. In just a short time, he'd be drinking real milk in a sippy cup, but for now, she'd hold on to the small things, letting the baby be a baby for as long as possible.

An image flashed of Justin in the hotel suite, holding Connor and giving him a bottle in the wee hours of the morning. There'd been a sense of calm and peace and normalcy when the three of them had been together. Kat had tried to absorb that feeling…she'd never before felt such stability.

"I've got a few appointments with contractors lined up today, if you're up to it. We'll start on the kitchen first, since it's in the worst shape."

"Oh, dear," Aunt Mattie said, glancing at the chipped kitchen cabinets and the flooring with big hunks of vinyl missing. "Where do we begin?"

"Well, we could gut it all and start over."

Aunt Mattie shook her head. "I don't need newfangled everything. There's a lot of…of memories in this kitchen for me. I remember looking out that window and seeing the boys playing catch out there. And well, my Ralph built me that hutch over there with his own two hands. I don't want everything gone."

"Aunt Mattie, that's fine. I sort of figured you'd feel that way. We'll take on one project at a time. You can pick new cabinets and floors and we'll get you a few new appliances, ones that don't spark when you turn them on. We'll pick out new paint and counters and we can keep everything in the same place. It'll just be updated and sparkling new. Would that make you happy?"

"Yes, with your help, sweetheart…I think that would suit me just fine."

Kat reached over to squeeze her hand. Aunt Mattie wasn't her mother, but she was a dear woman whom Kat had come to love. "Well, then, why don't you rest up a little bit. The first appointment isn't until the afternoon. Then we'll get cracking."

"Cracking, yes." The older woman's face beamed just a little bit brighter. "I don't know what I've done to deserve you in my life, but I'm sure glad you're here, Kat. You and Connor make life worth living."

And it wasn't a big surprise to Kat that she felt exactly the same way about Mattie Applegate.

Justin appeared at the front door two hours later in a pair of black dress slacks, a white shirt rolled up at the sleeves and opened at the collar and black boots coated with a thin layer of construction dust. Startled and a little awestruck, Kat didn't particularly like the emotions clicking away at the immediate sight of him. "Justin, I didn't expect to see you today."

Kat opened the screen door to let him in.

"Where is everyone?" he asked, striding in, removing his hat and tossing it on the sofa. His ink-black hair shone almost blue-ish as sunlight trailed after him.

"Connor's napping and Aunt Mattie is reading in her room," she said, wiping her hands on a kitchen towel. "I was just tidying up the—"

Justin's expression stopped her cold. He had a devastating look on his face. Hunger burned in his eyes. Kat's throat constricted and she took a hard swallow.

He grabbed her hand and she didn't protest when he led her into the kitchen. With his back to the farthest wall, he tugged her to his chest and wound his arms around her waist, planting her firmly against his taut body.

"Oh," she breathed quietly. "This—this isn't a good idea." As she said the words, her body called her a liar and softened to him immediately. And her fool heart... her heart had leaped in her chest the second she'd found him at the door.

"Tell me about it," he said, right before his lips claimed hers. "I've been thinking about you for two days, Kat. Ever since the wedding." He gave her another kiss that she eagerly returned. "I've had meeting after meeting and I can't concentrate on anything but you." He cupped her head in his hands, using his thumbs to caress her cheeks, and stared deep into her eyes. "I've missed you. I came here thinking we could talk business, but the second I laid eyes on you..."

"Mattie could walk in any second," she was quick to point out.

"I know." He had a hopeless look on his face now.

"We shouldn't—"

"Be quiet, Kat." He coaxed her into silence with another passionate, intoxicating kiss. "Don't waste what time we have."

She couldn't argue with him. She'd craved him, craved seeing him again, and she hadn't known just how badly until he'd walked into the house today.

His mouth moved to her throat and her skin prickled when he pushed the material of her blouse aside to touch the sensitive skin there with his lips. "Oh, Justin."

He was aroused and determined and oh-so-hard to resist. "I need to see you again, Kat. I want to be alone with you."

He planted tiny kisses up and down her throat, sending her nerve endings soaring. If she wasn't careful, his sweetly spoken words could get to her. He could fill her head with all sorts of crazy ideas. He could make her believe in a man again, after so many failures, so many disappointments.

"Come to me tonight, Kat. Come and be with me."

This time his kiss was filled with persuasion, with dire unabashed want.

How easy it would be to fall for him in a big way. But Kat had more than herself to think about. She had a son. And a dear friend who needed her. She wasn't going to mess this up.

She found the strength to push him away slightly, mere inches, but enough to grab his full attention. "I want that, too, but it can't be just about sex, Justin. I can't be your horny soldier booty call. It can't be that."

Justin lowered his head. His gaze went to the floor and he stared at her bare feet. She was thankful her toenails were polished cotton-candy pink.

Then he slowly lifted his head and their gazes locked. His deep-set eyes were rich with sincerity. "That's not what this is about, Kat. Not at all. I'm no sex-starved kid and I'm assuming you aren't, either."

"Maybe just a little. With you." Kat was dreadfully honest.

A smile trembled at the corner of his mouth. "I think we both know how serious getting involved might be for us. We have a child together, a son that we both love. I'm not going to blow the one shot we might have at this. I think we have a chance at something here." He pushed a hand through his hair. "Or am I reading too much into what happened between us the other night?"

Kat squeezed her eyes closed. She was about to take a giant leap of faith. "No, you're not reading too much into it." She focused on him now and nodded. "It was... special for me."

She'd connected to Justin in a way she hadn't connected to another human being. She'd listened to him admit things that hadn't come easy for him. He'd given her that much trust and she wanted more from him. She wanted a solid chance, but up until this point, she hadn't believed it could happen.

There were major forces working against them right now.

"Is it possible?" she heard herself ask.

"I think so." The look he cast her wasn't lust now, but something else, something that touched deep within her heart.

"But how?"

He shrugged a shoulder casually, as if the answer were simple. "We'll start dating."

"Dating?" She heard surprise rise in her voice. "We can't."

He hoisted her chin with the pad of his thumb so they were eye to eye. "We can. It's a natural occurrence. Returning lonely soldier meets gorgeous young widow and child and is besotted."

"Besotted?" Kat laughed and Justin kissed away her amusement.

"Humor me, okay."

"I thought I heard voices in here," Aunt Mattie's called from the parlor. "Kat, are you talking to someone?"

Kat jumped three feet back, her eyes wide and focused on Justin's big silly grin.

He gathered himself up first and stepped out into the doorway to the parlor. "It's just me, Aunt Mattie."

Aunt Mattie ambled a little farther into the room, just

enough to spot both of them. "Oh, hello, Justin. It's good to see you. I didn't expect you to pay us a visit today. Did Kat tell you we've got several appointments this afternoon? We're going to start remodeling the kitchen."

Justin gave Kat an innocent look. "No, she didn't mention that. Actually, Kat and I were discussing something else entirely."

Aunt Mattie darted a look her way and then returned her attention to Justin. "Oh? Something I should know about?"

"No!" Kat shook her head.

"Yes, actually," Justin said.

Her blood pressure elevated when Justin contradicted her.

Voice laced with enough charm to convince a mob boss to go to confession, Justin spoke directly to Aunt Mattie. "It's something I think you should know. Something I hope you'll take kindly to." He bumped shoulders with Kat as he reached around her waist to draw her close. She instantly relaxed, the tension seeping out of her pores. For some reason, it felt right, even though there was potential for disaster. But Kat wasn't a coward. She would take the risk. Besides, judging from the stubborn look on Justin's face, there was no stopping this now.

"Kat and I are going to start dating."

Aunt Mattie stared at both of them. Seconds clicked by. Kat hoped the news wouldn't hurt Mattie. She hoped she wouldn't feel threatened in any way.

"Well, that's good news, but you don't need my permission. I've seen the looks you two give each other. I think I'll go back to my room so you two can resume fooling around."

"Aunt Mattie!" Kat's face flushed with heat.

"You saw that?" Justin's eyes beamed with admiration.

"I'm not blind as a bat. Just got a bad ticker."

After Justin had a good chuckle and Kat's embarrassment ebbed, he said, "Please don't leave because of me. Stay. I'd like to discuss our progress on the retreat."

"Yes, stay and talk to us," Kat said to Aunt Mattie. "I'll fix lunch right after I check on Connor. He should be waking up soon."

"Well, all right. That sounds nice."

Kat left the room and returned five minutes later with a diapered, dressed Connor in her arms. She found Justin and Mattie sitting at the kitchen table. Mattie was entertaining him with tales of life on a hog farm. His gaze followed Connor and her into the room and Kat's heart leaped again, this time seeing the love and pride Justin had for their son. "Justin, would you mind holding Connor while I get Aunt Mattie her pills and throw some lunch on the table?"

The big strong man lowered Connor down into his arms. "Not at all. Come here, little buddy."

And Connor went to his daddy.

Without complaint.

The screen door slapped closed behind Justin as he walked outside the Applegate house with Kat. "It's official," he said, taking her hand and dragging her down the porch steps. "We're dating."

Her gaze darted in three different directions, looking for errant workmen who might, heaven forbid, see them holding hands. But there wasn't a soul in sight at the moment.

"You sort of bamboozled me into it. Like I have time for dating."

He didn't try to hide the grin spreading across his face. "You'll find time."

"You're so sure of yourself."

"Sort of reminds me of the time when we first met. And you told me you didn't date soldiers."

"You charmed the pants off me."

He leaned against the hood of his car, folding his arms across his chest. "I did, didn't I?"

Kat's mouth turned down in a tempting pout. In a pair of light blue jeans and some kind of billowy blouse she'd probably designed, she looked sensational. She flattened her palms against his chest and shoved playfully. "You think you're so clever. Clever Mr. Slade."

"I think…I'm lucky."

She batted her eyelashes. "Yes, well, there's a difference between *getting* lucky and *being* lucky."

"I plan to do both."

She shook her head slowly. "Sure of yourself, aren't you?"

He leaned forward, away from the hood. His lips hovered near her beautiful mouth. "Admit you're glad about it."

She leaned back and scanned the grounds again. She nibbled nervously on her lower lip. "I'm not sure yet."

He clasped the back of her neck and brought her up close. Their noses touched. Hell, she smelled good. Her scent nearly killed his restraint. "You will be." And then his lips came down on hers. He kissed her long and hard and didn't give a damn who saw them playing house.

After they broke apart, Kat spoke in a breathless whisper. "Why are you so darn cocky?"

A chuckle emerged from his throat. There were things about Kat he found vastly entertaining. Her way with words, for one. And the way she'd filled out his shirt the other night, for another. "When I get you alone again, I'll tell you."

"What does that mean?"

Around Kat, his willpower wouldn't win awards, but he summoned every shred of it and set her away from him. On a sigh, he said, "You'll have to wait and see what I have cooked up. But believe it or not, I brought you out here for another reason. There's something I want to show you and I need your input."

He'd scouted locations on the property and found a hilly rise that overlooked the entire facility—the perfect area to build a monument in Ralph and Brett's honor. He wanted Kat's opinion before proposing it to Aunt Mattie. "Connor is in his playpen, right? Do you think Mattie can watch him for a few minutes?"

Kat blinked. "We have the guy from Kitchen Redo coming over in half an hour."

"I'll have you back here in plenty of time. We'll take my truck. It's important, Kat."

Her brow lifted curiously. "Okay. Let me tell Aunt Mattie what's going on. It'll just take me a sec."

"Tell her it's our first date. Then she'll be sure to allow us time to *fool around*."

"I *will not* tell her that." He caught an eyeful watching her hip action as she sauntered away. *Man, oh, man.* There wasn't a woman alive who filled out a pair of jeans as well as Katherine Grady.

Several minutes ticked by. Justin glanced at his watch, then at the front door. What was taking her? Gut instincts told him either Connor needed his mother's attention, which happened more times than not…or something was wrong. Justin reached the porch steps when the screen door flew open. He immediately saw the look of panic on Kat's face. "It's Aunt Mattie. She's having tightness in her chest and feeling weak. I have her resting on the sofa. Come inside…I can't leave her another second." She whipped around and went back into the house.

Justin followed her. "I'll call for an ambulance. Does she take nitroglycerin?"

"Yes, I've given her one already. It's almost time for the next one."

Connor sat in the play yard, holding his little beetle bug

toy. He was occupied right now. Justin made the phone call and was assured the paramedics would be here shortly. Kat had already done all the right things, according to the dispatcher on the phone.

He walked over to the sofa and knelt down beside Kat. She held Mattie's hand. "Aunt Mattie, it's Justin. You take it slow and easy now. Help is on the way."

"Okay." Her eyes were closed, her voice weak. "I don't know…what happened. I was feeling fine when I woke up this morning, just a little tired." Moisture pooled on her forehead and at her hairline, darkening her bright red roots.

"You just rest now and don't fret about a thing."

Kat slid a worried glance at Justin.

He could only return the look.

The ambulance arrived. Two paramedics and an EMT hooked Mattie up to oxygen, poked her with IVs and did a thorough assessment. Justin knew something about following medical protocol. He didn't doubt Mattie needed observation and treatment at the hospital.

They worked on getting her ready to leave, bracing her head and limbs with restraints. Bravely, she did what she was told. They transferred her onto a gurney and rolled her carefully out of the house.

He took Kat aside. "You go with her in the ambulance. She shouldn't be alone."

Troubled, Kat glanced at Connor. "But the baby—"

"He'll be fine with me. I know the routine. I'll get him ready, pack up his clothes and bottles and meet you at the hospital. Just leave me your keys so I can use the car seat."

Kat's eyes closed. Seconds ticked by. Finally, she nodded. "Okay, I know you'll take good care of him."

Thank goodness she was going to let him help. She didn't need to be alone right now. "I'd give my life for him, Kat. So don't worry. I can figure out the small stuff."

She lifted on tiptoes and brushed his cheek with a kiss "I know you can."

She picked up Connor and covered him with kisses before setting him back in the play yard. "You be a good little boy...."

Connor's sweet face crumbled with tears. Poor kid. Three strangers wearing white uniforms marching into the house must've confused the hell out of him. "Maybe I shouldn't go," Kat said. Her loyalties were clearly split in two.

"Go... Mattie needs you." Justin walked over to Connor. He lifted him out of the playpen and situated him in his arms. Then he rocked him like a melodic pendulum swing, to and fro. The baby's inquisitive eyes widened, his crying stopped. Connor's cooperation proved Justin's point. "There, you see, I can handle him. I promise I'll be a few minutes behind you. I'll meet you at the hospital."

Kat agreed with a nod and grabbed her purse. Digging her hand inside, she came up with her keys and handed them over. "Here you go. Thank you... I'd better run." She smothered the boy with another round of kisses. If Connor wasn't his kid, Justin would be jealous. "I don't want to delay the ambulance." Kat hurried out the door.

Justin hugged the baby tight to his chest. "Looks like it's me and you now, son."

Nine

When the doctor asked Kat to leave the room so that he could examine Mattie again, the older woman gave her a small brave smile that nearly broke her heart. Reluctant to go, Kat pushed through the emergency room doors on wobbly legs and ran her hand through her hair. It was hard leaving Mattie alone. She'd almost lost it in there seeing her tied to all those machines.

Poor Mattie. She didn't deserve this.

After a short walk, Kat reached the waiting room at Silver Springs General Hospital. Framed pastel landscapes decorated the beige walls, and the chairs were cushioned with durable mauve material. It was a whole lot more cheery than the room she'd just left. Not that any of it mattered—the most important thing was Mattie's diagnosis and aftercare.

She scanned the room and immediately honed in on Connor in the crowd. He was lying across Justin's broad chest, his head nuzzled under his father's chin, sleeping soundly. What a sight. The two of them were a matched set. So incredibly alike. They looked beautiful together.

Happy endings rushed into her mind.

Kat had never had things go her way before.

She'd never had smooth sailing in her life.

Because of her father's abuse, her young life had been filled with fear, mistrust and poverty. Her mother died years before her time and Kat had had to scrounge and fight her way to a decent existence. Under her wavy blond hair and flashy clothes was a scarred, frightened woman she concealed from the rest of the world. For Connor's sake, she'd been strong, and done things that wouldn't gain her sainthood. She'd thought them necessary at the time.

Looking at Justin and Connor now and picturing the three of them together as a unit…as a real family, could be a foolish move. Did she dare to hope for something she'd never really had before? Kat wouldn't risk it. The hurt she carried inside still smarted like a son-of-a-gun.

Don't go there, Kat. Don't start believing.

Justin lifted his head; there was a question in his eyes. She put a finger to her lips as she approached. He nodded and understood she didn't want to wake Connor right now. Phones rang, nurses' chatter filtered into the room and elevator bells pinged. More power to her baby if he could continue to sleep through the noise.

She eyed the seat next to Justin. Her weary body welcomed the rest and she plunked down into a chair and closed her eyes.

She had some serious praying to do anyway…for Mattie Applegate.

Kat had held her hand in the ambulance, reassuring her with soothing words. "I'm going to stay with you," Kat told her. "You're going to be just fine." She wasn't sure Aunt Mattie had bought her Pollyanna act, but she'd nodded and her tired eyes had lit briefly with gratitude. Kat couldn't stand the thought of losing the dear spirited woman.

When Connor woke up, she explained to Justin that they were running tests to see if Mattie had suffered a mild heart attack or if it was a case of her meds needing adjustments. Kat hoped it was the latter. At any rate, the doctor said that she wouldn't be coming home anytime soon.

Images popped into her head of another hospital, another time, holding hands with her mother, and reassuring her, too, that all would be right soon. But her mom's battered body hadn't been able to fight off the bacterial infection that led to the complications that finally took her life.

A tear dripped from Kat's eye and then another and another until her cheeks burned. She wiped at the droplets with the back of her hand. If only she could've protected her mother. If only she could've defended her from a man who wouldn't control his rage.

Kat would never be a victim again. She would never let anyone hurt those she loved. But Kat was helpless now. She couldn't do anything for Aunt Mattie.

She sobbed.

She felt a hand on her arm and knew it was Justin. His gentle touch seeped into her skin and released some of her pain. She absorbed his warmth and tenderness and drew strength from it. He slowly moved his hand along her arm to her hand. She opened her eyes as he entwined their fingers. Once their hands were joined, he tightened his hold. The connection brought her peace. His strength made all the bad things in her life disappear.

She gazed into his dark eyes—her son's eyes—and was hit with a jolt of awareness. A single moment elapsed, and in the very next instant, Kat knew. There'd be no talking herself out of this. She couldn't wish it away. No amount of mental hammering would pound this out of her brain.

She loved Justin Slade.

She was deeply in love with him.

And she'd never felt anything so potent, so wonderful and so incredibly scary in her life.

"Come back to the ranch with me tonight," Justin said to Kat in the parlor of Aunt Mattie's home. "Connor would love it and I'll make sure you have everything you need."

Kat sighed quietly. He already did have everything she

needed. She had to disguise her new feelings for him…
they were just that…new, and she needed time to work it
all out in her head. "It's tempting. But you know I can't."

Justin frowned.

It was terribly tempting. He'd asked her to stay at his
ranch yesterday, too, and she hated refusing him a second
time. So she clarified her reasons. "It's easier for us to be
here, Justin. All of Connor's stuff is here. And this house
is closer to the hospital in case Aunt Mattie needs me. I
have to take care of the place for her."

It turned out that Mattie had had a mild heart attack
after all. Luckily, there wasn't too much damage to her
heart, but she was weak and they were still in the process
of observing her and adjusting her medications. The doctor
had informed Kat that it would be at least a week or two
before Mattie was released to come home. She'd probably
have to spend time in a rehab facility.

Justin approached her. He slanted a quick look over his
shoulder at Connor banging away at the new baby key-
board piano he'd given him. "If I was still into betting, I'd
bet that I could change your mind."

Musical notes and baby sounds zinged from the piano.
Justin zeroed in on her.

She faced him head-on, holding her ground. Okay, mel-
lowing a little. Gosh, he was hard to resist with those melt-
your-heart dark eyes and sharp handsome features.

His hands snaked around her waist. He drew her up
against his body and the fit was darn near perfect. Kat
blinked as he leaned in, touched his lips to hers and kissed
her tenderly.

When the kiss ended, Justin said, "I don't think you
should be alone tonight. I'm going to stay here with you.
I'll sleep on the sofa."

Last night, Justin had been a dream, taking her home
from the hospital after visiting hours were over. He'd

helped her settle the baby down and get Connor off to bed, then stayed until very late, comforting her about Mattie's medical condition.

"Justin, that's a sweet offer, but are you sure you want to do that?"

Justin was quick with a nod. "The sofa's a heck of a lot nicer than some of the places I've slept during the last nine years. I'm good with that. I want to be here for you and Connor."

There was no way she could refuse his generous offer. Having him stay over and lend support meant the world to her. "Thank you. I would like that very much."

Later that evening they fed Connor, gave him a bath and put him into his pajamas. Justin got down on the floor and played with him for a long time while Kat did the dishes and took care of some Babylicious business. As soon as she could, she joined them, and when nine o'clock rolled around and the baby rubbed his eyes, Justin rocked him to sleep in his arms. "Little guy is tuckered out," he said softly, brushing a kiss to his forehead.

"Wonder why?" She grinned.

Kat marveled at how close Justin was getting to Connor. Not too long ago, she'd forgiven Justin the lies and deceit of that New York weekend. If that weekend had never happened, she wouldn't have Connor, her precious little boy and the one really good thing she'd done in her life. How could she continue to hold a grudge against the father of her child, especially when she saw them together like this?

"Let's put him down," she said.

Justin transferred the baby into her arms and they walked to her room together. Kat laid the baby down gently on his back in the crib. He stirred for just a second before falling asleep.

It was sweet to see Justin stare at Connor and watch him sleep. "Still can't believe it."

"I know," she said on a sigh. "He's a miracle."

"He is." Justin took her hand and led her away from the crib. They stood just outside the doorway. "I know how concerned you are about Mattie."

"I'm worried sick about her," she said.

"From what I can tell, she's a strong woman. She'll pull through." He ran his hands up and down her arms with reassuring strokes. It felt like heaven having him touch her with such warmth and caring.

"You should get some rest while Connor is sleeping," he whispered.

"That's a good idea. I'm beat."

"I'll be here if you need me," he said.

She was grateful that he'd sacrifice his comfortable king-size bed for a bunch of pillows and blankets on a lumpy sofa to stay over tonight.

He reached out and tipped her chin up with his thumb. Then he lowered his mouth to hers and she squeezed her eyes shut, absorbing the taste and feel of his tenderness as he kissed her. "Good night, Kat."

"Good night," she said and before she opened her eyes, he was gone.

Justin thrashed back and forth on the sofa. His breathing was rapid and sweat pooled on his forehead and ran down his brows. He struggled to wipe away the drops.

It had happened again. He'd dreamed of the firefight and the day Brett died. The dream was mixed up, a concoction of his brain, where saving five men in that village coincided with Brett's death. It had all run together somehow and he'd been a part of it. This time, Brett was one of the men he'd rushed in and saved that day. Brett was alive in his dream. Justin's heart pounded. The rest of the dream jogged his memory and he trembled.

In real life, Brett had been taken out by a sniper's bullet.

He sat up and opened his eyes. Darkness surrounded him, but in that instant he remembered he wasn't with his platoon. He wasn't in Afghanistan. He was in Brett Applegate's home. He planted both feet on the ground, his head in his hands as he leaned forward.

"Justin, are you okay?" Kat rushed into the parlor, her concerned expression illuminated by a sliver of moonlight streaming through the curtains. She sat down beside him.

He sighed. "I didn't mean to wake you." Keeping his voice calm, he told her, "It's just a bad dream."

She leaned over to stroke his arm. He was amazed at how much comfort she packed into that touch. "You've had a lot of those lately."

"Some. It's getting better."

"I'm sorry," she said.

"I didn't mean to disturb you."

"It's okay. I want to help."

She bent to kiss his cheek. The sweet peck calmed him like nothing else could.

"Would you like me to stay with you for a little while?" Kat asked gently.

He took a swallow and nodded. There wasn't anything he wanted more at the moment. He didn't have the strength to refuse her or deny himself the comfort.

She nestled close to him and he wrapped his arms around her shoulders. In her light flowery scent and the warmth of her skin, he found a keen sense of peace.

"I'm here for you, too, if you need me," Kat whispered. The woman was good for his soul.

His eyes drifted closed.

Hell, he was quickly coming to the conclusion that he did need Katherine Grady.

In his life.

Always.

* * *

Justin checked in on Connor taking quiet sweet breaths in his crib for the third time in a span of thirty minutes. His little boy was tuckered out. A smile emerged on Justin's face and his boots hit the floor quietly as he walked out of the room.

Kat was visiting Aunt Mattie again at the hospital tonight and babysitting duties fell to him in her absence. The boy was responding to Justin more and more each day, giving him smiles and allowing him to hold him without instantly reaching out for his mama. Yep, he had mad fathering skills now. Pride tipped his heart off kilter. The love he felt for Connor was immeasurable. It kinda blew him away, these powerful feelings he held inside.

He glanced at the broken cuckoo clock on the wall that told time without the usual fanfare. No cuckoos, just clock. It was almost nine. Kat should be home within the hour.

He missed her.

Strolling over to Aunt Mattie's thirty-two-inch television set, he picked up the remote, making a mental note. Her wall was big enough for a flat-screen television almost double the size of the old TV she had now. He'd make sure it was part of her remodel.

He lowered himself down on the sofa and clicked on the TV. He had ten solid minutes until another bunk check on Connor.

Leaning back, he stretched out his legs and surfed through a limited choice of stations, searching for any kind of sports. Baseball, golf or basketball highlights? Nothing looked appealing and he was about to shut the darn thing off when he came across an entertainment news show where ace Arizona Diamondback pitcher, Doug Broadmeyer, was being interviewed about a possible move to the Los Angeles Dodgers. Broadmeyer was big news to Douglas County sports fans. He was a local high school boy who'd made his way up the ranks from the minors to the major leagues. Justin leaned back settling in for a few minutes of tube.

It wasn't long before the show's host steered the conversation to the pitcher's love life. "Is there truth to the rumor that you and Mia are talking wedding?"

"Oh, man." He should've known the host wouldn't stick to sports news. *Leisure and Luxury Lifestyles,* or *LLL* for short, was pure tabloid TV. He put his finger on the remote's off button.

"And in luxury news," the English-accented male host announced as he moved on to the next segment, "owner and CEO of *the* Golden Hotels, Michael Golden, is dating another Marilyn look-alike. Yes, that's right, this time it's Belinda Brubaker. We all know her as Charity McGrath on the nighttime soap opera, *Avenue M.*"

"What's up with *that,* Michael?" the TV host asked rhetorically.

A split screen flashed two photos, side by side…on the left, one of Belinda, the woman the hotel mogul was presently dating, a dead ringer for Marilyn Monroe, and on the right…a picture of Kat?

Justin blinked rapidly. His brain scrambled for some sense. He slid forward onto the edge of his seat and focused on the photograph again. Yeah, there was no mistaking it. It sure as hell was Kat. She was holding Connor and gazing happily into the camera with Golden by her side.

What the hell?

"This rare photo of Golden with his ex-fiancée, Katherine Grady, is proof positive that Mike certainly doesn't stray too far in his taste of women," the *LLL* host was saying. "Too bad this happy little trio never made it to the altar after a year-long engagement. Rumor has it Golden was heartbroken that his instant family didn't work out. Maybe actress Belinda Brubaker will have better luck snaring the insanely wealthy bachelor. We're sure *Avenue M* fans want her to have a happy ending."

The host's words banged like a drum in his head. He tuned out the rest of his dribble about Golden's preference for blondes and punched the off button on the remote.

He'd seen enough.

Kat had been engaged to Michael Golden? For a whole damn year?

True, Justin had been overseas for the past nine years, but hell, he knew the Golden name. His own brother had been married in one of the hotels, for heaven's sake. The Golden Hotels were everywhere in the United States. Even an out-of-touch soldier knew the power and influence that name wielded.

He ground his teeth together, hating that his heart ached so badly. Hating that his soul was seared with the truth Kat didn't tell him. The truth he'd had to hear on a gossip television show.

His initial instincts about Kat were correct. She was a social climber, a woman out to snare a rich man. When she'd thought he was Brett, she'd made it clear she wanted nothing more to do with him. One fling, one weekend, and that was that.

Her lies and bone-sharp betrayal made bitter acid churn in his stomach.

He bounded off the sofa and paced the floor. Everything made sense now. She'd dumped the man she'd thought was a hog farmer, refusing him knowledge of his baby, and didn't waste time getting engaged to the hotel giant. Was that it? Was it all about money? If it wasn't, then why hadn't she told him about Golden? Hell, he'd poured his heart out to her, telling her things he'd never told another human being. He'd given her a piece of himself with his confessions about Brett.

He heard the rattle of the screen door and a key turning

in the lock. The scent of gardenias preceded Kat into the room. He breathed her in, for a second remembering only the past few days of their lives together. He'd been a fool to believe in her in the first place. His instincts had been dead on. If only he'd listened.

"Justin." Her soft voice floated over him as she smiled and walked inside the house.

He braced his nerves. This wasn't going to be pretty. He stood facing her by the front door.

"How did it go? Did you get the baby to sleep?"

"He's napping," he said curtly. He was glad he didn't have time to stew about this. He wanted this out in the open, pronto.

"Everything okay?" she asked, her smile slowly fading.

"He's fine. Go check on him. We need to talk when you get back."

"Oh, okay." She swallowed and narrowed her eyes, watching him curiously as she brushed past him. Justin stayed rooted to the spot, hands on hips, breathing hard.

By the time she walked back into the room he'd calmed his nerves a little bit.

"He's so beautiful when he sleeps. I could stand there and watch him forever." There was a sweetly whimsical quality to her voice when she spoke of Connor that seeped into Justin's soul.

He glanced away.

"What is it, Justin?" She walked over to face him by the sofa, her eyes troubled. "What's wrong?"

"Were you engaged to Michael Golden in New York?"

She jerked back as if he'd hit her. A gasp sprung from her mouth. "How did you…?"

"Does it matter how I found out? *You* didn't tell me. Is it true? You lived with him for a year?"

She shook her head. "Not a year."

Justin rolled his eyes. "So *LLL* got it wrong. How long were you with him?"

"*LLL?* The television show? Are you telling me that you saw it on television?"

Justin pursed his lips before saying, "The host was happy to share a rare photo of the three of you together."

"They showed a picture of Connor? How? Why? I don't understand."

"He's a famous man. He's in the gossip news, that's how. Apparently, he has a thing for beautiful platinum blondes. No one in the public eye can avoid scrutiny, Kat. If you lived with him, you should've known that."

"But he promised me Connor would never be exploited. He promised me he'd protect us from the media."

"Well, something's changed, hasn't it?"

Kat opened her mouth to say something. But no denial came forth and slowly her lips came together again as a glimmer of knowledge flickered in her eyes.

She was holding something back. Her expression closed up tight. "Aside from the obvious, what aren't you telling me?"

Kat lowered herself down onto the sofa. It was as if she couldn't hold herself upright any longer than her need to sit. "I saw him the day after Logan's wedding."

"You saw him? As in, spoke to him in person?" Now Justin needed to sit. Did he know this woman at all? Who was the real Katherine Grady? He wished to hell he had the answer.

He lowered himself onto Mattie's chair and uttered a curse.

Kat's gaze found the floor. "I'm sorry, Justin. It wasn't planned. I bumped into him outside while I was…I was waiting for you. I guess I didn't realize how much I'd hurt him. He'd gotten attached to Connor."

Her eyes lifted to him. At the mention of his son's name,

Justin's mind clicked back in gear. "Why'd you do it, Kat? Was it just about the money?"

She shook her head vehemently, causing all that gorgeous blond hair to fly around. "No."

"Why don't I believe you?"

The light in her green eyes dimmed. "It's not that simple."

"Lies never are."

Her pretty face crumbled. "I know."

She should just spit it all out and lay the truth at his feet. It might even be liberating for her.

"Explain it to me."

"I, uh, well, I've already told you about my childhood. About the abuse and the way my mother and I lived in fear for years. Keeping one step away from my father messed up our lives. We never had anything of value. My mother's car was twenty years old. We were lucky it ran and if it didn't, we were at the mercy of some kind soul who would fix it for us. Those things most people take for granted. We never had that luxury. We were fortunate to have a roof over our heads. Thanks to the women's shelters and the generosity of friends, we had clothes on our back. Mom and I loved each other. We were very close. We never let my father's abuse come between us.

"As I got older, I saw the toll it had taken on her. She was worn out and sickly before she reached forty. It was hard to watch, you know? As a kid, I thought she was invincible. She was my strong, solid, rock.

"When I was a teen, I started playing around with fabric, using material from donated clothing that didn't fit. I used kitchen shears to redesign our clothes. I had a real talent for sewing and I loved every aspect of design. I was determined to make something of myself. Mom and I moved to New York and I promised her we'd live better. It was time for me to take care of her. I got a job at an upscale store and later started working behind the scenes with designers. I had talent, but no connections and no money. It's a competitive field, hard to break in. I was struggling."

"That's where Golden came in. He had money and connections."

"Fast forward a few years. I met Michael for the very first time a few weeks after you and I were together. If you recall, I had a blind date that never showed."

"And I was the fill-in."

She sighed. "I didn't look at it that way. Michael had been called out of town on business. I was lonely and grieving my mother's death. That's when I met you." Despite the situation, she gave him a warm smile. "You… you were amazing."

He frowned. "So amazing you slept with Golden a few weeks later?"

Her chin lowered and she shook her head. "It wasn't like that. We started dating and he was charming. I was flattered. When I found out I was pregnant, I did really try to find Brett. I wrote him and I never heard back. I was with Michael at that time, and we were becoming serious about each other. But I decided to tell Michael about the baby right away. Michael can't have children, so he knew he wasn't the father. I offered to end our relationship. I told him I'd understand if he didn't want to see me anymore. Instead, he was overjoyed at the news of my pregnancy. He wanted us to be a family. As the weeks went on and I didn't hear back from Brett, no news at all, I continued to see Michael.

"I was frightened, Justin. I didn't have a dime to my name. I didn't have a way to support my son. I didn't want Connor to have the same life I'd had growing up. I know you won't believe this, but my thoughts back then were only for my baby. I saw a way for Connor to have a good life. I was enamored with Michael."

"With Michael or his money?"

Her cheeks flamed red against her creamy complexion. "You think you've got it all figured out. But you have no right to judge me. You grew up wealthy, having everything at your disposal. You had money, friends, influence. I had none of those things…and it didn't look as if I was going anywhere in my career. My dreams had to be put aside… for the baby's sake. What I did wasn't right, I know that. But in my heart and at that time, it was my only option."

"The truth is always an option."

Tears rolled down her cheeks. "I'm telling you the truth now."

"Would've been nice if I didn't have to hear it on TV first. Would've been nice if you'd come clean when we'd first met in Silver Springs. You passed my son off to another man. He had the time with Connor I missed out on."

Her eyes squeezed shut. "I'm sorry about that. So sorry, and if I could go back and change things, I would. If I'd known who you were…but you lied to me, Justin. You can't forget your part in this."

"I know," he said, quietly agreeing. "I can't deny that. But you've had all this time to tell me about your past. Here I thought you were all alone, struggling to survive with a baby in New York. Wasn't that the impression you wanted me to have?"

"No, it's not." She opened her eyes; they were beautifully green and brilliantly clear as she focused directly on him. There was clarity in her voice, as well. "You're a good man, Justin. A good father to Connor. I know I messed up. I know that you probably h-hate me."

Justin rose from his seat. Hell, he didn't hate her. He hated her lies. He was halfway in love with her before all of this happened. His fingers dug into his scalp. "I don't know how I feel about you right now, but that's not important. What's important is to get all the facts out. If you had everything you wanted with Golden, then why'd you leave your perfect little setup? Why did you come here? And don't tell me you had a stroke of conscience."

Her hand lifted to wipe away her tears and she drew in a deep breath. "Michael started getting very controlling."

"What?"

She nodded. "When things didn't go his way, he got nasty. He's a man who expects his demands to be met. He'd been 'yessed' all of his life. While we were dating, he was the most attentive man I'd ever met. I thought I was falling for him. He thought he loved me. After Connor was born, things changed. He was smitten with Connor. He wanted a child very badly, but things started going downhill between us. He started ordering me around. He wanted things for Connor I didn't approve of. He tried to completely take over my life. I started feeling…suffocated. Like I was being choked with his orders. I won't go into details, but at one point it got so bad, I trembled with fear whenever he walked into the room. I never knew what he'd find to pick on, what he'd find wrong.

"It was as if I was reliving my past with my father. Michael got verbally abusive with me. That's how it starts. I'm not saying that Michael would've physically abused me, but his harsh words were enough. I knew it was a matter of time, before Connor…Connor… Oh, my sweet baby… I couldn't subject him to a life like that."

The veins in Justin's neck popped. His nerves jumped, picturing that big man verbally slashing Kat, trying to undermine her self-esteem and confidence. And Connor? Anyone who called himself a man wouldn't bully a woman and child.

"We fought like crazy and I hated subjecting the baby to all that arguing. Finally, Michael agreed to let me go. I was afraid he would follow me because of Connor. I never told him where I was going and I'm grateful he never tried to find me."

The blood pumping in his veins simmered. "I'm trying to wrap my head around all of this."

"Justin?"

"Is this all the truth, Kat?"

"Yes, I had to leave him. I couldn't go back to that kind of life."

"Leaving that jerk was the right move."

"It was the only move I could make."

He looked deep into her eyes. "Answer me this one question, Kat. Were you deceiving Matilda Applegate with your intentions? Were you using her to put a roof over your head hoping to ingratiate yourself into her life?"

Her face crumpled, and her voice fell to barely a whisper. "You know the answer to that, Justin. I love Aunt Mattie. Connor loves her. And when we came here, we believed her to be Connor's great-aunt. Remember, it wasn't until you showed up and revealed *your* lies that I found out Brett Applegate wasn't Connor's father. So no, I wasn't using Aunt Mattie in any way."

All of this was hard to digest. There were so many lies, so many omissions. "Then if that's the case, why didn't you tell me about your engagement to Golden?"

"Because I knew you'd think what you're thinking now. That you'd look at me the way you're looking at me now."

Justin clamped his jaw tight. Her suspicions were justified...he didn't trust her.

"If I'd told you right away...wouldn't you have thought that I was only after Michael's money? That I was desperate and wanted a secure life for my son at any cost?"

"Maybe. Maybe not. Your explanation makes sense to me. But you didn't trust me enough to tell me the truth. I had a right to know another man was raising my son."

"I thought I was doing the right thing, Justin. What's happening between us is new and special and—"

"You didn't want to muck it up with the truth."

"I planned on telling you…one day."

He stared at her and sighed. Shaking his head, he spoke quietly. "Kiss Connor for me when he wakes up. I'd better go."

Kat rose and braced her hands on the back of the sofa. Unmasked fear entered her eyes. "I hope you understand, Justin. I didn't mean for anyone to get hurt. Especially you."

"I guess you paid me back for the lie I told you in New York."

Kat's eyes closed. "It wasn't like that."

"Look, I get it. I really do." He was dizzy from the different directions his mind was going. "I don't know when I'll be back."

Harsh words.

Twin tears rolled down her cheeks. "I hope it's soon."

His shoulder lifted in a shrug. He'd never abandon his son. Connor would always be in his life.

Kat, on the other hand, was a different matter.

Ten

Connor's chunky feet hit the floor and he pushed off, springing up and down in the seat of his baby bouncer. His smiles seared her heart and the sweet sound of his cackling echoed against the parlor walls. "He's loving this," Kat said.

The new bouncer, decorated with giraffes, lions and monkeys, was a hit. "I think our son likes his new toy."

"He's a natural. Maybe there's some bronc busting in his future." Justin stood a distance away watching him. "I'm glad he likes it."

"It's generous of you."

Justin's eyes remained glued to his boy. He didn't look at her much these days. His shut-out was a cool blast of reality. How long could he continue to freeze her out? "It's only the beginning. I'm making up for lost time."

His comment grated on her jumpy nerves. At least he was still speaking to her. That was something, wasn't it? "Thanks again for coming by and watching Connor every day, while I visit Aunt Mattie."

Five days and counting.

"He's my son. I'm not going to abandon him, because things didn't work out between us."

Wow. Point taken and heart crushed in one single blow. Justin must've been a good soldier—he had killer instincts.

Connor went even higher in his bouncer and his giggles rang out.

A smile broke the barrier of Justin's tight lips. At least Connor could do what Kat hadn't been able to accomplish... make Justin happy.

"How do you like the new kitchen floor?" she asked hopefully. She'd had a crew in here yesterday and they'd worked into the night to get the floor finished. Tomorrow, the cabinets would be replaced and the new granite counters came after that.

He slid a glance from the baby to the kitchen tiles poking out from the doorway. "Whatever Mattie wants is fine with me. The floor looks good."

That wasn't exactly a glowing endorsement. But what did she expect? Justin wasn't giving her an inch.

"I hope she's happy with everything. I've been gradually getting her to make decisions about the remodel. The good news is if all goes as expected, she should be home from rehab in two weeks."

His eyes lifted to hers. She soaked in the impact of his gaze. "Two weeks? So she's better?"

"Apparently...if they're sending her home."

"That's good."

"She asked about you."

His gaze shifted to Connor. "Give her my best."

"You should go see her. Talk to her. She'd like that." Kat knew the reason Justin didn't visit her. Guilt about Brett's death still managed to dictate the terms of his life. But she loved him enough to want to see him unburden himself from the pain eating him alive.

"I will. Soon."

Kat kept her lips sealed. It was difficult keeping her thoughts to herself these days. She wanted things back to where they were before. No, that wasn't true. She wanted to go back in time, and tell Justin the truth from the very beginning. If only she'd been less of a coward.

"It's difficult, you know."

So much for biting her tongue.

A frown creased his forehead but didn't say anything. Kat pressed on, summoning her inner diva. "Having this distance from you is worse torture than not being able to touch you. Or have you touch me."

Hot sparks flashed in his eyes. Good. She'd hit a nerve. Finally. "Sheesh, Kat. Don't you think this is killing me, too? It's eating me alive. It's just too much, all at once. There's too many lies between us. Torture goes both ways."

"But that's a good thing, isn't it?" she asked. "It means we still care about each other?"

Their gazes locked and held for a few beats. She was teetering on the edge here, hoping he wouldn't push her over.

Then his jaw clamped tight and he shook his head. "Leave it alone for now, Kat. If you're going to visit Mattie today, you should go. I'll take care of Connor while you're gone. When does he get his next bottle?"

Her hope vanished. It was hard keeping her voice light and breezy. The only thing that helped was looking at Connor's smiling face as he played in the baby bouncer. "In an hour. It's ready in the fridge. Just take it out ten minutes before, like you always do, to take the chill off."

He nodded with more enthusiasm now. He couldn't wait to be rid of her. "Got it."

"Okay," she offered softly. "I'll be going now."

She moved toward Connor, bent to kiss his cheek and whispered, "Be good for your daddy."

Feet planted, knees bent, Connor sprang up again. His baby laughter filled all the holes in her heart but one. That one only Justin could repair.

* * *

The house was lonely in the mornings. She missed being with Justin. She missed cooking him breakfast, and having him make French roast coffee for her. They'd lived that way for only a few days, but those days had been magical.

"That's what love does to you, sweet baby," she said to Connor in his crib. He tried a few times to stand up and then plopped back down. She smiled. "Makes you believe in magic."

She tied her pink cotton terry bathrobe around her waist and put her cold feet in her slippers. Even though it was still only late fall, there was a winter chill in the air and she shivered. If it were up to her, she'd have eighty-degree days every day. "Let's go get the newspaper," she said.

She wrapped Connor up in his blanket, plucked him off the crib mattress and marched the short steps down the porch to a patch of dirt where today's copy of the *Douglas County Sentinel* lay. Rural living meant no newspapers delivered on the penthouse doormat but she didn't miss the high life as much as she thought she would.

A crisp, cool wind followed her inside the house and she closed the door. "Wow, that's cold. Brrr," she said to Connor. "Momma's gonna put you in thermals today right after we eat."

The thermostat cranked up the heat in the house as she made Connor breakfast. His breakfast today was creamed oatmeal mixed with pureed pears. Mixing a little sweet with the healthy went a long way.

Her cell phone rang as she spooned the last bite into his mouth.

She wiped his oatmeal mustache away with a napkin and answered on the third ring.

"Hi, Kat. This is Audrey."

Kat glanced at the clock. Seven in the morning was kind of early for a social call. Audrey Thomas was usually tending the animals at this hour of the day. "Hi, Audrey. It's great to hear from you. How are you feeling? Everything good with the baby?"

"I'm feeling fine. Baby's doing yoga inside my belly."

"It's a wonderful feeling. I remember those flutters and waves of movement. Just wait until he does karate in there."

"Uh…Kat, I'm sorry to have to tell you this." Suddenly, Audrey's voice turned somber. "Last night one of the reporters from *Insider Buzz* flew into town and sort of ambushed Justin for an interview. He was caught off guard outside the ranch gates. Apparently, the reporter recognized you from that *LLL* show and asked Justin about his relationship with you. The guy was a real sleaze. He'd dug into your past and all Justin would tell us was that the questions were not flattering to you."

She took a sharp breath. "Oh, no."

"Justin was furious with the guy. There was a shouting match and Justin threatened to toss the guy back to New York on his ass. Oh, Kat, I'm sorry to say, there's a story on the *Insider Buzz* website and an article about the altercation between Justin and the reporter in the *Sentinel* this morning."

"The *Sentinel?*" She slid a glance at the newspaper on the table. "Is it…horrible?"

"No, I wouldn't say horrible, but there's speculation about Justin being Connor's real father. It lays out some fine points that aren't disputable, putting Justin in New York at the time of Connor's conception and mentioning rumors that the baby looks just like him. There's a bit about your relationship with Michael Golden, too."

"Oh, Audrey…I'm sorry I didn't tell you about Michael. It was a time in my life I didn't want to dredge up. I've made…mistakes."

"It's okay, Kat. You don't owe me an explanation. But

how do you think a reporter from New York found out about you and Justin?"

"Logan's wedding was at the Golden Hotel. We were together there and well…the next day I saw Michael. It was rotten timing—he was coming as I was going and we talked briefly."

"That six degrees of separation thing?"

"Maybe. Either the reporter really did his homework or Michael was behind leaking some information. I can only guess what terrible things were written."

"The Slades' phone has been ringing off the hook. Justin asked me to call you to explain."

"Oh, wow. He's doing my damage control." Tears stung her eyes. Her life had just gotten messier and now she was dragging Justin's good name down.

"I haven't lived here long, but I do know gossip travels fast," Audrey said.

Her heart dipped down to her stomach. "Aunt Mattie?"

"If she's got friends in Silver Springs, the grapevine will reach her."

"Oh, no. I've got to talk to her. I've got to explain everything."

"I think that's a good idea. Good luck and give little Connor a hug for me."

Kat pushed the button to end the call and her phone clicked off. Hesitating, she stared at the copy of the *Sentinel* on the table and scolded herself for not being braver. *Take a look. See what was written about you.* The chicken in her didn't want to pick up the newspaper. The chicken in her wanted to pretend this never happened.

Putting her phone down, she turned to the high chair. "Uppie arms," she said to her son. He waved his hands high in the air and she was quick about sliding the high chair tray off. Then she lifted Connor out of the seat, poured him a bottle of formula and set him down in his play yard.

"Drink your bottle, sweet boy. While Mommy…" She gulped. "While Mommy sees what all the fuss is about."

Picking up the newspaper, she plopped onto the sofa and opened it, turning the pages until she found the headline: War Hero Doing Battle at Home. She scanned the article quickly; it was just as Audrey had described.

She went into her sewing room, steeling her jumpy nerves as she opened her laptop and went to the *Insider Buzz* website.

The first thing she saw when she clicked on the article were two photos that took up about a quarter of the screen. The first had been taken at a charity gala when she was seven months pregnant. Her belly protruded from the silver satin gown she was wearing. She remembered how Michael had proudly told her she looked elegantly pregnant that night.

Then she scanned down to the second picture. It was a shot of Justin in full dress uniform—white gloves, white cap and all. Photo credit was given to the web archives of Medal of Honor recipients.

She did a quick read of the article. "Bleached-blonde social climber" stuck to her like Scotch tape, while Justin was described as a decorated war hero and Michael Golden as the injured party in their broken engagement.

Mortified, she bit back tears as she realized her entire pitiful life, minus anything that would paint her in a good light, was out there for all the world to see now.

She was only glad that no one had figured out the whole truth about Connor yet, and Matilda Applegate's name had not been mentioned in the article. But that didn't mean Aunt Mattie wouldn't hear about this or worse yet, read it herself. She'd find out from a gossipy neighbor or a well-meaning friend that Kat hadn't been entirely truthful with her. She'd find out about her engagement to Michael Golden and hear speculation regarding Justin's role in her life.

She tried to rein in the tears dripping down her cheeks as best she could. Connor shouldn't see her sobbing. He didn't need to see his mommy's grief over how she'd made a mess of things and the people she loved were being hurt.

One thing she knew for sure: she had to tell Aunt Mattie the truth. And she prayed it wouldn't send her back into cardiac arrest.

Or worse.

Justin kept a watchful eye on the rearview mirror, making sure he wasn't being followed. He had something to do. Something he should have done months ago. It was time for all of the truths to come out. Today, he was going to set his life to rights. No more secrets, no more lies.

He steered his truck through the gates of Silver Haven Cemetery and parked by the Tombstones of Soldiers monument. Climbing down from the cab of his truck, he didn't hesitate. His boots hit gravel as he moved to the grassy area, reading one tombstone after another. He should've guessed Brett's headstone would be the shiny new one, the one that wasn't ravaged by inclement weather and time. It felt odd, being here, about to talk to his friend this way. But he needed to wipe the slate clean. It would take a few swipes and today he was determined to see it through.

Removing his hat, he knelt on both knees. He no longer held back the tears. Unexpected relief came as they ran down his cheeks. He opened his mouth and the words he'd rehearsed over and over in his head flowed freely.

"Hello, buddy…I've got a few things to tell you. Now, it'd be too darn weird if you had something to tell me back, so don't spook me. Let me get this off my chest. First off, I miss you. The world isn't a better place without you. I'm sorry you're not here. For months I've beat myself up about my decision that day. I wish I could go back in time and piss you off royally. I should've kept you in the infirmary, out of action. You weren't fit for duty and I should've second-guessed myself. If I had, you'd be back on your farm again with your aunt Mattie. She's a kick in the pants, by the way. I've come to know her and she's as great as you said. I'm doing my best to protect her. In fact, I'm going to see her today, pay her a little visit. Oh, and there's one more thing I wanted to tell you. I've got a son. A sweet little boy named Connor. Man, I'm so thankful I lost that bet to you, you have no idea...."

Pungent scents of alcohol, medicine and sickness filled Kat's nostrils as she sat on the edge of Aunt Mattie's bed. The older woman's hands were small and fragile in her grasp. Mattie's skin was soft as butter though.

The Silver Springs rehab center was a halfway house for the infirm, but it was no royal palace. Aunt Mattie needed to get out of this place—the sooner, the better.

"I'm sorry about all of this, Aunt Mattie. Really, I am."

The *Sentinel* lay across the bedspread, open wide to Kat's personal living obituary. At least it felt that way to her, when she'd carefully explained the circumstances of Connor's birth and read the entire article to Aunt Mattie.

"I'm sorry, too."

"Everything in that article about me is t-true." Heavens, this was hard. A biting chill raced up and down her spine. Mattie's welfare was at stake. Kat wouldn't protect herself by easing up on her confession. Mattie needed to hear the truth from her lips. "I didn't try very hard to find Brett, I'll admit that to you. I didn't want to be tied to a hog farmer from a small town. In my mind, I'd come too far and I didn't want to backtrack. Michael doesn't know about Brett's bet with Justin so that part wasn't printed in the article. Thank God. Could you imagine if Connor found out how I met his father—how he was conceived—in a newspaper article when he grew up? But the rest is true about me, Aunt Mattie. I did do all those things. I wanted to provide a good life for Connor but I went about it the wrong way."

"Oh, dear girl, it's a lot for me to take in," Aunt Mattie said.

"I know. I'm sorry, Aunt Mattie. Please don't be upset. We, Justin and I, were afraid of your reaction when you found out. We didn't want you to get hurt. I was terribly afraid that if you knew the truth about Connor, you would have another health scare."

Mattie smiled for the first time today. "You thought I'd have another heart attack."

Slumping on the bed, Kat whispered, "Yes. I'm still terrified of that."

"Don't be scared. I'm not as fragile as I appear." Mattie squeezed Kat's hand hard to prove her point.

"I was stunned, angry and frustrated when I found out that Justin was Connor's real father. For almost two years of my life, I'd lived one lie, only to find out I'd really been living another. I can only imagine how hurt you are, learning that Connor isn't, isn't…"

"I love that boy. Nothing will change that, Kat."

"I know you do. You have to b-believe me…." Her voice cracked with a sob. "When I came to Silver Springs, I really did believe Brett was Connor's father. I didn't know anything about his bet with Justin Slade until he showed up that day." Kat sighed. "We've really made a mess of things."

"Not so much of a mess," Aunt Mattie said. Hinging forward on the bed, she released Kat's hand. "You see, I have a confession to make too." She paused and rubbed her temple. "I've always sort of known that Connor wasn't

Brett's boy. In my head, that is. In my heart, Connor will always be mine."

Air puffed out of her lungs. What was she saying? Kat wasn't sure she heard right. "What do you mean?"

"My Brett was built like his uncle, solid and wide. He had reddish-brown hair and freckles across his nose. His eyes were bluer than mine. Connor looks nothing like him. So I had my suspicions. Then I went into my pack of old letters from Brett and found one where he spoke about a bet he'd won with his commanding officer. They'd switched identities for one weekend in New York. Brett had a great time going to movies and eating in expensive restaurants by himself. He never mentioned a woman. When Justin came knocking on my door and introduced himself, I got a chance to see him up close next to Connor. That boy is the spitting image of his daddy."

Kat's mouth dropped open. She hadn't expected this. "Why didn't you say something to me?"

Aunt Mattie pulled the material of her bed robe tighter. "If my suspicions were correct, I figured you'd tell me when the time was right."

"But you invited me to stay with you. To live at your house even when you weren't sure I was telling the truth."

A warm beam of light brightened her eyes. "Honey, I took one look at you and that little angel standing on my doorstep, and knew you needed my help. My goodness, I've lived a long, long time. I know despair when I see it. You needed me. And I wasn't about to turn you away." Aunt Mattie leaned back against the pillows on her bed. Immediately, Kat rose to straighten them out and fluff them to make her more comfortable.

"There, you see," she said. "You've come into my life and only made it better. You're always helping me."

"I lied to you."

"To protect me."

"I'm not a good person."

Her eyes lifted to the ceiling. "Dear Ralph. Are you hearing this? You've seen her goodness. You've seen Kat help me with the cooking and cleaning. You've seen her make sure I take my medications on time. You've seen her work into the night to earn her keep. And Ralph, I swear to you, if there's a better mother in the entire world, I've not met her."

Aunt Mattie's gaze lowered to meet Kat's eyes. "Not only do I love Connor," she said, her gravelly voice smooth and silky now, "but I love you, too, Kat. You're like a daughter to me."

Warmth and joy ran laps inside Kat's body and she couldn't get the words out fast enough. "Oh, Aunt Mattie. I love you, too."

Kat put her arms around Brett's aunt and hugged her carefully. Moments ticked by as Kat counted her blessings and good fortune in meeting Mattie Applegate.

"I'm so glad everything is out in the open," Kat said softly into Mattie's ear. "But I want you to know Connor will always be your great-nephew. You will always have a place with us. You are part of our family."

"That makes an old woman very happy. No heart attacks today for me."

Kat squeezed her tighter. "You promise?"

"I can surely promise you that."

Justin stood behind the partition in Mattie's rehab room listening to her to talking to Kat. He didn't mean to eavesdrop but he also didn't want to barge in on their private conversation, so he stood quietly waiting for the right moment. He'd heard every word Kat had spoken and now his boots propelled him forward and he stepped past the hospital curtain. "Hello."

His eyes reached Mattie first. She smiled back. "Hello."

"Am I interrupting?" he asked her.

"Not at all. We're just chillin'."

He couldn't hide a grin. Mattie was as feisty as ever. She must be feeling better. She knew the truth and was okay with it. That said something wonderful about her character.

"Chillin' is a good thing."

His gaze slid to Kat. Her eyes softened on him. Her lips parted and she did that innocent little gesture with her hand in her hair that rocketed through his nerve endings. His breathing quickened and something powerful clicked inside his head, pounding sense into it.

His heart squeezed tight.

He'd been wrong about Kat. He'd come to that conclusion after his sorely bruised ego had healed up. He'd seen her side of things for the first time. She did have a rough life, and despite her hardships, she'd always done what she believed best for their son. He had to give her credit where it was due.

What he'd just witnessed now told him in a thousand different ways that she was a good woman. He didn't care about her past. She was strong, a survivor. Just the kind of girl a tough-minded former marine should pair up with.

"Come join us, Justin," Mattie was saying.

Kat rose quickly from the hospital bed. "Actually," she said to her, "I've got to get back to the house. Audrey was nice enough to babysit Connor. I told her I wouldn't be gone too long."

Slipping her purse over her shoulder, she leaned down and kissed Mattie's cheek. "You and Justin should talk. I'll be back tomorrow."

She spared him a glance as she strode toward the door.

"Kat? We need to talk, too," he said.

She stopped and focused her gaze on the floor, refusing to look at him. "I can't tell you how sorry I am about all of this." Then without another word, she brushed by him and slipped out the door.

Justin turned his head and peered down the hallway, but Kat was already out of sight. Sighing, he swiveled back to Mattie. Grabbing the only chair in the room, he swung it around to her bedside and straddled it backward so he was facing her.

"You know about Connor now?"

"Kat explained everything to me." She gestured toward the newspaper. "I imagine this isn't easy for you, either."

"I couldn't care less about myself. It's you I'm worried about. You know, Kat and I didn't want to see you hurt."

"Yes, I know. Kat made sure I understood. I don't blame either of you for keeping the truth from me. You were both trying to protect me."

"Kat more than me," he said. He had to be honest. "I wanted to claim Connor as my son, but Kat insisted and I finally agreed it would be best to hold back the truth until you were fully recovered."

"It doesn't matter, Justin. I already love that boy like my own. I always will. Kat assured me that I'd always be a part of her family. That's all I want."

"You got it. You're Connor's great-aunt, as far as I'm concerned."

"Thank you. It means everything to me. My Ralph always would say, the truth shall set you free."

Justin took a big swallow. It was time to shed light on one more truth. It was time to unburden himself of the heavy weight he carried. He faced his fears and forced the words out. "There's one more truth, Aunt Mattie. It's about Brett and how he died that day. I'm afraid it's my fault."

"Oh, dear boy. I doubt that very much."

Justin set out to change her mind. He spoke to her now, leaving nothing out about the events leading up to Brett's death. He held Mattie's hand and confessed, pouring out his guilt, baring his soul and crying tears of enormous grief. "H-he was a good man and a fine soldier. Maybe too good a soldier. He was so damn eager to get back to active duty. He loved being a marine," he finally concluded.

"He did love it." Tears filled Mattie's eyes. She tried not to show it, but she was in a lot of pain.

"I'm sorry. I'm sorry. This is too much for you all at once," he said.

"I'm going to be just fine, Justin. Lordy, you've held this grief inside for so long, boy."

She rose from her bed and came around his chair. He wanted to tell her to stay in bed, to take care with her fragile body, but she set her jaw firm and filled her eyes with determination. She cradled his head and gently ran a hand down his cheek. Her fingers were touches of peace to his tortured spirit. "Please don't feel responsible. Brett was a stubborn one. He wanted what he wanted, when he wanted it. He told you he was ready. He made that decision. He did. Not you," she whispered. "Not you, Justin."

"But when we got to the schoolhouse, I ordered him to go back. That's when he got shot."

"You saw that he was sick. You sent him to safety." She lowered her weary body down on the edge of her bed. The warmth in her eyes spoke of forgiveness. "You were being a friend and a good commander. Brett would always say the unit was only as strong as the weakest link. I miss that boy something fierce, Justin, but I won't see you torture yourself with regrets. If Brett wasn't up to the task, it was your duty to send him back. You didn't know what would happen to him."

"I, uh, don't know what to say. I've dreaded having to tell you about Brett for a long time. I thought you'd hate me."

A kind smile parted her lips. "Now, how could I hate Connor's real daddy?"

He lowered his head and stared down at her bed slippers. "You're a good woman, Matilda Applegate."

"Too bad I'm too old for you."

His chuckle rose up from his mending heart.

"But if you're looking for a really fine woman, I've got me a roommate I think you'd like."

He searched her knowing eyes. "I like her just fine."

"You love her. Don't know if you realize it or not."

Oxygen whooshed into his lungs and he blinked.

"She's kicking herself in the behind about the mess she's made. I think a fine upstanding man like yourself could undo that mess with three magical words."

He gave a shake of his head. "I don't know."

She frowned. "Those aren't the three words." She took his hand in hers. The pressure she applied was forceful, much stronger than he gave her credit for. Then she looked him dead in the eyes. "If you have any doubts about Kat's intentions or her character, ask her about Lowery's."

His brow furrowed in confusion. "What's that supposed to mean?"

"Ah, it's not for me to say." She gave him a final squeeze of the hand and a quick nod of the head. "You go see her first thing tomorrow morning and ask her. You won't be sorry."

Tomorrow morning worked for him. He had some unsettled business that he needed to tend to tonight before he spoke with her. "Okay, I'll do that."

"Good. Now, if you'll excuse me, I think I need my beauty sleep."

She climbed into bed and he helped her get settled in the sheets. Then he gave her a little kiss on the cheek. "You couldn't get any more beautiful, Aunt Mattie."

"Hush now. Talk like that will surely get my heart pumping too hard."

He smiled. How could he ever repay her generosity? Not only had she helped him rid himself of his guilt about Brett's death, but she'd given Kat and his baby son a roof over their heads and unconditional love when they'd needed it the most.

Matilda Applegate was turning out to be his savior, his conscience and his couples counselor all rolled up into one.

Justin left the construction site at the Gateway Equine Retreat and headed east on foot. A walk would do him good. He had things to say to Kat. And he wanted a clear head to say them. Pulling the brim of his hat down, he shaded his eyes from the morning sunshine peeking out through scattered gray clouds.

He glanced at his watch. Seven-thirty. Was it too early to show up unannounced at Mattie's house? Suddenly, he was a teenager again, full of nerves and anxious as all get-out to see his high school crush.

The Applegate house came into view from fifty yards away. Movement on the porch caught his eye. He stopped abruptly and shoved his hat off his forehead to get a better look. Straining his eyes, he narrowed in on a brown-haired woman entering the house with his son. Who was she? He didn't recognize her. Was she someone else from Kat's past that he didn't know about?

"Damn it." His gut told him something was wrong.

It was too early for a social call from one of the neighbors.

His boots ate grass and gravel getting to the house. Heart hammering, he pushed his way through the unlocked front door. He'd have to caution Kat about keeping the door locked later. "Kat? Connor?"

"We're in here," Kat called out, her voice sounding as sultry as the day they'd first met.

Relief swooped down to replace his fear. He crossed the parlor and strode down the hallway. Once he reached Kat's bedroom, he blinked and refocused his eyes.

The woman who'd just finished diapering Connor

turned to face him and his mouth fell open. It wasn't the rosy-lipped, wavy-haired, platinum-blonde seductress, Katherine Grady, staring back at him. It was a clean-faced, green-eyed natural beauty with straight ordinary brown hair.

As the seconds ticked by, his heart bludgeoned his chest. He couldn't take his eyes off her. "Kat?"

Her lips trembled and turned down. "This is the real me."

A slow nod moved his head up and down. "O-kay."

"I'm a fraud, Justin."

Man, oh, man. She looked so different. Equally beautiful, but different. "No, you're not."

Her gaze landed on Connor in the crib. She handed him his bottle.

Justin walked over to stroke his head and watch him take the first few gulps. His little mouth sucked hard, drawing the formula out. There was nothing more precious in the world than his son. Justin stole a glance at Kat—they were his family.

Kat took a step back, away from the crib. "Yes, I'm the worst kind of fraud. Anyone who knows anything about Michael Golden knows he likes platinum blondes. He had this thing for Marilyn, you know. My blind date had been set up a month in advance. I invented my look. I designed clothes for myself that would give off a certain impression. I transformed myself into someone else just to gain the attention of a certain rich man."

Justin didn't care about any of that. It was never clearer than right now. "So what?"

"So what? Aren't you afraid that I'm only here for your money? Aren't you—?"

"No."

"You're not?" Her eyes opened wide.

"No, I'm not."

"Why not?"

A smile spread across his face. "Because I know you."

"You don't know the real me."

"I know you're a scrapper. I know you truly care about that old woman. I know you've worried about her, taken care of her, protected her even when it was probably in your best interest to tell the world Connor was a Slade. I know you'd do anything for our son. I admire that about you, Kat."

She gulped. "You admire me?"

"Yes, I do." He took her hand and tugged. She landed up against his chest. He wrapped his arms around her waist and then moved them lower. As he flattened his hands against her buttocks, a tiny gasp escaped her throat. "I like you as a brunette, sugar. You're still gorgeous."

"I'm not flashy anymore."

"Flashy is so twenty minutes ago."

Her eyes beamed and a chuckle burst from her lips.

He brought his mouth to her hair and kissed her there. "Mattie knows the truth about everything now."

She pulled away from him. "You spoke to her about Brett?"

"I did. Yesterday. It was one of the hardest things I've had to do. But I made my peace with it all. Thanks to you."

"Me?"

He spoke from deep in his heart. "You helped me through a tough time, Kat. You were just what I needed. Your encouragement guided me in the right direction. You didn't condemn me, not even when I had the worst suspicions about you."

"I'm glad I was able to help," she whispered. "Very glad."

He brought her hand to his lips and kissed it. "I have a confession to make."

"What's that?"

"After what you told me about Michael Golden, I suspected him of having leaked the story to that reporter at *Insider Buzz*. There was something about that guy that didn't ring true. He flew in from New York to get a story about you and me? Then he deliberately provoked me? None of that added up. I'm sure it was a setup. Since then, Logan's been helping me dig into Golden's past. My brother found out some things about Michael Golden that wouldn't go over well in the public eye. Let's just say there's a few women from his past who'd also been harassed and abused."

"Really? I guess that shouldn't surprise me. Michael is very good at hiding his true colors. And it's only recently that he's become a focus of the media. When we were together, he promised to keep Connor and I out of the limelight."

"Golden is out of your life now. He won't be causing you any trouble."

"How do you know?"

"To a man who deals with the public, bad press is worse than a bad economy. It's the kiss of death. He's not the only one who can leak a story. His PR people must be going crazy right now, worried their stock will drop if some of those women come forward and Golden Hotels' squeaky clean name gets tarnished."

"I guess the moral of the story is, no one should mess with a Slade."

"Got that right."

"Me included?"

"*You* should always mess with this Slade."

His hand moved through her silky straight hair, cupping her head as he brought her mouth close to his. Her flowery scent tickled his nose. He pressed his lips to hers and touched softness. He poured everything he had into that kiss, his heart, his mind, his soul. He could go on kissing her for hours, but he wasn't through with all the truths yet. Summoning his willpower, he stepped back, breaking their connection. "Tell me about Lowery's."

Her pretty green eyes rounded and her voice turned breathless. "H-how do you know about that?"

"I don't know much. I'm asking you to tell me."

Her shoulders fell. "Aunt Mattie must've flapped her gums to you yesterday."

"I wouldn't blame her if I were you. She was singing your praises to me. Not that I needed to hear any of it. I'm already crazy in love with you. I don't think I could possibly love you any more than I already do."

"Justin," she whispered through pale pink lips. Her head tilted upward and she ran her hand through the strands of her hair again. The gesture didn't need blond roots to turn him on. "You really love me?"

Unable to resist, he kissed her again. "With all my heart."

Her eyes softened and her hand came to rest on his cheek. "I love you, too."

A wide grin spread across his face. He reached for her waist with both hands and in one swift move, lifted her in the air. Her hands came to his chest as he twirled her around and around. Her laughter filled the room and he joined in, bellowing his happiness. When he lowered her down and her feet hit the floor, tears spilled from her eyes.

"Why are you crying, sugar?"

"Because I love you so much, Justin, and I never thought you'd love me back. It means so much to me that you told me before you found out about Lowery's."

He took her hands in his. "You'll never have to doubt my love, but I'm dying to know what's up with Lowery's."

"Wait one more second." She stepped out of his arms and went to her dresser. Pulling open the top drawer, she lifted out a handful of letters. "I've kept this secret for two weeks. Even before Aunt Mattie took ill. Even before I thought there was any hope for us."

Her gaze fastened on one letter in particular. "You know how hard I've worked to make a success of myself. I've told you about my designs and my dreams. I've been rejected by every major department chain." She took the envelope out of the drawer. "But one. Lowery's Department Store offered to buy my line of baby clothes for their stores. It's a lucrative contract. More money than I've earned in over ten years of struggling. More than I ever imagined. I'd be financially independent."

Walking over to her, he gave her shoulders a squeeze. "That's your dream, Kat. Congratulations."

"But it's not my dream anymore, Justin. That's just it. I thought I wanted it and sure, I needed some security for Connor's future, but I couldn't bring myself to accept the offer."

"Why?"

"Because it meant leaving Silver Springs. It meant leaving you and Aunt Mattie. I just couldn't do it. I couldn't bring myself to leave the people I love. I'm happy here, Justin. I've finally figured it out. I'd transformed myself on the outside, but inside, I never really changed. All I've wanted in life was a shred of happiness, a family to love and a way to earn a living. I have the start of a great online business with Babylicious. I can develop that right here. I thought I needed wealth to make me happy because of the way I grew up. But all I really want is a simple life."

He peered deeply into her eyes. "I hope that simple life includes me."

A smile radiated from her face. "Of course it does."

"Well, then, let me introduce myself properly," he said. He entwined his fingers with hers. "I'm Justin Slade, filthy rich war hero and a man who loves you beyond reason." He brought her fingertips to his lips and kissed each one.

"Nice to meet you, Justin," she said, her voice barely above a whisper. "I'm Katherine Grady, a scrappy survivor who has finally found her true self."

Justin didn't need another second to think about this. He loved Kat and Connor and wanted them with him for the rest of his life.

His knee hit the floor right there in Kat's bedroom, beside the crib where his young son lay. His sweet baby breaths were the music that soothed Justin's soul. Lifting his face to Kat, he saw love enter her eyes. He knew this was right. They had come down a very jagged path to find each other, but now he'd do everything in his power to keep them together.

"Beautiful Katherine, will you marry me? Will you become my wife? Will you and Connor be my family?"

"Oh, Justin. Yes. Yes. I'll marry you. We already *are* your family."

He rose to his feet and smiled. How lucky could he get? He kissed her deeply, soundly, and let his lips linger on hers for long moments after.

"I can't wait to make it official," he said, gazing into her eyes. "The sooner the better for me. Do you think you'd like a double wedding? Luke and Audrey wouldn't mind if we tagged along. I've already hinted at it and Audrey was all over the idea."

Her voice broke tenderly. "Really? You've discussed this with Audrey and your brother?"

"Yeah, late last night."

"But their wedding is coming up fast."

He gulped air. Was he pressing her? "Too soon?"

She braced both hands on his chest and nestled closer to him, laying her head on his shoulder. "Not at all. I'm a simple girl, remember? I don't need a fancy wedding. I just need you and Connor."

Soft whimpers rose up from the crib. His son had good timing. "He's agreeing."

Kat moved away and bent over the crib to lift the baby up. Cradling him in her arms, she whispered, "He's smart as a whip."

"Takes after his mommy."

"I won't argue with that." Her lips pressed against Connor's eyebrow and Justin kissed him on the other one. Then he wrapped his arms around the two people he loved most in the world, huddling them into his embrace.

"Family hug," Kat said, laughing.

Connor's lips formed a big smile and Justin's heart zinged. "I don't think I could be any happier."

Connor shifted from Kat's steady hold and leaned toward Justin with arms outstretched, waving for his attention. "Oh, look. He wants his daddy."

Justin reached for him and Kat made the easy transfer. His son nestled into his chest, spreading warmth.

Standing back, a warm loving beam entered Kat's eyes. "That just looks right. I don't think I could be any happier, either."

Justin grinned.

All the secrets were out.

The three of them were where they belonged.

And finally a family.

Epilogue

Kat's engagement ring caught sunlight and sparkled, dazzling her almost as much as the man standing at the podium on the front steps of the Douglas County office. Dressed in a fitted dark suit and tie, his Congressional Medal of Honor pinned to his lapel, Justin addressed the thousands of townspeople who'd honored him with a parade through the main street of town. All five of the servicemen whose lives he'd saved stood behind him, a living, breathing testament to his bravery. Aunt Mattie, holding Connor in her arms, sat beside Kat in the front row. Luke and Audrey, Logan and Sophia were seated directly next to them.

"Thank you. Thank you." Justin's voice was filled with gratitude. "For all of you who have come here today, it's an honor to serve you and my country. I have to say I'm humbled by the turnout. Your generosity and support mean a lot to me. Though I didn't want all the hoopla—and certainly when I commanded my unit in Afghanistan, a parade in my honor wasn't something I'd ever dreamed of—I do appreciate what you've done for me today."

He sent Kat a nod. She rose from her seat and he waited while she picked up Connor. As soon as they reached the podium to take their place beside Justin, the baby, dressed in his little blue suit, opened and closed his hand, waving to the onlookers. Sighs and giggles rang out.

Justin's prideful chuckle boomed over the loudspeaker. "And before I go on, I want to introduce you to a very special woman…someone who's made a big difference in my life, someone who, by this time tomorrow, will be my wife. Katherine Grady."

Justin set his hand on her waist and drew her close. Their hips bumped, and she smiled at the crowd. She didn't want the attention—this was Justin's time to shine—but he'd insisted she stand up here with him. He wanted to put to rest once and for all the rumors and innuendo from those scandalous articles. He wanted a fresh start and to show the world he was behind her one hundred percent. He wanted to introduce his family. "And this little tyke, who's got his wave down pretty darn good, is our son, Connor Brett Slade."

Applause broke out. "I know," Justin said over the noise, "he is pretty darn cute, isn't he?"

Justin waited for the noise to settle down, his big smile warming her heart. Oh, how she loved him. She could hardly believe tomorrow she'd be Mrs. Justin Slade, wife, mother and Babylicious clothes designer.

Justin went on. "We gave our boy the middle name of Brett, because it means something real important to all of us." Justin's gaze flowed over to Mattie. "Brett Applegate was a buddy of mine, a damn good marine and a great person. Brett lost his life in a firefight in Afghanistan. To honor him and his uncle Ralph Applegate, who was also a veteran, along with all of the great men and women who've served our country in the military, I'm happy to announce that come next spring, a project I'm very proud of will be opening its doors in Silver Springs. On the spot of Brett's family farm, we're building an equine retreat for veterans called the Gateway Equine Retreat. Soldiers helping horses, horses helping soldiers. Can't think of anything better. The construction is already in the works thanks to the cooperation and help of Brett's aunt, Matilda Applegate. It's going to be something remarkable and I hope you'll join us at the grand opening."

After concluding his speech, Justin pulled Kat aside, grabbing her hand and taking her back behind the county building. He trapped her against a wall, his hands braced on the building bricks behind her. "Thanks for standing by my side." His lips tenderly touched hers.

"Always."

He smiled. "You're beautiful."

She lifted a hand to a wayward lock of his hair and set it in place. "So are you."

"I can't wait to get you alone tonight."

"Mmm, sounds good. But you're not getting me alone."

His eyes opened a little wider. "I'm not?"

"Nope. Sophia has invited me and Audrey over for a good old-fashioned night-before-the-double-wedding girls' party. After tomorrow, we'll all be Slades. That's something to celebrate. I'll be staying at Sophia's cottage tonight."

"And what will I be doing?"

"Well, you, Connor, Logan and Luke can have a boys' night."

"You mean I'm babysitting?"

She tilted her head to one side. "I thought you'd like that."

A smile broadened his lips. "I love it. But I'll miss you."

"I'll miss you, too." Her fingers walked up his chest to his collarbone and she massaged the hollow spot there. "What if I make it up to you?"

"Keep talking."

"I think I'll leave it to your very vivid imagination."

His eyes burned hot and hungry. "Man, oh, man, I love you, Kat."

She'd never imagined this much happiness could fill her

life. It beamed inside of her. She'd never forget her past, but now she had the promise of a wonderful future ahead with no detours or roadblocks in her path.

It was smooth sailing from here on out.

Kat smiled.

"I love you, too, Justin."

He covered her hand with his and led her toward a life as brilliant and beautiful as a Nevada sunset.

* * * * *

LET'S TALK

Romance

For exclusive extracts, competitions
and special offers, find us online: